RAVE REVIEWS FOR
OUTLAW JUSTICE

"Having spent the past 25 years devouring everything I could lay hands on regarding motorcycles, outlaw bikers, and the biker lifestyle, K. Randall Ball's OUTLAW JUSTICE, in my opinion, truly captures the gritty essence of the outlaw phenomenon like no other book I've ever read. I literally could not put the book down from the thrilling beginning to the climactic finale. Every chapter is crammed with Ball's lifetime experience with the biker lifestyle. This book is one bad-ass ride!"

   –*Dave Nichols,*
   contributor to Easyriders, Biker,
   In the Wind, and VQ magazine

FINALLY, a kick-ass action/adventure novel written by a biker! Every word of this mother rings true. Hell, you can almost smell the hot leather and burnin' rubber! If you aren't a biker when you begin OUTLAW JUSTICE, you just may consider a change in lifestyle by the thrill-packed conclusion! Live to ride!

   –*Toecutter,*
   on the road somewhere

It's more than a coincidence that you hold this book in your hands. The story is more than a parable pitting greed and deception against honor and justice. It is a tale that goes beyond the good, the bad, and the ugly of our world, to a place of true metamorphosis!

   –*Rev. Chris Stevens*
   Church of Two Wheels

K. Randall Ball is a master of weaving a modern western etched with the very code of the West that still lives in the heart of honest men. Following in the engineer bootsteps of Ball's first novel, PRIZE POSSESSION, OUTLAW JUSTICE continues this truly original genre. Within these bigger-than-life pages you'll find action and adventure blastin' atcha with the kick of a sawed-off shotgun at close range!

   –*Phantom*
   Seattle, Washington

WHERE LIFE HAS NO VALUE ... DEATH SOMETIMES HAS ITS PRICE. INTO THIS WORLD, THE OUTLAW BIKER WAS BORN.

They returned from war to a home that had forgotten them. Their need for high-octane thrills fed a passion for motorcycles, high-speed adventure, dirty sex, and ultra-violence. Outlaw bikers spread across America like a virulent plague to the straight world. By the 1970s, the so-called one-percenter's motorized mania had become an entrenched way of life for the few who dared risk everything for the white line fever and thrills found behind the chrome ape hangers of a chopped Harley-Davidson. OUTLAW JUSTICE is a modern-day western from the first gut-wrenching bar fight, to the ultimate showdown pitting a ragtag band, held together by brotherhood and honor, against an army of drug-crazed outlaws.

LOYAL TO NONE, SWORN TO FUN

The Night Hawks were born to raise hell, a charismatic band of hard-fighting, hard-drinking, hard-riding womanizers living for the credo, "Live Hard, Die Fast!" There was the club's no-nonsense, slick-dressing, knife-wielding president, Fast Eddie. The club's vice president and enforcer, Hank, with a gaze as deadly as a rattlesnake. The club's streetfighter, Big John, 6 foot 2 inches of unleashed muscle. Old Man Jason, the forever drunk or high daredevil, and Fireball, the stocky redhead with a temper like a lit stick of dynamite.

A MAN OF HONOR IN A WORLD GONE MAD

Danny Lonsdale proudly wears the club patch of the Night Hawks M/C. Harley oil flows in the veins of this laconic biker and vet. Danny learns too late that the road to brotherhood is often a cracked and bleeding freeway of broken dreams and betrayal. Danny lives by a code of loyalty few hold to and less understand. He is a man of honor whose world explodes one sultry Southern California night only to awaken on a blood-soaked barroom floor, on trial for a murder he didn't commit.

RUNNIN' WITH THE BIG DOGS

Blade was the very visage of the devil himself. He stood in the shadows of the infamous fortress/clubhouse. "We've been doing business with the Los Cuchillos for years," he screamed, "and you've interrupted all that, and cost us thousands. I say off the bastard who killed the Cuchillo, and end this bullshit!"

The room was as quiet as a mausoleum. Every outlaw eye was on the small group of Hawks from the L.A. basin. "Well?" Blade demanded. "Are you faggots going to say something, or should we just kill the lot of you and get back to business as usual?"

"This is horseshit," Jesse barked. "We were invited here, and I'd rather fight to my death than give up a brother. So let's fucking get on with it."

Blade looked Jesse up and down with a humorless grin. "Well," he said, "this one's got heart. You oughtta make a decent prospect." Blade's words were direct and blunt. "Snitches are killed quickly, punks are thrown out, and each man in each chapter has to be able to fight strongly and instantaneously. If a man hesitates, he could lose his patch or his life—no questions asked, no explanations accepted. Is that clear?"

BETRAYAL IS A BITCH

Dixie entered the living room in a sheer, black teddy. Danny just stared, recalling the two years since he had seen a woman nude, present, and in the flesh. Her eyes were pools of liquid, her lips parted, her long, red hair moist. With coke-sharpened senses, Danny let his fingertips dance along her youthful flesh. He tasted one nipple, then the other, and each brightened under the candlelight, becoming excited and erect. Lost in an avalanche of alerted senses, and fueled by the drug, their marathon lovemaking went on for days.

Outlaw Justice is published by 5-Ball, Inc.
5-Ball, Inc. grants discounts on the purchase of 12 or more
copies of the same title. For further details, please write to:
5-Ball, Inc.
2934 1/2 Beverly Glen Circle, Suite 410
Bel Air, California 90077

Printed and manufactured in the United States of America
First Edition: October, 1997

Cover Illustration by Eric Herrmann
Book design by Melissa A. Colton, MacDab
Library of congress Catalog Card Number: 97-090730

ISBN: 0-9651605-1-3

BIOGRAPHY

A motorcyclist enthusiast, tireless rider, skilled builder and prolific writer since adolescence, K. Randall Ball was among the original staff of *Easyriders* magazine—the most unusual and influential publication in the industry—at its inception in 1971. Ball was the first manager of ABATE, the pioneer motorcycle rights organization, and his involvement in riders' rights issues continues to this day. In addition, he was a member of the *Easyriders* motorcycle land speed record team that achieved the present record of 322.150 mph in 1990.

Today K. Randall Ball remains the original and reigning "Bandit" of *Easyriders* magazine, as well as being vice president and editorial director of *Easyriders'* parent company, Paisano Publications, overseeing the production of nine specialized motorcycle-oriented magazines in five languages, and continuing his lifelong dedication to bikes and the people who ride them.

Calling upon a lifetime of firsthand experiences, Ball has produced another novel of exceptional power and excitement. His first novel, PRIZE POSSESSION, was published in 1996 and kicked off a fist-fighting series of biker adventure novels. OUTLAW JUSTICE is number two and soon-to-be followed by SAM "CHOPPER" ORWELL, a story of bikers in the future trying desperately to find peace and open roads. Then comes CROSS COUNTRY, the tale of five young bikers on their first transcontinental adventure. In short, he writes about what he knows, telling his tale with a gripping and accessible style born of real-life experiences.

K. Randall Ball lives in Southern California with his wife, Rebecca.

DEDICATION

*This book is dedicated
to a former love, Elizabeth,
who was stricken by cancer
and fought successfully for her life,
my writing mentor Tex Campbell and
our female counterpart Randi Rivers, Mark Lonsdale,
and to all the club members I've known
over the years who have found themselves
on the wrong side of deals that cost
them their lives or freedom.*

May wide open roads await them on the other side.

WILD IN THE STREETS

*D*anny ducked beneath the razor-sharp, stainless steel blade that slashed at him in the dark. An inch closer, and the deadly edge would have altered the pitch of his voice forever. Grabbing a rickety wooden chair beside a teetering barroom table, Danny swung it in the direction of the oncoming steel. The flimsy chair shattered against a smaller Mexican man. At the same instant, a beer bottle lit fireworks in Danny's skull, and he collapsed into the sawdust and beer bottles covering the well-worn tavern floor.

Earlier that evening, Danny and fellow members of the Night Hawks Motorcycle Club had ridden into a small Hispanic suburb of Los Angeles. Spotting a chopped Harley parked outside the Red Robin Bar, the club's president, Fast Eddie, signaled to the group of eight riders to pull up and park in front. As the pack rolled up to the curb, the Harleys sounded like a herd of rhinos on reds, popping and snapping like bullwhips, exploding like rounds of gunfire splitting the warm night air. The club members, each adorned in black and fringe, or roughed-out leather, and toting evil-looking knives on their belts, dismounted, hollering, shoving, and threatening to kick the ass of any citizen foolish enough to cross their path.

The time was shortly after 11 p.m., Saturday night in May, 1984. Every member was high on his drug of choice. Some were primed with crank, others with pot, still others with beer and whiskey. Although no one knew it at the time, it was the beginning of a very long night.

As the Night Hawks entered the bar, a short member of the Los Cuchillos Mexican Motorcycle Club slipped off to the narrow hall in the back of the dilapidated saloon. As he lifted the receiver on the marred pay phone, a single red light shone above his head while he dialed. Then he whispered into the cracked mouthpiece. A husky voice at the other end of the line responded abruptly. The biker hung up quietly, as Bo Diddley responded to the quarter shoved into the juke box. In the few minutes since their arrival, the Night Hawks had taken over the sloppy saloon and were ordering, hollering, and hassling the joint's only waitress. Meanwhile, the small, dark man slipped out the back door and disappeared down the alley.

Within minutes, more motorcycles arrived. Tough-looking Hispanics dismounted their chopped Harleys in groups of two and three. Their rides glistened with excessive chrome and vivid, multi-colored, metalflake paint jobs. The scooters were flashy, but the riders were dead serious. They moved quietly into the bar through both the front and back doors, sliding up against the walls and into the corners. They spoke to no one.

The Los Cuchillos were new to the urban streets of Los Angeles. The chapter was founded by a group of the original Los Cuchillos from the central valley to the north who had moved south to Culver City to set up drug operations. They recruited bad-ass local riders or Latinos looking for a group to ride with. The harder, older men taught them the streets, but not the business enterprise they intended to operate on their newly acquired turf. These newcomers knew that they were on Night Hawks' turf, but the older members from 150 miles to the north were playing hardball. Both groups were stoned, and itching for a fight.

Neon hung from the bar's windows, flashing garish images of different brands of beer. Cheap paneling lined the dim room. Sawdust and peanut shells covered the unforgiving concrete floor, and battered Formica tables with brightly upholstered chairs were scattered around the pool table. The room smelled of piss and stale beer.

Fast Eddie instantly recognized the infiltration of the other gang. It was one of his responsibilities as the president to stay cool, alert, and on guard. Fast Eddie wasn't big, but he was tough and, at age 33, he was older and craftier than most members. Eddie projected a certain slickness, with his leather pants, black western shirt, and black contoured vest. His slick, black hair was long, and pulled into a ponytail that accentuated his bony features, the narrow slits of his eyes, and his carefully trimmed goatee. He was no taller than 5 feet, 10 inches, but he was 185 pounds of speed and quickness. And he knew the Buck knife in the black, hand-tooled sheath on his hip better than most people know their key rings.

Unobtrusively, Eddie nudged a couple of the club members sitting near him. They took notice and passed the word. Bent over a pool table, Danny listened intently as one of his brothers whispered in his ear, "Watch the fuckin' Mexicans, man." At an even 6 feet and 200 pounds, Danny was muscular, tan, and blond. But he was also young, foolhardy, and a born romantic. Thick, wavy hair fell over his shoulders and around his eyes, to overlap with his bushy mustache and a week's growth of stubble. Gradually, the bar grew quiet. Outside, two more bikes roared up to the curb, and soon two more armed outlaws swaggered into the bar.

Eddie inhaled the stench of stale suds and old sweat, fully aware of the growing hostility and the diminishing odds inside the little beer joint. Instinctively deciding that offense was better than defense, Eddie deliberately picked out the biggest Mexican, and walked straight toward him. But before he reached the man, the small member of Los Cuchillos who had made the call earlier entered from the back of the bar. Puzzlingly, he strolled directly up to Eddie as if he knew him.

"You people got to leave," the small man said in a surly tone. "I got business to take care of here." The man's narrow eyes glinted in the murky room. Although shorter than the other biker, he showed neither fear nor concern as he stared eyeball-to-eyeball with Eddie.

"We're not going anywhere, asshole," Eddie fired back, jabbing his index finger into the little man's chest. But the dark-eyed stranger didn't budge, and suddenly Danny saw something leave the small biker's waistband, glinting momentarily in the light. Grabbing the nearest beer bottle, Danny launched it at the diminutive Mexican. The longneck shattered against the bar, its explosive crash a signal for the brawl to begin.

Eddie reached for his knife sheath with his right hand and blocked with his left. Confident of Eddie's ability to hold his own in any altercation, Danny smiled to himself as he ducked the first chair flying his way. The stale air in the beer coffin abruptly seemed choked with the eye-watering sting of smoke after a grenade explodes in a foxhole. In the chaotic confusion all around Danny, everyone seemed to be swinging something at somebody.

Spinning with a pool cue in both hands, Danny fended off a scarred wooden chair aimed at his head, snapping two of the legs and cracking the cue. He dropped the broken stick, then drove a hard right fist into his opponent's nose, demolishing it in an eruption of blood. A beer bottle spun past like a kicked football, missing his head by a fraction of an inch. Across the room, by the juke box, two Los Cuchillos were pounding on John, Danny's club brother, a muscular former bouncer with massive arms and the club's name tattooed up each of his triceps.

Fighting well, Danny dodged a trio of attackers, feinting and eluding his adversaries while planting a road-worn engineer boot to the side of a slim Cuchillo's knee. The biker's kneecap snapped like a dry twig. The thin man with a Fu Manchu mustache and shoulder length, wavy hair, screamed, grabbed his destroyed knee and caved to the deck. The thin man's partner, considerably heavier and wearing a large, striped T-shirt and a denim cutoff that smelled as bad as it looked, was surprised and infuriated to see his brother go down. No color remained in the oil-soaked vest worn by the overweight Mexican. The garment was a maze of tattered and faded club patches that stamped him clearly as an outlaw biker, a devotee of drugs and a veteran of numerous bizarre sexual exploits. Enraged, the Mexican turned in Danny's direction and pulled out a knife. The weapon's rusty blade flickered briefly in the gloom, reflecting the neon and the swinging light fixture above the pool table. But before the Cuchillo could react, a single punch from John's anvil-sized fist drove the man to the sawdust-covered cement floor.

Near the front door, another Cuchillos trio swarmed all

over Jesse, a Night Hawk with the build of a small tank. Jesse reached inside his cutoff and jerked a countershaft sprocket from a concealed leather pocket and slashed the face of the young Hispanic foe nearest to him. Immediately, blood sprayed his companions, causing them to flinch for an instant. Their hesitation allowed Jesse, aka "Fireplug," to move within striking distance of another Cuchillo.

Jesse, 5 feet, 7 inches of stout primal strength, had saved a brother's life at a swap meet when a gang of 15 attacked them. When Jesse was knocked to the ground during the brawl, he reached for something in the nearby piles of motorcycle parts, coming up with the tranny sprocket. After the fight, he had the part chromed and engraved with the words, "Fireplug's Tool." Jesse had a leather pocket sewn inside his vest, where he always carried the odd weapon.

Danny jumped suddenly, barely avoiding the thrust of a switchblade. After his enemy's flailing arm passed, Danny grabbed the knife-wielder's wrist, encircling it with the strong fingers of his own right hand, and yanked the arm straight. He then drove his left fist, the fingers adorned with six jagged rings, into the locked elbow. With an audible crack, the bone broke and the arm went limp as its obese owner pissed himself and passed out, hitting the floor with an arm suddenly—and permanently— double-jointed.

Jesse's chromed sprocket slashed into the denim-covered crotch of the remaining attacker. Blinding pain hit the terrified Mexican like a lightning bolt to the shorts, causing him to grab his balls and scream hoarsely. Jesse raked the gasping Mexican across the face with the chromed sprocket just as a hissing pool cue slammed him squarely in his bulldog neck. The Night Hawk staggered backward, dropping the bloody gear to the floor. A sneering member of the Los Cuchillos seized the moment, stepping forward to drive his right fist into Jesse's jaw. The veteran biker stumbled, but his deep-set blue eyes remained sharp and focused.

The Night Hawks were set against four-to-one odds, but

they considered themselves true one-percenters, and lived up to that rowdy reputation whenever challenged. Sometimes they fought for fun, and sometimes for survival, but they were always ready to take on anyone, at any time. The Hawks fought cops, straights, bikers, cowboys, jocks, oil workers—you name it. They fought in the streets, in bars, at events, whenever and wherever. Their vocation and life consisted of the club, their club brothers, and their bikes—nothing else. Few worked; few knew how. Most had street girls who supported them, or else they cut deals as needed, or collected bad debts for loan sharks. They were just as tough first thing in the morning as they were late at night, fighting whenever they felt like it. And when they were high, they always felt like it—and they always won.

From the corner of his eye, Danny glimpsed the assault on Jesse. Instantly, he dropped the broken arm and lunged at the man preparing to swing the cue stick again. From behind, Danny yanked the stick free from the gloating Mexican's hand and, remembering his Shore Patrol training, gripped the laminated wood in both hands. The surprised biker, his club insignia toward Danny, attempted to turn to face the Night Hawk, but was too late. Danny wrapped the hardwood cue around the man's neck, seizing him in a choke hold.

Gagging and gasping loudly, the once-cocky Hispanic clawed at the unyielding wood. Danny leaned the man back against his out-thrust hip, pulling the young Cuchillo off his feet. Nearly unconscious, the helpless biker stopped struggling, allowing Danny to thrust the limp body at a charging Mexican brandishing a knife. Danny dodged the blade, grabbed a chair, and crushed the man to the floor.

With invisible suddenness and brutal force, a Budweiser bottle cracked against Danny's skull. Unceremoniously plunged into the enfolding shadows of tunnel vision, Danny stumbled backward, away from the unconscious Cuchillo at his feet. Faintly, as if from far away, he thought he heard someone scream. The fury of the bar fight seemed to be slowing and, as he crumpled to his knees, Danny was vaguely aware of people running out the front door. He felt the sawdust floor against his cheek an instant before everything was swallowed by blackness.

THE TRAP

Danny was unconscious for five minutes. Before opening his eyes, he touched the side of his face with his twisted right hand. His throbbing temple was gooey wet with blood. A spasm of fear ran through his body, and his eyes jolted open. The juke box, though lying on its side, continued to spew out a Led Zeppelin tune. For as far as he could see, scalpel-sharp glass shards glistened on the floor. No one was in sight. The bar appeared deserted—but something was wrong. Danny moved his head against the smell of spilled beer and stifling sweat. His cheek pushed against bits of glass, cigarette butts, beer, and blood. Nearby, he heard someone breathing erratically, and gurgling as if his lungs were congested with a terrible cold.

His skull throbbing like a jackhammer, Danny rotated his head in the opposite direction. Two feet away, the wiry biker who had fought Eddie lay on his back in a pool of dark liquid. A knife handle protruded from his chest. His mouth opened and shut like a fish out of water, and his bloody hands encircled the carved wooden hilt and brass bolsters. Dazed, Danny stared at the rosewood handle, wiping at his eyes, trying to force them to focus. The realization hit like a gunshot. He groaned, desperately reaching behind his back to his sheath. His knife was gone. With his dying breath, the slight Mexican struggled futilely to release Danny's own blade, buried deeply in his chest. Danny rolled over to assist, bringing himself up on a bruised elbow and wrapped his good hand around the specially carved grip. At that precise moment, the doorway to the bar burst open and a barrage of flashlight beams entered.

"Police!" a young officer shouted, just as his baton struck the side of Danny's head. "This one ain't going nowhere," another anonymous, uniformed voice boasted.

"Except to trial—for murder," the sergeant commented

grimly, looking at the Mexican and the unconscious biker holding the knife.

The young Cuchillo exhaled a final time, and his hands relaxed their death grip around the polished wood and fell to his sides. His last gasp sounded like the final wisp of air escaping from a flat tire. Three Emergency Medical Team members pulled Danny off the body and heaved him onto a waiting gurney.

Danny was one of a kind, a biker to the bone ever since he was a kid. In high school, he sketched motorcycles and dreamed about the day he would own one himself. And when he could, he hung out with a biker who lived a few streets away. His folks drove him hard, both at school and on the field. He was good at sports, performed well in the classes that challenged him, and was recognized as a tough guy on campus. But school wasn't his thing. He didn't get along well with his teachers, and he was impatient with required courses. For Danny, the mechanical won over the scholastic. At home, his mom disapproved of the group he hung out with, kids who lowered cars and slicked their hair. But his dad, a hard-working machinist and tool designer in the oil fields, enjoyed seeing his son get his hands dirty, and make things work, like when Danny replaced the transmission in his first car, a 1948 Nash.

Two days later, Danny woke up in the hospital ward of county jail. As he fought to regain his bearings in the fog filling his mind, a nurse disappeared from the room and two uniformed officers entered, one pushing a ramshackle wheelchair.

"Get in," the older cop ordered. His partner began reading Danny his rights as he struggled out of the bed and stumbled into the rusty wheelchair. His head was swollen with a concussion, his side throbbed from a slashing knife wound. Nausea welled up in his stomach.

Danny's head swam, and faintly he heard a disembodied voice, intoning, "You have the right to remain silent, you have the right to an attorney." He pitched violently against the armrests as a uniformed officer jerked the wheelchair out of the room and into the brightly lighted hall. Danny passed out again as the cop finished reading his rights, but when the chair came to an abrupt stop in the middle of the glaring hall, consciousness returned. Trying to open his eyes, Danny squinted at the neatly pressed uniforms flanking him, then at the hazy succession of white smocks moving quickly up and down the polished linoleum hall. He was baffled, uncomprehending. His mind refused to function, and every bone in his body ached.

One of the cops stepped directly in front of Danny, and in a loud voice announced, "Danny Lonsdale, you are under arrest for the murder of 24-year-old Sancho Gomez. Do you understand? Do you understand?" The cop was shouting, startling everyone in the hall, and causing many to turn and stare at the young ruffian, his form bent and twisted in the chair, confused and in pain. Nurses shook their heads in disgust; doctors shrugged, returning to their work. Danny's body shook, and he slumped down in the wheelchair, his eyes closing involuntarily.

Danny had graduated from high school primarily because his mom was hell-bent on his getting an education. But immediately after receiving his diploma, he joined the army to study helicopter mechanics, spending the next two years flying operations in and out of Vietnam jungles. The service affected him much like high school—he hated every restrictive moment and pointless routine, longing for the freedom of the open road. Wounded, decorated, and disliked by his superiors at the age of 22, he left southeast Asia for home, already beginning to grow a beard before the plane lifted off for San Francisco.

To straight citizens, Danny's life appeared to go directly into the toilet. But in Danny's way of thinking, the next couple of years were the best of his life. The G.I. Bill paid his tuition for classes at the local community college, as well as for welding training at Trade Tech, in Long Beach. His hair was long, and his untrimmed beard grew down to his chest. He tore an old cop bike to the ground and rebuilt it. He spent his days working on bikes and going to school. He spent his nights in the wind, alone, searching the midnight hour for loose women and action. Danny found plenty of both.

Danny awoke when the two officers rolled the wheelchair into a tiny, 5-by-7-foot cell and dumped him on the bunk. His knees smacked against the hard, metal frame, jarring him awake.

"Whenever you come around, scumbag," the younger cop hissed, leaning close to Danny's blinking eyes, "you'll wish it was you who died. In case you hadn't heard, that Mexican kid croaked with your knife stuck in his chest."

Danny blinked, then stared unbelievingly with wide-open eyes. "I didn't kill him!" he gasped, before passing out again on the thin, cotton mattress.

Danny slept for 18 hours. When he awoke, he rubbed his eyes groggily, struggling to sit up on the sagging, spring-supported mattress held by the angle-iron frame. Surveying his bleak surroundings, he realized he was alone with his thoughts, fears, and confusion. Barely 25, and with no record, except for being known as a member of the notorious Night Hawks, he had never been in jail before. Nonetheless, he was well aware that his patch was an automatic two strikes against his sorry ass. Another day passed.

"Lonsdale, your girlfriend is here to see you," an officer shouted down the line of holding cells. Danny got up, stretched his 6-foot, 1-inch frame, splashed water on his face, and did what he could to make himself presentable. Dejectedly, he tugged at the bandages on his head, elbow and side, all of which were beginning to fall off. Looking at his reflection in the polished stainless steel sheet bolted to the wall, he didn't know what to make of anything. Except that he was sure he hadn't killed that Cuchillo, and that he had no business being in jail. Still, he knew instinctively that things looked bad, and that the Man was looking for someone to take the fall. Facing this sort of crisis for the first time, he was scared, as well as concerned about his club brothers. He felt isolated, out of the loop.

The cell made Danny claustrophobic and depressed. Its cramped confines held no TV, no chair, no shelves–just the stainless steel commode, sink, and dingy bunk. The heavy, steel door slowly opened, and Danny stepped into the long, concrete hall. At the end of the corridor, another iron door opened, and he was led into a small concrete room whose only furnishings were three chairs and a large, rectangular oak table with a low partition down the center.

Dixie sat on the far side of the table, her baby face trembling slightly. She was petite, 5 feet, 1 inch tall, with round features and straight red hair. Dixie had eyes that could melt a battleship, and a pair of soft, pouting lips. As Danny entered the room, she jumped to her feet and ran around the table to hug him. For an instant, he felt her warmth against his body, and her full tits pressed against his chest. Then, just as quickly, a guard burst into the room and separated them. "Sit down, dammit, on the other side of the table," the guard barked. "No contact. You've got ten minutes to talk, then you gotta leave." He paused dramatically, then slammed the door. But Dixie's charms had their effect on the guard. Even as the last words blurted from his mouth, his expression softened as her moist eyes and terror-ridden features began to soften his harsh demeanor.

"How are you, baby?" Danny asked.

"I miss you so much," Dixie said, whimpering.

"Can you bail me out?" Danny asked.

"You're going to be arraigned for murder today," she replied, bursting into tears. "They may not give you bail."

"But, goddammit, I didn't do it!" Danny shouted, slamming his fist down hard on the grimy wooden tabletop.

"I know, honey," Dixie murmured soothingly. "But they found your knife in the Cuchillo's chest. It's starting a war between the clubs."

For the briefest instant, Danny sensed a hint of treachery, along with confused feelings of fear, uncertainty, and resolve. He looked down at his hands clenched on the table's oak surface. Feeling strength returning to his soul, Danny stared at the young, street-savvy girl sitting across from him, and wondered what was next. It was all he could handle just to process what was happening to and around him.

"Honey," said Dixie, lowering her voice, "the guys want you to know that, if you hold your mud—well, you know."

"There's nothing to hold my mud about!" Danny shouted, pressing his sweating palms against the worn grain of the tabletop. "I didn't kill the guy, and I don't know who did!"

"Keep to that, and you'll be OK," Dixie whispered, leaning forward, so that his tired eyes could explore her cleavage.

Danny loved Dixie's honey-in-your-mouth lips, the delicate,

childlike softness of her skin, her guileless immaturity, and the kid-like glee she usually displayed. She was born to party, and had done just that. At night, she played, availing herself of whatever drugs were available. During the day, she pored over the classified ads, looking for neglected animals. She would adopt rabbits, chickens, ducks, cats, dogs—anything that was being given away. Their half-acre plot of land had evolved into a menagerie of homeless animals, but she cared for each one with tremendous love. In spite of Dixie's genuine affection for animals, there had always been a hint of larceny in her eyes. She seemed to relish being involved in dangerous drug deals, and shoplifting thrilled her. For the most part, Danny regarded her eccentricities as merely signs of a good-hearted, ready-to-party, biker woman. Nevertheless, from time to time, he wondered if the innocent-looking sweetie wearing those cute, farmer overalls, and sporting her ever-present dazzling smile, was all peaches and cream.

"I love you, baby," Dixie said, reaching across the counter and bending lower to reveal her braless chest. "I'll be here for you until they cut you loose."

"Are all the others all right?" Danny inquired. "They're fine, except for a few cuts and bruises," Dixie replied, brightening, "It was all over the papers."

"Who's coming down to see me?" Danny asked, wondering when his brothers would show up.

"They're all lying low right now," Dixie muttered, averting her eyes. "Did I tell you that the Devils Own have come to their aid?"

"No. Whaddaya mean?" Danny asked, puzzled. "Some of the Devil's Own don't like the Los Cuchillos either," the girl replied, softly. "A few of them came to the meeting the other night."

Danny scratched at his beard and reflected. The Devils Own was the most notorious club of all, with the most sought-after patch on the planet. Everyone who had ever straddled a Harley longed to be a Devil sometime in his life. As a Night Hawk, Danny enjoyed his one-chapter club, but he was still strongly attracted to that embroidered, flaming Devil's head. There was always the hope in the ranks that the Hawks would be absorbed by the Devils Own, but it was more a dream than anything. Undeniably, he enjoyed the tough intrigue, the close calls with the cops, the fistfights and the empty city streets late at night. Bitterly, he ached to be free. For a fleeting moment, Danny's thoughts escaped his prison predicament, his mind returning to his life in the club, as if he was still on the streets.

Dixie left in a shower of tears, and within an hour, Danny had been afforded a shower, donned a pair of blue prison overalls, and stood in front of the walnut counter of the arraignment judge. He was shackled, his wrists and ankles chained to the heavy leather belt encircling his waist. The courtroom was almost empty, and as quiet as a coffin. Still disoriented, Danny shivered, feeling numb and sleepy in the chill of the cold room. He was startled back to wakefulness by the bailiff's announcement of the judge's entrance.

"All rise," the officer boomed to the empty room. "Court is now in session, the honorable Judge Ray Ralston presiding."

A grim-faced, humorless-looking elderly man mounted the steps up to the desk and tossed a file on his blotter. "You may as well remain standing, Mr. Lonsdale," the imposing judge said, sitting back and peering scornfully over the top of the half-lens reading glasses perched low on his nose. "I have a first-degree murder felony complaint against you, Mr. Lonsdale. How do you plead?"

"Not guilty," Danny mumbled, his knees weakening. The reality of his predicament was truly beginning to hit home.

The judge frowned and glanced around the courtroom, apparently just then noticing that Danny was alone. Danny vaguely recalled talking to some guy in a suit not long after he woke up in jail, but except for a couple of phrases like "advised of your rights," "subpoena witnesses," and "petition for a continuance," he remembered nothing of their conversation. "Do you have legal representation?" the judge barked, seeming to imply that Danny deserved none.

"No, sir," Danny responded.

"Then your appearance here today is evidently another clerical error," the judge said, sending a withering glance in the court clerk's direction. "Very well, the court will assign a public defender for you. Any questions?"

"Thousands," Danny said. "But this isn't the time to ask

them, I guess. Any hope of bail?"

"No bail in a murder complaint," the judge spat down at the accused, "unless there are extenuating circumstances."

"How about if I'm innocent?" Danny snapped back. The judge cut the biker off sharply. "That will do, Mr. Lonsdale," he said sternly, glaring over his reading glasses like a vulture eyeing its prey. "A public defender will contact you within twenty-four hours. He will have ten days to prepare for your preliminary hearing, although in your case, I don't anticipate any extensive investigation. At that hearing, the judge will determine whether this complaint is reasonable, then you have fourteen days to prepare for rearraignment in Superior Court."

"But when do we get down to the trial?" Danny asked, uncertainly. "After your hearing in Superior Court, your attorney has 60 days to prepare for trial, or request a continuance. Thank you, Mr. Lonsdale," the judge abruptly concluded, standing up and leaving the room.

Danny felt a freezing chill penetrate to the marrow of his bones. Listening to his fate declared from the pinched-face, gray-haired judge, he felt more vulnerable than ever before in his entire life, more apprehensive than on a Vietnam mission. Even while his helicopter was under fire and he was trying to rescue fellow grunts caught in a crossfire in a burning village, Danny hadn't been this fearful of a disastrous outcome. Even as the airframe lifted from the smoke, grossly overloaded, with guys dangling by their armpits from the landing gear while the enemy sprayed them with automatic rifle fire, Danny wasn't this scared. In combat, his efforts may have seemed hopeless at the moment, but at least he had been able to move, to take whatever evasive action he could. Stymied in the confines of the courtroom, Danny felt terrified and helpless. He couldn't make a move.

Glumly, Danny realized he was stuck, his hands tied, separated from his brothers by a wall of hostile opposition. As the judge had pronounced the crime for which he would be tried, Danny's heart sank. He knew, the D.A. knew—and his public defender would soon discover—that he was in very deep shit indeed. He had no defense, no money, no witnesses, and little or no hope.

In the simplistic view of the law and the public, Danny was an outlaw biker. And bikers deserved the worst.

STREET JUSTICE

*T*he Night Hawks rode their machines down the alley behind the run-down bungalow on the edge of Culver City, two miles from the blue waters of the Pacific Ocean and south of its celebrated coastline. Earlier, as the group rolled past the pier and the million-dollar high-rises overlooking the sea, the last thing on the minds of the scruffy bikers were white, sandy beaches and the tidy lawns of Santa Monica. As the streets wound inland, the size and ostentation of the homes steadily diminished, until finally, 1,200-square-foot bungalows, built barely five feet apart, lined the narrow streets. Still, even these ordinary citizens felt privileged to own a cramped stucco house in the coastal community on the Gold Coast.

Big John rented the dilapidated bungalow to be close to the girls in the night clubs down by the beach. The exterior stucco was cracked, and the house was bare inside, except for two ancient black leather couches and a steel-bodied coffee table. Above the marred wooden floors, the walls displayed club flags and paraphernalia. In the kitchen, a freshly-painted Harley-Davidson rigid frame custom glistened in the center of the linoleum floor, resting on a plastic milk crate. The middle-class house had two small bedrooms, one tiny bathroom with white, ceramic tile walls and floor, a back yard not big enough to park the average sedan in, and one miniature, two-car garage.

A hulking brute with the power and grizzly attitude to go with his size, John was nothing short of a fist-fighting madman. He stood 6 feet, 2 inches, with tree-trunk-size limbs, a full, dark chocolate beard, and a greased-back hot rod hairdo. Older than most of the members at age 35, John was a legendary street fighter, a veteran tattoo collector, and a dedicated womanizer who cared only about getting high and fucking. He took no special pride in his motorcycle–as long as it started and got him to the bar and back, he was satisfied. John's parents were southern-bred alcoholics who drifted from job to job, looking for easy work and a fast high. In a drunken domestic battle while John was still a boy, his father shot his mother. Then, realizing what he had done, he turned the gun on himself. Throughout his life, John had always been terrified of long-term relationships.

John signaled the brothers to pull their bikes into the garage from the narrow alley, and enter the house by the back door. Officially, the club was at war with the Los Cuchillos, so everything—including parking the bikes in the garage–was handled in a serious, high-security manner. John was an imposing, formidable sight as he stood in the center of the narrow alley, wearing jeans and a black club T-shirt reading, "Snitches are a Dying Breed" under his tattered Levi's club vest. The sleeves had been cut off to display his massive, tattooed arms, which now made slicing motions across his throat, indicating for the members to shut off their engines and coast quietly into the garage.

With the bike's long, upswept exhaust pipes and fishtail tips shattering the quiet night like a runaway train, Old Man Jason roared around the corner and into the alley on his rigid-frame chopper. Fishtails—finned ends to pipes that looked traditional, but were actually unmuffled—created a slapping sound, as if Jason's earsplitting, outrageous exhaust was smacking each citizen he passed with its rancorous, stinging sound.

Jason gunned his bike, and the discordant din exploded in the narrow alley, reverberating from the uninsulated garage doors and stucco buildings like an artillery barrage. He enjoyed calling attention to himself, so he kicked over a trash can, yanked at his clutch, revved the motor again, and dropped the hammer. The bike bellowed deafeningly and flew into a wheelstand. It was an impressive stunt, but John's reaction wasn't at all favorable. Scowling, he ran to the center of the alley, making slashing motions with his bulky hand and hamhock forearm, all the while looking like a madman pantomiming his intention to decapitate his victim.

Old Man Jason was the real item—a genuine, no-shit, wild outlaw who loved riding his motorcycle, creating a "scene," and tearing up the town. In the service, he had learned to operate heavy equipment and cranes, but he was a rebel and a party animal, first and foremost. His discharge from the Navy came after an officer caught him smoking dope while getting a blowjob in one of the ship's compartments.

If Jason had played it cool, he might have talked his way through the incident and walked away. But his gut reaction was to threaten the officer. "Snitch me off, and I'll kick your sorry ass," he had snarled menacingly, continuing to smoke while holding a petite Asian woman in place with his free arm. He was a man on the move—tough and good-looking, with kinky, prematurely gray hair and a full beard. After the service, he worked for a while in the harbor, operating cranes until he was fired for being drunk on the job. Soon thereafter, he decided that the life of an outlaw didn't mix with having a steady job.

"Shut that motherfucker off!" John shouted, finally breaking his own silence, and adding to the pandemonium in the alley.

"Fuck anybody who don't like it!" Jason shouted, slamming on his brakes and sliding to a sideways stop a foot away from John.

"Listen, asshole," John growled between clenched teeth, "we've got some serious shit to deal with here. The last thing we need is the whole fuckin' neighborhood checkin' us out."

"Fuck you," Jason slurred, obviously drunk. He got off his bike and reached inside his vest for his flask of Jagermeister. "You take this shit too seriously, brother. Besides, any of these so-called neighbors give us any shit, I'll take care of 'em personally. Now, let's party."

John said nothing, simply shaking his head and closing the door after Jason had shoved his bike inside, joining the rest of the cooling iron in the garage, an impressive collection of Big Twin engines, flame-covered gas tanks, swastikas, and chrome.

Inside the house, the seven members gathered in the living room, drinking beer, smoking pot, snorting lines, sharpening a knife, polishing a handgun, or waiting quietly. Other than Jason and Fireball, the group was subdued. A few members, nervous with anticipation, fidgeted as they swigged from a bottle of Jack Daniel's being passed around the room.

Fireball, as everyone called him, had no other name. It seemed a perfect tag for this flamboyant rider whose short, stout body and brassy, red hair made a striking figure as he flashed down the freeway. Years earlier, his socialite parents had tried to accept their son's wild ways, but when they could no longer cope with his increasingly nonconformist—even anti-social behavior, he simply laughed at them and rode away. Now, he dealt drugs on a lightweight scale and ran a performance Sportster shop. He loved to ride fast and to build fast bikes. Funny, jovial, and easygoing, Fireball was the kind of guy who could laugh at a knife fight he was losing, a guy almost impossible to dislike.

Sitting back in the heavily padded, black leather chair, Fast Eddie sharpened his Buck knife with a small, worn whetstone he carried in his slick leather vest. Inside the black borders of the small, rectangular patch sewn above his pocket, black letters against a white background spelled, "President." A single pin adorned the front of his vest. The silver claw of a hawk holding a tortured skull glinted in the night's gloom.

The same silver claw and screaming skull composed the centerpiece of the Night Hawks' back patch. Above that, arching across the rider's shoulders, was a rocker bearing the club's name, while the bottom rocker simply read, "Los Angeles."

Originally, the bottom rocker read, "South Bay," but as the Night Hawks' influence grew—along with their fearsome reputation and intimidating notoriety—the club dropped the suburb's name in favor of the entire metropolis. Fearless, the Hawks pretty much did as they pleased, bluntly challenging anyone who didn't like it to do something about it. Publicly, there were no takers. But privately, more than one bike club—including the Los Cuchillos—had other ideas.

Only one club wore colors with "California" emblazoned across the bottom rocker, and that was the Devils Own, the oldest, most feared, most notorious motorcycle club in the country, and no patch was more coveted than the one its members proudly wore. Curiously, however, there was no chapter in the Los Angeles region, leading some of the Night Hawks to hope secretly that the Devils Own might absorb their group, so that ultimately, they would become the L.A. chapter.

Eddie came from Southern California. His attorney father abused his mother, and taught his boy that the world was a dog-eat-dog struggle, and that his survival would depend on his being unrelentingly cunning, while simultaneously maintaining a strong facade and taking care of business. Now 33, Eddie had once been married, back when he was still trying to mold himself in his father's image. He had abused his wife, beating her, and forcing her to have sex with him at his whim—anyplace, anytime. Unfortunately, his wife's father was also an attorney. He threatened legal action, as well as public humiliation, for the offense. Eddie's father was so devoted to his lifestyle, and so protective of his public image, that he coerced Eddie into quietly divorcing the woman, and leaving the community. By imposing his will on his son, Eddie's old man avoided having his reputation tarnished by the violent cruelty that was his legacy to his son. Away from the smothering confines of the straight world, Eddie found outlaws to be less judgmental than the people back home. He could rape and pillage at will, and no one would say a word, nervously aware that Eddie's knife could cut off all opposition—literally.

Eddie was unruffled by the news that the Los Cuchillos wanted no talk of peace. He sat in the large leather chair completely relaxed, exuding an aura of quiet strength. Eddie's powerful presence was enhanced by the outlaw garb he wore with obvious pride: polished black boots, black Frisco Levis with narrow legs, black western shirt with pearl buttons, and a custom-made black leather vest. His black, shoulder-length hair was carefully combed back, and his goatee was neatly trimmed. Eddie always looked sharp—as sharp as the knife he skillfully stroked across the narrow whetstone—the knife that had originally entered the Cuchillo's torso, the knife the real killer had wielded so skillfully that humid night in May.

Eddie was confident that the now-notorious incident would capture the attention of the Devils Own. He was both right and wrong.

Inside the house, the group sat on the floor, on couches, and overstuffed chairs, filling the room with the smell of drugs, smoke, and booze. Eddie called the meeting to order, opening the proceedings with an admonition to all the members. "Nothing said in this meeting tonight leaves the room," he said, forcefully. "Everybody got that?" Eddie watched the assembled bikers nod their agreement, then continued. "I talked to those Cuchillo cocksuckers, and they got nothin' to say. So, brothers, we're at war." A low murmur passed through the room, followed by a few scattered cheers. Gradually, the room became quiet, as each biker pondered what lay ahead.

"What the fuck does that mean?" said Hank, his low, menacing voice seeming unnaturally loud as it shattered the fragile silence from the dark corner where he stood. Eddie and Hank were close—their partnership secured Eddie's position and prevented ambitious power plays. His pockmarked face was hidden by shoulder-length, wiry, salt-and-pepper hair. His full beard was also graced with touches of gray, and it concealed most of his less-than-handsome face. Hank was a quiet, direct man. But he was also mean, cruel, merciless, and—by a very substantial margin—the most dangerous man in the club. "I ain't gonna stop riding my bike!" Fireball shouted. "I'm a Hawk, and ain't no one takin' that away from me!"

"There's half a dozen of those guys to every one of us," Big John said, gulping down the last of another beer. "And the bastards are spread all over downtown L.A., Burbank, and Long Beach. What the fuck can we do?"

"We ain't gonna do nothin'," Eddie said, rubbing his blade against the sharpening stone, pausing only to stare eyeball-to-eyeball with each member. "Unless, of course," he continued, "we run into any of them scumbags. In that case, kill the cocksuckers, or fuck 'em up and take their patches. No fucking slack! Got that? We'll teach those bastards to fuck with us."

"Got ya, boss," Old Man Jason shouted, slamming his flask of Jagermeister on the steel coffee table. "Hell, brother, why don't we go find us a couple-three tonight?"

"Hey," Fireball barked, interrupting the war talk. "What about our brother downtown? Shouldn't we be puttin' bail money together, so we can spring him?"

From a dark corner of the room, his form indistinct and barely discernible among the shadows, Hank spoke again. "Forget him!" he snarled. "He's fucked. The bastard shoulda stayed on his feet and got the fuck outta there like the rest of us." Scowling, he turned his attention back to the 9mm Browning pistol in his hand, using a clean shop rag to wipe on a protective coat of Hoppe's gun oil.

"What the hell ya sayin'?" Fireball butted in. "Because he got sucker-punched while tryin' to keep a brother from gettin' his ass kicked, we ain't gonna help him?"

"All I'm sayin' is that he's up against the big one. We can't bail him out, and the cops are hot for a speedy trial." Eddie's tone was not encouraging. But the strained silence that followed his response to Fireball's question perturbed him a bit. Momentarily abandoning the speech he had intended to make, Eddie began to improvise, his words depicting Danny as the Fortunate Fuck-Up, a dumb-luck guy who breaks the law, but gets away with it in spite of himself. Or, in Danny's case, as Eddie explained to his rapt audience, it's a guy who acts irresponsibly, then leaves it to other people to deal with any negative or heavy consequences. Eddie concluded by saying, "Think about it. The Los Cuchillos are a buncha pricks anyway, but we're at war with 'em because Danny blew it at that bar. The rest of us are gonna have to figure out how to stay alive until this mess can be straightened out. But not ol' Danny. He don't have to worry, 'cause he's—well, he's safely under protection."

"Shit!" Fireball barked, contemptuously. "I'd rather be on the streets, fightin' Los Cuchillos daily, than cooped-up downtown." Fireball stared at the club's president as if he were seeing the "real" Eddie for the first time, an Eddie who showed little compassion or concern for his locked-down bro.

In the thick, tense atmosphere of the room, the two men glared at each other without blinking. Dumbfounded by the unexpected confrontation, the other Night Hawks exchanged puzzled glances. After all, hadn't it been Eddie himself who had lectured them on the absolute necessity of closing ranks, of displaying a united front to the enemy club? Fireball's angry voice broke the awkward silence. "Well, fuck you, Eddie-Boy," he sneered. "I still think we should do something—go see him, make sure he's got a lawyer an' all that shit. What the fuck good is a so-called brotherhood, if the first time somethin' goes wrong, your brothers just dump you? Lemme tell ya, asshole, I'm beginnin' to think your attitude is fucked!"

Hank stared intently at Fireball, sliding back a little farther into the darkened corner. Eddie made no response to Fireball's angry remarks. Instead, he simply began to stroke his knife along the sharpening stone, as if to taunt his fellow Night Hawk. "Why, you pansy motherfucker," Fireball growled, enraged by Eddie's silent insult. The angry biker leapt to his feet and charged toward the far corner of the room, spilling beers and overturning ashtrays in the process.

In an uninterrupted, flowing motion, Hank straightened his slender torso, popped the clip into the automatic, and quickly worked the slide to chamber a round. Stepping out of the darkness behind Eddie's padded chair, Hank held the gun with both hands, its barrel leveled directly at the sternum of the raging biker. Fireball stopped short, the gun poking against his chest. "Go ahead, hotshot," he sneered. "Kill another brother!" Undaunted, he slapped the pistol aside and flung himself toward his brother Hawk. But Eddie wasn't known as "Fast" for nothing. The agile biker spun out of his chair with remarkable quickness, leaping toward the wall, and leaving Fireball embarrassed to be grabbing handfuls of empty air instead of his adversary.

WHORES AND KNIVES

*T*he blast from Hank's pistol was deafening, the report driving all the brothers to their feet instantly, as the heavy slug missed Fireball's head by two inches before tearing through the stucco wall and on into the darkness beyond.

To add insult to injury, Eddie made a show of sitting back in his throne and continuing to sharpen his precious knife, even as several members thrust themselves between the men to keep them apart. When everyone was seated again, Eddie cleared his throat to signal the resumption of the meeting. "There's another matter to consider," he said quietly, tugging thoughtfully at his long goatee. "We're expecting a meeting tonight with some of the Devils Own from up north. Hank and I will get together with them, and we'll talk over ways of handling the shitstorm Danny caused. But for now, we're not moving against the Los Cuchillos, unless we happen to run into one of them. That's final. If you see one on the streets, go for it. But no hunts." Taking his time, Eddie surveyed the faces of his audience before continuing. "And don't worry," he said in a mildly conciliatory tone, "our lawyer has already been in touch with Danny. Now get your ass over to the bar before the cops show up here. Hank and I have business to take care of."

As the bikers scrambled for the garage, Hank approached Fireball. "Hey, brother," he said, "don't sweat about our takin' care of Danny. Dixie went to see him this morning, before he was arraigned. And the lawyer was there for the hearing."

Hank's voice was normal, but the glint in his eyes was insincere, treacherous. He liked to give people the impression that he knew something no one else did, but Fireball saw through the act, and wouldn't take the bait. Nor would he accept Hank's apology. Instead, he simply patted him on the back and laughed, as he always did. Walking across the neglected, tattered lawn to the garage, Fireball tried to sort things out in his mind. Hank was the drug dealer, on good terms with numerous other clubs, including the Devils Own, his connection for crank, women, and—supposedly —information that made him an invaluable member of the Night Hawks. Maybe that's true, Fireball thought. Or is Hank actually an invaluable spy for others? Fireball's musings were abruptly cut short by the distinctive wail of sirens in the distance, the sound growing louder by the second. Neighbors had called the police, and two cruisers, lights flashing and sirens blazing, were speeding down Washington Blvd. toward the rented house that very moment, even as the brothers frantically pulled on their jackets and leathers, before kicking their machines to life.

"John," Eddie shouted, "you and Jesse go north on Washington and double back on Santa Monica Blvd. We'll meet you at Oil Can Charlie's later. Fireball, you and Jason head south to Ocean, then go west. Now, git!"

Big John and Jesse roared north through the alleys for several blocks, speeding down side streets without slowing to check for oncoming traffic. They flew through intersections, jumping dips and knocking over trash cans while their bikes screamed against the night. They hung an abrupt left on Sawtelle, shot over two streets, then turned toward the freeway at the light on Washington, just as the police cruisers wheeled onto Washington, heading in the opposite direction.

The other two riders were long gone as Hank and Eddie picked the next parallel street and headed west, then north on Wilshire, toward Beverly Hills and Hollywood. From Sunset Blvd., they took Highland south, into the back yard of Hollywood, where small photo studios and sound recording warehouses lined the drab streets. Whores and druggies mingled at every corner, while transvestites roamed the alleys in packs, taking comfort in the company of people with the same tastes.

For the average citizen, the area was a dark and foreboding world of freaks roaming the back streets and alleys of Hollywood. But for outlaw bikers, this was a candy store full of undesirables to hassle, beat up, or rob. Tourists and straights might find these Hollywood creeps scary, but bikers regarded them with such disdain and contempt that these wretches would literally shudder at the sound of a big Harley, especially a chopper. The prostitutes knew that their pimps could offer no protection from these wild riders who splashed on violence like straights put on aftershave. Among street people, the outlaw bikers were universally known to be vicious, unpredictable—and very dangerous.

Eddie and Hank pulled up in front of a nondescript brick building on one of the many darkened streets lurking behind the glitter of Sunset Blvd. As they came to a stop, a double-wide, roll-up door creaked and began to rise. Waving them inside with a long, coiled bullwhip held tightly in his mammoth fist, was a menacing biker wearing a wild, fringed vest, even wilder hair, and empty spaces in his mouth which several of his front teeth used to occupy. They pulled in slowly and killed their engines. Rotten Ron, 6 feet, 3 inches, 235 pounds, a veteran outlaw biker and longtime member of the Devils Own, let go of the chain holding the door. It dropped immediately, slamming against the pavement, startling Eddie, who had never met these men before.

In the darkened photo studio, Eddie was barely able to make out a murky form rising from a chair and turning to walk in their direction. Looking past the vague silhouette to the studio behind, he observed small spotlights illuminating an ornate bed where two women posed for the camera, their faces buried in each other's pussy. The eager photographer captured each darting tongue, hardened nipple, and arched hip. Both women were knockouts—tanned, buxom, and obviously eager to get nasty together. Between shots, they teased one another, rubbing and kissing. The photographer gave directions to his assistant, who adjusted the lighting for each pose, then stood back and watched intently. The girls were too engrossed in their erotic play to notice—or to care.

Everything here—the girls, the studio, the photographer—was among the benefits of being in the drug business. Because the Devils Own supplied meth to the photographer, the club had a standing invitation to attend whatever lurid photo session might come up. And, from time to time, the club members met the female stars up close and personal—another perk of big-time drug business.

Rotten Ron stared at the Hawks without speaking, idly

fumbling with his bullwhip. A second Devils Own appeared out of the darkness and motioned for everyone to follow him to an adjacent room, just off the studio. Silently, he led them into an all-white dressing room full of lingerie, make-up, and props. Rotten Ron followed the two Night Hawks and shut the door. Everyone else remained standing in the narrow corridor. While they waited for one of the other bikers to begin the meeting, Eddie and Hank tried to drink in their surroundings without being too obvious about it. The most prominent feature of the long, rectangular room was a counter surrounded by lights running its entire length. Along its Formica top, a variety of cosmetics and make-up brushes lay scattered in a sea of crumpled Kleenex tissues. The smell of cheap perfume hung heavily in the air. Standing closest to Eddie and Hank was Miguel, a massive Mexican with large, muscular forearms, and long, black hair pulled into a thick ponytail. Even his patch seemed impressive and foreboding. Eddie knew that these outlaws were veterans of several wars, and their track record, he remembered, was perfect. They didn't lose, they didn't quit, they didn't back down. What they did do, was anything—literally, anything—to prevent disgrace to themselves or to their patch.

Suddenly, Miguel turned to face Eddie directly. "Just what the fuck do you people think you're doing?" he snarled, contemptuously. "We do business with the Los Cuchillos— lots of business. The fuck we need you turds for?"

Eddie sized up the huge Hispanic with the narrow sunglasses and the drooping mustache looming over him. Remembering his goal of someday becoming a Devils Own reveling in the sheer sense of power known only to those who ride with the biggest, baddest club in the country, he held his fear in check. "With all due respect to your patch," Eddie began, calmly, "if I'm partying in a bar, and a bunch of assholes tell me and my brothers to leave, I'm fightin' the sonsabitches, and that's all there is to it. I sure as hell ain't gonna wait to ask 'em who they buy their drugs from."

"In fact," Hank chimed in, supporting his brother, "if you do so much business with these guys, why don't you do a better job of controlling them?"

Miguel ignored Hank's comment and stepped close to

Eddie, his massive bulk looming above the smaller man. At the same time, Ron came up behind Hank and threw a coil of his worn, braided bullwhip over the other biker's head and around his neck, pulling the lighter man into a chokehold, and cutting off his wind.

"We'll control anyone we like, motherfucker," Ron hissed into Hank's ear. "And right now, we're controlling you."

Eddie was impressed by the guts and poise shown by these two tattooed monsters. Obviously, they had no fear of the newcomers, and Eddie felt his knees tremble slightly. Suddenly, as fear closed in around him, he forgot the enticing sight of women's clothing scattered around the room, forgot the erotic memory of the two girls making love for the camera less than 30 feet away, and forgot the exciting smell of lust permeating the room. Miguel's breath enveloped his face, only inches from Eddie's nose. These weren't negotiations, Eddie realized. These people didn't want to know what happened at the bar, nor were they interested in discussing details of the Hawks' becoming members of the Devils Own. And worst of all, just behind him, his brother was being choked to death. It was time to act.

Moving quickly, Eddie grabbed Miguel's hand and turned the big man, smoothly slipping beside him as he pulled his knife and shoved it under his opponent's vest. Miguel winced as the blade's point pierced the flesh near his kidney. Instinctively, Eddie knew this wasn't going to be a two-punch fight. The four of them would likely go at it like hungry mountain lions crazed by the scent of fresh meat. And, in all probability, the two Night Hawks would lose. "Let him loose," Eddie snapped.

Miguel, spinning aside and pushing the blade away from his body, slapped Eddie like he was an insolent teenager. "You've proved you can handle yourselves. But don't ever make a move on a Devils Own again, 'cause it will be your last."

Miguel had been a Devils Own for 20 years, and it wasn't his nature to give in. He quivered with anger, right down to his elaborate mustache. He wanted to kill both Night Hawks in the dressing room and leave. But he knew from his own experience that he often found his best brothers in similar situations. And anyway, he had other priorities for this meeting.

Hank gasped for air. "Let him go, Ron," Miguel muttered.

Rotten Ron hesitated, then loosened his grip. Hank tore himself free of the bullwhip, choking and coughing. But Hank was no fool—moments before Miguel told Ron to release him, even as he gagged and struggled to get his breath, Hank reached into his vest and clicked off the safety on his 9mm with his right thumb. He was beginning to draw his weapon when Ron relaxed his hold on the braided bullwhip.

Miguel was furious, but he nonetheless had a new respect for the two men, "We've got a deal for you guys to consider," he said, curtly. "provided your members have the heart you two do, and can back it up." He paused, staring grimly at the two Night Hawks. "Give up this bullshit with the Los Cuchillos, and we'll consider your club for a charter."

"But this shit won't just go away by itself," Eddie objected. "What about the Los Cuchillos themselves?"

"We'll take care of them." Ron's voice came from behind Eddie, but the Hawk made no move to turn and face the man. Instead, he maintained his direct, eye-to-eye concentration on Miguel.

"Well?" Miguel asked, impatiently.

Eddie was both pleased and surprised at the same time. He was certain that his club would gain some recognition, but he had no idea matters would progress this fast, nor in this way. Still, he remained unsure about many things, so when he responded to Miguel's question, he was cautious. "I'll need to discuss this with my club brothers," was his terse reply.

"You are the president, aren't you?" Miguel asked, scornfully. "We could kill the two of you right now, let the Los Cuchillos kill the rest of your members, and just forget you creeps. So make a fuckin' educated guess, asshole—we ain't got all night." Miguel spoke with such confidence that Eddie took a step back from him. The man simply radiated strength. Power emanated from his pores like a poisonous gas.

Choosing his words carefully, Eddie said, "Of course, we'd be honored to become The Devils Own."

"Then someone's got to fall for the dead Cuchillo," Miguel said, bluntly, motioning for Ron to open the door. Clearly, the meeting was over.

"What do you mean?" Eddie inquired.

"Think about it. You'll figure it out," Miguel said, turning to leave. As Ron stepped forward to show Eddie and Hank out, Miguel paused, then walked back to the two Night Hawks. "Listen, we've got some other business to take care of," he said with a slight smile, gesturing toward the back of the studio, where the girls continued to writhe on the bed. Suddenly friendly, he gave Eddie an unexpected pat on the back. "Maybe next time we meet, circumstances will be different. And by the way, good move with that knife. You're fast." Not waiting for a reply, Miguel spun on his heel and walked away, his full patch in Eddie's face.

As Ron led the two Night Hawks back to their bikes, Eddie glanced back over his shoulder. Miguel had already disappeared into the dark shadows of the studio.

Chapter 5

SHOWDOWN

*T*he killing occurred in May, and in the blink of an eye, the first of June had come and gone while Danny racked his brain for information, and strained his burning triceps and abs doing push-ups and sit-ups on cold concrete. While Danny sweated through self-imposed, tortuous workouts, and pushed the iron of his will, his brothers were dealing with the strange experience of being involved in a street war between factions who didn't know one another, nor where their enemies lived, though rumors and paranoia abounded. For most of the club's members, the notion of "kill or be killed" was a new sensation. Indeed, Danny was the only one of the bunch who had faced life and death tension in the war zones of Vietnam. This was different.

Club meetings were filled with intense talk of weapons. Big John bought two Swedish automatic rifles—vintage guns from sometime in the 1940s—along with spare clips and several boxes of ammunition. The weapons hadn't been fired in 20 years, but the dents on the cooling jackets around the barrels, and their sloppy chamber action testified to their active past. John, Jesse, and Jason borrowed a battered Toyota, and rolled into the hills behind Oxnard to experiment with their new contraband. The three skidded along the winding highway weaving between the coast and Ojai, the surrounding terrain overgrown with scrub oaks, manzanita bushes, and poison oak. John leaned out the window, cocked the weapon, and fired it into the brush alongside the road. The gun blurted and jerked as flames spewed from the barrel. Even in John's massive arms, the automatic recoiled violently from the powerful bursts ripping through the underbrush.

"Jesus Christ!" John shouted, the firing halting abruptly. "What happened?" Jason hollered from the back seat, swigging from a half pint of peppermint schnapps.

"This bastard's a monster," John replied. "But it quit on

me." He pulled the weapon back inside the Toyota, and turned it on its side. The clip was gone. "Stop the car!" he shouted.

Jesse hit the brakes. The three husky men in the dusty compact pitched forward in their seats. "Back up!" John barked, sweat glistening on his high forehead.

The men were aware that possessing or firing a fully automatic weapon constituted a federal offense, and for all they knew, these battered guns could have been used in any number of crimes in the past. Jesse backed up quickly, searching the expanse of the road for the foot-long, olive drab clip.

"Fuck," John growled, "if we don't get the damned thing before another car comes along, we could be in Shit City."

"Relax," Jesse said. "We'll get it." He rounded the last bend confidently, as if certain no one was in the vicinity. The clip lay in the center of the roadway, and Jesse veered until it was directly alongside the Toyota. "Grab it, John," he said.

John opened the door and retrieved the clip without getting out of the car. "Let's get the fuck outta here," he said nervously. "At least we know this one works. But we better tape the fuckin' clip in place, so it'll be there if we ever have to use it."

"That artillery is bad shit," Jason muttered, wide-eyed, still gulping his alcohol-candy-in-a-bottle. Jesse nodded as they rolled down the hill, the three burly figures in the small Toyota looking incongruous, yet ominous, as if the car and the men were from two different planets. The bikers were all big-boned, muscular badasses with beards. Somehow, they looked as if they should actually be outside the tiny vehicle, pounding on it with sledgehammers, instead of riding down this picturesque road on their way to the coast highway. It was a bizarre sight, yet they managed to avoid detection.

Later that week, Fireball stockpiled dynamite and blasting caps stolen from a construction site in the mountain community of Big Bear. Though the men bragged about their new weapons, their smiles faded once they left the security of their homes and companions to venture into the city streets alone. Nonetheless, to a man, they refused to back down, or to remove their patches, or to slink along the city streets in cars.

Danny faced his preliminary hearing like a blind man, uncertain what to expect. In the cold and lifeless courtroom, Danny massaged his freshly shaved chin while the judge assessed the evidence and interviewed witnesses. Against his attorney's advice, Danny had kept his mustache, but his hair was combed carefully and tied tightly at the base of his neck. Since he faced only the judge today, he wasn't allowed street clothes, and therefore stood behind the long oak table in orange prison overalls, his wrists shackled to a chain around his waist. The gray-bearded judged glared at Danny from his oak perch. "Do you know what special circumstances are?" he asked sharply.

Danny was momentarily caught off guard. Just recently, his cocky attorney announced a manslaughter deal, and suddenly he was facing premeditated charges. Fearful that, if he responded quickly in the affirmative, the judge might conclude that he was fully aware of the magnitude of special circumstances, Danny froze.

"No sir," Danny said humbly, his knees rattling like loose pistons. Frightened of the outcome of this stage of the investigation, Horowitz was already aware that the judge was forced, by law, to evaluate the possibility of special circumstances, and he was afraid to confer with his client on the matter, leaving Danny in the dark. But Danny knew in his gut that, in order to tag him with special circumstances, the D.A.'s office would be required to prove to the judge that he had acted with malice of forethought, that he actually planned the death of the Mexican biker. Danny knew that wasn't the case, and that the prosecution lacked the witnesses and evidence to make such an extreme charge stick. Still the Assistant D.A. was going to give it a shot, arguing his case for special circumstances to the stern-faced judge.

If Danny were found guilty of murder with special circumstances, he would face a minimum sentence of Life Without Parole (LWOP). Special circumstances also prohibited any chance of a deal with the court for a reduced sentence. Danny scribbled on a pad, then shoved the note in front of Horowitz, who paled visibly as he read the words Danny had written. "David, don't fuck this up. They have no witnesses, no proof of premeditation. The bar was a mess—it was a fucking brawl."

"I know, I know," the lawyer muttered, standing to respond to the Assistant D.A. "Your honor, my esteemed colleague knows that he has no evidence of any plan to harm Mr. Gomez. There is, however, substantial evidence of a brawl, and no witnesses to the actual crime."

The judge pondered the attorneys' statements, and glanced at the three officers poised in the seats behind Danny like a loyal cheering squad on the 50-yard line at a home game. Danny could sense their alertness, monitoring the judge's every gesture, right down to the way he spun a pencil between his hands. Danny further sensed the judge's rapport with the prosecution, and his contempt for the defense attorney's comments. Every time the judge jotted a note, Danny felt the energy level at his back intensify. As the judge prepared to issue his ruling, a slight shiver caused the hair on the back of Danny's neck to rise briefly. "Gentlemen," the judge said, shuffling through his notes, "I don't see any reason not to hold Mr. Lonsdale over for Superior Court. Before then, I will decide whether or not this is a murder case with special circumstances. Mr. Lonsdale, if you are found guilty of first degree murder with special circumstances, the minimum sentence will be LWOP. Do you understand?"

"Not exactly, your honor," Danny replied softly. "Will you be so kind as to explain how I can get jumped in a bar, and end up with LWOP?" He struggled to stay calm.

"Find out from your attorney," the judge barked, slamming his gavel against its oak base with a crack that reverberated against the unforgiving walls. "Court is recessed," the judge announced, abruptly rising to his feet. "Bailiff, I'll hear the next case in one hour." Danny sensed that the man was grappling with misgivings concerning his integrity, versus the will of the three officers sitting behind him, and the prosecution's recommendations. After the judge left the room, the youngest of the officers squealed, "The judge will bury this clown."

"I'm not so sure," the middle-aged veteran beside him said, straightening out his lanky frame and stretching.

"What do you mean, you're not sure?" the young one

persisted. "We saw the bastard holding the knife in that wetback's chest." The third officer, a robust man working on a substantial tire around his midsection, lowered his voice after his companion's indiscreet use of the term "wetback" had proclaimed his prejudice to everyone present. "We got this kid dead to rights. He's a worthless piece of shit, and meant to kill that kid."

Quietly, the three cops continued to debate the matter as they exited the courtroom. Danny was returned to his cell, desperate and glum.

As the middle of June rolled past, a huge, annual custom bike show was planned for the Los Angeles Sports Arena. Posters hung in the windows of every bike shop in L.A. Rock radio stations excitedly blurted ads for the weekend affair, which would feature bands, wet T-shirt contests, custom bikes galore, beautiful babes, and bike-riding celebrities. Another ad had just poured from the radio in John's garage, as Jason and Big John wrenched on a stripped Harley, while Fireball cleaned guns. "What do you think? should we go to the show?" John asked the club's president.

"Why not—you afraid?" Jason snapped back, pumped with a new confidence built by his superficial alliance with the Devils Own.

"Could be a problem," John said, adjusting the valves on his Shovelhead, his hand full of open-end wrenches. Jason bent over and held the chromed pushrod cover out of the way. Highbars jutted two feet above the chromed Wide Glide front end. The sleek bike sported a glimmering club emblem on its jet-black Sportster tank. The custom motorcycle was originally a Long Beach police bike before John bought it at an auction on Signal Hill, an industrial area on the outskirts of downtown.

When he was a younger man, John had cared for the bike like it was his Rolls Royce. But his nature was changing. The scoot still meant more to John than any other material possession, but drugs, violence, and cheap thrills were getting in the way. What once had been his ticket to women, the key to his unbridled mobility, and his vehicle on the freeway to freedom, now shared the limelight with whiskey and white powder. His patch and the bike were John's only property, his brothers, his sole companions.

"If any of those Mexican motherfuckers show up," Fireball said, stroking a spotlessly clean 9mm Browning automatic, "there will be a problem. We'll need to find a way to get some weapons inside."

"That's not necessary," Eddie said, entering the garage, prompting the other outlaws to stare at him inquisitively. Through the open garage door, the single light hanging from the rafters of the garage spilled a soft glow into the dark alley.

"Fuck it ain't," Fireball said, standing up defiantly. His glossy red hair flashed in the brightness of the 100-watt light bulb suspended above them. "You know as well as I do that they'll be there. We need to be there. Sure as hell, there's gonna be a fight."

John looked into the dark alley, seeing another light collide with the glow from the garage, as a highly polished Lincoln with mag wheels and blackwalls skidded to a stop outside the open door. The car's back door flew open, and Miguel leaned forward, reaching into the night with a handful of sinister-looking gold rings on each thick finger. "Eddie," he said, "get in. We need to talk."

Eddie walked toward the menacing-looking Lincoln. Everything about it, from its lowered body, to its dark magnesium wheels and tinted windows, looked intimidating. The door shut hard behind Eddie, and the car disappeared into the night.

Although it was dark in the speeding sedan, Miguel wore narrow sunglasses, his impassive face showing no emotion as the vehicle screeched around corners. "Eddie," he said quietly, "I like you. And your people could make good members in my club. But you've got a problem."

Eddie ordinarily never lost his cool, never got rattled. But the thought of becoming a Devils Own unnerved him. His eyes grew wide in anticipation of what the veteran outlaw might say.

"We could give a shit about these Los Cuchillos here in L.A.," Miguel continued. "They shouldn't be here, but we do business with the Los Cuchillos in the Central Valley, so they run errands for us from Southern California, north. Now ... what about our deal?"

"What do you mean?" Eddie blurted, instantly wishing he hadn't.

"What the fuck do you think I mean?" Miguel shouted. Reaching inside his vest, he withdrew a chromed and engraved 9mm automatic. He snapped off the safety with a flick of his thumb and said, "Maybe we shoulda killed you back at the studio. I told you we would take care of the Los Cuchillos, and that you can back off!"

Miguel shoved the muzzle of the pistol into the sensitive hollow spot at the base of Eddie's neck. "Let me spell this out for you one last time," he said. "We told you that this mess would be taken care of, provided you gave up your boy in the joint. That doesn't mean you start buying guns and ammo, and blow up Mexicans whenever you run into them. If one of their members goes down, you'll be on your own. Understand, fucker?"

Frozen-eyed, Eddie stared sideways at the stout man holding the weapon to his neck as the Lincoln bounced and swerved through the dark streets. The right bump, enough of a jolt, and the 9mm would turn Eddie's brain into Alpo. But his fear was all but overcome by the realization that Miguel and his people knew that the Night Hawks had been buying hardware prior to attending the upcoming show. How did they know?

"What's the name of your member up for the beef?" Miguel asked, although he already knew the answer. The car sped west through Santa Monica, then north along the Pacific Coast Highway toward more isolated regions and remote, winding canyons, inhabited only by a few gun nuts and aging hippies.

"Danny," Eddie replied tentatively, staring expectantly into Miguel's dark glasses. His mind flooded with thoughts of one-way rides into the hills and news accounts of dumped bodies. What did Miguel want with Danny?

"There's a number of options here," Miguel said, relaxing his grip on the gleaming handgun and shifting his position on the seat so that he was facing straight ahead once again, looking out the front window over the huge shoulders of the fellow member who was driving. "We could let this deal pan out—probably leaving some of you dead, some of them, too, maybe. And we'd just go about our business with whoever was left standing." Miguel paused for effect, studying Eddie out of the corner of his eye, stroking the weapon in his lap. "I could take you into Topanga Canyon and off you," he continued. "Then I'd make a deal with them to end this thing. Eye for an eye—they'd love it. See, even if everybody in your club turned in their patches and became Devils Own, that wouldn't solve your problem. And we don't want new members with problems. Know what I mean?"

"Yeah, I can dig that," Eddie said, dry-mouthed, but excited at the idea of joining the celebrated club. For a biker, becoming a Devils Own was similar to a sailor entering the Navy Seals, or a college football player being drafted into the NFL. "But what about Danny?"

"Danny is going down for the murder, right?" Miguel asked quietly, still fondling the automatic.

Eddie nodded, his eyes glued to the lethal handgun. "We can go to the Los Cuchillos and tell them that the guy who caused all the problems is going down," Miguel said, wiping the 9mm with his handkerchief. "I'll tell them that their problem was with him, not your club—and especially not with you. If your people have the heart to become Devils Own and our partners in Los Angeles, that will help in the long run. But you've still got to stay away from the Los Cuchillos for a while. So what do you say? You can speak for the club, can't you?"

Eddie's mind was reeling, and he couldn't believe how poorly he was handling the situation. He didn't know what to say—whether to go for the patch and the deal, fight the Los Cuchillos with the Night Hawks and risk a war with the Devils Own, or try to fight all these motherfuckers in the Lincoln and somehow get out alive. Realistically, his choices were clearly limited.

Eddie liked to fight, but on his own terms. And this mess posed too many options to sort out on his own. He couldn't back down, of course, but he couldn't fuck up, either. He liked the idea of his club becoming Devils, of the end of the war and more direct drug profits, but what about Danny? "Listen," he said, improvising. "It sounds all right to me. We were thinking about kicking Danny out because of this mess, anyway." As he uttered the words, Eddie knew they were wrong. Nonetheless, they kept coming. "But I want to run the deal down to the club, first."

"That's your problem. Just handle it," Miguel said, turning toward Eddie quickly. "This is your chance to show the Devils Own that you can make decisions and control your people."

"But what do I tell them?" Eddie said, anticipating the answer. "I can't just tell 'em the war is off."

"You tell them they're Devils Own hangarounds" Miguel said, forcefully. "You tell 'em we're calling the shots now." Miguel's intense stare seemed to bore into Eddie's brain. "Well, does that mean you'll handle it?" Miguel asked, gesturing to the driver to turn around and head back to the city.

"Yeah, I'll handle it," Eddie said, drawing himself up, confident with his verbal commitment from Miguel safely in his back pocket.

"Let's get back," Miguel said to no one in particular, "so Eddie can prevent any more trouble." His voice had an edge like a razor. "Tell your members we've taken a look at your club, and we've concluded that they're Devils Own material. You and I will worry about that Danny turd later."

"But you don't know the other members," Eddie remarked, uncertainly. "We know all we want to know," Miguel said curtly, shoving the piece back into his vest as the Lincoln entered the city limits. "Anything we don't know, we'll find out when we're ready."

"How we gonna exchange our patches?" Eddie asked, trying to press for more commitments from Miguel.

"You've got a long ways to go, pal." Miguel chuckled lightening up. "You'll need to bring the chapter to the Bay Area to meet with my people. We'll party down, see how it goes."

The big car lurched to a stop in front of John's garage, where Jason and Jesse were still working on his bike. As Eddie began to climb out, Miguel leaned forward and reached into his vest once again. Eddie stiffened, then relaxed, as Miguel drew an envelope and slowly opened it. Eddie breathed in fast, shallow gasps, watching Miguel withdraw a new bottom rocker sporting the California name. The rocker was sewn to a small, bright orange, satin flag. "Hang this in your clubhouse," Miguel said casually, shutting the door behind Eddie before the car vanished into the night.

Big John looked up to see Eddie standing proudly in the center of the dark alley, bathed in the glow from the garage, illuminating him as if he were some bandit legend who'd dropped out of the sky to unfurl the banner he held above his head. When the satin banner and its implications sunk in, John, Jason, and Jesse all leapt to their feet and ran into the alley. "What's it mean, brother?" they asked excitedly.

"If we don't fuck up, we'll be Devils Own in a few months," Eddie said with obvious pride. The four men hugged and shook hands. "Call for a meeting tomorrow night. We've got something to celebrate."

By the time the brothers pulled into John's garage, the air was already thick with rumors and speculation. Hank pulled Eddie away from the raucous din of the party and into one of the small stucco bedrooms. A few motorcycle parts lined the stained carpet. A queen-sized mattress with dark satin sheets occupied a corner of the room.

"What's going on?" Hank asked with his confident, treacherous air, as if he already knew and was just checking Eddie's story.

"They're getting serious," Eddie announced, pulling at his long goatee. "Except for Danny, that is."

Hank peered hard into Eddie's dark eyes for the truth. "Eddie, that's bullshit," he stated flatly. "What's the bottom line?"

"They want us to stop any conflict with the Los Cuchillos, so they can get back to business," Eddie began in a hushed voice. "So if we give up Danny, they'll take care of things, end the war, and we'll be in the drug mainline."

"Yeah," Hank growled indignantly, pacing back and forth in the small room. "But what if Danny isn't convicted?"

"He won't become a member just now," Eddie mumbled evasively. "They need someone to blame the war on, and as long as he's down, the Los Cuchillos will be satisfied."

"I don't know," Hank said skeptically, as if pushing Eddie to make another decision.

"Miguel will call us within a week and invite us to a party

in the Bay Area," Eddie said, a grin creeping across his narrow lips.

"Uh-huh," Hank grunted, unconvinced that the issue of Danny was resolved. "Fuck it—let's go face the club."

Hank stood in his corner behind Eddie, his arms folded across his broad chest, looking over the group like a man studying ivory chess pieces on an enameled board, considering his next move. Peering over the top of his glasses at the restless group filling the room, he wondered how they would react to the news.

"OK, pipe down," Eddie said, bringing the club to order. "We've talked about becoming a chapter of the Devils Own for years, and, finally, something has come up that might make that possible." Listening to Eddie talk, Hank could tell that he had created a script to follow. "This conflict has created some problems with other clubs and a major opportunity for us," Eddie went on. "The Devils Own met with me and Hank, and we got to know a couple of members. They know our reputation, and how we handled ourselves with the Los Cuchillos. They're impressed, but there's a catch."

Hank stiffened and pulled on his salt-and-pepper beard, believing Eddie intended to break the news about Danny and worrying that it could backfire. He knew what power, influence, and drug business being a Devils Own could bring. "If we decide to become hangarounds, they want us to back away from any problem with the Los Cuchillos, so you can knock off buying weapons and explosives."

There are three stages on the path to membership in one–percenter clubs. The first, the hangaround stage, allows a biker to come around the club with no formal affiliation. Hangarounds are the low men on the totem pole, a few eventually progressing to the second stage—official prospect. Prospects are allowed to wear only the bottom rocker to indicate their allegiance to the club. Full membership comes only after extensive testing.

Obvious relief swept through the dark room from the brothers who had joined the club for fun, wild times, and girls. They might enjoy a fist fight from time to time, but a war was something else altogether. Many had never seen war, battle, or military service, and were relieved to hear the hostilities were ending.

"The Devils are planning a party in Menlo Park," Eddie explained. "And if we come up, and they like us, they'll take a vote the next day. We may ride back as members." He said the last line with a buoyant enthusiasm that caused most of the members to cheer.

"We ain't gonna prospect, are we?" Jesse asked, though still excited. "They either take the lot of us as members, or none of us," Eddie stated, forcing the issue of Danny's membership.

"But what about, Danny?" Fireball asked, his nostrils flaring in anger. "Danny's the only one who'll have to wait," answered Eddie. "He got us into this mess by killing that Cuchillo. As long as he's in the joint, the Los Cuchillos are mollified."

A few of the group murmured, seemingly to signify agreement. "Why not Danny?" Jesse asked. "He's the one doing time." "Listen, asshole," Eddie snarled, "we've got a major opportunity here. We'll be here when Danny gets out. Then he can join." His menacing voice clearly indicated he wanted the discussion to stop.

"Seems too easy to me," Fireball sneered, finishing off another beer and passing a joint to Big John.

"It won't be," Jason said, leaning close to a mirror on the table to snort a line. "But it will be a helluva party. We'll need to stick together."

The festive mood darkened momentarily, then Eddie broke the spell. "If we play our cards right, in a couple of weeks we'll be on our way to becoming Devils Own. It's real important that we get to know as many members as possible while we're there."

As if a heavy fog had lifted, the dark room brightened with renewed enthusiasm. Congratulations, questions, and general euphoria floated through the house. Everyone was relieved to know war was now handled. The brothers drank more than usual that night, picked fights at the bar later on, rode faster and more recklessly than before, and looked over their shoulders less frequently, acting tougher and more ominous than ever. They felt invincible. No longer were they going to be a one-chapter bunch of rebels and misfits, roaming the streets of Los Angeles. Soon they would be a part of the most organized, powerful gang of motorcyclists in the state.

Chapter 6

SENTENCING

On July 15, Danny was again before the court. It was Friday morning, and he was again shackled and marched into the courtroom.

Danny, of course, knew he was innocent and should be freed. But while his hand, as he laid it out on the table, offered various options, instant freedom simply wasn't one of them. It was as if he were sitting at the slot machine of life, and was about to drop every quarter he could muster into one final pull of the handle. He could win a little, he could win a decent payoff, but his chances of hitting the jackpot were several million to one. He was charged with murder, and if he persisted in pleading innocent, and pulled the handle before a jury, his chances weren't good.

As he studied the law and his situation, Danny determined that this particular Friday morning was far more crucial than any trial that might follow. If he were charged with special circumstances, he'd have no choice but to take his case to trial, and trial was risky. If he insisted on fighting it out in front of a jury, the system would make him pay. Ironically, the system seemed to work backward. If Danny went to trial, they'd muster the toughest prosecution possible, and attempt to bury him in prison for life. As Danny dragged his chains through the courtroom like Marley's Ghost in *A Christmas Carol*, he reflected on the fact that, apparently, it wasn't so much the money, but the effort involved. If they had to work, they would make him pay. If he wound up being charged with manslaughter, his options increased considerably, from several degrees of involuntary, to a voluntary charge.

Wearing their starched, crisply creased uniforms, the three cops marched into the courtroom, confident their capture would result in the defendant taking the maximum fall. The judge signaled the bailiff, who turned to the assembled participants and said, loudly, "All rise. The Superior Court of Los Angeles is now in session, Judge Raymond Shuster presiding."

"Be seated," the judge said, sinking into his leather chair. "Mr. Lonsdale, remain standing please." The stern-looking judge opened a large manila folder and, gazing over the top of his glasses at the crumpled contents, said, "I'll make this quick, so the attorneys can confer and we can set this matter for trial. Mr. Lonsdale, you are charged with the murder of Sancho Gomez. However, after reviewing the evidence and circumstances as presented by the prosecution and your attorney, I have decided that you will be tried for..." The judge's words seemed to come slower and slower. Danny could feel his knees weakening with every syllable. Danny's heart raced, and his breath became labored as he listened.

"...voluntary manslaughter," the judge continued, "punishable by a minimum of two years and a maximum of four years in state prison. How do you plead?"

Danny was stunned. He almost stumbled, feeling his attorney's relief through body language and his audible sigh. Danny stood alone with his attorney, while Dixie sat in the back of the courtroom, trying to be as inconspicuous as possible. The place made her skin crawl. She wanted out, but the club had insisted that she come to the hearing and report back.

"Well, Mr. Lonsdale," the judge snapped, impatient with Danny's failure to respond, "how do you plead? You're not the only case on the docket today." With the cops all sitting slack-jawed with disbelief behind him, glaring angrily at the judge, Danny could see that the haggard old man wanted to move off the hot seat and on to the next case. As the three uniforms saw it, the judge had just betrayed the brotherhood of the badge—he had taken the word of a biker over the word of a cop. The three stood simultaneously and stormed out, fuming and cursing under their breath.

"Not guilty, your honor," Danny said confidently.

"Trial is set for 60 days from today's date. Is that satisfactory for both sides?" the judge asked.

"Yes, your honor," both said in unison.

Danny pondered every word during the brief process. With his attorney at his side, he professed his innocence. As an outlaw, he knew the deck was still stacked against him, especially with three police eyewitnesses testifying for the prosecution. To Danny, the circumstantial evidence looked like a massive concrete headstone. Although he couldn't remember what had happened, he was positive that he wasn't responsible for the Mexican's death. Indeed, he was more certain with each passing day, as he trained his body and cleared his mind.

Horowitz glanced at Danny with the look of a man who wanted out. He would much prefer to deal with the Deputy D.A., thereby avoiding days in court, confronting the three officers and dealing with numerous blood samples and a menacing murder weapon that belonged to his client. He had little doubt that the young, muscled man at his side was guilty. "Can I make a deal?" Horowitz asked Danny as his moment before the court ended and preparations began for the following case. As he stared at his immaculate surroundings, Danny thought of how odd it was that such a flawless environment housed such a lowly class of people. He supposed the buildings represented the iron will of the law, the supremacy of the establishment over the common criminal. Looking over his shoulder as two deputies arrived to escort him back to his cell, he saw that Dixie was already gone.

Danny shook his head in dismay and turned back to his lawyer. "Not yet," he replied. "Let me think about it. For the time being, tell 'em we want a trial."

Danny looked at his frightened attorney, who turned his timid gaze to the polished floor and sighed deeply. "Convince them that we're going for a trial," Danny said, as he was led away, "even if you have to act like you're not going to do the job."

It was a 50/50 risk whether a jury would find for or against Danny. For weeks, he had mulled over the possible deals, the facts, the financial aspects of the battle, and the overall risks. Poring over the case documents, he had studied each transcript, every report and statement for clues. But even the jailhouse lawyers failed to come up with anything. He considered calling his folks, but when he recalled his dad's furious harangues about bikers, he abandoned the idea.

When Danny was 16, he had asked his dad if he could buy a motorcycle. "I hate bikers," his father had barked, leering at him across the dining room table, his fists growing taut against the glass tabletop. "A few years back, some new hotshot bought a bike. I saw him riding to work. As the weeks went by, he drove faster, his hair got longer, he quit wearing his helmet, and he began swerving in and out of traffic like a goddamn lunatic." Danny's dad took a swig of the last beer in his first six-pack of the evening, then slugged Danny in the arm when his attention strayed to a customized car cruising past the front window. "Listen to me, shithead! I was following this punk one day when the car in front of him stopped abruptly. The bastard lost control and dumped it in the street. I stopped, got out of my car, and walked over to him. I said, 'Are you OK, buddy?' He looked up at me and nodded as he pulled himself out from under that piece of shit. Then I told that motherfucker, 'Good, 'cause if you hadn't done this to yourself, pretty soon I was gonna pull your ass offa that scooter and beat the lazy, no-good piss outta you myself.' Now, if you want a motorcycle, I won't stop you. But by God, I won't help with loans, insurance, nothin'. And you better take the responsibility yourself. If I catch you ridin' without a license, registration, or insurance, I'll kick your butt and throw that piece a shit in the ocean."

Danny shrugged his shoulders and picked at his threadbare denim shirt, remembering how hard he worked to get his first bike. Even that little Honda received its share of Danny's customizing talents, but he had always kept it insured—and away from the old man.

A banging against the bars jerked Danny's attention back to the present. The cell smelled of ammonia and greasy food. He had been locked down since May, and it was already approaching the end of August. Danny reflected on the irony of how slowly the wheels of justice turn. Not long after his last appearance, Danny's lawyer fell in love with a young grad student. Their marriage cost Danny a month. Then the District Attorney's mother died, causing another delay.

September rolled past, and Danny stewed about the excuses and delays. He heard from Dixie that the club was being considered for a Devils Own charter, and the prospects looked good. That news kept him pumped, and highly respected on the floor. Still, because of the nature of his alleged crime, and the fact that the county jail was basically a holding facility for criminals waiting to be shipped off, long-term friendships weren't possible.

Although Danny made no real friends among the other prisoners, a curious relationship began to develop between him and a particular guard. The officer was black and big, a reasonable man who had begun to respect Danny's singular determination to keep himself ready for whatever lay ahead. The guard watched Danny do his exercises, never missing a day. He worked out for two non-stop hours, regardless of court delays or his attorney's missed appointments. Danny remained focused on his own body and spirit.

This guard was somehow different from the brutish creeps roaming the halls, banging on cell doors with nightsticks and harassing prisoners, especially the blacks and Mexicans. Guard Raymond Black was a disciplined family man who trained young children in martial arts and was studying for his master's degree in Criminology. Envious, the other guards talked about him behind his back.

Over time, Black came to admire Danny's dedication to researching his case and developing the knowledge necessary to understand the complex process. "Hey, badass," the guard called playfully, interrupting Danny's afternoon reading. "What's with the studying? What's your scam?"

"No scam," Danny replied, calmly. "Just studying the facts, trying to figure out what happened."

"You're guilty, you mean," Black said, pulling at the wide leather belt around his narrow waist. The cell door opened with a deafening clang as another guard at the end of the narrow hall released the locking solenoid. "You're just looking for a loophole."

"Listen, man," Danny said, standing up straight. "I'm not talking to you about my case. That's a no-win proposition, so let's drop it."

"You oughtta drop it, make a deal, and get it over with," the guard said. He had heard every conceivable scam during the five years he had worked at the county jail, and couldn't be conned. "They don't arrest people unless they're guilty."

"Look," Danny said, putting the papers aside, "tell you what. Get off my back, and I won't bore you with my side of the story. If that ain't fair, just leave me alone, and I'll deal with this shit, do my time, and get on with life."

The guard evaluated the young biker. Danny stood firmly

in place, staring at the guard eyeball-to-eyeball. "I'll think about it," Black replied, handing the prisoner three dog-eared magazines. "Your girl said you're going to trial this week."

The next morning, Danny awoke to another uneventful day. As he sat on the edge of the bunk, he wondered where his attorney was. He wondered if such a job was the equivalent of a prison term, marching back and forth to a steel-and-cement office daily. Danny heard the iron door at the end of the concrete hall clang and creak open. Then he heard footsteps, and a barely audible whistle. He knew it was deputy Black.

"I got some news for you, Lonsdale," the guard said. "Your case was postponed again—for a month this time." The guard had been impressed with Danny's response to the bad news, taking it with a grin and a joke, without crying about the cruel world, or making slams against a society turned against him. He was beginning to wonder about Danny. He didn't pace, curse his bad luck, wallow in self-pity, or try to kill himself with cigarettes or smuggle drugs like so many of the guilty did. And he didn't act like a man who knew he was going down for a long stretch.

Danny's attorney came by the next day. "You know why they keep postponing the trial, don't you?" Horowitz asked, after the jailer had left them alone in the attorney-client discussion room.

"Cause I won't make a deal?" Danny replied, already knowing the answer.

"That's right," Horowitz said, opening his briefcase.

"Isn't it your job to see that I get a speedy trial?" Danny spit back at him. "And why didn't Dixie come in yesterday?"

"I don't know," Horowitz said, squirming around in the chair. He wouldn't make eye contact with Danny, and his furrowed brow was covered with tiny beads of sweat.

"What's the deal?" Danny inquired. He pushed forward on his iron bunk, slipping closer to the attorney.

"I was hoping you'd ask," Horowitz said, his mood suddenly brighter. He was dressed casually, though he appeared depressed. He moved back in his seat as Danny moved forward, finally skidding the metal chair backward, away from Danny's penetrating gaze. Fumbling through the mass of papers in his briefcase, the lawyer said, "It's about time you came to your senses. Maybe now we can."

"I won't discuss a deal with the fucking court," Danny interrupted, leaping to his feet. "What's the deal with you, her, the club what the fuck is going on?" He loomed over Horowitz's trembling form, his fists clenched. "I'm fucking sick and tired of sitting here day after fucking day waiting without any indication that someone is working for me on the outside."

Horowitz panicked, dropping the papers and scattering them around the cell. He raised his trembling hands above his head to protect himself from the big man hovering over him. As he leaned away from Danny, the chair buckled, dumping the attorney on the concrete floor. For the first time, Danny noticed Horowitz's dilated pupils, the red rings around his eyes, and the crusty particles of white powder around his nostrils. "I'm calling the guard," the lawyer whined, fumbling for both his words and his balance.

"Is there a problem down there?" the guard at the end of the corridor shouted.

Danny stared down contemptuously at the yuppie on the floor. "Tell him, 'No problem,'" Danny hissed, bending close to the attorney's clammy face. "Or I'll tell 'em you need a drug test, and then you'll be sharing a cell with a hundred guys instead of being here."

"Ah," Horowitz blurted, trying to regain his composure. "No problem, deputy. Thank you."

Danny turned his back on the ivy league punk. "Well, Horowitz," Danny said, "I need some answers."

"I don't know what's happening," Horowitz said, tentatively. "But there's no more money from the club for your defense. In fact, Eddie doesn't want much to do with you—some problem with another club." The lawyer's voice was choked with fear. "I went to the Deputy D.A. about a deal, and I'll follow through, if you'll listen. You can owe me until you get out, but I can't afford to go to trial with this. Anyway, you'd lose. I can't get anyone from the club to testify that you didn't do it."

"All right, what's the deal?" Danny demanded, glaring down at the wretched man at his feet. Here was a guy who had the opportunity to go anywhere, and he let drugs dictate his crumbling life. Danny began to relate to a man lost behind his weaknesses. Looking down at his only comrade in his plight, a troubled loser of an attorney, Danny felt lost from his brothers.

"The D.A.'s office will reduce the charge to voluntary manslaughter without aggravating circumstances, and you'll be sentenced to two years. You'll actually serve only about half of that, minus the time you've already done here." Horowitz waited expectantly.

"OK, I'll think about it," Danny said, leaning against the tarnished stainless steel sink. "Now, go home and clean up. I mean really clean up. You're on the outside, so get some help and get off the shit."

Horowitz nodded, and turned to signal for a guard to let him out. "I'll stop by in a couple of days," he assured Danny.

"Well, biker boy," Raymond Black said after the attorney was gone. "You gonna make a deal now?"

"Is it always like this?" Danny asked. "A guy gets arrested, everyone abandons him while he's awaiting trial, his attorney turns to shit, and the court wants his ass too much to take the time to do him justice. Finally, he's forced to accept some fucked deal just to save his people, money, the court system, time, and his attorney, the effort."

"That's usually the drill," the guard replied, "unless you've got millions. In that case, you can dig up all the ugly shit that happened to you as a kid, and spread it all over the courtroom, in hopes the jury will decide that what you did was cool." Suddenly, surprisingly, Raymond felt ashamed of the system he worked for.

"Listen," Danny said, trying to concentrate on something other than his plight. "One of the other officers mentioned that you train kids in martial arts."

"That's correct," Black said.

"Since I'm going down for the count anyway, do you think you could give me some pointers?" Danny asked, looking at the poised black guard standing five feet from his cell door, his tautly defined muscles showing through his tailored uniform. "I need to keep focused," Danny said, dropping his gaze momentarily.

"All right," the guard said. "But what I teach is as much spiritual as physical."

"I'll be a sponge for both," Danny stated, standing at attention to indicate his respect for the man's discipline and knowledge.

Each day, Danny picked deputy Black's brain about the discipline of martial arts and Zen. Raymond taught Danny basic moves, blocks, punches, katas, and stretching exercises, which Danny integrated into his workout routine immediately. One day, while Danny worked out in his cell, Raymond interrupted to say, "I have two gifts for you today, number one student."

Instinctively, Danny stepped back and into the defensive position he was taught, while Deputy Black reached into his briefcase. "I have a book for you. It's called *Zen and Martial Arts*. It combines the two disciplines simply, and compares them with everyday dilemmas."

Danny stepped forward and respectfully accepted the small paperback, bowing to Raymond as he said, "Thank you, sensei." Danny studied the black and white photo on the cover—a man in a martial arts stance, in a studio that seemed to reflect the solitude of his own cell.

"If you listen to the words, you will learn much from this book," the guard said, in a low voice.

"What's the second gift, deputy?" Danny asked with concern. "I have no proof, and I know that you have only one visitor you rely on," Black said, with a somber expression. "But I sense that this person may not be working in your best interests. Oh, by the way, you're going to court tomorrow."

The following morning, Danny took great pains to shave as cleanly as possible, to be as immaculately groomed as possible. Thoughts of what the guard had said to him spun through his mind. He pulled his long, sandy-blond hair behind his head and tied it.

"Lonsdale," someone shouted from the guard shack, "Time to see the man." The black guard, who was always crisp and clean, poised and polished, appeared at the door and studied the figure before him. "Well," he said, "you look innocent, whether you are or not."

"I'm afraid that's not the issue today," Danny said, uncomfortable with the wait before going to the courthouse.

"I'll tell you two aspects of that book that might apply today," the guard said, while he cuffed Danny's wrists in front, and began to lead him up the hall. "Two words: Wa and Ri. Wa is the atmosphere around you. Never let anyone disturb your wa. If someone tries to get to you, you move this buffer zone, or move physically, so the individual isn't trespassing on your wa. It's your area, your place of peace and ultimate control, and no one can penetrate it. Ri is the ability to see beyond obstacles." Raymond stopped in the hallway to elaborate on the concepts he had been explaining to Danny. "When martial artists break wood," he said, "they do not think about breaking the surface of the wood, but well beyond it. The goal is not to attack the obstacle, but to think about the success beyond it. Your Ri will help you find a way."

The long corridor from the jail to the courthouse was polished and sterile. As the two men exited the prisoners' tunnel leading into the courthouse, where Danny would be transferred to the custody of another deputy, Black spoke one more time. "This is a house of emotion," Raymond said softly, nodding at the deputy in charge of the prisoner from this point forward. "Try to avoid the level of fear that consumes the people here."

"What can you tell me about prison, Raymond?" Danny inquired. "You must have worked at one or two."

"Stay disciplined, stay to yourself and read that book," the black man replied, opening the oak door to the courtroom. "And use your time wisely. It's still your life."

Danny glanced back at Deputy Black as he was led through the labyrinth of passages ultimately leading to the defense table. Along the way, Danny was allowed to change into a suit he was told had been left for him by Dixie. In the courtroom, the deputy removed the handcuffs, and gestured for him to sit down. Ten minutes passed while Danny sat alone at the table, studying the ominous architecture of the room. The massive Seal of California was directly above the elevated judge's bench, and the United States flag and the California flag flanked the judge. The bailiff, a short, overweight deputy sheriff, scuttled around the room, preparing for the judge's arrival. Sweat rolled down his balding head as he ordered the clerks to take their positions.

Danny ran Raymond's words around and around in his head, wondering what use they could be to him that day. Lost in thought, he plucked at the fabric of the suit he wore. It fit OK, but the arms of the coat were a bit short, and the pants legs felt tight against his muscled thighs. It was then that he realized the suit hadn't come from Dixie, but rather his attorney, who was much shorter and thinner than Danny.

Sensing someone entering the room, Danny turned around and saw Dixie taking a seat in the back row. She huddled in her seat unobtrusively, apparently scared to be there. Danny caught her eye, and for a moment she perked up. A faint smile crossed her face, but was it masked in fear, or concern? Danny couldn't tell.

For a split second, Danny felt her fear penetrate his being. Then he remembered what Raymond had told him about his wa, and it all fit perfectly. If he pushed her look of concern and fear back away from him, it could no longer affect his thinking. The bailiff called for all to rise, and Danny turned forward again, just as the judge entered the room.

The man who was to decide Danny's fate stood less than six feet tall, with thinning hair as white as Xerox paper. He had a sparse beard and irritable eyes, surrounded by a sea of straining wrinkles. Above his narrow, pursed lips he scowled at the world through beady, blue/gray eyes. Even at a distance of 25 feet, Danny sensed the smell of death in the air. The old man took one deliberate step after another to reach his position of power behind the oak pedestal, where he flopped in the high-back leather chair as if he would never rise again. "What's the first case?" he snapped, grabbing a file from the clerk. As he read his notes, he occasionally glanced over his wire spectacles at the biker behind the table, sitting next to his squirming attorney.

Danny looked at the wheezing old judge, and then at his own fidgeting attorney. The judge seemed to be glaring darts at Horowitz. Nonetheless, Danny felt a stronger, more solid sense of the lawyer's being—he had straightened up, although he was still obviously nervous and clumsy.

"Hey, what the fuck's happening here?" Danny asked in a low voice.

"We had a serious disagreement yesterday," Horowitz explained, uncomfortably. "He caught me on a technicality. Almost busted my ass."

"That was yesterday, asshole," Danny whispered, catching the fumbling man in his gaze and holding him steadfast.

"Today, my life is on the line. Do you have your shit together? I'm a man of my word and he's a professional, whether he looks half dead or not. Take a deep breath."

"You're right," the lawyer said, sighing deeply. "This is a formality," Danny continued. "The real goal is to survive the reduced sentence you're supposed to obtain for me." Danny patted the man's shoulder encouragingly.

"Regarding the case of the state versus Danny Lonsdale," the judge began, half-heartedly, "in the interest of justice and a speedy trial, I'll ask if you, Danny Lonsdale, plead no contest to the crime of involuntary manslaughter."

Danny and his attorney were on their feet, as was the Deputy D.A., a conservative-looking Italian who appeared too slick to be a lawyer for that public office.

"Yes sir," Danny said, hesitantly.

"Then you understand that you have waived your rights to a trial by jury. Do you have anything to say, Mr. Lonsdale?" the judge spat at him. "This is your last opportunity before I impose sentence."

Danny's mind raced, flooded with the words he desperately wanted to say. He could hear them echo through his brain. "Yes, your honor, I do. I am a self-employed motorcyclist, or a biker who is a member of a motorcycle club. Those are my only real crimes. I don't have the money for a proper defense, so I'm throwing myself on the mercy of the court. I may have been in a bar brawl that night, but I never stabbed anyone."

Choking back the words he wanted to shout at the old bastard before him, Danny heard himself say, "No, your honor." "This court will recess for 15 minutes," the judge stated. "I will return for sentencing at that time." He struggled to his feet and painfully descended the steps to the floor.

"All rise," the bailiff announced officially, as the judge stood up. Instinctively, Danny looked toward the back of the room. Dixie was nowhere to be seen.

The door shut softly, like a time lock on a bank vault, sealing the hysteria and anxiety of the courtroom from the quiet, reflective richness of the judge's chambers. Horowitz turned to Danny and said, "What do you think?"

Once again, Danny turned to face the young attorney, who was sucking on his upper lip. "What's wrong?" Danny inquired. "We made a deal, right?"

"I'm afraid his track record and his demeanor this morning don't seem in keeping with our deal," the lawyer said, pulling at his starched collar and fidgeting in his chair.

"If you feel that strongly," Danny said, his eyes fixed on the attorney's darting pupils, "I suggest that you wait outside for the judge to return. You have a long way to go before you're free of your addiction. Only then your confidence in yourself and mankind will return." Horowitz grasped the significance of Danny's stare, and stepped away from the defense table, heading toward the back of the room.

The next 14 minutes seemed like an eternity. Danny pondered various scenarios, but tried to force his mind back to what sentence a fair judge would impose under the circumstance.

"All rise," the beer-bellied bailiff shouted once again, shattering the library-like quiet of the room. In the ensuing silence, each rustling paper sounded like a thunderclap, and felt like a bolt of lightning. The harshness of the sounds was augmented by the slick floors, the wooden chairs, the paneled walls, and the hardwood counters—not a single soft surface to absorb sound.

Once again, the judge gasped as he went from one step to the next, struggling to climb up to the bench, his commanding perch. Slamming the file down on the counter that no one ever sees, the magistrate said, " In the case of Danny Lonsdale versus the state of California, the court finds Mr. Lonsdale guilty of voluntary manslaughter, and imposes a sentence of—" For a moment, the judged paused to raise his balding head and look past Danny and the lawyers, all the way to the back of the courtroom ... "two years incarceration at a state facility to be determined within one week, plus one year of probation, subsequent to release, with three month's credit for time served."

With a harsh rap of his gavel, the judge indicated that the court system was finished.

SWITCHNG WORLDS

*T*he ride to Menlo Park, south of San Fran Miguel, was 350 miles of adrenaline rush. The Night Hawks rode with pride, a false dignity, a veil of fear, and an ammunition belt of Harley Thunder. Never in their existence was the group as unified into an organized team as now—although admittedly a bit rough around the steel and chrome edges. Like a small band of mercenaries, they swung off the freeway in a torrent of screaming pipes, wild mounts carrying a motley crew of motorcycle pirates. At Valparaiso, the group turned, heading into a dilapidated industrial park. Away from the scenic highway, the area provided a grotesque contrast to the seaside panorama of colorful restaurants, art shops, and coffee houses. The massive clubhouse was situated on Alameda De Las Pulgas Road, a street that revealed a society trying to hide real industry from the Disneyland facade of the tourist industry.

The nondescript buildings were little more than enormous blocks of concrete, one next to the other, as if built in the fear that the community would vote to move them even farther out of town, or to push them even closer together, or to simply eliminate them completely. They were like industrial wagons drawn into a circle for protection–with one notable exception. The Devils Own clubhouse was simultaneously abject and intriguingly gothic. Originally an ordinary industrial building of moderate size, the wealthy club had the exterior sheeted in large steel panels, and painted them a dark, battleship gray. Gnarly molten welds and massive industrial rivets held the armor in place. Shaped like an enormous shoebox, the clubhouse had no windows, and looked like a huge rusting vault set in the center of the block. A handful of motorcycles were parked out front, as well as the ominous, dark Lincoln that Eddie knew from that dark night at John's garage.

Fast Eddie, ambition running high, signaled for the band of

rowdies to pull over and park together. They dismounted together just as the iron door of the clubhouse creaked opened, and Miguel emerged. "Right on time. I like that," he said, walking out to greet the bikers.

Stepping forward, Eddie introduced each member. "Miguel, this is Hank, our vice president, that's Big John, and next is Jesse, Fireball, and Old Man Jason."

Miguel shook hands with the members, staring directly into each man's eyes to see if he could unnerve any of them. "Come on inside," he said. "Let's get started."

Inside, the clubhouse seemed even more ominous. The floor was polished hardwood, and at the back of the room, a massive, hand-carved oak bar from the 1920s stood centered against the wall, with two doors carved from heavy wood on either side. Behind the heavy-pillared bar, a massive, beveled mirror reflected low overhead lights. In the center of the mirror, the club's logo was intricately etched into the glass. The flamed Devil's profile seemed to thrust out at anyone who dared to stare at it. The hollow, mocking eye spoke of pain and death, and the powerful flames flowed down either side of the creature's head to encompass a motorcycle wheel. By itself, the club's trademark icon would send chills up any straight's spine. The first Devils came from a disbanded fighter group in the South Pacific in 1942. During a battle for the city of Manila, a B-52's flight crew scrambled ashore while off duty, and smuggled four Filipino women back to the ship. The crew and pilots stashed the women on their flying boat, and proceeded to pimp them out to other crews. The women flew raids with the men, and it was said that the babes were taught how to operate the 50-caliber machine guns, using them to gain a bit of retribution against the Japanese. The team, known as the Devils Own, became legendary, bringing luck to the crew—until another pilot spotted one of them firing on a Jap Zero from a tail bubble while over one of the Philippine Islands. He reported the crew, who were arrested as soon as they touched down. But the pilot who turned in the report was tossed overboard before he could testify. Eventually, the women were returned to their homeland, and the crew, among which were a few motorcyclists, was sent home. As a tribute to their brave, fighting whores, the crew founded the motorcycle club in Long Beach, California, in 1944. Or so the story goes.

Burned by the Navy, these men who had fought valiantly for their country returned to the states as outcasts from their families and friends. Now, they had only each other, a bottle of booze, and their bikes. They learned to ride hard, fight hard, and stay on the run. In time, the ragtag group grew into a solid organization of renegades who had no use for society, and the establishment came to fear them.

Through the years, the group's reputation had grown, primarily because of their violent behavior and take-no-prisoners attitude. They weren't thieves, and they had their own unique, ironclad code of integrity; nonetheless, they had a tradition of underhanded dealings and treachery. The Night Hawks regarded them as the baddest of the bad, and in outlaw circles generally, they were the masters of the night, the toughest men on two wheels, the nastiest of the nasty. Of course, the bottom line was power and respect, backed by whatever violence it might take to maintain the bottom line. So each man entered the Devils Own inner sanctum fully aware of the risks involved.

The room was broad and deep. The walls held pictures of past members, all deceased, and over each picture was the man's patch, framed against a blood-red velvet backdrop. The oak frames matched the bar, the floors, and the tables, which were arranged in a square with a 100-square-foot vacant area in the center. Officers from every chapter in the state sat at the tables, quietly observing. No one stood up to greet the Hawks, or in any way acknowledged their presence. No music, no girls—just silence and an occasional cloud of smoke wafting from one of the long tables. Thirty men, each sporting some form of facial hair, sat impassively—watching and waiting. They looked rough and ready, like a roomful of pirates who had just captured a band of young toughs. Each officer projected an aura of violence and leadership, and there was a quiet threat in the air. Each man carried some sort of scar, testifying to his veteran status. A member's nose had obviously been broken numerous times, another wore a Devil earring, above which, the faint pattern of old stitches was visible on his shaved head. Most had thick, wavy hair, shoulder-length or longer, and wore a black vest so road-worn that the Devils embroidery, as well as patches sewn on years ago, had so completely blended with dirt from the street, grime from the freeway, and blood from fights, as to be barely distinguishable.

Old Man Jason entered the room, and Miguel shut the door, silently returning to his seat near the head of the table. Sitting in the center of one of the tables was a small man, one of the few men present with closely cropped hair. His long mustache was trimmed closely, giving the appearance of two daggers running alongside his narrow mouth. Jaws clenched, he stood up slowly, then abruptly kicked his chair back. "What makes you think you can go to war with any club in the state without our permission?" he bellowed. His angry gaze was aimed at the new group of men who had been allowed to enter the Devils hall, but had not been asked to sit down. Uneasily, Jason noticed two guards slip behind them to secure the door, making them more prisoners than guests.

"We've been doing business with the Los Cuchillos for years," the man screamed, slamming his fist against the heavy oak table, "and you've interrupted all that, and cost us thousands. I say you off the bastard who killed the Cuchillo, and end this bullshit." The room was as quiet as a mausoleum. Every eye was on the small group of Hawks from the L.A. basin. "Well?" the small man demanded. "Are any of you faggots going to say something, or should we just kill the lot of you and get back to business as usual?"

"Listen," Eddie began, only to be interrupted by Jesse, who shoved him aside, and stepped forward, intentionally putting some of the bikers sitting around the table on their guard.

"This is horseshit," Jesse barked. "We were invited here, and I'd rather fight to my death than to give up a brother. So let's just fucking get on with it."

The tanned man with the mustache looked Jesse up and down. "Well," he said, "you ought to make a decent prospect."

"Let's fight now, party later, and I'll ride home tomorrow a Night Hawk, and proud of it!" Fireball shouted, nervous and mad. "We came here to be voted into your club, not to prospect—we did that shit years ago. Either take us as we are, or leave us be." Fireball felt insulted. Moreover, the rules had changed, and he wasn't prepared for this test, though he had no preconceived notion of what was supposed to happen.

Wearing only Levi's and a vest over his tanned and buffed torso, the man with the mustache stepped around Miguel, who sat next to him, and walked toward the irregular line of tense Hawks. He stepped up to each man individually, and snorted in his face. "We're going to vote," he snarled, "but your guy in the joint doesn't become a member—you got that straight?" The man with the mustache punctuated this last line by poking Jesse in the chest. Immediately, Jesse responded in kind, popping the man in the chest with both gloved palms. When the man stepped back, every officer present was on his feet at once. Chairs were kicked or tossed out of the way. At every member's side was an engraved baseball bat, and each man's hand was wrapped around the grip.

"It's all right," Blade, the president, said in his stern, unforgiving voice. "This one's got heart."

"Why don't you and your brothers step into that room over there," Blade said, stepping up to Eddie and Hank, and motioning for them to stay, "and I'll talk to my club." Miguel and Rotten Ron stood up and huddled with Blade, then Eddie and Hank followed their members into a large, comfortable, party room, where a prospect offered them drinks and speed. "This is a first, if they vote you in," the prospect said, in a low voice. He was young and slick, and already he seemed to carry himself with a suspicious confidence, like many of the leaders in the meeting room. Jesse and Fireball looked at each another, saying nothing. The party room was clean and yet more club paraphernalia was displayed on the walls. But, unlike the meeting room, the place smelled of drugs, a consequence of years of smoke and booze permeating every surface. A small bar occupied one corner of the room, and black leather couches lined three of the four walls. The prospect was aloof, and Jesse, who was beginning to dislike the atmosphere around the Devils, wondered what made this kid think he wouldn't kick his ass. In view of the apparent absence of brotherhood, as well as the overt threats, Jesse was close to saying that it just wasn't worth it, regardless of the ego boost of riding with this patch.

Ten minutes passed, with little conversation among the Hawks. Jesse sat quietly, observing the various plaques and evil-looking club emblems carved in wood, etched in glass, or engraved in steel. Unlike some clubhouses that were no more than ramshackle ghetto dwellings littered with beer cans and decorated with girlie posters, this place was a genuine command center. Power seemed to emanate from the very grain in the hardwood floor, and violence seemed to hang on the walls alongside plaques honoring dead or longtime members. The Devils Own patch was crimson and gold, the only color scheme displayed in the clubhouse, except for the chrome and oak furniture and bar. No motorcycle parts or calendar girls and, apparently, no exits.

"This place has class," Big John said, interrupting Jesse's thoughts. Fireball shot a frowning glance at John, cutting short any idle conversation. They waited in silence, while the wiry prospect sat in a corner, watching them as if he were keeping an eye on prisoners.

"You got any other problems besides the one we discussed outside," Miguel inquired of Eddie, "or any other reasons for not becoming Devils Own?"

"No," Eddie replied tonelessly, looking from one menacing face to another.

Blade's words were direct and blunt. "Snitches are killed quickly, punks are thrown out, and each man in each chapter has to be able to fight–strongly and instantaneously. If a man hesitates, he could lose his patch or his life—no questions asked, no explanations accepted. Is that clear?" Blade looked around the room, as most of his lieutenants nodded vigorously.

"Yeah," Eddie said. "But don't you guys ever have fun?" The comment took Blade and Miguel by surprise, and some of the officers snickered.

"We have fun when we're ready," Blade said, grabbing Eddie's vest and pulling Eddie's face within inches of his own. "When we're ready, we have more fun than anyone. We'll take a vote. Now get the fuck outta here," he said, pushing Eddie away abruptly.

Before Eddie could follow Blade's order, Miguel grabbed his arm, spun him around, and thrust his face an inch away from Eddie's. "We've been following you guys for years," he snarled. "You're veterans, you know the streets of L.A., and you ain't afraid. But this is a new ball game now. You're responsible for more than just your chapter. We'll be watching. We've got a business to operate, and you're gonna keep your members in line, or we will."

Eddie stood his ground, unblinking. Miguel sidestepped to Hank, then whispered in his ear. "That bastard in jail. He'll be taken care of when he gets out. No problem, right?"

Hank could already feel the patch on his back, and a sense of power welled up inside of him as he looked deeply into the cold eyes facing him. "No problem," he said, without a pang of conscience.

"Then we vote," Blade said, spinning on his heels to face the officers from a dozen chapters blanketing California. "All in favor, say aye!"

In a release of the tension that had gripped the room for so long, the members shouted their support. Bring your members in and let's party!" Blade shouted.

SLOW-MOVING CLOCK

Six months had passed since Danny was led, chained to 24 other inmates, into a black and white school bus with wire-grate windows and steel rings on the seats for securing handcuffs or chains. The aging bus clunked and banged along the Interstate 5 freeway, north from Los Angeles, heading home to Tehachapi Prison. When the I-5 split away, south of Bakersfield, the bus stayed on Highway 99. It was hot, and getting hotter, when the bus stopped outside the Bakersfield courthouse to pick up more ill-fated felons, mostly young Hispanics. Parked on the street while the deputies shot the shit in the shade, the steel structure baked. Danny was still in a daze, but he tried to keep himself centered on the new challenges ahead. Finally, the officer mounted the steps of the blistering bus, and soon they were turning toward Highway 58, heading east over the dry Walker Basin, then along the arid Caliente Creek bed, into the town of Tehachapi.

Danny awoke in his cell startled, dreaming about that long, hot ride in the unair-conditioned bus through California's agricultural Central Valley. In September, the hottest month of the summer, the air drove through the bus like a blast furnace with its door open. The smell of cow shit, hay fields, and sweat mixed with anxiety to form a stew of despair on this one-way trip to one of the state's model prisons.

Tehachapi was built as a woman's minimum security prison in the 1920s. An earthquake in the '40s caused the three-tier building to become two stories. Many of the prisoners fell victim to the quake and lay buried at the facility's gun range. A level-two yard was built in the '60s with an ultra-modern high security yard. The facility is broken into seven buildings—one for administration, one for prisoner processing, which takes between one and six weeks, and six modules for various levels of criminal behavior. The levels went from One, the so-called country club for the white collar crime group, up to Level Six, housing violent repeat offenders.

In every nightmare, Danny attempted to escape, although he awoke each time before the conclusion. During the dream, the anxiety-saturated ride in the dilapidated bus would overwhelm him, jerking him back to the heart-pounding reality of his present fate and the gray walls less than eight feet away.

The escape nightmare was one of many sleeping apparitions, and Danny would get up to splash water from his stainless steel sink onto his face, hoping to wash the nightmare from his confined mind. In truth, he was actually living the horrifying phantasm a day at a time, determined to survive and leave a stronger man. Danny dressed in dungarees and a denim shirt, reading quietly in his cramped cell for an hour while the other inmates on the row woke up gradually, dressed, smoked, taunted each other, and prepared for breakfast.

Processing involved several tests and background checks to determine Danny's abilities, aptitudes, and the module in which he would do the remainder of his time. He made a point of being straightforward with the interviewers, regardless of their skepticism. But Danny's candor, direct gaze, and tattoo-free arms couldn't overcome his motorcycle club affiliation or the stigma of the manslaughter conviction. Eventually, he was assigned to the Level Five module, housing hardened, violent offenders and gang members.

With a metal-against-metal screech as irritating as chalk on a blackboard, all the cell doors in the row opened simultaneously. The inmates stepped out of their cells, were checked by guards, and then assembled for breakfast outside the cafeteria. As he entered the line of black and Mexican gang members, Aryan race proponents, and minor Mafia thugs, Danny nodded to a couple of bikers on the block. He knew the people he had to hang with to survive—the members of other bike clubs, and the violent loners and drug dealers. He quickly discovered that the Devils Own had the power inside. Three members from three different chapters ran the biker population—Nick, a steroid monster, Big Al, an older member doing time for three murders, and Crusty

Craig from the Bay Area Chapter, the leader of the group.

"Hey, brother," Nick said, breathing heavily. "You pumpin' iron today?" Nick was the bouncer type, big as a house. In reality, Nick was soft inside, but he was all muscle and power on the surface. He had torn the sleeves off all his prison shirts to reveal the club tattoos on his arms, and because his muscles split the seams whenever they were flexed anyway. His 58-inch chest and 20-inch arms kept even the biggest blacks at bay in the yard. In the prison population, bikers were known for their general cunning, their ability to think and react quickly, and for their violent and unforgiving ways. They were edgy and unpredictable, especially Crusty Craig.

Craig, the chapter president from Benecia, was busted when a young member became a confidential informant and disrupted the club's methamphetamine business. Craig wound up taking the fall for his chapter. Although the joint was hundreds of miles from his home turf, he nonetheless ruled with an iron fist. A slight man with short, curly blond-red hair and a shortly cropped full beard, Craig stood no more than 5 feet, 9 inches tall. Even so, he was an imposing figure, with eyes like welding torches burning hotly in his scarred and pockmarked face—a coiled rattlesnake 24 hours a day.

Big Al, on the other hand, was older and more mellow. He was a leader, tough but quiet, like a knife with a scalpel-sharp blade carefully placed in a lined leather sheath. He wasn't called Big Al for nothing—6 feet, 4 inches and 250 pounds of gristle, sporting a full salt-and-pepper beard and long, wavy black hair. Al was well-kept, well-read, and well-trained, but he knew better than to be the first one into the wrong fight, preferring to assess the situation and make his move carefully, as he had one fateful night in a boisterous beer joint in far northern California. Another club had surrounded the snowbound tavern where Al and his brothers were drinking. Everyone would have died that night if Al hadn't made his way outside and killed three of the rival bikers before they could torch the building. His brothers were deeply indebted to him, but the community was determined to rid the streets of all bike-riding outlaws. So Al was found guilty of three counts of involuntary manslaughter, and pulled a two-year sentence for each count.

"Yeah, I'm lifting," Danny replied to Nick's question, as they moved along the line of food bins. Craig moved in front of him to the scrambled egg server and stared at the small black inmate serving him. "Gimme three scoops," he demanded, "or I'll catch ya in the yard and butt-fuck ya in front of your buddies."

The young black hesitated. "Listen man," he said, pleadingly, "I can't." Al leaned forward and glared at the man, ready to underscore his threat. But their dispute had stopped the line, and a guard quickly arrived to see what was holding things up.

"What's the problem?" the bulky guard asked, pulling out his billy club and looking at the black. The guard was a sizable man, considerably taller than Craig. Officer Hollis was devoted to working out and getting bigger, and bikers knew steroids. Guards were often violent, but none were as hair-trigger touchy as the Devils Own. When the guard spotted Craig behind the Plexiglas counter, bending his tray against the tubular steel runners, he slowed immediately.

"What the fuck you gonna do with that thing?" Craig snapped, gesturing with a short nod of his head at the guard's nightstick.

"You're out of line, buster," the guard said, lamely. He then turned to the black behind the counter and barked, "Just give him the eggs."

Several blacks in the line grumbled about white pigs, but the tension subsided. After chow, Danny and the bikers went to the yard for a workout. While the three Devils Own and Danny alternated sets on the bench press, the workout area began to fill with blacks. Jabbering constantly, some appeared to be waiting for the bench, their massive arms folded impatiently.

Lying on his back and engrossed in his set, Danny pressed 250 pounds off his chest, bouncing the bar off his rib cage slightly for momentum. Nick spotted him while Craig looked on. Grunting out the last rep, Big Al leaned down and said, "Looks like we got company."

Danny sat up straight, spun off the bench, and walked up to the nearest black man. "What's the problem?" he asked.

"Da problem seems to be dat curly-haired boy there," the man replied. The small black stepped forward, followed by 20 more. "We don't take shit from any white-ass fucker."

Danny sensed the movement nearby while he spoke. "Look, we're just working out, so leave..."

Danny's words were interrupted by Craig's jumping forward, angrily thrusting himself directly in front of the black, in the man's face like a close shave. "Listen, motherfucker," he growled, "we'll do whatever the fuck we wanna do. If I want extra eggs, give 'em to me, and shut the fuck up. Now, if you slimy bastards want trouble, go for it. Otherwise, leave us the fuck alone." Without warning, a massive Negro moved to Craig's side and shanked him just below the ribs. Blood spurted over the big man's hand, and Craig groaned. But he stayed on his feet, turning, with the knife still in him, to face the monster who cut him.

In the blink of an eye, two men jumped Nick from behind, as Big Al traded blows with another two. As if training, Al punched each man in rapid succession. But others moved in to surround him. Danny turned back to the bench, wondering where the guards were, but remembering that he had noticed only black guards patrolling the area earlier. The power structure in prison is complex, and black inmates usually have connections with black guards. Today, they had tipped off the guards, persuading them to switch positions for a half hour with some of the white force. After all, black guards don't like white bikers any more than their incarcerated brothers.

Danny yanked 125 pounds off one end of the bar, catapulting the bar directly toward the confrontation, and creating a loud, explosive sound as the cast iron plates crashed onto the rough asphalt. He knelt quickly, picking up a 10-pound plate and threw it like a deadly discus at the monster black who had stabbed Craig. The flying weight split the big man's jaw, knocking him backward. Craig, stumbling unsteadily, swung at the man, but missed. In painful desperation, he reached for the blade in his side.

Danny spun around once, swinging two 25-pound plates and launching them over Craig and into the crowd, knocking several men back from the collapsing biker. Wasting no time, he leapt from the bench, grabbed another bar at his feet, and swung it with all his might at the crowd. "Back off, goddammit!" he shouted. "Back off!"

Though they tried to duck, the heavy steel bar caught two men as they approached, driving them to the asphalt and scattering teeth everywhere. The gang of blacks, now intimidated by the actions of this crazy-eyed madman with the long, wildly flying hair, slowly backed away. Danny's adrenaline surge lasted long enough for the white guards, now aware of the brawl, to muster and break up the melee.

"Call the medics!" Danny shouted over the blare of alarms to the guards, and knelt at Craig's side. "You'll be fine, Craig," he assured his wounded brother. "Just lie still."

"You're all right," Craig wheezed, his breathing labored and his eyes glazed. "No niggers gonna fuck with Devils Own. We run this fucking joint, and it ain't gonna be no other way." Even badly wounded, Crusty Craig maintained the outlaw attitude.

"Take it easy, brother," Danny said. "The medics are on their way." Danny crouched beside the bleeding biker, holding him in one trembling arm while trying to stop the bleeding with his denim shirt. Nick and Al stood guard as medics brought a stretcher from the infirmary and loaded Craig onto it.

"You did good, junior," Al said, walking with Danny back to the cell block. "You might make a Devil yet." Danny looked at him, his heart still pounding in his chest. The yard alarm was still blaring, and guards armed with riot shotguns were herding the blacks back into the cell block. After six months in the joint, these men were beginning to treat him as a brother, and Danny needed the company. His girl wrote infrequently, and even then, her cards were short and sweet. He heard nothing from his brothers, except occasional gossip whispered by another inmate. News came in unreliable, distorted fragments.

Danny spent most of his time reading, studying Zen in the prison library, because his faith in Christianity had been severely trounced, along with his trust in his family. His trust in his fellow man was at an all-time low, and he questioned his own understanding of human nature. In time, he got to know a young Chinese drug dealer who had a deep, traditionally Oriental upbringing, but who turned out to be the black sheep of the family. He had been moving major shipments of cocaine into San Francisco, unaware of the political structure organized crime employed to govern the flow of coke into the Bay Area. Tong was a street tough from a solid family line in Hong Kong, who couldn't resist the rock 'n' roll lure of America. He had hatched a get-rich-quick scheme, and went into business without the permission of the established crime families.

As a maverick drug smuggler, Tong had two options—take the fall and the heat for the additional drugs appearing on the wharf in San Francisco, or take a swim wearing a chain wet suit. He went down behind enough cocaine to put him away for 40 years, and now he lived inside the deep, peaceful Zen legends. Martial arts was his armor against hostile factions in prison. After a Las Vegas hood tried to make a move on the slick-skinned young Asian, Danny stood with Tong in a fight with a couple of wiseguy Italians in the showers. Danny's presence prevented others from joining in, but Tong's poise, balance, and discipline made the swarthy Italians look like limp-wristed faggots who couldn't fight their way out of a used condom. Too late, the men realized that they were way out of their league. Tong gracefully jammed nuts into abdomens, palm-heeled noses into foreheads, and drove one man's Adam's apple to the back of his neck.

Danny and Tong met in the library every afternoon, often saying only a few words to each other. Tong suggested passages from several books on Zen philosophy for Danny to study. Although practicing martial arts was strictly forbidden, each day, as the library was closing, Tong would show Danny another move, block, or exercise behind the long banks of books. Danny stood respectfully, in a Chimbe martial arts stance, his fists clenched against his thighs, his knees bent slightly, and his feet shoulder-width apart. The two men would practice a single strike, block, throw, or defensive movement 10 times. Each time, Tong pointed out different aspects of the move until he was satisfied that Danny understood the nature of the man. Then they would bow to one another, and return to their respective cells.

After lights out, Danny would practice the move 100 times, the first 25 with his eyes open, analyzing each and every aspect of the act. He would perform the next 25 with his eyes closed, imagining perfection, feeling his muscles work, and concentrating on reflex and power points. The next 25 would be done with eyes open, executing the move as if he had an opponent. The final 25 he would perform while moving in various directions, as if fighting multiple opponents. Then he would sleep and allow the knowledge to enter his subconscious.

In the morning, Danny would detail each move in a notebook, jotting down every aspect of the motion he could remember during the fleeting instruction. Then he would practice the new move 10 more times, followed by rehearsing each of his other moves five times, then the new move 10 times again. This workout took less than 10 minutes the first week, but with each passing week, the number of forms increased, as did the time consumed by his workout. Other inmates became annoyed as the workout expanded from half an hour, to 45 minutes, and then to a full hour. But Danny was religious, unrelenting, and devoted. For the first time in his life, he began to feel that he was making an improvement in himself. Even more than pumping iron, martial arts training taught him self-esteem and confidence.

After dinner, Danny returned to his cell. On his bunk was an envelope bearing Dixie's return address. He opened it quickly and eagerly extracted the card inside. On the front was a color photo of a thong-clad beach babe, shimmering with sheer voluptuousness. Danny opened the card and read the message, written in Dixie's childlike, loopy hand: "I'll take you to the moon, baby." Danny smiled and closed the card, thinking of the tanned curves he missed so much. Reopening the card, he read the note on the facing side. It read: "Baby, I miss you so much. There are always members around here from up north. The brothers got their patches. They're full members! Everybody seems busy now, but Jesse doesn't like it. The others are going wild, though. I wish you were here with me. I'll write again soon. Love forever, Dixie."

Danny read the card over and over. His brothers had been a constant for five years. Sure, there were squabbles, disputes, and hassles, but the members always stayed together. Danny couldn't understand why Jesse would be unhappy, or why he hadn't written. He read the letter one more time, then went to the library.

Tong was sitting quietly at their usual table. Few inmates used the run-down library. Tables with small reading lights occupied the center of the room, flanked by rows of wooden book shelves donated by a nearby college after it remodeled one of its reading rooms. The sturdy oak tables dated from the '30s, and had withstood years of abuse at the hands of the young. Now they were used only occasionally, and by men who weren't trying to pass any test, just the time.

"Tong," Danny whispered across the table. "Read this, will ya?" Tong took the card without comment.

"What do you make of the note inside the card?" Danny asked, still whispering.

Tong read the message twice. "Was your club young?" "No, we've been around for a while," Danny answered. "But my brothers just became Devils Own."

Tong's eyebrows lifted slightly. Barely 5 feet, 8 inches tall, Tong was slim and, like Danny, in his mid-20s. Tong's jet black hair, pulled tightly back from his face, was about the same length as Danny's. His features were soft but angular, and his mouth was a narrow slit that seemed patterned after his eyes. When he was intense, he took on the appearance of a man two decades older.

"Let me tell you a story," Tong said, shifting slightly in his chair and lowering his voice. He became statue-like in his concentration, imparting great wisdom to Danny, who was mesmerized by the man's presence and poise. "I faced a similar situation recently. Although I am Chinese, and good at my trade, I disrupted the product flow in a ruthless game. For that I was not accepted, but tested over and over. The gangs in Chinatown knew nothing of brotherhood, but only of the drug business and paranoia. Gang members killed people in their own families in order to move up the ladder. I was dismayed, but fought for what I believed was right. Wrong—it was incorrect to intrude. If I wanted in, I should have walked slowly behind, but it was against my nature to follow, and against their nature to trust, even their own people. Maybe

Jesse is going through the same ordeal, trying to rock a very old boat. Now let's train. It's getting late."

Danny had trouble focusing on his training routine while pondering each word of Tong's tale. As he lay down in his bunk that night, it dawned on him.

Jesse hated drug dealing.

SLOW-MOVING CLOCK

*F*og hung heavily over the coast on Valentine's Day, but for half a dozen outlaws, there was no romance in the air—only the chill of violent change. This was meeting night, or "church," as the club members called it, Wednesday, 8 p.m. The brothers braved the February fog to attend their meeting at Big John's pad, where the mood was solemn and the room quiet, unlike gatherings during the month following their becoming members of the Devils Own. At that time, they celebrated constantly, partied harder than ever before, and made certain that the bike community knew that the Devils Own were in town.

Eddie and Hank began to make trips up north constantly, and members from that region dropped in from time to time. More and more drugs appeared, and Fireball and Big John were getting high more often. The conflict between the Los Cuchillos and the Hawks was forgotten and women were plentiful. But there was an edge, like a knife blade fresh from the sharpening stone, cutting through the ranks. Jesse pulled up in front of John's house, shut off the Shovelhead's engine, and dropped the kickstand. He remained astride the bike long enough to straighten his new vest with the pristine Devils Own insignia sewn on the back, then walked to the house. His fireplug physique had taken on a new significance. He was training hard, and his stout forearms were bigger and stronger than ever. He pounded on the front door with jackhammer blows of his powerful fist.

"What the fuck are you doing, asswipe?" John shouted, flinging open the door.

"Tryin' to see if anyone was awake around here," Jesse barked, delivering another pile-driver blow to the door, tearing the heavy slab of oak from John's hand, and driving the door knob into the wall behind it.

"Goddammit!" John bellowed, rapidly losing patience with

Jesse's behavior. "What's the fucking problem, dickhead?"

"We'll talk about it at the meeting," Jesse said, brushing past John, and heading for the refrigerator. "Got any beer?"

"Yeah," John said, obviously higher than a kite. "And coke, if you want some." A reddish ring encircled each of John's bloodshot eyes. "I hope we can get this meeting over fast–I've got a couple of broads comin' over, and we're gonna git down."

Jesse shook his head and dropped into a black leather armchair in the living room. "I thought this goddamn meeting was supposed to start at eight," he said, kicking the glass-top coffee table hard enough to send it sliding into the wall. Jesse could never tolerate drug dealing and substance abuse. Sure, he liked to party as much as the next guy, but not every day, every night, every weekend. He knew that some of the brothers sold drugs, but as long as they were discreet about it and left him out of it, he was cool. But what was happening to the club he once knew and loved wasn't cool—not by a long shot.

Jesse grew up in the South, deep in Louisiana, with a cop for a father and a mother who was a competent, devoted housewife. Both his parents worked hard, fought hard, and drove their offspring hard. But shortly after his father's 40th birthday, he changed, drinking heavily and pushing around both his sons. But it was Jesse's mom, a stout, corn-fed woman with long blond hair, German blue eyes, and a voice that could melt butter, who took the brunt of the ol' man's anger. Jesse never figured it out—at least, not entirely. As a teenager, he benefited from the solid position his father enjoyed with friends and family members. The ol' man came across as an upstanding, honest citizen, and his mother mirrored the same qualities.

But something broke the code of integrity his father shared with other cops. Jesse could only guess that it had something to do with his dad's last partner, one of the first women on the police force. They had been partners for only two years when she was found face down near the New Orleans shipyards, shot behind her right ear with a .38. It was no secret that she was about to testify against a handful of cops who had executed a private bust on a drug ring, kept the money and the drugs they seized, and set up their own business. Jesse's father went downhill fast after the murder.

One day, his mother packed the two boys in their station wagon, saying they were going to visit relatives. But both Jesse and his brother, Brian, knew better. Observing the way she packed the family wagon, and seeing the tears rolling down her cheeks as she pulled away from the curb, they knew they'd never return. She never contacted the stout cop again. But a year later, he died mysteriously, and soon she began to receive his pension checks, because they had never divorced. Rumor had it that he drank himself to death, or committed suicide. Jesse and his brother stuck with their mom throughout high school, and although Jesse was a rebel and a biker, he never could tolerate substance abuse, lying, or betrayal.

As John turned to snap at Jesse, he heard the roar of two Harleys rumbling up the street. It was Fast Eddie and Hank, riding to the meeting in tandem. They had been inseparable for the last four months, and they swaggered into John's pad draped in a black cloak of evil confidence. Both had become a different level of outlaw, and one of the perks was their simultaneous offers on homes. Neither had jobs, but their income had increased tenfold. The world of the motorcycle club was once composed of hard-fighting rowdies who often couldn't contain their violent urges. They cared nothing about a job or a family. The only things that mattered were their brothers, their bikes, and a piece of ass. Until they changed their patch, the Hawks embodied the essence of that breed. Although the Devils Own displayed the same anti-social, threatening behavior, it was a shrewd disguise, concealing an even more sinister activity—drug trafficking.

Jesse sat scowling in the corner, nursing a beer while Eddie and Hank nodded to John and followed him into one of the back bedrooms. Behind the closed door, the bedroom windows were shrouded by lengths of black velvet to prevent outside scrutiny of anything in the room. "How the fuck are you, John?" Hank inquired. "You been dipping your nose into the profits?"

John smiled, his nose running slightly from the effects of snorting. "Well, sure," he replied. "Man's gotta party. And at the price I can get this shit, I just party all the fucking time."

Eddie spun around on his cowboy boot heels, grabbing John with his left hand, and slamming him against the wall.

Simultaneously, his Buck knife was out of its sheath and in his right hand, instantly open, the blade's point indenting John's neck just below the jawbone. "Listen, motherfucker," he hissed, "we got a good thing going here, and you're not gonna fuck it up or put us in a cross by snortin' the profits." With the flick of his wrist, Eddie snapped the knife closed, thrust it back into its sheath, and gave John a quick forehand-backhand slap across his nose. The action took only an instant, but it scared the living shit out of John.

"Fuck!" John screamed, grabbing his nose with both hands. His sinuses burned from Eddie's slap, and involuntary tears rolled from his eyes. "I'll quit! I got control!"

Hank handed John a scarf with the Devils logo silk-screened on it. The design depicted the evil devil's profile, surrounded by flames. John dabbed at his nose, expecting blood.

"Sit down," Eddie commanded. John sat, trembling slightly. He was beginning to lose his bouncer physique because of snorting coke. Under stress, his paranoia grew to epic proportions. He would sweat gallons of fluid while taking in almost none, so his hands shook perceptibly, and he was unable to maintain an erection.

"You got the money?" Eddie asked.

"Yeah," John snorted through the scarf. "It's in the top drawer of the dresser." Eddie opened the drawer and withdrew a gray tin cash box. It was locked. "Gimme the key," Eddie said. "How many of your girlfriends know where this box is?"

"None," John replied, handing over the key. Eddie opened the box, counted the bills, then paused thoughtfully. After 15 seconds, he sighed, slipping two hundreds back into the box before shutting it. "You're OK this time," Eddie said somberly. "But you're not gonna make it if you keep on moving such large amounts, and only come away with a couple hundred to live on. And we can't afford brothers who can't stay in business."

Eddie counted the money again, then stuffed the bills into a concealed pocket inside his jet-black leather vest. He maintained the look of an outlaw, but beneath that exterior he was physically unimpressive. His arms were thin and his legs weak, but he was fast with a knife—and he was mean.

Hank pulled his Levi's up over his black riding boots, and extracted a freshly sealed bag of coke from each boot. "Break out your scale," he said.

Big John bent down and reached under his bed. He pulled out a sensitive, digital scale, cleared off the top of the wooden dresser, and began weighing and bagging small amounts of coke.

The sudden and unexpected sound of loud banging on the bedroom door froze Big John where he stood. Eddie snapped open his knife, and Hank pulled his Browning from his vest, flipped off the safety, and pointed it at the door.

"Who the fuck is it?" Eddie shouted.

"It's Jesse. Are we gonna have a meeting, or just sit around a table and snort our goddamned brains out?"

Hank put away his automatic, and was about to respond to Jesse's annoyed question, when Eddie nudged him with his elbow. Whispering, Eddie said, "That motherfucker don't get the plot. He's beginning to get on my nerves."

"We'll be right there, brother," Hank said through the door. Turning to his companions, he said quietly, "Let's finish this up after the meeting."

"We shouldn't just leave it here," Eddie said.

"Why the fuck not?" demanded Hank. "Just members in the house."

"Yeah, I know," Eddie said, returning his knife to the black sheath, as if tucking a deadly snake back into its bed. "A couple of more members like that one, and we might go for a face-down swim in the Santa Monica Bay." Eddie glared at John. "Get that shit off your nose and let's have a meeting." The living room was now adorned with Devils Own paraphernalia—flags, banners, and pictures—surrounded by Big John's array of knives and weapons. Jesse sat in the corner, his young face etched with lines bespeaking his determination. Fireball sat with Old Man Jason, sharing laughs and a half-pint of Schnapps, paying no attention to Jesse's sour mood.

Eddie sat in his usual chair, and opened a small crystal flask brimming with high-grade coke. In a single fluid move, he drew out his trusty knife, snapped open the blade to the locked position, dipped the point into the flask, lifted it to his pointed nose, and inhaled. Eddie offered the flask to the room, but not the knife. Everyone indulged, with the notable exception of Jesse, who declined the euphoric drug. "Let's get the meeting going," Eddie announced. "We've got business to do."

Big John entered the room, still dabbing at his nose with the scarf, and sat down with a glass of whiskey.

"You collect the dues?" Eddie said to Fireball.

"Yeah, it's a done deal," Fireball replied, snorting the coke and chasing it with a hit of Schnapps.

"Well," Eddie began, "We're in a different league now, so-"

"Oh yeah?" Jesse interrupted. "What the fuck league is that? We drug dealers or bikers?"

"What the fuck is it to you, buttbrain?" Eddie shouted, his still-opened knife pointing at Jesse.

"What's that, asshole?" Jesse shot back, gesturing toward Eddie's knife. "You gonna stick your brother like you almost did to John over a pile of bullshit blow?"

"Why the fuck not, motherfucker?" Eddie bellowed, getting to his feet.

"I thought this was a brotherhood, fuckface," Jesse barked, his eyes bright with anger. Nostrils flaring, he vaulted to his feet. "Come on, pig-sticker, let's see what you can do with that fucking knife."

Eddie wrapped his thumb and forefinger around his nose and snorted, driving any residual white powder from his nostrils into his sinuses. The rush produced by the 80 percent pure powder slamming into his brain sent Eddie's confidence level skyrocketing. He knew how fast he was with a knife, and the coke magnified the perception to a superhuman scale. Poised and determined, he moved toward Jesse. The room fell deathly silent. Every eye was glued to the murderous blade clutched in Eddie's hand, its razor-sharp edge distinct and deadly even in the dim light. Never taking his eyes off Eddie, Jesse moved along the wall until he came to a standing lamp. Big John had painted it the club colors, maroon and gold, and stenciled the Devil's profile and flames on the shade. Jesse grabbed the base of the lamp and swung it at Eddie, snapping the cord and yanking the plug from the wall socket in a shower of sparks. The base of the lamp swept through the air, catching Eddie's left biceps. Moving to block the attack, he lashed out with the knife. Jesse leaned back, holding the lamppost in the center, and dodging the glistening blade. Using the lamp as a defensive weapon, Jesse slammed the shade into Eddie's face in a shower of glass as the bulb exploded under the impact. Stunned by the blatant attack, Eddie backed away. One moment he felt invincible, yet the next, in the slumping decline of the cocaine rush, his self-assurance gave way to uncertainty. Eyes wide, he slashed at his opponent erratically. Jesse cocked his left arm, and struck again and again, first to Eddie's head, and then to his knife arm.

Eddie stumbled, and Jesse followed, slamming his target until Eddie dropped the knife and fell to the greasy carpet. "You lightweight motherfucker," Jesse sneered. "You and your fucking knife piss me off. You've been my brother for five years, and now you've turned to shit because of some fucking white powder. Screw it, I'm outta here." With that, he ripped off his patch and threw it at Eddie.

"Hey, wait a minute," Fireball said, standing. "You don't have to quit."

"The hell I don't," Jesse said, heading for the door. "This is just the start, and I ain't gonna be around for chapter two."

Jesse tore open the door and stomped off, followed by the house-rattling sound of the door slamming shut.

Eddie pulled himself to his feet. "That cocksucker, may be right," he said, still recovering from his defeat. "So if any of you other motherfuckers ain't up for the job, now's the time to hit the streets."

Fireball and Old Man Jason looked at each other, their expressions radiating amazement, questioning, and doubt. All they had was the club, their patches, and their bikes. For years, they had dreamed about becoming members of the Devils Own, but now they wondered what this signified, and whether Jesse was right, or just scared, and whether Eddie was their brother, or Satan.

Looking over at Hank standing quietly in the corner, Eddie probed between his teeth with a toothpick, and sipped at a glass of Jack Daniel's. Hank raised his eyebrows. Together, they knew what they were doing, what ladder they were attempting to climb. Moreover, they were confident that none of the men in the room constituted a real problem worthy of their concern.

HOMECOMING

*J*une was an exceptionally hot month for California in 1974. The state was experiencing one of the worst droughts on record, necessitating severe cutbacks in water, allocation for crops in the central regions of the state. Danny had not slept comfortably for a week. His hands perspired constantly, and the stress caused his joints to feel disconnected. He was three days away from release.

When he began serving his sentence almost a year earlier, he was anxious, afraid, and purely pissed off. He counted the slow-moving days, looked hard on his fellow inmates, and ground his teeth at night, but discovering martial arts, learning from Tong, and being accepted by the brotherhood of inmate bikers pulled him out of his slump, and he began to do his time one long prison day at a time. He learned the prison lifestyle, and melded into the graybar society, adjusting to its severe restrictions and uncomplicated routines. Prison life was simple, but in 72 hours he would face another transition, and he was apprehensive about returning to society and a world of unknowns.

Dixie's letters were upbeat and excited, but brief and superficial. She and Danny remained friendly, but without the deep emotional bond he desired. From long-time convicts, he learned about prison relationships with the outside world riddled with uncertainties, shot full of treachery, and dependent on a paper-thin foundation of emotion without physical touch. A great many prisoners received the notorious "Dear John" letter while serving their sentences.

After his martial arts workout, Danny sat on the edge of his bunk and reread Dixie's last letter. "Dearest Danny, The brothers are riding to Santa Barbara this weekend to celebrate their first anniversary as Devils. Everyone's excited. Jesse quit. I'm sorry. I liked him."

"They have a bike for you, for when you get out, but Hank

said something about some business you have to take care of before you can be a member. I'm not sure what it is, but it's probably nothing much. I can't wait to see you again. Love, Dixie."

Several members from the northern half of the state called Eddie with an invitation for his chapter to come to Santa Barbara and celebrate their first anniversary. Higher than kites with the strings snipped, the remaining five brothers rode along the coast whooping and hollering, taking slugs of whiskey and snorts of coke in bars and behind gas stations. Eddie and Hank led the pack, John and Fireball rode behind, and Old Man Jason brought up the rear. Their bikes screamed against the Pacific Coast Highway cliffs, the sound shaking the local residents like a seven-point quake. Citizens pulled to the side and into the emergency lane, fearful of contact, or even the glares darting from the eyes of these madmen on two wheels.

The president's bike was as sharp as his knife. Eddie rode a late model Super Glide Harley, stripped to the bare bones—the frame raked, the narrow glide front end shaved and chromed and, adorned with 6-inch risers and drag bars. On each side of the jet-black, hand-rubbed lacquered tank, the bike displayed the club's foreboding profile of the Devil's head wreathed in flames and wearing a top hat. Hank's machine was a more traditional chopper, but just as black as Eddie's, with flames licking the devilish logo, and the motto, "Ride With The Best Or Die With The Rest," pinstriped onto the front fender. Hank's bike sliced through the traffic less than a foot from Eddie's, the wide glide rigid with its tall apehanger bars framing his wild, salt-and-pepper locks lashing in the wind behind narrow sunglasses. He rode with a stern expression, as if always prepared for the worst, and he was. He was learning fast, understanding that his future was centered on his contacts to the north, and on Eddie—and even Eddie was suspect.

Big John rode a massive, old, modified police Shovelhead, stroked and slammed into a rigid Harley-Davidson frame. Behind the rider, a long dixiebar thrust into the air, complementing the extreme highbars. As he licked his mustache for the residue of cocaine running out of his nose and into the coarse hairs below, his flashy, chromed, upsweep exhaust pipes slapped those he passed with insults of noise. His hair was short, his face coarse and round, and drug abuse was beginning to take a visible toll on his features and his eyes, still big and brown, but now red-rimmed and sunken. With only a pair of black sunglasses for wind protection, his shades provided further contrast to the white T-shirt he wore under a black club vest.

Motioning for the brothers to pull over at a rest stop overlooking the ocean, so that he could retrieve his vial and pack his nose, John geared down and coasted to a stop in the parking lot. The bikers retreated to an isolated corner of the scenic overlook, and John broke out the dope. This time, everyone indulged.

John lit a cigarette and leaned back against a rock. "This is the life, brothers," he said. "No one fucks with us, we got the best shit in the world, and women love us. What more could we want?" He flicked the butt into the dirt, stretching his tattooed arms to the sky before taking one more toot of coke through each nostril. He had lost much of his muscle tone, and was on the way to becoming a fat oaf who no longer cared about anything except lines of white powder. He had the drugs, the glaring patch, and the bike to bring the women home. He was riding high.

"We don't want to be late," Eddie said, cutting through the idle mood before it consumed them all. "Let's ride."

Old Man Jason held back as the bikers fired up their motorcycles, watching for cops and traffic, like a sergeant at arms is supposed to do. As he waited for them to hit the road, he felt anxious, and uneasy with the idea of a meeting outside their turf, and he squinted through his dark, oval wire glasses for some sign of trouble. His new bike was low and red, short and bright, with small, narrow handlebars and a narrowed and stretched gas tank. The rear fender was an English ribbed job, shortened, and mounted to the frame with a small dixiebar. The bike ran drag pipes, and Jason, known for riding on sidewalks and pulling pranks most riders only dream of, could pull donuts in the street all day. His jacket was made of old, natural brown leather, and he wore a fringed, tan vest over that, with a maroon scarf tied around his neck. Clean

Levi's and boots contrasted with the rough and natural exterior of his jacket. He rode fast, and liked the danger, although he was more of a hippie than a badass. Still, a fight was never altogether out of the question.

No one rode like Fireball; he was in a class by himself. His thinning red hair flashed in the sunset as the staccato bark of the drag pipes on his new Sportster filled the air. Fireball treated the bike like a woman who needed a good beating. His talent with engines was his life raft for staying on the road, and he pushed his power trains and drive lines like a drunken stagecoach driver whipping his team, until it collapsed. When an engine was thoroughly flogged beyond its tolerance, he'd rebuild again. Fireball wore Levi's and engineer boots, a T-shirt, and a Levi's vest over a standard black motorcycle jacket. His bike slid to the left in the soft sand, throwing pebbles and road debris backward at Old Man Jason. As he pushed the power band through first, his rear wheel spun against the pavement and jumped, lifting the bike into a wheelstand. Fireball enjoyed drag racing, and had been a devoted enthusiast until cocaine overcame his preference to snort fuel instead of drugs.

They had been instructed to ride past the downtown off ramps leading to the affluent, seaside community of Santa Barbara, and to get off on Painted Cave Road, a mile before Goleta, and then to head inland. Once away from the coast, the terrain became more winding, strewn with scrub growth and underbrush. Soon there were no homes, the featureless landscape broken only by an occasional farmhouse. Rolling through the hills, Eddie kept his eyes peeled for some sign of the designated turn-off. Finally, he spotted a gate over which was a small sign designating the place as the Ghost Ranch. A maroon and gold scarf was tied around a post just next to the sign.

Eddie raised his left arm, signaling the turn, and in unison, the small pack of bikes followed him onto a dirt road, and then a mile or so through a winding gorge that prevented the farmhouse from being seen from the road. The trail ended at a clearing that spread out for 20 acres. Except for a small house and a barn, no structures interrupted the landscape. Several bikes were parked in front of the fading red barn.

Eddie pulled up alongside them and shut off his bike, as did the others.

Pulling open the massive creaking door, the bikers walked inside as a group. Two club members were standing at a makeshift bar in the far corner, washing down shots of tequila with chilled cans of Tecate. Rotten Ron turned to the arriving group and gestured for them to join the drinkers. "Hey," he called out, "come on over and get a beer, unless you're afraid."

Eddie said nothing, nor did Hank, but John shouted, "We're Devils—we ain't afraid of nothin'!"

"That's what I like to hear," Ron snorted, taking a slug of beer.

Old Man Jason was the last inside, and he carefully but unobtrusively checked out the entire barn as he entered. The fact that there were six bikes out front when they arrived, but only two members inside, bothered him. His stony eyes continued to sweep the inside of the two-tiered barn. Farm equipment and animal stalls occupied half the area inside, and hay bales filled one corner of the dilapidated building. Except for the drinkers, the broad, open area was empty, but the shafts of afternoon light slanting in through several loose boards, indicated to him how easily someone could observe the barn's interior from outside. "Where are the other riders?" Jason said, looking around.

Miguel turned around abruptly. "What the fuck's it to you, you hippie motherfucker?" he said, pushing back his stool and standing up aggressively, feet wide apart, hands twitching at his side. "You got no business being in this club. Go smoke your dope somewhere else."

Jason froze, as did the other members. Instantly, his suspicions that this gathering was more than a simple one-year anniversary celebration were confirmed. He rapidly weighed his options for escape and survival, disturbed that his brothers stood motionless. It was as if Eddie and Hank weren't there. They hesitated momentarily before turning away and grabbing a couple of beers from the galvanized tub full of ice behind the bar. As they did so, they nodded to the brothers from out of town.

"You might be right, asswipe," Jason said, moving away from the other members for a straight shot at Miguel. "But I ain't going that easy."

Miguel's long, Fu Manchu mustache and slick features were framed by long braids of wavy, jet black hair. His attire—black T-shirt, black vest, black Levi's, and shiny black cowboy boots—made him look like a paid assassin. Indeed, he seemed downright frightening, like a gunfighter waiting to cut another notch in the handle of his six-shooter. Nonetheless, Jason stood his ground. Since they had joined the Devils, Jason had became aware of the brutally enforced pecking order within the massive organization. Moreover, he also noted that if a brother had a problem with members from the northern part of the state, that member no longer had brothers. Instead, he was just one man surrounded by strangers. The Hawks had stood up for one another, no matter what. Suddenly, he felt very much alone.

The two men stared at each other without blinking. Miguel sized Jason up from his tan boots to his frizzy hair, and all the while, the man stood fast. That, of course, was exactly what the confrontation was about—to determine whether these guys had the *cojones* to be Devils. Miguel turned around and picked up his drink. "Come on, you old fucker, have a beer." His half-hearted attempt to pass off the incident as a joke left a violent cloud hanging in the air. Silently, everyone devoted their attention to cold beer, waiting for whatever would come next.

Eventually, with the help of plentiful supplies of cocaine and beer, the tension subsided, replaced by something like a party atmosphere. Outside, the setting sun cast long shadows across the floor of the barn as the brothers talked of fights, rides, and women. But Old Man Jason noted that Rotten Ron and Miguel weren't consuming alcohol at the same rate as the others, while Eddie and his sidekick seemed detached from the pack. Meanwhile, Fireball and Big John were going at it hot and heavy, when two more Devils Own walked in the door.

"Hey, Big John," called Rico, a member from up north who had a well-known reputation within the club as an enforcer, an all-occasion, dirty-deeds man. Striding forward till his menacing presence loomed over Big John, he spoke in a low voice with an unmistakably sinister tone. "Where the fuck you hiding our coke?"

The room fell silent again.

"Whaddaya mean, brother?" John asked, with an unconvincing, nervous chuckle. "I ain't hiding nothin'."

With the lidless intensity of a rattlesnake's gaze, Rico stared at John as he pulled his long, dark brown mane of hair into a ponytail at the base of his weightlifter-thick neck. Steroids pumping with drugs through his veins, his biceps twitched as he coiled a rubber band around the thick strands. Wearing only jogging shoes, Levi's, and his black leather club cutoff over a bare chest, Rico's abs rippled as he brought his hand around to his chin to stroke his long, pointed goatee. Without warning, he and his steroid monster partner charged John like two furious bulls.

Old Man Jason moved to intercept the powerful pair, but Miguel stepped in front of him, firing him an intimidating glare that could freeze boiling water. Jason stopped short, not out of fear, but from the realization that he needed time to evaluate this unforeseen turn of events. Fireball, too, attempted to intercede, but Eddie and Hank held him fast. "There's nothing you can do," Eddie whispered in his ear.

The behemoth bikers hit John like dual pile-drivers, knocking him to the dirt of the barn floor. Eddie and Hank didn't budge while the two outlaws beat John unmercifully, battering him with their fists and kicking him repeatedly before tearing off his patch and throwing him outside. Painfully, John struggled to his feet as his tormentors ordered him to haul his ass out of the area pronto. Dazed and bleeding, he struggled onto his chopper, kicked it to life, and weaved slowly down the road leading out of the ranch beaten and distraught.

"Now we can have some fun," Ron said, sneeringly. But his anticipation of a celebration was short-lived.

Handing Ron a beer, Miguel said, "Before we can enjoy the night and I can give you your one-year plaque, we need to settle one more score. That member who's doing time in Tehachapi—he'll be getting out soon, right?"

Fireball and Jason, still stunned and shaken by the sudden and unexpected violence and accusations, simply nodded. Jason observed that Eddie and Hank seemed aloof and undisturbed by what had happened, and he was determined to find out why. "Hey, Eddie," Jason said, "you've been in touch with Dixie. When's our brother getting out?"

Eddie shot Jason a hard, baleful glance. "He ain't our brother no more," he said through clenched teeth. "He was the one that got us into that shitstorm with the Los Cuchillos, and—"

"That's bullshit," Jason interrupted, angrily. "He was a stand-up guy, and he took the fall for all of us, and he's doing his time like a man. Shit—you and I both know he didn't kill that Mexican."

Miguel assessed the situation, then looked at the president of the chapter. "It's your deal, asshole."

"You're right," Jason interrupted again. "It's his deal. And he's our brother, and he's getting his goddamn patch when he gets out. We hung back and let him take the fall by himself. It's fuckin' high time to show some class and let him back in."

Eddie saw his personal arrangement as well as the respect of the northern chapters dissolving before his eyes. And he had no doubt that he would be the next on the knock-'em-out line if he didn't resolve this mess right away.

Miguel challenged Eddie with his eyes and his words. "Well, motherfucker," he sneered, "that wasn't the arrangement, and you know it. So who do we deal with on this—you, or Jason, who frankly, is more of a man about it? Or do we just pull all your patches, thump your pussy asses here and now, and leave?"

Jason's head was reeling, unable to believe what he was hearing, at a loss to understand his own behavior. One of his brothers had just been beaten within an inch of his life, stripped of his colors, and sent down the road humiliated, and yet they had done nothing to stop it. And it was now obvious that another brother had been a patsy in some fucked deal, and these bastards were threatening to take everybody's patch. For a moment, he looked at Fireball, who seemed as perplexed as a kid locked in a holding tank for the first time.

"Listen, you slimeball motherfuckers," Jason growled, striding directly toward Miguel, "I don't give a fuck how many other chickenshit assholes you got planted in the weeds. We've been brothers for years, and that's all that matters in my book. If this is nothing more than a business, and we're supposed to trade brothers for profit, I'll split now. But if we're going to call ourselves brothers and mean it, then the brother who took the fall and is doing time for us right now, doesn't get tossed in the garbage like a worn-out oil rag. You can side with me on this, or you can call this bullshit game a business and I'll turn in my patch this minute."

Eddie eased his hand down to his knife sheath, but Miguel grabbed his arm. "Let's go outside for a minute," he said softly.

Miguel held on to Eddie's elbow, leading him toward the door. "I'll get a piece of you yet," Eddie snarled over his shoulder to Jason, as they left the barn.

"I'll be right here, buttface," Jason returned, holding his ground. During the next two or three minutes, he heard indistinct fragments of their heated conversation outside. Then the door opened, and the two men reentered the barn.

"All right," Eddie said. "When Danny gets out, we'll have a bike and a prospect patch for him, but he's got to go see the Los Cuchillos honcho and straighten this mess out before he can become a Devil."

"What the fuck does that mean?" Fireball demanded, stepping forward defiantly. "Another trick bag?"

"No trick," Eddie said. "Just an understanding we need to have between the clubs in order to keep the peace. OK, enough of that shit—let's party!"

Miguel grinned and slapped Old Man Jason on the back. "I got to hand it to you, hippie," he said. "You stood up well back there." The two shared a beer, and Miguel grabbed a maroon and gold plaque from behind the crudely assembled bar and presented it to Eddie. "Let's see if you bastards survive another year. In the meantime, stay away from John—we're not through with him. He owes us ten grand and the shithead's slipping deeper into the bag every day."

Jason knew the whole story hadn't been laid out on the table just yet. He wandered out to his bike and uncovered a silver flask of peppermint schnapps. Taking a deep slug, he pondered the evening, alternating shots of schnapps with tokes on a fat joint. Heaving a sigh, he concluded that he just couldn't figure it out. For years, he had partied with his brothers, fought with them, and worked with them. Yet inside a year, the group was crumbling, as if someone had poisoned the beer. For Jason, the celebration rolled into the night on a sour note.

Danny woke up with a start. "Hey," the guard barked. "Here are your street clothes. Get dressed and haul ass down to the mess hall and get some chow. Then I'll walk you through discharge, right out through the goddamn door." The guard paused, spinning his baton in his hands, watching Danny, then added, "I'll be back in fifteen—be ready."

Danny looked at the Levi's, T-shirt and denim jacket he wore when he arrived at the prison. His waist had shrunk from 38 inches to 35. The dungarees were sloppy, but Danny's thighs were stronger than ever, due to hours of squats. The T-shirt was tight over his biceps, and he was unable to button his jacket over his 48-inch chest. He was tan and clean-shaven, except for the mustache. Gazing at his reflection in the stainless steel mirror, he detected the signs of passing time on his face. He had matured in the short period he spent in prison.

Danny showered and dressed, pulling his thick, sandy-blond hair into a ponytail, before collecting the few items around his cell that he was allowed to take with him. Earlier, he had given most of his books to the prison library, or to other inmates. He surrendered his *Penthouse* and *Easyriders* magazines to the Devils Own he had befriended, and offered two books on Zen to Tong.

"You keep them," Tong said, politely declining the books. "Take every step with care, my friend." For the last few weeks, Tong had taught Danny the art of observation, training him to recognize hidden meanings, veiled threats, and the like. "Now is the time for the test," Tong said with finality. He bowed and shook Danny's hand.

"If there's ever anything I can do for you on the outside," Danny said to his friend, "don't hesitate to ask. I'll stay in touch."

Danny's goodbyes from the Devils were bear hugs and slaps on the back. "We'll put in a good word for you," Craig said. "You deserve a fair shake. You took the heat and stood tall."

Danny had always wanted to ask them what they thought was going to happen, but never did. Nevertheless, since they had never volunteered any information regarding the club or his release, he had a hunch that there might be reason for concern. Although they had treated him with respect, no one had ever called him brother. He remembered Tong's warning about stepping carefully, but only momentarily, a passing thought in the midst of his pre-release excitement.

As he walked to the outer gate, Danny was uncertain whether or not his brothers would finally break their silence. Based on her most recent correspondence, Danny suspected that Dixie was partying too much—some of her letters were up, some down, and their generally erratic tone suggested mood swings. The last letter was so scattered that he had found it simply incomprehensible.

Danny reflected on his long walk to freedom. He looked at the walls behind him, at the clean concrete path and the manicured lawn on either side, wondering if he wouldn't be happier inside than face all the snares and uncertainties on the street. The tower guard hollered down, and Danny came to the gate. "Thought for sure no one would come to pick up your biker ass," the officer at the gate sneered. "But it looks like you lucked out this time." Danny stepped through the opening to find the same stretched Lincoln that had greeted his brothers in the alley.

Walking through those iron gates almost nine months after Danny was brought through the booking entrance in back, shackled to 20 other prisoners in a depressing black and white bus, was undeniably a memorable experience, but one he wanted way behind him. Danny's eyes met with brown-sugar hills, trees so green and alive they seemed to wave at him simply out of sheer vitality.

The land around the prison seemed to go on forever, and the air smelled fresh, as though filtered through a woman's exhilarating perfume. Danny found everything stimulating, invigorating. Though he wasn't a religious man, many of Tong's teachings came to mind at this moment—teachings about how man should treat himself and the land. Dropping to one knee, he scooped up a handful of soft soil and looked at it as it ran down between his strong fingers. "I will respect myself and the land," Danny murmured quietly.

This panorama of nature also contained less pastoral elements—like the long and low, black Lincoln idling outside the prison. Danny could detect the heat waves generated by the car's big engine rising from the hood. The darkly tinted windows made the vehicle look even longer and more menacing. He took another step, feeling his way along, as though he was an infant having to test every texture, color, smell, and taste. The passenger-side rear door opened, and Dixie emerged, almost falling down, as if someone had pushed her. Regaining her balance, she stood and straightened her miniskirt, revealing tanned, supple legs.

Dixie's timid smile enhanced a naturally naive countenance, although she was actually about as innocent as a whorehouse madam. A petite, 4-foot, 11-inch tall woman, she was perfectly proportioned for her height. She looked thinner than Danny remembered, which accentuated the shape of her legs, her narrow waist, and the whole, tightly wrapped package. Bending slightly and pushing the hem of her skirt back into place as if she had never worn a slinky garment like this before, Dixie raised up slowly until her eyes met Danny's. Instantly, a smile that could make flowers bloom spread across her full lips. Danny's heart overflowed with the sight of her, and as she smiled, he recognized the innocent Dixie he always loved and cherished. In an instant, she bolted toward him, like a small child running to greet her seafaring father, returned home at last. As Danny's arms encircled her body, he felt as if an earthquake shuddered through his body. Even dressed, he could feel her form beneath the fabric, and his mind recycled the many times he had held her naked body. Dixie was a tempting package, complete with all the trimmings that made her so enticing. Having her was like buying a sports car that comes complete with racing mirrors, an embroidered sweatshirt, scarf, and the hat to match. Having purchased such a total package, when you slip into the leather driver's seat and plug the cloisonné key fob into the ignition, your experience is a complete encounter, from the Pirelli tires to the leather-laced steering wheel.

Danny tried to concentrate on Tong's words as his lips met the soft warmth of Dixie's neck while he inhaled the familiar scent of her perfume. Her smooth skin, her aroma and just the way she felt in his arms melted Danny's resolve like a stick of butter tossed on a fry cook's grill. Dixie was small and unassuming, with a habit of blinking her eyes shyly, and dressing like a kid in junior high. She told Danny about growing up as an abused child with alcoholic parents, leading to her running away at the age of 13, and moving in with a bike club member who took her under his wing. He treated her rough at times, but was always there for her. Those years made for a story of innocence and tender love. But his resolve was lost then to her untainted delivery and buttery flesh. Now, as he held her in the summer heat, Danny never wanted to let go, but he knew better. Danny's resolve weakened. If it weren't for her out-of-touch letters, he would have melted into a slobbering mass of amorphous manhood, succumbing to any of her desires right there in the middle of the street.

As their lips met and her mouth opened gently to let his tongue inspect that particular cavern, he remembered the first time they kissed, recalled the passion, the searching, the longing, the connection. His right hand rested on the soft depression between her waist and the curve of her hips. He felt like an adolescent holding his first girl, driving his senses into overload.

He felt perspiration coming through her dress, and she broke free, saying, "Let's get out of the sun," in her too-sweet, Alice in Wonderland voice. "I have something for you inside the car."

Danny returned to reality—the reality he had trained for during the previous nine months. And the return carried a jolt like a bucket of ice water in the face. Turning her toward him as she attempted to return to the Lincoln, he looked straight into her nervously beautiful eyes. "Where we going?" he asked, seeking information, a sign, anything.

Dixie studiously avoided making eye contact with him, though only moments earlier they were locked together like magnets. "Home," she said, evasively, volunteering nothing more. She held the door for Danny, and he stepped into the plush interior of the big car. The interior was a sea of thick, deep purple velvet, cooled by a mammoth air conditioner under the hood. Every handle inside—from those on the drawers under the seats and door frames, to the passenger handholds at the back of the front seat, was set with Burlwood inlay. In the center of the spacious passenger compartment was a console on which a bottle of champagne and several chilled glasses rested. On a small silver plate alongside the champagne was an impressive chunk of uncut cocaine and a silver straw.

As he attempted to take in everything he saw, smelt, and felt, Danny found himself on sensory overload again. Through the open partition between the driver's compartment and the passenger area, Danny was greeted first by Fireball, smiling broadly and waving for him to sit down. Old Man Jason held out his hand, but didn't smile. Dixie sat across from him. In the briefest instant of panoramic vision, Danny took in the coke, noted the handle of an automatic pistol protruding from inside Fireball's vest, observed the Devils Own insignia on Old Man Jason's cutoff, and the one year bar pinned next to it. At the same instant, through the tinted windows he took in the brightness of the outdoors, the clarity, openness, and fundamental goodness of the fields, and what they offer all mankind. With a conviction born of indisputable insight, he realized the Lincoln was idling in the brilliant light, enveloped by a cloud from the dark side.

Behind the wheel, Eddie waited until the door slammed shut, then threw the car into gear and peeled out in a small explosion of scattered gravel and squealing tires. Danny hugged Fireball and shook Old Man Jason's hand heartily. "How ya doin' brother?" Fireball inquired.

"A lot better, now," Danny returned. "Who's at the wheel of this barge?" Danny asked, shooting a glance at Jason, who avoided Danny's eyes.

At the first stop, Eddie turned in his seat and nodded to Danny. "You look like the time did you good," he said.

"Time can be good for the body," Danny replied, then asked, "How come you're driving—ain't you the president?"

Eddie abruptly pulled the Lincoln to the side of the road, jamming the chrome shifter into park as he turned around to face Danny. "Yeah, I'm still the president," Eddie said, ignoring Danny's question about why he was the driver. "And I owe you a word or two of explanation, although you caused us a helluva lot of problems, including nearly going to war with the Los Cuchillos. That's why we couldn't come around during your trial or visit you in the joint." Eddie wore his most intimidating expression. "We need to talk about all that when the party's over. But for right now, we know you did the time, and we're proud of you. So get high and enjoy yourself while—"

"I served time for someone's else's crime," Danny interrupted. "Why should I have been the one to take the fall?"

"Listen, goddammit," Eddie replied, stammering slightly, "we want you in the club, understand? But we've got a problem, and we're asking for your help. Right or wrong, the Los Cuchillos think you're the guy who killed their member, and things ain't gonna be right till the matter is closed. We want you to ride up to Fresno and straighten it out with the club's president. Do that, and we'll get you a patch."

"There's always a catch," Danny said, an edge of disdain creeping into his voice. "Aw, screw it—it's damned good to be out of there."

"Fuck this!" Fireball interjected. "Let's party. We can deal with that shit later." Danny relaxed. At last, he was with his brothers, and when he was with them, he had nothing to worry about. He felt certain that they would take care of the conflict with the Los Cuchillos, and Danny would be riding with his brothers again.

Dixie seemed edgy and apprehensive, almost frightened as the car lurched away from the dusty shoulder, and returned to the road. Not surprisingly, she did what came naturally when her survival was the issue, she knelt down on the floor of the car, wiggled her head between Danny's legs, reached up, and unzipped his fly.

Fireball shifted uneasily in his seat, his eyes wide and fixed with uncertainty and fear, not for himself, but for Danny. When Old Man Jason uncorked the champagne with a loud and hollow pop, Fireball jerked around in surprise, his hand halfway to the piece whose handle Danny had observed earlier. Jason poured the pale, sparkling liquid into slim glasses, handing them to the others when all were filled. "You have brothers, now," he said to Danny, the grim expression on his craggy face indicating that the brotherhood ended at the back of the driver's seat. "But we're in a big club now, and the priorities are altogether different ... if you know what I mean."

The truth was that Danny didn't know what Jason meant, but he nodded affirmatively anyway, saying nothing in reply. He was confused by the conflicting signals he seemed to be picking up from his brothers. "Well," he said to no one in particular, "I've waited for this day a helluva long time. So let's have some fun." Raising his glass high, he downed the champagne in one gulp just as Dixie took his cock in her mouth.

PARTY TIME

*F*ive hours later, the Lincoln slid to a stop behind a massive warehouse on the outskirts of Marina Del Rey, adjacent to the ritziest seaside development in the L.A. Basin, and less than five miles from Los Angeles International Airport. The building had originally been solidly constructed in the '30s by Howard Hughes, and used initially for airplane design work, then for making movies. The club had rented the least visible segment of the block-long building—a secure unit, in a corner that saw few cars and even fewer people. The rest of the huge structure, situated half a mile from any major street, and surrounded by acres of overgrown seaside marsh land, was rented by fledgling movie producers, artists, and computer techheads.

In L.A. County, finding a piece of land not crammed with stucco homes, strip shopping centers, malls, industrial parks, apartments, and high-rise office buildings, was a feat in itself. But this area, less than two miles from the beach, close to the airport, and surrounded by nothing, had somehow remained a haven for artists in spite of runaway growth elsewhere. The outlaw bikers recognized another benefit of renting their segment of the sprawling building—it provided them a commanding view of the surrounding area. A single prospect, perched on the roof, could give the members six to eight minutes warning of anything heading their way.

By the time the Lincoln pulled up at the mammoth building, everyone was stoned out of their heads, hooting and hollering as they poured themselves out of the car—everyone, that is, except for Eddie who had driven, and monitored every word said along the way. Fireball and Old Man Jason had been very careful about what they said to Danny. And though they made a couple of cryptic statements behind the coke, weed, and champagne, they had learned over the years that being high was no excuse for running your mouth.

Eddie honked the horn outside the enormous double doors constructed of steel and wooden slats. The doors were big enough to allow a fighter plane to be rolled in or out easily. As the Lincoln entered the building and the doors slid shut, the lights of the big car swept across a draped object, behind which, Danny observed, were stairs leading to offices above. Inside, the evening sun shone through the tinted panes of glass that formed a massive mechanical skylight along the length of the building. The concrete floor was painted, and the walls were made of industrial-quality steel and wood. Motorcycles lined the left side of the interior, and a tool bench, bike lift, and parts inventory were carefully stored next to the bikes. The other side of the room held an ornate bar, copped from Merlin MacFlys, a pub in Venice, after it shut down.

As Danny dragged himself out of the car, he sported a brand-new prospect patch sewn along the bottom of an equally new, black leather vest. Hank stepped out of the shadows and, without saying a word, strode to the shrouded object Danny had observed when they entered. Hank lifted the tarp, revealing Danny's new custom chopper, a 1955 Harley rigid frame with fatbob tanks, a quarter-inch raked neck, and painted with resilient black enamel. The stripped and chromed wide glide front end was eight inches over stock, the rear fender had been shortened and chromed, and the license plate and taillight were integrated into the fender straps. As Danny preferred, the bike was without a sissybar and front fender. Chromed shotgun pipes gleamed against the black paint job, and the wide handlebars soared t10 inches above the bike's 6-inch risers. No question—this motorcycle was bad. Each side of the tanks had been painted with sinister Devils flames, but without the face, and under each set of the lapping flames, the word "Dannydog" had been executed in fine pinstriping. The machine seemed to blast down the freeway just sitting there on the floor.

Jesse had rebuilt the engine before leaving the club, and it was nothing but raw horsepower, and plenty of it. Even without sitting on the bike, Danny felt high, sensing the power of the patch, the thunder of the machine rocking through his bones. Already he had begun living a biker's dream, days filled with sex in limos, coke by the pound, and violence by the truckload—the dark side slipped into his being like jelly spread onto peanut butter. Dixie sidled up next to him, and he swore he could smell her sex. For a moment, he wanted to bend her over the bike and fuck her right there in front of everyone standing around the huge, open warehouse.

"Before we cut you loose on that thing, let"s talk," Eddie said, motioning for Danny to follow him and Hank upstairs to the windowed offices above. They had already painted the club logo on the windows, with the words, "Devils Own" above it, and "Los Angeles" below. And to the side were the words, "Dead men don't talk." Danny walked up the stairs, but none of the other members followed, and Dixie stayed behind as well. "The night's still young," she whispered in his ear at the foot of the stairs. "We'll be waiting." She lifted her tits and caressed her nipples. Danny shook his head in frustration.

Inside the office, Hank offered Danny a seat without saying a word, while Eddie poured them shots of Jack Daniel's. "I know you must feel bad about being a prospect," Eddie began. "But it should be only a week or so before you get your patch. The rest of California needs to know that you still have the heart for the job. All you need to do is meet with the Cuchillo president, fight him, whatever, then we're off the hook, and you're a member."

Danny was high, drunk, horny, and in no mood to cut deals. "Off the hook sound like the operative words," he said, his tongue thick, and slurring the word slightly. "But what the fuck, let's party now and I can go up and meet with this asshole next week."

"That's not possible," Eddie stated, turning around holding a short straw and a small mirror piled with coke. He headed for the black chairs that Danny recognized as John's. "This has to be handled right away. You're leaving Sunday morning." It was Friday night.

"I can't do shit until I see my probation officer," Danny said.

We'll handle that," Eddie replied, snorting a thick line before offering the mirror to Danny, who shook his head, declining. Hank took the plate and inhaled twice, vacuuming a line of the white powder into each nostril. "The sooner you get this taken care of, the sooner you get your patch."

There was something unconvincing about Eddie's words, but just then Danny didn't care. He was free, and had a week to register with his probation officer.

Having served about half of his time, including the credit for county time, Danny was released to begin the probation part of his sentence. He was obligated to see a probation officer once a week for the next year. Hanging around or being affiliated with a gang, leaving town, or doing drugs were just three of the transgressions that gave cause for revoking probation, but at this moment Danny didn't give a shit about anything but being a Devil, getting high, and fucking Dixie's brains out.

Danny studied Eddie's face, then Hank's, but didn't care what they had to say. Hank had always been Eddie's man, and he kept fairly quiet. But he was altogether silent now, and both men looked older. Eddie stroked his long, black goatee, staring at Danny as if he wasn't there, as if he were dead and gone. Danny shoved his drink back toward Eddie, saying, "Well, fill me in—times, locations, and so on. I don't have a lot of time."

"Nope," Hank said, finally breaking his silence. "You don't." He glanced briefly at their president. "But let's party now—you'll get the details soon enough."

Danny had known Hank for years. He was always quiet and with a touch of evil somewhere about him. He cultivated the image of himself as club hit man, although no one was ever killed. Danny was surprised to note a hint of compassion in his words, and decided to make the most of the moment.

"Isn't this Big John's furniture?" Danny inquired, staring at Hank, who said nothing at first, but instead breathed deeply and closed his eyes momentarily. When he opened them, both dark, dilated pupils were locked on Eddie. He slipped his hand inside his vest.

"After he left the club," Eddie said, pausing to speak before snorting another line of coke, "he disappeared. His landlord called and told us to get all his shit outta his pad if we didn't want it tossed."

"He was our brother for five years," Danny reminded

Eddie, sitting up straight on the couch, and looking somberly at one man, then the other. "And all you can tell me is that he disappeared? What the hell is that supposed to mean?"

"Hey, look," Eddie said, groping for a reply and becoming more frustrated by the minute, "I feel as bad as you do, but..." At a loss for words, Eddie simply shrugged his shoulders and reached for the mirror. Frowning, he carved off a small chunk of coke and began chopping it into fine granules.

"Listen, Danny," Hank said in his usual dry fashion, while pushing his thick, salt-and-pepper locks back from his face, "Big John ripped the club off, so I'm not sorry he lost his patch. We're in a different league now—you wanna play, or talk about bad drug deals?"

"Let's play, for now," Danny replied, unwilling to accept the idea that his brothers had done the right thing, but anxious to move on.

"You need to meet with Pito Flores in Fresno," Eddie explained. "He's the president of the Los Cuchillos. The plan is to leave Gorman Sunday morning before it gets too hot. From there you'll ride into the Central Valley, meet with Flores, tell him your story about the fight, and take whatever they dish out, even if it means gettin' your ass thumped a little. Then you're to ride to Menlo Park, where you'll meet with the officers of the northern chapters of the Devils Own. They'll check you out, and if you pass, you'll get your patch."

Danny poured himself another shot of Jack Daniel's from the crystal decanter on Eddie's desk. "I've done the time," he said once again. "Now I want to party, dammit." He walked over to Hank, who stood behind Eddie, as always. Hank never sat at parties or meetings, adhering to some odd, personal code that required him to stand, regardless of the circumstances. Hank was strange, but strangeness is the essence of the outlaw's uniqueness. Danny walked up to Hank and slipped his hand inside his cutoff, and pulled out a polished, 9mm Browning. "I've waited over a year to get this patch," he stated. "And I'll do whatever it takes to make it mine. So lighten up."

Danny snapped the magazine free from the weapon's handle and worked the slide, kicking out the chambered round. Snapping the magazine back into the grip, he shoved the uncocked auto into the waist of his Levi's, where his denim jacket covered the small of his back. "I'll probably need this, Danny said, casually. "So I'll be hanging onto it. You don't have a problem with that, do you?"

Hank fumed, every muscle taut with the effort to control himself. Beads of sweat formed on his forehead. His anger was obvious, but he couldn't give in to it. "No," he growled through clenched teeth.

"OK, enough's enough," Danny said, turning his back on the two men and walking toward the door. "I'm gonna have a drink with my brothers, get laid, and catch some sleep before I get myself into another shitshower. All this serious crap is taking the edge off my buzz." Danny looked back at Eddie and Hank, downed a last slug of whiskey, and headed down the stairs.

Below, Danny found Old Man Jason and Fireball leaning against the bar, while Dixie was playing bartender. "Jack on the rocks, baby," Danny said. Another pile of coke rested on a mirror at the corner of the bar, and Fireball pushed it down the polished wood surface toward Danny, who once again declined with a terse, "Not yet."

"Those guys are awful serious," Danny remarked. "We used to party till we puked, but now it's all this business bullshit."

Fireball, his ruddy features brightening, turned and leaned over his drink. Jason's eyes darted toward Dixie for an instant, then back to Danny. "Politics with the big boys up north," he said quietly.

"No shit," Danny said, seizing his drink and walking over to the new bike. "We meeting back here Sunday morning?" Danny asked over his shoulder, studying the new motorcycle, then sitting on it. "We got papers for this thing?"

Eagerly, Fireball grabbed an envelope at his elbow, and brought the paperwork and the key to his newly freed brother.

"Hey, amigo," he whispered earnestly, "we'll do anything we can for you. You gotta understand that this shit is out of our hands."

"You're to meet Hank and Eddie in Gorman on Sunday," Jason said. "I'll take you to my house tonight—everything's all set up and ready for you. Then I'll come back and crash here."

Fireball opened the gates as Danny kicked the Shovelhead

to life, then tried the controls. Dixie climbed on behind him, and they followed Jason out of the building. It had been almost two years since Danny had felt the power of an 80-cube stroker flowing through his body. Choppers were second nature to Danny, who melded to the tan leather solo seat instinctively. The bike smelled of fresh oil, new parts, and fresh paint. Every muscle and bone cried out for the ass, the ride, the action, and the adventure he'd been missing. Danny followed Jason to a house on the edge of Redondo Beach. The place wasn't much, but it was clean. They locked Danny's bike in the garage, then followed Jason as he showed them in through the back door. Dixie stuck close to Danny, remaining quiet and unobtrusive. In the small, sparse living room, Jason had laid out fresh clothes for Danny. "Here's some supplies for your ride," he said. "There should be a lot more there than you'll actually need. Take anything you want, and if you don't see something you want, just look around. His eyes locked with Danny's. "Whatever's mine is yours."

"How about some 9mm ammo?" Danny requested.

"Can't help you there," Jason said, dropping his gaze and glancing at Dixie. They hugged and said their goodbyes. Dixie and Danny stood on the curb in front of the 50-year-old Spanish California bungalow to watch Jason ride away. When they could no longer see him, Dixie turned and reentered the house. Inside, she scurried about, lighting candles, and when Danny came in, on the coffee table lay another mound of coke on another mirror, a bottle of Jack Daniel's, a bucket of ice, and a tumbler. He heard the shower running.

Pouring himself a stiff Jack on the rocks, Danny took the old army blanket Jason had left and began preparing his bedroll. Figuring a couple of days for his excursion, he threw in two pairs of socks and underwear. In a small towel, he rolled up a handful of tools and extra spark plugs, securing the kit with two short bungee cords. Another towel held a bar of soap, a razor, and a some hotel samples of shampoo and deodorant. As Danny packed the tube of toothpaste, he noticed that the box was the large, economy size. And it seemed unusually heavy. Danny was momentarily puzzled, wondering why Jason would purchase such a big-ass tube of toothpaste for a two-day ride. One end of the box had been taped closed, and when he worked it open, he saw two 9mm clips. He shoved the box into the towel and wrapped it with another bungee cord. Lastly, a pair of Levi's went into the mix, along with two T-shirts, and a sweatshirt, each sporting "Support Your Local Devils" designs.

Dixie wandered into the living room in a sheer, black teddy. Danny just stared, recalling the two years since he had seen a woman nude, in the flesh. The diaphanous material seemed to make Dixie's body even more stunning, and Danny moved toward her. Her eyes were pools of liquid, her lips parted, her long red hair damp. Her clean, flawless skin and her damp hair pulled back from her face made her look younger than ever. They embraced, and she helped Danny disrobe, then laid a blanket on the living room floor. With coke-sharpened senses, Danny let his fingertips dance along her youthful flesh. He spent 15 minutes adoring her navel alone, and when her tiny soft hand caressed his cock, he thought he would explode. Gradually, he lifted her top, touched and kissed her flesh above her soft tummy, and under her pert breasts. He tasted one nipple, then the other, and each brightened under the candlelight, becoming excited and erect. Slowly, he slipped off her filmy teddy and skimpy panties. They snorted lines of coke and made love on the living room floor, then snorted more coke, and he kissed her sweet pussy in the hallway. At 4 a.m., they whispered fantasies to one another as he slipped inside her while she lay on the kitchen table. As the sun rose, they fondled each other in bed, oblivious to the daylight creeping in under the shades. Lost in an avalanche of alerted senses, and fueled by the drug, they continued to explore one another until noon Saturday, when the drug could no longer replace their fatigue and renew their energy. They fell asleep in each other's arms.

The pair slept through Saturday evening and on into the night. Danny was up at 5 a.m. Sunday morning, packing the bike, checking it over carefully, and securing the bedroll to the handlebars. At 6 a.m., he returned to the house, greeted by the smell of hot coffee. "Baby," Dixie said in a low voice, "do you really have to go?"

Danny poured himself a cup of coffee and sat down at the Formica-topped kitchen table before looking up at her and speaking. "I've dreamed of this opportunity all my life, Dixie," he said. "It's not right that I have to fight a man over a killing I didn't do, but I can understand how things went down—I know how these clubs work."

"Are you sure?" she persisted, her eyes downcast, locked on the scrambled eggs, sliced potatoes, and sausage in front of her.

"I'm sure I want the patch, babe," Danny replied, "if that's what you mean."

"Dixie made no response. After a lengthy silence, she asked, "You want some coke to take along?"

"No, thanks," Danny said, wincing at the thought. "I don't ever want to see that shit, except when you and I party. Listen, I'm in enough jeopardy already—packing, hanging out with the club, going up north without seeing my probation officer. Each of those could send me back to the joint. You got a problem with the bag and your nose?"

"It's been so long since you were here," Dixie whimpered, beginning to cry. "I forgot how you treated me, how we were together. Don't go."

"Is that it?" Danny said, getting up to put on his old army jacket with the vest over it. "You're in the bag, in a big way, aren't you?"

She sobbed, falling into his arms. "You've got to get some help," Danny said firmly, "or you'll end up someone's whore, or like John." He felt her shudder, but didn't want to ask more questions. Leaning down and kissing her forehead, he said only, "I gotta go."

GORMAN

*D*anny hit the 405 freeway running at 6 a.m. while the sun was beginning to rise. He rode directly into the spectacular blues and fiery oranges of a perfect California morning. He was locked and loaded, and the bike purred like the finely crafted machine it was. The construction and workmanship spoke to Danny in the cool morning air. Someone had cared, and that realization compounded his feeling of being on top of the world. The freeway was deserted on Sunday morning, he was out of prison, free, and flying on his favorite wing, a chopped and stroked Harley-Davidson lightened by 200 pounds.

Danny's eyes watered behind dark sunglasses as he headed east, inland toward Interstate 5 north. Alone with his motorcycle, taking solace in his thoughts, Danny pondered the conversations, the mission he faced, Dixie, and the risks he was already taking. As he passed the interchange for the Hollywood Freeway, he considered for a moment the possibility of making the turn and disappearing into another world, a world far away from patches, drugs, and warfare. He knew it would require nothing more than a hand signal for a lane change, a long, bending right turn onto another freeway leading to another life. But this was his life, the style he dreamed of, the excitement he adored. For Danny, being a Devils Own was everything, and he was within a few hundred miles of achieving that goal. In the heady excitement of the moment, his ass barely touched the seat.

Tong had taught him that the world was composed of many different lives. In addition to lives filled with hate and destruction, there were lives of adventure and love, creativity and caring. All a man had to do was choose. It wasn't as if Danny was trapped in a dead-end lifestyle. After all, he was young, strong, and intelligent. As he passed the interchange, Danny felt confident he was making the right decision, certain that he would be successful in his mission and return

vindicated, a credit to the club, and a full-fledged member—all
in time to meet with his probation officer. Then, he believed,
his life would be secure as a Devil, and he would work hard
for the welfare of the club. The sun climbed higher in the
clear sky, bathing Danny in its radiant warmth. Still,
something clawed at his mind as he headed north, navigating
the six-lane-wide I-5, and abruptly the pleasant blanket of
warm rays became a smothering shroud of relentless heat.
Although he tried to push aside his memory of furtive,
cunning eyes and indirect, evasive answers from his over-
confident mind, he couldn't escape thoughts of Big John's
disappearance and Jesse's leaving the club.

Danny looked down at the speedometer between the two
fatbob tanks and noted that he was cruising at 90 mph. When
his eyes shifted to the rearview mirror, he saw another cycle,
and it was closing in on him fast. Backing off the throttle, he
signaled his intention to change lanes and get out of the way.
At that moment, the lights of the highway patrolman's
motorcycle began flashing.

"Shit," Danny muttered to himself as he moved to the right.
He was acutely aware of the many probation violations he was
committing—more than enough to send him back inside for
an additional couple of years. Breaking out in an angry sweat,
he felt a wave of relief envelop him when the officer sped
past, only motioning for Danny to slow down. Adrenaline
pumping through his body, Danny took his time getting back
up to speed, realizing that the warning was a wake-up call
saving him from a stupid mistake that could torpedo the
whole mission. He knew that, whatever he had to face in the
next couple of days, those days had to be low-key, or they
would be his only days of freedom until he was 25. The
thought made him shudder.

Danny pulled off the freeway in Newhall to top off his gas
tanks and give the newly rebuilt engine a brief respite. The
July sun was already softening the tar in the streets, and the
next hour would be spent on a constant three-degree
ascending grade into the Los Padres National Forest,
separating the vast Central Valley region from the Los
Angeles Basin. Danny glanced at the off-ramp leading to
Magic Mountain, for a moment remembering rides taken

years earlier, when Newhall was nothing more than a truck stop. Then some forward-thinking individuals decided Disneyland needed competition, and just as Walt put Anaheim on the map, Magic Mountain put Newhall and Valencia there, thanks to attractions like Colossus, the roller coaster from hell. Millions of people came, and a city grew up where none had been before. Danny reflected on the energy expended by mankind, and speculated about how Tong would point out that such energy may be channeled toward good or evil, used to build up or to tear down, to flourish or to stagnate.

At the gas station, Danny studied the bike, beginning at the front wheel by rocking the 425-pound scooter on its sidestand. He asked a kid returning from the rest room to spin the front wheel, and he jerked the front end from side to side to check its neck-play and the neck bearings. He examined the engine, the supports holding the Shovelhead in place in the frame, and the carb. Next, he checked the exhaust system for loose clamps, observing that the shotgun pipes were mounted so securely that he could lift the bike by the pipes without harm. He inspected the brake linkages, the gas tank mounts and fittings, the rear wheel, and the fender supports. Lifting the seat to check its mounting, Danny noticed a line of tiny gold pinstriping on the bottom of the seat pan that read, "Ride Safe, Bro Jesse, DF/FD."

That simple message hit Danny like a sledgehammer. Jesse had invested his heart and soul in the machine before he left the club, and he knew what Danny would be facing when he returned. As he replaced the seat, Danny felt complete confidence in this machine to the core of his soul. Standing back from the Shovelhead, he studied its simple design, its solid lines, and its intimidating styling. Satisfied, he tossed a leg across the seat, kicked the bike to life, and pulled out of the gas station. Like a cosmic blast furnace, the sun elevated the heat by a degree or two with each mile Danny rode. At the station, he had removed his green army jacket and strapped it to his bedroll. Now he was flying toward the mountains wearing nothing but his vest over a striped T-shirt, the picture of a two-wheeled pirate. Danny's hair was pulled back into a ponytail, and his mustache was plastered flat by the wind against his face. The highway rolled into the curves of the hills, and Danny watched the foliage change as he climbed higher and higher, his dark glasses shielding his eyes from the brutal glare of the sun.

Less than an hour passed before Danny saw the sign informing travelers that Gorman was one mile ahead. The town was little more than a truck stop watering hole at the top of the Tejon Mountain Pass—two restaurants, two hotels, five residential houses, and seven gas stations, a sanctuary for the weary, a pit stop for the mechanically challenged, an emergency exit for overheating vehicles, and a gas stop for choppers with small gas tanks. Transients on or in a variety of vehicles stopped to huddle indoors and escape the heat, the cold, or the long road ahead. Danny pulled off the freeway, just as he had done a dozen times before, and refueled at the first station. That done, he rolled the bike to the restaurant adjacent to the gas station, parked it carefully, and went inside.

The restaurant was a linoleum holdover from the '50s, as were many of the buildings in the area. With its red and cream checkered floors, its matching Naugahyde tuck-and-roll booths, and its red and cream marbleized countertops, the place was awash in nostalgia. Danny sat at the bar. The truck stop diner was busy, even at 7:30 on this Sunday morning. The air was redolent of grease and coffee, but the sight of the fry cook sweating over the blistering grill caused Danny to remember that it had been two years since his last meal in a restaurant.

"Can I get you something to drink?" the waitress said as he began to dismiss his thoughts of the road ahead, and lose himself in the warm odors emanating from the kitchen.

"Sure," Danny replied, looking into the bright blue eyes connected to the crisp, clear voice. The waitress was blond, her thick tumbles of hair pulled into the mandatory bun and secured by a hair net. Her cream-colored uniform with red piping matched every other item in the joint except the food. She was tall, maybe 5-foot, 8-inch, maybe taller. Danny gazed into pools of blue set into a pretty, alert face. "Coffee. And, uh, let's see ... a tall glass of milk."

"There's the menu," she said, pointing to a cracked chalkboard, bordered in red and cream, on the wall near the entrance. "The specials are the items in yellow. I'll be back in a minute to take your order." She smiled, raising one eyebrow slightly. Danny could swear he noted a romantic gleam in her eye.

As she turned away, Danny observed her shape, obscured to some degree by the country girl uniform and the white apron. He noted her order book, as well as the pens she carried in the pocket of her apron. In spite of the uniform, Danny could see enough to appreciate her lush figure, and for a moment he wondered why a good-looking blonde would work for peanuts in this godforsaken truck stop in the middle of nowhere. Looking over the red and cream menu, then the chalkboard, he decided to order more eggs, since he hadn't eaten anything during the drug-and-sex fest on Saturday.

"Is that your bike out there?" the waitress inquired, looking through the front window.

"Yeah," Danny replied. "I just got it. A brother built it for me."

"You ride a lot—like maybe riding is your life?" she asked.

"Yeah. I guess you could say that," Danny returned.

"I'd like to ride someday," the young woman said, wistfully before snapping back to her duties. "I'm sorry. I'll quit bothering you and take your order."

"No problem," Danny said, studying her intently. He couldn't decide whether his interest stemmed from her attractiveness, or was a consequence of his heightened awareness of women since being released, or the fuck-and-suck marathon with Dixie before he left. "I'll take an order of scrambled eggs and some wheat toast. Now, I have a question for you."

"Sure, go ahead," she said.

"This is gonna sound like a bullshit come-on," Danny began. "But you seem really sharp, to say nothing of being good-looking. So how come you're working at this hash house?"

"It's a long story," she replied. "When I'm not working, I go to college in Bakersfield. Maybe someday I'll get the chance to tell you the rest." She walked off, and Danny watched her slip his order under a retainer on the stainless turnstile sitting on the ledge at the order window. She buzzed off to get the coffee, topping off other cups on the counter while on her way back to Danny.

"My name's Elizabeth," she said, smiling softly and extending her hand.

Danny took her hand in his and was captivated by the softness in her eyes. And in the brief instant they touched, a connection was formed. Danny sat up from his relaxed slouch. "A pleasure to meet you," he said, holding her hand a second more than might be expected. "That meant a lot to me. Oh, and my name's Danny."

She spun on her heel, seemingly lighter on her feet than before, floated to the order window, and added butter and garnish to Danny's food. She returned to his booth and slipped the plate in front of him as he watched, hoping to catch her gaze once again, since it had affected him like a warm blanket thrown around his shoulders, protecting him from the elements. In the brief time since he had entered the diner, a brief handshake had somehow transformed her from an ordinary waitress into a romantic interlude.

Danny didn't know whether to eat or watch her every move, and he ended up pushing his food around his plate, idly picking at it. Elizabeth watched him for a while, then came to his counter. "Is the food OK?" she asked, catching him lost in thought, unaware that for the last five minutes, he'd been playing with a forkful of cold eggs.

"Sure," Danny answered, momentarily tongue-tied. "Uh, right ... sure—it's great."

"Hey," Eddie shouted, without warning, from the entrance to the restaurant. "Let's roll!"

Like darkness drowns light, Danny's soothing reverie shattered instantly. He slid out of the booth and stood face-to-face for a brief moment with heaven even as hell waited at the doorway. Elizabeth turned and saw Eddie at the door. She had seen him earlier in the day, and she recognized him now.

"He was here ear-" she began, attempting to inform Danny, in case it might be important.

"Goddammit, it's blistering out here!" Eddie shouted, silencing Elizabeth by the sheer volume of his voice. "Move it!"

Danny reached in his pocket to pay and only then realized that he had very little cash. Elizabeth reached out and laid her hand over his, still partially thrust into the pocket of his jeans. "I'll take care of it," she murmured.

"But meet me for a second at the cash register."

Elizabeth bent over behind a stainless steel register almost as big as a safe, then came up with a red and cream book of matches. Handing the matchbook to Danny, she punched some keys on the face of the register, and the drawer shot open. She looked up at Danny one more time, then said, in her best professional voice, "Thank you sir, please come again." She closed the drawer and walked away. Danny had no time to open the matchbook, so he stuffed it into the back pocket of his Levi's and headed for the door.

Outside, Eddie, Hank, and Miguel stood waiting. "Danny," Eddie said, pulling on his mustache, "this is Miguel from up north. He's gonna tell you what's up."

Danny reached for his hand, but Miguel ignored the gesture, turning around and motioning for him to follow. "Listen, asshole," Miguel began, "you created the problem, whether you think so or not. So you're the one that's gonna take care of it, if you want to be in the club." Miguel stopped alongside a black-primered van and stared at Danny straight in the eyes. The stranger's long and scraggly black hair hung over his shoulders, and he pulled at his nasty Fu Manchu mustache that curved well below the downward-turned corners of his mouth. Miguel's dark, Hispanic skin was slick, and his narrow eyes were hidden behind dark, narrow shades. "We've held this war business off 'cause your brothers are flyin' our patch now," Miguel said sternly. "But the Los Cuchillos still know who was involved, and they ain't gonna let the guy they think was responsible just walk away. And I can't have you jeopardizing our members over this. So if you can go to Fresno and meet with this guy Flores and straighten this out, you've got half a chance at that patch."

"Let me get this straight," Danny responded, trying not to lose his temper. "They may want to kill me, but if I can convince them not to, you might consider me for membership?"

"They're not gonna kill you—you're with us, so they know better," Miguel assured Danny. "Besides, we've set up a meeting. Flores knows you're coming."

"I need some cash," Danny said. "And where's the information I need?"

Miguel handed Danny a piece of paper with the address he

needed, along with $200 in cash, and a small but heavy object wrapped in a Devils Own scarf. Danny opened the cloth carefully. Inside was a blued, S&W .38 with a 4-inch barrel and a full box of shells. He re-closed the scarf and looked at Miguel expectantly. "OK," Miguel said, signaling the conclusion of their business. "You better get moving. They're expecting you." He glared hard at Danny. "Just keep your cool. The president is an older guy, and you can talk to him. You may be forced into a fist fight, but that's all. Your brothers are looking forward to your return, and having you become a member. Some of 'em even speak highly of you."

"Thanks," Danny said, searching Miguel's hardened features for clues to what was really going on.

"Oh, yeah," Miguel added, opening the door of the van and reaching inside. "One more thing. Take this and give it to what's-his-name—their prez." His tone was disrespectful, edged with sarcasm. He handed Danny a 2-inch-thick, rolled-up plastic bag full of white powder.

"What the fuck is this?" Danny demanded.

"You know what the fuck it is," Miguel shot back. "It's a fuckin' peace offering, and you're gonna carry it up there." Miguel turned away and walked back toward the restaurant.

Danny watched Miguel approach the other members, and while their attention was momentarily diverted, he tossed the bag back into the van. "If Flores needs a peace offering, someone else can deliver it," Danny murmured under his breath as he straddled his motorcycle. He kicked it over, racked the throttle a few times, then peeled out of the parking lot without so much as glancing at the others. His own brothers had said very little to him, nothing helpful, anyway, and his instructions were vague. But he didn't give a damn if they wanted to fuck with him in this chickenshit fashion. He was determined to succeed; nothing could make him fail.

Inside the restaurant, Elizabeth watched the activity in the parking lot. She recognized the outlaws from earlier that morning when they were talking to some Mexican members of another club. She wondered how all this connected, and had to admit to herself that her interest in the day's events stemmed from her concern for the young rider she had just met.

For a brief period, Elizabeth had been married to a military officer stationed in Long Beach. He had abused her, and ridiculed her drive and ambition. She had written two screenplays, and was making a little headway in the movie industry maze, when her husband returned from an overseas assignment, and beat her badly the first day back. Afraid for her life, she fled to Bakersfield, taking a job in the restaurant in Gorman. The beating had made Elizabeth suspicious and defensive around men. She hadn't dated for a year while taking courses at the local community college and working long hours at the truck stop. But she knew something was different about the man she just met. There was something soft in his eyes, a questioning and a sincere concern. She hoped that somehow she would see him again.

RIDIN' IN

*A*s Danny's motorcycle barreled up the on-ramp, the other Devils Own parted company. Eddie got in the van and drove to the south, back to L.A., while Miguel and Hank rounded the corner of the restaurant and boarded a rent-a-car with two members of the Los Cuchillos. Elizabeth watched the group swing by the front of the restaurant and pull onto the freeway, going north. She was curious, but none of it made sense to her. Nonetheless, her marriage to the Navy officer taught her a few things about military tactics, politics, and treachery. She knew that Rule One was to be constantly observant, accumulating as much information as possible. If not now, chances are the information would come in handy at another time.

Danny was equally curious as he rumbled into the heat. The temperature gauge outside the Texaco station was boiling past the faded 90-degree mark when he pulled onto the freeway, and the temperature would rise to 105 within the next hour. The heat would be relentless until around 5 p.m., before receding a couple of relieving degrees. As his hair flapped in the wind Danny felt a forgotten sense of belonging, and he realized how much he missed it while in prison. He gained a sense of brotherhood and strength from the bottom Los Angeles rocker sewn carefully onto the lower half of the black leather vest he wore. He was confident about his mission. Other than feeling nervous about the risk to his future freedom if he was caught out of the city, violating the terms of his probation, Danny was excited, certain that what lay ahead would answer all his questions about the uncertain future.

Danny understood the code of taking care of business. He had been in the Hawks for two years when a young Irish kid began hanging around the club. When he eventually asked to join, the club called on its connections with the Santa Monica Police Department to run a background check on him.

Inquiries about whether he paid his bills for bike repairs and service were made, his girlfriends were questioned, as well as certain members of another club he rode with for awhile. The background check turned up a problem, revealing that 18 months earlier, he took a hot-tempered redhead, a local topless dancer, to a party where she shot off her mouth to one of the members. The biker, an obnoxious, drunken brawler named Disco, smacked the girl, but the Irish kid never responded to the assault.

The kid was told that if he wanted to ride with the Hawks, he'd have to seek out the guy and finalize the beef. He could handle the matter however he wanted, but the Hawks made it crystal clear that he had to return a stand-up biker before he could hope to ride with them. He could return with the man's patch, the guy's blood on his knuckles, or with a formal apology to the club and to the girl. Two Hawks escorted the kid to the club's digs, where the confrontation had occurred. The two men met face-to-face and came to blows over the unresolved incident. This time, the Irish kid stood up for his date, ripping the clubber's patch from his back, and gave it to the Hawks. Danny, who was present when the kid brought back his trophy, returned the man's patch to the president of the Southsiders MC because there was no problem between the clubs, and no reason to create one. The kid had proved himself, and rode home proud. Although he never made it into the club, he rode with them frequently, until one winter morning a green Cadillac centerpunched him on Washington Blvd, killing him instantly. The driver simply told the cop he hadn't seen the motorcyclist.

Danny shuddered at the memory as he rounded another sweeping corner on the multi-lane highway before it began its harsh decent into the blistering valley below. He had been instructed to call Dixie, twice a day and report his progress. Although the letters she sent him in the joint had gradually become distant, he was once again assured of her loyalty once her lips met his. Her eyes had brimmed with love, although her body quivered as much for the drug as for him.

Danny looked over the sheer precipice to his right and into the valley below. Bakersfield held little promise for anyone but oil field hands, and the oil industry was currently the mainstay of the Bakersfield economy, supplemented somewhat by a handful of sawdust ranchers and small farmers who were driven from the L.A. Basin by rising land prices. Now, they scratched out a living in the blistering heat of the Bakersfield summer and the bitter cold of its winter. Danny looked down the dizzying cliffside at the massive boulders strewn along the base of the mountain, and at the sparse shrubbery and white-hot terrain. Suddenly, a car cut into his lane, forcing him to veer close to the dusty shoulder of the highway and the 3,800-foot drop to certain death beyond.

He wanted to look at the sick sonuvabitch behind the wheel, but was unable to do anything but keep his eyes riveted on the distant valley below—where he was headed. His wheel bit into the soft dirt of the shoulder and slid sideways. For a split second, Danny thought he recognized a diamondback rattlesnake trying to avoid his careening wheel. He counter-steered the bike back toward the sizzling asphalt, but the bike's rear wheel was already sliding toward the rim of the canyon. He knew his brakes were of no use in this situation, and he fought the front end in his desperate effort to return to the pavement. But as his rear wheel lost traction in the soft shoulder, the bike began to slide out from under him at 60 mph.

Frantic, Danny planted his left foot on the edge of the road in a last-ditch effort to avoid being pinned under the bike. This was the first motorcycle he had owned or ridden in two years, and he didn't want to lose it. The chromed primary cover screeched against the asphalt, sending a shower of sparks in his face as the bike went down. The handlebars hit the pavement next, jerking the grips from his gloved hands, and dropping Danny on his ass, sliding in the dirt and sand covering the 5-foot-wide emergency lane. Spinning on his denim-covered butt, Danny tumbled headlong into the mass of brush, rusting beer cans, and jumbled trash alongside the highway until he was brought to a stop by a steel object. Still conscious, he sat bolt upright, discovering he was still alive. But his right leg dangled over a small boulder inches from taking the rest of him along to a crushing death against the granite and sand below. The chopper's still-spinning rear wheel was also precariously close to the devastating drop.

Getting to his feet, Danny looked down the road, but the car was long gone. Dizzy, he dusted himself off and knelt beside the bike.

The condition of his scoot was far more important to Danny's survival than bruised and raw flesh. He quickly shut off the engine and dragged the hot machine away from the cliff, then heaved it upright to assess the damage. His chromed primary cover was smashed and pushing against the clutch, so he removed it, loosening the 14 screws that held it in place, and tossing it to the distant grave at the base of the cliff. The tin shield clanged against other dead steel relics rusting into oblivion, tributes to reckless driving on the Grapevine. Danny was grateful that the handlebars, though scraped, were not bent. His left gas tank sustained some road rash, marring the carefully painted logo. When he pulled his bandanna out of his back pocket to wipe the tank, something fell to the ground. But he had no time to think about anything but the condition of his bike and himself. He wiped off the tank, and checked his shift linkage, then he wiped the blood seeping out of the dirt-packed wounds on his elbows and hands.

The pack of matches Elizabeth had surreptitiously handed to Danny in the restaurant fell out of his back pocket and lay on the ground. The amber and cream design with the name of the restaurant—Dolly's—was foil embossed into the cover and glistened in the sunlight, in distinct contrast to the backdrop of faded land and dark asphalt. The effect was striking, but fleeting. Left for any length of time in the intense heat and bright sunlight, it would rapidly fade and shrivel, until it blended in with the parched dirt and the faded trash. Danny mounted the bike and kicked it over, his shock from the fall gradually subsiding. The monster came to life on the second kick, and he sank onto the seat, relieved that he wasn't stranded alongside the road in the brain-boiling heat. Before dropping his shifter into gear, he decided to check the linkage from the transmission to the foot controls for possible damage. Below the metal rods and chrome, something shiny lay in the dirt. He bent over and spotted the matchbook, noting that something protruded from the cover. Dropping the kickstand, he leaned the idling Harley against solidly

packed dirt, and picked up the matchbook. Inside the already
fading flap was Elizabeth's phone number, and stuffed behind
the rows of brightly colored matches was a folded $20 bill.
Danny paused briefly to look back toward Gorman,
envisioning her face and remembering the touch of her hand
and the gentle curves of her body. For a split second, he
imagined that she was looking out for him. He carefully
placed the matchbook and the bill in his wallet, jumped on the
bike, and hit the road.

LOS CUCHILLOS

*T*wo hundred miles north of Danny, in the town of Clovis, a massive Mexican, named Pito Flores, held court in the back of a downtown body shop owned by his family for two decades. Pito had ruled the Los Cuchillos Motorcycle Club with an iron fist for more than a decade. Under the rule of his 6-foot, 3-inch, 300-pound authority were more than 50 members of the club. Unlike the tight, controlled Devils Own chapters, the Los Cuchillos had amassed their impressive membership largely from street gangs and car clubs. Pito, the massive guardian, was getting along in years, and his hold on the members was slipping. Moreover, the club was changing both character and emphasis.

In the early years, the organization was composed of family-oriented riders and kinky motorcyclists who came together to build their choppers out of bits and pieces. They were poor agricultural workers, body and fender men, and mechanics who sought a different identity, who craved to belong, and who loved to ride. At that time, they could hardly be called a bike club in the outlaw sense—at worst, they drank cases of cheap Mexican beer and occasionally stole a motorcycle from some passing touring rider. But primarily, they simply wanted to protect their families by means of the club's unity and the members' loyalty to each other. They were capable of petty theft, but lacked the larcenous core and the scary unpredictability of the true outlaw. Pito's leadership protected them from warring street gangs, car club melees and organized crime.

Over the years, the more ambitious members of the club longed to associate themselves with the violent power of the Mexican Mafia, wanting a piece of their lucrative drug business. If these members had paid attention, they would have seen how the gangsters routinely used and abused small car clubs, forcing members to deal more and more drugs, and killing off unprofitable members. Eventually, the club would fold, and the Mafia would move on, seeking fresh meat. But the attraction was too strong for some of the tough guys, bikers who craved power, sex, and big profits. Inevitably, a faction within the Los Cuchillos began to deal drugs—primarily heroin—to seek out opportunities to enhance their violent reputation, and to indulge their taste for the dark side with members of the Mexican Mafia.

The Mafia had infiltrated the Los Cuchillos with a couple of slick hit men who loved to control, capture and kill—and they also rode bikes. The last few years had seen a drop in club membership, largely because of internal dissension. The splitting factions were causing members to drop out, some permanently disappearing, others becoming so strung out on drugs that they killed themselves or turned themselves in. Under the debilitating influence of drugs and organized crime, what once had been a strong family of Hispanic riders had become a loose amalgamation of treachery and betrayal. Pito remedied the problem by attacking the Mexican Mafia in his area during a bloody gun battle in a downtown bar. He forced his straying members away from the heroin trade and back into the fold—or so he believed. The two infiltrators abandoned their Mafia upbringing, deciding that Pito had better stay, leaving them the entire fertile valley as a customer base. But they needed a new source and a product. That product proved to be cocaine, and the source, the Devils Own.

This time, there was no overt enemy. The problem came from within the ranks. Emilio and his throat-slitting partner, Romeo, made the connection with Rico, the monster who beat John, and the Devils Own. Soon, they began moving coke from the Bay Area down to Los Angeles. They feared little except the Devils Own themselves, and business was brisk until the incident with the Night Hawks. They drew heat due to the war, and the Devils Own didn't like what was happening. Miguel and his club made peace with the Hawks in order to lessen hostilities and open the lines of communication and commerce again.

When the Los Cuchillos were founded, Pito was barely 30 years old, tall, ruggedly handsome, and muscular, with thick wrists and massive hands. No one fucked with him—his gargantuan size was a guarantee against that. But his demeanor toward every member was that of a father, consoling them during family squabbles, assisting them with employment, giving them money when they were broke, and fighting for them if anyone tried to harm them. As the years passed, he became even more good-looking, although a sprinkle of gray appeared around his temples. He despised drugs, and each violent confrontation to protect his club's involvement took its toll. The last few years hit Pito hard. His empire was crumbling, his solid brothers were dying or retiring, and most of all, both his influence and the family he built were vanishing. Now, only 30 members remained, although they continued to be the only outlaw motorcycle club between Los Angeles and San Francisco, and thus far maintained a haphazard control of the Central Valley.

Only 10 members milled around as Pito sat behind a small, paint-splattered table in the back of the bondo-dust-covered body shop. "What's going on here?" he shouted at his brothers as the afternoon heat penetrated the tar roof and settled into the dark room. Two shop fans blew any remaining cool air out of the shop. He was sure that some of his brothers were selling drugs through the Devils Own, but it was a subversive operation, and none of the Devils were seen doing business with members. He had never encountered one in his territory, nor did he want to. He wanted nothing to do with dealing drugs, but he knew that his power was waning as his eyes scanned the men in front of him—they were the weaker ones who looked to him for guidance. The other members weren't in attendance because they took their orders from Emilio and Romeo, and while the old blowhard let off steam, they were taking care of business. Pito turned to Emilio and stared, his face growing grim. "What the fuck's going on, wise guy?" Pito demanded, exasperated.

"The club is growing and changing," Emilio began, "and we-"

"Bullshit," Pito interrupted. "My club is splitting apart and shriveling up. We were once a brotherhood, a family..." Pito's voice trailed away in frustration.

"Times change, old man," Emilio said. "We either change with them, or we die." He paused and looked threateningly at each member in the room. "Right now, we need to discuss the gringo who's riding through our territory carrying drugs. What should we do about that? He's the one who killed Sancho."

Pito could smell the evil on Emilio's words, but he detested the Night Hawks, recalling the brief war with them and the one who killed his young, hotheaded brother. And he detested the Devils Own as well, primarily for their involvement in big-time drug dealing. The members seated in front of him looked expectantly at the big man, anticipating his decision to go after the drug runner from the other club. "We don't have a problem with the Devils Own," Pito replied to Emilio's question. "And we don't need to make one."

"Fuck, man!" Emilio spat. "He's the ex-Night Hawk who killed our brother. He ain't no fuckin' Devil. They just gave him a prospect patch." Emilio spoke slowly, as if laying each word in front of Pito like pictures of his hottest fantasy, teasing him. "The Devils called. He's on his way to meet with you. Remember their promise when our brother was killed? They said that they would make the Hawks members of the Devils, but the killer would be ours."

"I never understood that deal," Pito said, frustrated. "We should have killed all of them. This whole business with the Devils just doesn't make sense. And you're sayin' we can kill this asshole and avenge our brother?"

"You got it," Emilio stated. "And at the same time, send a message to the Devils about drug dealing." Emilio was truly a silver-tongued snake.

"Does this rider have any idea what's going on?" Pito asked.

"No," Emilio replied. "His assignment is to sell you drugs and thereby get the ball rolling for doing a regular business with the Devils. If he blows it, he doesn't become a member." Emilio was jerking Pito around, manipulating him like a marionette, and he relished each word.

"I'll take care of him myself," Pito growled, inhaling deeply on a Marlboro, "the lowlife, murdering, drug-peddling cocksucker." His face radiated his fuming temper. His dilated eyes peered out at the group of men in front of him, who remained unmoving. They prayed that their older brother would side with Emilio and Romeo, and take action. They prayed for brotherhood and unity to return to the Los Cuchillos. "I want to know where this bastard is at all times. I told those goddamn Devils years ago that we wanted no part of any drug shit, and to keep the stuff out of our territory."

Emilio listened impatiently, dying to get to a phone.

"We don't always get along, Emilio," Pito remarked. "But do I have your support on this one? Whoever finds the bastard is to bring him to me, dead or alive."

"*Si, jefe*," Emilio said with respectful graciousness, bowing slightly. "We'll find this *cabron*, and keep you informed all the way."

The men passed around *cervezas* while congratulating Pito on his decision to eliminate the drug-wielding gringo heading into their territory, and for his willingness to go after the man who downed their little brother, Sancho. Emilio slipped out the metal side door of the shop, and headed for the pay phone at the corner, alone in the blistering sun. He stepped inside the suffocating booth and dialed a Bay Area number.

"Yeah?" It was Rico who answered the phone.

"The trap is set," Emilio said, looking around. The phone booth baked in the sun, and the black receiver immediately dripped with sweat from Emilio's palm and cheek, and his dark glasses clouded over.

"Good, it's about fucking time we resolved this," Rico said in his most irritating tone of voice. "No more than 24 hours from now, we should be in business, and then we'll turn that ragtag bunch of wetbacks into productive citizens."

Emilio flinched at the term wetback.

"Let me know when the funerals are held," Rico added. "And don't call me with bad news—we got shit to do."

Rico hung up, wiping his sweating palm on his black Levi's as he headed back to the relative cool of the shop to meet with his unruly brothers. The auto body shop was on Rainbow Street, near the old town of Clovis. Rainbow was an industrial street running parallel to Clovis Ave., half a block to the south. From Clovis, the riders were only five miles from Highway 99, running north through the Central Valley and on to the Bay Area. A block up from the body shop was the Skyline Bar, a regular biker hangout controlled by the Los Cuchillos. No one fell in love at the Skyline—its role was purely functional. Bikers went there to catch a buzz before riding into Old Town to Jim's Saloon for western dancing, or chasing women. The place had been a trucker/biker dive for years, offering little more than beer, pool, and fist fights. Not much else happened in the neon-adorned bar with the baby blue exterior.

Emilio motioned for a few of the members to follow him up the street to the Skyline. He included Romeo, who usually sat quietly in the back of the room, picking at his fingernails with the stainless stiletto he carried in his boot sheath. Romeo was small, narrow, and evil. He grew up in Tijuana, in a large, disheveled family headed by a pimp who also was a member of the Mexican Mafia. His father was cruel, and treated his whores even worse. At an early age, Romeo learned the reality of fear, and the power of terror. He loved to select some member and then intimidate him at every opportunity until he left the club. Wiry and short, with close-cropped hair and a thin mustache, Romeo lacked finesse. He didn't have the flair and style of his brother, Emilio. But he was twice as evil, three times as dangerous, and possessed a tenth of his partner's social graces. He wandered around behind Emilio, waiting for someone to show up he could pounce on. He wore old Levi's and a denim cutoff, a motorcycle belt, and a T-shirt, usually torn and tattered, like the one he wore that day. But looks can be deceiving, because he had more money stashed in coffee cans inside, outside, and around his ramshackle pad than any two drug-dealing members saw in six months.

Emilio and Romeo insisted that two of Pito's followers come with them to the bar, where Emilio bought a round of Coronas with limes. He reached under the waitress' short skirt and slipped a finger under her panties, pushing a small bag of coke between the cheeks of her ass. She jumped, and her mane of bouncy curls shook as she bent down to reveal her full, round tits, blooming over her frilly top, for the other members to appreciate. "I'll need a blowjob after this meeting," Emilio informed her, whispering and biting her earlobe. "See that no one bothers us." His deep stare met her shallow eyes, and she nodded, her eyes moist at the very thought of injecting the white powder into her veins. Her pussy grew damp at the thought of the rush.

"Now listen up, you motherfuckers," Emilio said, addressing a group of younger, more impressionable members as Romeo sat back in his chair and observed. "Just 'cause Pito is going along with the program doesn't mean you're in the clear." He leaned forward and stared at each man's face. These were the ones who stayed clear of the drug trade, seeking only simple brotherhood, beer drinking, riding, and broads.

"You can either get out there and prove yourselves by killing this white asswipe," Emilio said, on an evil roll, "or you can pack your shit and get the hell out of the club—and the sooner, the better. We're taking care of business now, whether you're with us or not. But you *pendejos* can give us a hand."

Three members sat across from Emilio and Romeo. All three were wide-eyed with fear. Escobar sat between the two other members, who were considerably smaller than the man in the center. Escobar grew up in Clovis and knew the shame this would bring him if he quit. He never planned on leaving this, his native area, and he wasn't about to begin now. The cotton fields, almond groves, and grapevine-heavy vineyards were his home.

"I been here all my life," he said. "I ain't goin' anywhere."

Instantly, Romeo jumped across the table, his stiletto flashing in the dim light of the bar. Slamming Escobar against the wall, he stuck the lethal point of the knife under his throat. "We'll tell you what to do and when to do it, *puta*," Romeo whispered. "You got that?" Escobar nodded, his knees shaking. "Now get your butt out on 99 and find that sorry sonuvabitch." Romeo withdrew his knife from Escobar's throat, and a trickle of blood followed.

"All right, you fuckin' *putas*, it's nut-cuttin' time," Emilio said. "This club is changing and growing up. So either you get with the program, or the program is gonna get you." He stood up, downed the last of his bottle of beer, grabbed the waitress by the elbow, and headed for the rest rooms.

One of the seated members, a heavyset Latino named Alonzo, got to his feet. "I'll find him," he declared. "I know every damned inch of that highway."

Romeo looked at him and snickered, as if he had just told a joke. Throwing Alonzo a contemptuous glance, he stood up, stretched, and wandered out the door.

CENTRAL VALLEY HEAT

As a precaution, Danny pulled into the first gas station/truck stop he came to. After refueling, he gave the bike a thorough examination. It broke his heart to see the freshly chromed primary ripped like a chunk of Wisconsin sharp after a visit from the cheese grater. The tank graphic bled, but held the fuel tight. Other than superficial wounds, it appeared to be all right. But Danny had learned from hard falls in the past to check everything twice, just to make absolutely certain that every mechanical component was in proper working order. He checked the mechanical brake linkage, the throttle, the clutch cables, and the condition of the wiring. Again, everything seemed OK, so he fired up the chromed beast and headed north. It was almost 11 a.m., and the sun was softening the tar in the cracks of the freeway. Some time earlier, Danny had peeled off his old army jacket and strapped it to his bedroll, and later he took off his T-shirt, until finally all he wore above his waist was the leather vest sporting the Los Angeles bottom rocker. While his skin felt the cleansing rays of the sun, he rode along the narrow ribbon of asphalt and concrete that split the massive valley in half all the way to San Francisco. The traffic continued to pour down two lanes on either side of a row of huge, colorful oleanders. Tourism and commerce rolled north and south along the center of the valley. Except for refueling, hiding from the sun, and obtaining something cool and wet, most people had no reason to stop anywhere along the this Highway With No Name.

Danny began to feel at ease again, holding on to the handlebars at 80 mph, whizzing past trucks, compact cars, and RVs, until something caught his eye—another motorcyclist heading the opposite way. He could hear the throaty scream of the twin, but he couldn't see bike or rider because of the erratic wall of multi-colored shrubs strewn thickly along the median. As the bike passed, Danny detected a change in the engine's scream, and then it seemed to die out altogether. He looked ahead, then in his rearview mirror. Finally, looking back over his shoulder, he saw another Harley tear through the tall oleander bushes as if they were colorful defensive linemen in a football game. The rider dodged the thick stalks of bush, found a hole, and sped through it, throwing dirt, sand, and debris in a roostertail behind his bike. Spinning, he completed the U-turn, and then peeled back onto the hard asphalt in a cloud of dust. Danny twisted his throttle and the bike sang against the heat. His thick mane of hair stood out like fire from a rocket as his bike rolled through the 80s and into the 90s. He considered the possibility that this biker was an emissary coming to show Danny the way to the meeting, but he wasn't going to pull over to find out.

The following bike was coming on strong. The young Mexican at the helm was Manuel, one of Emilio's inner circle who had been waiting for the *gringo* to come down from the mountain. From the flatlands, he could sit on any overpass with a pair of binoculars and watch vehicles follow the snake of concrete weaving down the mountain. His bike was lean, ideal for the chase, and he weighed less than 160 pounds to Danny's 200. He was aboard a stroked, high-performance Sportster with shortened front tubes and drag pipes. Compact and fast, the bike went through the gears swiftly, and was into the 90s before Danny could get up to a hundred. Ahead, a small rental car was parked to the side of the road in the rough asphalt emergency lane.

Still not sure the hell-bent scooter was pursuing his Shovelhead, Danny watched the biker's shaky image in the intensely vibrating rectangle of the rearview mirror. All he could see in the reflected blur was a small form behind drag bars. Thick strands of black hair flapped wildly in the wind, as did the denim cutoff Manuel wore in his tucked position behind the drag bars. The Sportster was ripping through the sparse traffic as if it didn't exist. Splitting lanes like an ax through a chicken's neck, the young Mexican cut through the traffic, steadily gaining on his target. Danny knew by the tingle creeping up his spine that this rider wasn't coming with a welcome mat strapped to his handlebars.

Crouching behind his bars, Danny listened to the recently rebuilt motor. It wasn't even broken in, especially for this level of abuse, and it screamed in protest against the asphalt. Behind his dark shades, Danny's eyes watered as he glanced from one side of the freeway to the other, looking for cover, hoping against hope for some sign leading off the freeway. No, nothing but miles of hay fields and cotton crops recently sprouting from the parched earth. The Sierra Nevada mountains loomed in the distance, but that haven was 50 miles away across dirt fields as open and visible as a bright, orange 5-ball alone on a sea of rich green felt. Facing forward, he twisted the throttle to the stops. Just as he did, the rent-a-car in the emergency lane abruptly swerved left into his.

Terrified, Danny sat bolt upright and hit the brakes, smoking the rear wheel against the hot pavement, and sending the bike into a slide. He had been burning the asphalt at just under three digits when the car turned into his smoking path at 20 mph. The bike slid sideways less than a yard from the tin stern of the little Jap junker. Danny could have touched the trunk as he instinctively raised his right leg to avoid being crushed between the flying motorcycle and the all-but-parked compact. He released the brake and clutch, and almost instinctively the bike straightened into the number one lane. Even so, he wondered if he could clear the compact without collision.

The following rider, pleased with the results of his chase, backed off momentarily to watch the deadly encounter ahead, then opened up the engine when it appeared that Danny might survive. Manuel was a short, tight Mexican of 25 whose family had fled Mexico as soon as he was old enough to handle a brisk 20-mile walk in the desert. To reach the family's destination in the States, he had to be able to climb in and out of dilapidated trucks and hide in secret panels in a bus without panicking or whimpering. The family stayed with relatives outside Bakersfield and worked in the fields until they could afford a place of their own, at which time they moved into two-room, stucco field-hand quarters for another three years before they could afford to rent an abandoned and battered house originally built for military personnel. Manuel's father was a drunk and a slob, always looking for an easy way out, while relying on Manuel and his four brothers and sisters to bring home the bacon. His wife worked as a maid for a cleaning service. For Manuel's family, working for slave wages in the California fields and dodging immigration officials while being ripped off by the wealthy landowners, was still an improvement over their meager existence in Mexico. But for a young teenager in tattered hand-me-downs, life was an insult. Finally, at 15 he kicked his father's ass and threatened his life if he ever again tried to fuck with him. A shrewd kid, he began dealing drugs in his teens, turning over his profits to the family, although he didn't see much of them. Manuel's efforts lifted the family out of economic squalor, and eventually, his mother was able to open a small seamstress shop and put his sisters to work hemming skirts and making clothes. Manuel retained the bitterness of those days of abject poverty, and anxiously waited for the day he could assist his brothers by turning the Los Cuchillos' low-rent drug dealing operation into a full-bore, high-profit business.

As he bore down on Danny, whom Manuel saw as the principal obstacle to the success of the drug operation—he could almost taste the sweet flavor of wealth and power on his dusty tongue. With his clutch hand, he pulled a 12-inch stiletto from his belt, twisting his torso so that he could reach out over his throttle arm and slash at the rider on his right. His timing was perfect, although he had hoped the small Toyota would cause the rider to slam into its quarter panel, squashing him like a fat bug. But the rider had shot past the fender like a bullet through the rifling in a gun barrel, his rear wheel smoking as he regained momentum. Manuel was close, so close that he could smell Danny's sweaty fear, feel the heat radiating from his Shovelhead, and taste big V-twin's exhaust.

Danny passed the car so close that he left a streak of blue Levi's against the white enamel finish. Fear mixed with anger as Danny glared into the vehicle where, to his astonishment, he thought he saw four bikers, but he passed the car in a blurred burst of speed that prevented his making out their features. "Chickenshits!" he screamed, facing the asphalt ahead.

As one of the men in the front attempted to hide his face, the driver reached for something concealed between the seats. In the back seat, a Mexican outlaw shoved a clip into an automatic. At that moment, Danny felt a blade slide across the back of his leather vest, near his neck. He ducked and spun, adrenaline pumping through his veins like a locomotive. He twisted in his seat and kicked out to the left. Delivered while Danny's bike was rolling at better than 80 mph, the blow caught Manuel's right knee and slammed it against his Sportster fuel tank. The Sporty shuddered and wobbled, forcing Manuel to drop the knife as he tried to control the careening bike. The deadly blade pierced his thigh, then bounced and clattered against the pavement racing by at 90 mph. As he reached for the bike's other grip for control, he was distracted by the sudden pain in his thigh. Panicking, he jammed his left foot hard against the brake pedal, and the bike slid to the side, the rear wheel coming around until the bike was almost 90 degrees from the direction of the highway. Sheer terror crossed his face as he remembered all the terrible stories of riders high-siding because they freaked and buried their boots and gloves in the brakes. Motorcycles are inherently stable—even crafty—when it comes to avoiding obstacles, but the extreme use of braking can be as devastating as it can be helpful. Manuel's fate flashed before his horrified eyes in the form a pumpkin-colored CalTrans street-sweeping truck poking along the median at 15 mph. He had a split-second to scream, but it was too late for anything but the realization that he was either going to high side, or hit the truck. His fear of high-siding made the decision for him, as he let up on the rear brake and the motorcycle's momentum at 80 mph took the Mexican hit man into the iron rear of the 3-ton rolling fortress. He was killed instantly, the motorcycle destroyed. The bikers in the rented compact were only the width of a lane away when they witnessed the explosion of Manuel and his bike against the huge, heavy, truck. The motorcycle burst into flames, and Manuel's body was cooked into its fresh paint, fused to the machine by heat and fire, a grisly spectacle for passersby. The street sweeper rolled to a stop, and the driver emerged from the cab to investigate whatever had slammed into his work vehicle. Jolted by this heavy dose of reality, the men in the white rental reacted with animated shock. "Jesus Christ!" gagged Hank, ducking involuntarily from the explosion as the compact sped past the fiery collision. Miguel, who was driving, turned to Hank. "Can you shoot that thing?" he asked, cool and unfazed by the mass of blood and flesh oozing down the side of the street sweeper while the truck driver bent over and puked into the dirt.

"Just get me into range," Hank said, a trickle of sweat running down the side of his forehead. He thought of himself as a tough guy, but he had never witnessed anything so violent. He fumbled as he jacked a .380 round into the chamber of the PPK stainless steel automatic. Miguel pushed his foot to the floor and leaned toward the steering wheel. For a moment, he wished he could throw out the two Mexicans in the back seat to lighten the load. He also anticipated sniveling from Pito about their crushed and charred brother, now adding blood and bone graphics to the side of the state highway vehicle.

"We need to get to a phone," the younger of the two brothers said. He held a 9mm Browning automatic in shaking, sweating hands.

"I'd rather see this motherfucker dead, wouldn't you?" Miguel snarled.

The two members of the Los Cuchillos in the back were Emilio's closest lieutenants. Pedro, the younger of the two, was dark and small, and his weakness for drugs made him his own best customer. Basically, he was not a violent man. But Al Potero, his partner next to him on the vinyl seat, was. Stocky, broad, and a no-holds-barred brawler with a taste for blood, he enjoyed crushing a man or woman with his fists. His face was pockmarked and scarred, his nose broken and twisted. Still, he didn't lose to his opponents often, and that was due to the simple fact that he cheated. Fighting dirty was one of the eight rules of close-quarter combat Danny learned from his Asian comrade in the joint. Al was a master of that particular rule.

"Can we catch him before we reach the city limits?" Al asked. "The rat bastard's killed two of my brothers now, and I know the club would be delighted if we could snuff the creep."

"If you don't," Miguel interjected, "I will."

The loaded compact gradually picked up speed until it topped out at 85. The motorcycle had slowed some, and they were gaining on him. But the freeway signs indicated that they were less than 18 miles from the city limits, which meant witnesses, more traffic, and cops. Miguel drove his engineer boot against the accelerator pedal till he thought it would go through the floor. The speedometer needle crept past the 85 mph mark and began to struggle toward 90. "We gotta get a shot at him soon," Hank said, "or we'll be in town." Hank was beginning to worry about the increased likelihood of witnesses and the consequences of that likelihood—prison. He checked the rearview mirror for flashing lights in the empty lanes behind them, then ahead at the speeding bike.

Trying to stay out of harm's way without overtaxing the motor, Danny pushed the scoot to 95 mph, blazing through the light tourist traffic and past interstate trucks. A searing pain in his neck forced him to let go of the throttle momentarily and grope for the source of the sudden torment. The bike slowed against the high-compression pistons screaming in the cylinders. His gloved hand came back wet with clotting blood. But he couldn't stop here, where nothing but the uncovered, vast fields lay on either side of him, leaving him open for another attack. He rode on, hoping for an off-ramp, the town, an emergency vehicle, or some form of cover.

The rental car continued to gain on the bike, now clearly visible in the searing heat of mid-day, but the waves of smoldering heat rising from the concrete made it difficult to focus on the Harley. "Shoot the motherfucker!" Miguel demanded.

Hank flinched and rolled down his window, inspiring Miguel to turn off the air-conditioning, thereby gaining another five mph. The bike seemed to be slowing and growing in their vision, and each man inside the small car found himself bathed in sweat from the fear, tension, and searing heat. "Shoot him, goddammit, shoot him!" Miguel ordered again, as the wavering image of the speeding motorcycle gained detail. "Shoot that punk motherfucker!"

Hank looked back, but the trailing cars were mere dots on the horizon. He looked from side to side, wondering first if he should kill Miguel and the others, but his fear of retaliation eliminated that thought, and he looked past Miguel to the brightly colored row of 15-foot high oleanders in the dusty median littered with retreads, hubcaps, and beer cans. To his right he saw only golden fields separated from the highway by a single barbed wire fence. He was alone with a sweaty, cocked .380 PPK. The custom rubber grip felt wet and slippery in his hand as he thrust his upper body into the 90 mph wind outside the passenger window. He lifted the piece into a straight-armed position, and stabilized his torso by pushing against the door frame with his left forearm. The wind whipped wildly against his aim, and its blast-furnace temperature immediately made his eyes water. With his arm straining against the wind, he took aim at the vibrating target 800 yards ahead and fired.

Danny ignored the wound on his neck and grabbed the throttle, the bike lurching as it began to climb to speed again. He heard the crack of the pistol, but it was so faint against the thunder of the motorcycle and the roar of the wind, that it barely registered in his mind. He wiped his brow with his left hand, feeling pain from the knife slash course through his arm. He was losing blood.

Hank fired again and again. Gaining speed, Danny was climbing above 95 when something hit his boot like a sledgehammer driven against his right heel, tearing his foot off the peg, and causing him to swerve to the right, onto the rough asphalt emergency lane. His heart racing, Danny fought for control of the bike, virtually willing it to stay upright rather than go down among the tumbleweeds and debris lining the road. One look at the ragged hole where the heel of his boot used to be, and he knew that the cracking sounds following him like a cowboy wielding a bullwhip behind a herd of cows were rounds from a pistol. He grabbed the throttle and turned it to the stops—new engine or not, he had to get the fuck out of there.

"Reload, you shit!" Miguel shouted. "We've got maybe 30 seconds before we catch the next pack of cars, or get too close to town!"

Hank jerked himself back into the smoldering interior of the car just as the Mexican outlaw in the back rolled down his window and shoved his weapon outside. "I'll kill that motherfucking *gringo* for both my brothers," he hollered over the howl of the wind. He rested his right arm against the side of the speeding compact, and sprayed a rapid-fire hail of bullets from his wildly vibrating semi-automatic pistol. The first round blew the sideview mirror off the door and onto the hood before it disappeared, whipped away by the screaming wind. "Fuckfuckfuck!" he screamed, firing as fast as he could pull the trigger.

Danny leaned tightly against the tank and prayed one of the bullets whizzing all around him wouldn't find its target. The men in the compact saw the mileage marker indicating only a half dozen miles to town. Hank fumbled with the clip, reloading. Miguel could see traffic ahead, and a cluster of billboards, a sure sign they were close to the outskirts of Bakersfield. Hank leaned out the window as the bike began to pull away. He cocked the weapon and took careful aim, aware that it was now or never.

Danny buried his torso against the his custom-painted Sportster tank, and twisted the throttle with everything he had. Ahead, he heard sirens and saw a sign identifying the first off-ramp. Danny had to make a decision fast. He was speeding, going almost twice the legal limit. He was packing. He was on probation and had yet to register with his P.O. He was out of town without permission. The choice appeared to be maintaining his speed, and in all likelihood, lose his freedom, or slow down, and lose his life. He could try to maneuver onto the first off–ramp, but slowing down would bring him more into range of the gunmen behind him. Moreover, getting off the highway could put him on slow streets through open fields. He peered out of his dark glasses, as if looking for answers.

A massive freeway road sign loomed ahead for an instant, then sped over Danny in a blur of vibrating visibility. The sign alerted motorists that the junction of I-5 and the 99 Freeway lay ahead. The Westside Freeway was newer, and could handle Danny's speeds better, but the off-ramp was a long, sweeping curve, and he would be forced to slow considerably. The newer, mammoth 5 Freeway, a direct route to the north, would afford Danny little protection. Anyway, at these speeds, he would soon run out of gas. A minute later, the junction shot past, gone like a lost opportunity. He stared ahead, watching the traffic become more dense the closer he got to town. He noticed another off-ramp and signs of city life. Out of nowhere, there seemed to be a multitude of billboards announcing the agricultural community of Bakersfield.

Danny knew he would need a straight ramp so he could maintain his speed until the very last second, before merging with city traffic and, he prayed, escaping his would-be assassins.

Billboards advertised small car dealerships, farm equipment, tourist information, and fast food joints. Traffic forced Danny to slow, allowing the others to close the distance between them even more. Bear Mountain Drive emerged on the horizon, coming at him like a missile at almost a 100 mph. Danny's eyes were watering in the harsh sun and floating dust, his vision worsening as he decided to split off the freeway. Hitting the off-ramp at over 90, then slowing, he heard the crack of gunfire again. Danny had difficulty letting off the throttle as he sped for the intersection at the top of the dust-strewn off–ramp. A hundred yards ahead was a boulevard stop. Abruptly, pickups and semis pulling massive loads seemed to emerge from the nearby truck stops all at once, forcing Danny to grab all the binders he had just as a bullet blew out his rear tire. He lost control, and the bike went into a slide. Sparks fired into the air like a ton of Fourth of July rockets when the handlebars encountered the pavement. Danny jerked his leg from beneath the screaming chassis, while the custom Shovel, Danny's dream machine, was being ground away against the harsh surface of the road. The bike slid into the center of the intersection, where it stopped. Danny rolled off the hot steel surface of the bike, jumped to his feet, and tore at the straps holding his bedroll. A hotshot semi driver screeched to a stop less than five feet from the bike. Limping, Danny dragged the bedroll to the cab. "Let me in!" he screamed at the driver. "I won't hurt you!"

Though startled and a bit frightened, the thick, tough-looking driver threw open the cab's passenger door. Danny tossed in his bedroll and jumped inside, slamming the door behind him. The Ford 1-ton diesel hauling the gooseneck trailer lurched around the downed bike, and continued down Bear Mountain Road.

The compact car skidded to a stop alongside the smoldering

bike as Miguel threw open his door, grabbed the PPK from Hank, and leapt out. In one direction, the fields were bare, except for perimeter fences, and in the other, Miguel saw only a truck stop and an adjacent gas station, busy with lumbering diesels, truckers, and roughnecks coming and going. He chambered the PPK in the pungent air, thick with the smell of gasoline and oil fumes from the dying motorcycle. Standing alone in the intersection, with the other outlaws sweating inside the suffocating rent-a-box, Miguel spit on the bike. "I hope that cocksucker can hear this," he said, shooting into the motorcycle until the clip was empty, and continuing to pull the trigger long after the bleeding Harley burst into flames.

Danny peered over the back seat of the 1-ton cab, looking out the back window along the trailer hauling a 50-foot oil well directional drill, a tool used for steering the direction of a well being dug. Mick, the driver, shifted gears, baffled and confused by the sudden intrusion of the blood-splattered stranger. Danny watched his motorcycle explode into flames, and felt his dreams die as he watched the bike burn. He had endured almost two years without riding, and hardly had he returned to the free world than his hopes of brotherhood and the lifestyle he adored melted in the sun. He had dreamed of becoming a member of the Devils Own every day he spent behind bars, only to watch another outlaw torch his motorcycle. Danny's mind was a jumble of conflicting thoughts and emotions. This had to be Los Cuchillos trying to take care of the president's business. Or perhaps he wasn't the man he was purported to be. He looked at the trucker, who was wearing a T-shirt that said, "Bones Heal. Scars Turn Women On. Pain Is Temporary. Honor Is Forever."

Danny smiled. "Where we headed?" he asked.

Chapter 16

WAR GAMES

*T*he phone rang in the back of the dark and dusty body shop. Pito walked toward a pay phone coated with years of bondo dust, but Emilio intercepted the overspray-covered receiver before Pito could answer. Pito, aging and mellowing out, grudgingly acquiesced to the secretive behavior occasionally seen in some of the club's members. From decades of being an outlaw, he knew how the game was played, understood the stakes, the pitfalls, and the snakes. And he smelled snake shit all over this deal. As he watched his supposed brother lift the receiver and turn his back on the veteran president so as not to be overheard, he remembered a similar situation eight years earlier, when an ambitious younger brother tried his hand at dealing whites to truckers.

Garcia, a flashy, young biker whose ego often overran his judgment, had been warned several times by Pito about the risks of dealing whites and bennies to the truckers passing through Bakersfield in need of a chemical boost to make schedule. Garcia ignored the warnings, and before long he was turning some pretty good money from his pill-popping enterprise. Evidence that business was good came in the form of a new Sportster and pickup truck, the wad of bills bound by a rubber band he carried in his back pocket, and the expensive sluts whose favors he could have never afforded prior to dealing speed. He was a welcomed regular at dozens of white cocktail lounges, kicker bars, and truck stops throughout the area. Everyone knew who he was and what he was up to, since he indiscriminately moved his wares all over the Fresno area. His connection flew in from Las Vegas once a month, and delivered the goods in a stretched Cadillac limousine. His suppliers were Italians from the east, exiled to Vegas behind a nasty penchant for bad drug deals. Garcia didn't know about their slimy background, and wouldn't have given a shit if he had. After all, he was a high roller, moving in circles he couldn't have dreamed of in the days when he was merely a lowly field hand.

One night, the Italians called him and told him that a deal had gone sour, that they were hot, and that he had to meet them in the desolate town of Mojave, at the junction of Highway 14, that rolls across the Mojave Desert toward Nevada, and Highway 58, rolling out of Bakersfield and south to Barstow. They promised him a stake and some of the finest uppers they had procured in years. With over $100,000 in cash in Garcia's new leather briefcase, he confidently drove his truck into the desolate wastelands. They met behind a gas station on the edge of town, and when the silk suits invited young Garcia into their limo, telling him they were going to get him fed and laid, he accepted. Garcia eagerly stepped into the car and out of existence. They found what was left of him three months later, with six .22 magnum bullet holes in the back of his head, left in the desert to rot.

Pito watched Emilio whisper into the receiver and remembered that losing Garcia wasn't the last of it. Every trucker, cowboy and college student in town who had invested in Garcia's last deal was pissed. College students were afraid to confront outlaw bikers, but soon after the disappearance, several Los Cuchillos found themselves surrounded by angry truckers in a local bar. Nothing much had come of that incident, but then Pito rubbed his graying mustache as a chill ran up his spine, recalling that dark night in Old Town Clovis, when two of his brothers entered a bar and were immediately jumped by a handful of cowboys. One of his brothers had been lured by a white woman in a pickup, who told him she liked bikers, especially Mexican outlaws. His eyes were attached to the cleavage spilling over the top of her blouse. Her bright eyes, and her flimsy silk blouse tucked into a narrow-waisted pair of Levi's sprayed over supple hips made him want to gnaw the paint off his bike. She told him she had friends, and to bring anyone he knew who was in the mood to party.

Outside the saloon, a younger Pito lit up a cigarette, then he heard the ruckus explode inside. Pito had no formal fight training, but had a natural killer instinct, and the powerful physique to back it up. It didn't take much to rile the big man, and once the switch was turned on, nothing short of a fire truck would stop him. As he entered the bar, six big shitkickers were taking pool cues to his younger brothers. Knocking half a dozen cowgirls on their asses, Pito grabbed their round, wagon-wheel table, and set it over his beaten brothers to protect them. Pito's sudden and animated arrival startled the cowboys, who were fatigued from fighting the two young Los Cuchillos before Pito jumped in, fresh and ready to stomp butt. Snatching a blood-coated cue stick from the paws of one of his brothers' hillbilly attackers, he broke it over his knee, tossed the light end at one of the fighters, and began to take batting practice on the cowboys. He broke six arms, three jaws, one kneecap, and never took a hit. When the fight was over, he helped his brothers back to the clubhouse, then drove to Los Angeles, took a loan for some whites, repaid Garcia's debt, and put an end to the trouble.

Pito was older now, and the stakes were higher with each new dangerous enterprise. His level of confidence for controlling these risky situations diminished with each passing decade. Still tougher than most members, he looked at his inexperienced brothers as young, naive punks with huge chips on their shoulders. Sometimes, it was up to Pito to knock the chip off, and take the errant member in hand. Emilio began to hiss and spit into the phone. Whereas he generally showed little emotion, this time, his richly colored face was red and flushed with anger. His hand clenched the receiver with strained-muscle, white-knuckle intensity, and his narrow, sinister features twitched with rage, "Here, take it," he growled, thrusting the phone into Pito's hands. "That fucking *gringo* killed Manuel. I told Gonzalo and Pedro to find the *puta* and kill him."

"What happened?" Pito shouted into the receiver. At the other end, Miguel took the phone from Al. "Listen, bud," he said. "This is Miguel. He may have spotted me, so now it's up to you to finish it." With that, he handed the receiver back to Al. While Al was talking frantically on the phone, Miguel and Hank got in the rent-a-car and headed across Bear Mountain Road, which spans Interstate 5 and Highway 99. They planned to escape along I-5 to avoid the accident.

"What the hell happened?" Pito barked into the phone's mouthpiece again, determined to get answers."

"We tried to stop the gringo, but he forced Manuel into a truck and killed him," Al said, lying because he feared getting on Pito's bad side. Sometimes, talking to Pito was like suggesting to General Patton that he consider surrender. The president was passionate about his family of bikers, and wouldn't take no for an answer. "We caught up with him on Bear Mountain Pass and destroyed his motorcycle, but he got away."

"What do you mean, he got away?" Pito screamed into the receiver.

"I'm sorry, *jefe*," Al apologized, his hands shaking even though he was 10 miles from the object of his fear. "He must have jumped on a truck, but we'll find him."

"And kill him!" Pito bellowed. "Then bring him to me, and I'll kill him again!" Pito hung up by smashing the receiver down so hard that the cradle cracked, then finished the job by jerking the cord from the wall and heaving the phone through a window.

Demolishing the phone apparently calmed Pito, since he seemed composed immediately. He turned to Emilio and asked, "Who's Miguel?"

"What do you mean?" Emilio replied, caught off guard. Pito wasn't aware until that minute that Miguel or anyone else was involved with this fight.

"You know what I mean, shit-for-brains," Pito barked, moving in close to Emilio, his anger flaring up again. "What the fuck does he have to do with our business? This is our business, our valley. What, in your mother's thoughts, is going on?"

"Nothing, brother, *nada*," Emilio stammered, afraid his plan was crumbling. "I swear, he's just a friend." "He don't talk like no friend," Pito snarled. By now, Pito was nose-to-nose with Emilio, although he stood 4 inches taller. His chest pumped rapidly, and the sweat generated by the smoldering tar covering the shop's roof ran down his brow. As he spoke, he punctuated his words with jabs of his right index finger to Emilio's chest. As if being whacked with a heavy iron poker, Emilio grimaced and backed up with every hit.

"Listen up, motherfucker. I raised you, I've saved your ass more than once, but I can bury you just as easy, if I find out you're dealing drugs with the Devils Own."

"I swear, brother," Emilio said, feeling his plan fading, "It ain't nothin' like that. Ya gotta believe me. We've been down *too* many roads together."

Pito knew a liar when he heard one. He knew Emilio's dark side, and he knew it was polished and glowing. But in the heat of the moment, Pito had a tough time turning on his own. Ultimately, he just hoped for the best. "Let's find the *gringo* and get it over with," he said, stomping off. "But if this goes sour, and we lose another brother over this piece of shit, I'm coming to you."

Emilio's black silk shirt under his shiny leather vest was drenched with sweat. He could smell his own fear, and his faltering confidence in his plan. The pressure was coming from several directions, and he felt his knees buckle slightly. Reaching into his vest, he pulled a small vial out of a hidden pocket. Attached to a 2-inch silver chain was a tiny silver spoon. He stepped into the paint booth and snorted two large spoonfuls of coke, one into each nostril. It wasn't like Emilio to get high on the job, but with Pito, the Devils Own, his dead brother, and this lucky *gringo* to deal with, his resolve faded. He needed an ego boost, and the white powder gave it to him ... and more.

As the drug filled Emilio's nostrils and entered his sinus passages, he felt the heat of the day dissipate, then the pressure began to bleed off. Finally, confidence returned, and Emilio detected the familiar taste of power and evil again. Once the *gringo* was gone, or had killed Pito, he would finish the operation. All he needed was patience. Just wait and stand aside for the fireworks to subside, then ... Emilio, on top again, tossed off an unspoken, "Fuck it" in his mind. Thanks to a couple of tiny spoonfuls of cocaine, he was king again. He stuffed he vial back into his vest, marched out of the paint booth to his bike in the body shop parking lot, mounted it, and rode away. Pito watched in wonderment. He knew Emilio was up to something, but he wasn't sure what ... yet.

Emilio rode a late model Shovelhead. Profits from drug dealing afforded him the first new bike owned by a Cuchillo club member. But riding wasn't his passion—power and sex were. The bike was an ordinary, factory stock model, except for the all-black sheet metal with the club's logo painted on the sides of the fatbob tanks. He rode south on Clovis Avenue toward 99, but when he arrived at the intersection of Clovis and Butler, he turned right and headed into the barrio section of downtown Fresno. It once was home to Fresno's working class—frugal, honest toilers who worked on the railroad, in the packing plants, and in the cattle yards adjacent to the railway station. Fresno was an agricultural center, and downtown was only a couple of miles to the north. The houses were small, neat California bungalows, built on large, tree-lined streets, until the nature of the area and its business changed.

The Southern Pacific became aware of the inexpensive workforce south of the border, as did the large land owners whose crops could be harvested cheaply by the Mexican hordes coming across the border and then migrating north for work and a place to raise a family safely. Fresno businesses gradually ran off the white, middle-class workers and replaced them with illegal immigrants willing to perform twice the work for half the pay. After all, if they didn't like it, they could return to their corrupt homeland, where jobs were scarce, extortion rampant, and infrastructure non-existent. They had little choice.

For Mexican males with anything going on besides a six-pack-a-day habit, and a field job, women were plentiful, bored, and ready. The lives of *muchachas* consisted of raising children from the time they were old enough to sit still and hold a baby bottle. Their only escape depended on their looks and education. The plain or ugly migrant females, along with the slow and illiterate, followed in the footsteps of past generations, raising kids and caring for the home from the time they were six or seven. As they grew into their teens, someone usually knocked them up, and the pattern would begin again. As their youngsters grew, they cared for the siblings, so mama could clean homes, pick fruit, do laundry, or virtually anything to bring in some extra change. Still, the lifestyle here was an infinite improvement over what *señoritas* could expect in Mexico.

For those girls with hot, Hispanic looks, there was the hope that someone would pay more attention to them, buy them things, perhaps even take them away from the pattern threatening to engulf them. Emilio had the pick of any woman in the barrio. Some liked the drugs, some the sex, some the excitement, and some just wanted money or clothes, and in order to get what they desired, would do anything he wanted. Emilio pulled up in front of a small Spanish-style home with a tile roof, lath-and-plaster exterior, and a one-car garage alongside the small lot. The grass was neatly cut, but strewn with small toys. He revved his engine and faces appeared at the door and adjacent windows. Little faces looked through the torn screens at the slick man on the menacing black Harley. Their large, round, and wrinkled grandma peered out the window and hollered, "Maria, your tough guy is here." She shouted toward the back of the house as Maria emerged from the bathroom, which she had held hostage for almost two hours. "When will you be back?" her mother asked sternly.

"He's going to take me to the park then to dinner, ma," Maria answered, entering the living room. Her thick make-up softened her dark skin tones, but her eyes sported heavy mascara and deep, black eyeliner. Above her black, garage-door eyelashes, her eyebrows had been plucked into dark slivers over her distinctive bone structure. Maria's long, jet-black hair was pulled tightly to the back of her head, and her bangs were cut at harsh angles. In Los Angeles, she would have been labeled a street whore. In Fresno, she was high style.

"I don't like that boy," her mother complained. "He never comes in, never talks to me. No respect." She knew instinctively that this was no walk in the park for her daughter. The girl was dressed in a satin miniskirt and a tiny top that held up her young supple torso like black lacquer on the curves of a gas tank. Her full bust was half exposed, and her waist was as narrow as a sparrow's. She wore no nylons, and her creamy legs were carefully shaven and oiled to a softness that would set mortal fingertips on fire. A hint of blush gleamed in her cheeks, while her Saturday night lips glowed as red as blossoming roses. At one glance, she was angelic, and at another, she was the youngest prostitute on the block.

Maria bounced out the door before her mother had a chance to say more, and jumped on the bike behind Emilio. "What took you so long?" he demanded, as she mounted the bike and her black panties snuggled warmly onto the narrow seat. "I don't have much time."

"Where are we going?" Maria asked, whispering in Emilio's ear and kissing the back of his neck. Just riding down the street for the neighbors, behind the vice president of the Los Cuchillos was an ego boost for the lonely girl.

"You know where we're going," Emilio said dryly. "And you love it. I have a treat for you, so hold on."

"Can we go out afterward?" she asked, nibbling at his

earlobe, hoping he would finally take her to dinner so she could show off the powerful biker to her friends and acquaintances in the community.

"We'll see," Emilio said, turning onto Monterey Street, and heading along a row of abandoned packing houses.

"Can we at least cruise downtown, so my girlfriends can see me?" she coaxed, her eyes sparkling behind dark plastic glasses. Each eyelash had been carefully combed and wiped with thick mascara.

"No time today, I have a lot of business to take care of," Emilio said over his shoulder. He realized he was bringing her down, so he pulled over on the wide, trash-strewn, industrial street, leaned back against her, and buried his tongue deeply in her mouth. "You look beautiful, baby," he said, after ending the kiss. "Let's swing over to Lupe's, next to the mall and get some beer."

The suggestion excited her. All the young men in the area hung out at Lupe's, and showing up with Emilio would cement her connection. And the young teenage girls coming out of the mall always walked past Lupe's liquor store to make sure the guys sitting on the curb, at the bus stop, and on the bench in front of the taco take-out window, saw them when they were dressed to kill. Even though the walk past Lupe's little building was a city block out of their way home, Emilio pulled up in front of the store and gave Maria a 20-dollar bill with instructions to buy a half-pint of Cuervo Gold, a six-pack of Corona, a couple of limes, a picnic-size salt shaker, and a bag of freshly fried tortilla chips. She bounced all 5-foot-3, 105 pounds of herself off the back of his Harley, strutted proudly past the assortment of young Hispanic men sitting on benches in the hot sun, and into the store. Emilio got off his bike and lit up a cigarette. He paid little attention to the young men and older drunks strewn around the hot cement that bordered the small store. Newer 7-Elevens and fast food joints were popping up everywhere, and this cracking stucco, mom-and-pop store was one of the last of its kind in the neighborhood.

Her fanny jiggled under the miniskirt's light material as Maria bounded up and down the narrow isles, looking for the tequila. The eyes of each man outside followed her every step toward the store, but avoided staring for fear of Emilio's wrath. But one particularly brave, particularly drunk 25-year-

old on the splintered and chipped park bench whispered
under his breath to his partner, *"Creo que la puta quiere
comer muchas vergas."*

Emilio spun on his heels and stared at the men on the
bench. "Somebody got something to say?" he challenged them.

"I just said that your girlfriend..." the young Hispanic
began, his remark trailing off in a drunken, surly tone of
voice. It was closing on three in the afternoon, and this out-of-
work, lonely immigrant had only one thing to do, drink
whatever anyone had to offer, and chase young pussy. He had
already been through a six-pack, and was sipping cheap
tequila with the 50-year-old at his side. The sun had half
cooked half of the six-pack out of him, and the other half had
been pissed against the wall behind the building. Only the
alcohol remained.

Emilio sensed the young man's lack of respect and flicked
his burning cigarette from between his thumb and forefinger
at his face. The guy ducked, but the ember from the butt
singed his forehead, and he pushed himself to his feet. Emilio
stroked his long Imperial and without batting an eye, he
pulled the silver stiletto out of his waistband at the center of
his back and cut the man's face, turned the knife bolster
toward his injured opponent, and snapped the shiny metal
against the man's forehead. He collapsed as Maria emerged
from the store.

Maria looked at the bleeding man lying face-down on the
sidewalk, at the others backing away, and decided not to
ask questions. Emilio sheathed his knife, took her elbow,
and carefully assisted her on the leather pillion. He then
stepped over the bike and started it. Several young girls
looked at Maria in awe as she and the biker sped off,
leaving the community corner store in disarray.

"Did he say something?" Maria asked, again whispering
into Emilio's ear as he pulled back onto Monterey Street.

"He didn't show you respect," Emilio said over his
shoulder. "He will in the future."

"Thank you," she said, hugging him, thoroughly impressed
by his valiant actions, yet uncomfortably aware of his violent
tendencies. Emilio rolled to a stop in front of a particular
warehouse and gave Maria the key. She dismounted silently,

and opened the massive padlock on the broad door to the building. The structure was all brick except for the wooden doors, wide enough to drive semis in and out of. The big room was vacant and featureless, except for a massive wrought iron bed, a couch, and a bathroom at the far end. Light streamed in from the skylights above. The bare floor was concrete, except for a small Indian rug between the couch and the bed. In the winter, Emilio parked his bike close to the bed for warmth. This time, he parked it far from the black framed bed. The air was still now, and years of hay and fruit had left a lingering odor of rotting plant matter.

Near the bathroom was an old refrigerator and a small counter. Maria put four of the six beers in the refrigerator, sliced the limes, opened the diminutive salt shaker and poured the chips into a stainless steel bowl. She also pulled a small mirror and a rusting, single-edged razor blade out of a drawer, and set them carefully on the countertop. Emilio approached her from behind, and wrapped his arms around her, running his narrow digits over her small belly and down to her crotch. One hand slipped around behind her, under her flimsy miniskirt and into her panties. His hand slid quickly down the crack of her young, rounded ass, over her asshole, and into her pussy without warning. When she jumped, he sensed fear, and he responded by yanking her black panties down around her knees.

For a moment, her throat closed. She enjoyed his power, but at the same time, it scared her. She knew the drugs and tequila would help her warm up to his strange behavior, and she hoped he would give her a chance to lose herself in the high before he got too carried away. Emilio pulled out his stiletto and cut her panties away, then, with the palm of his left hand, pressed her face against the countertop and stuck the knife into the wooden surface less than an inch from her pert nose. She flinched, and her fear turned him on. He kicked her patent leather, spiked heels apart, and raised the skirt above her ass. Leaning forward, he bit her butt, leaving a small set of teeth indentations on her smooth skin.

"Did it turn you on to see me cut another man?" Emilio hissed, pulling his .25 caliber automatic from his boot, and pressing it to the lips of her cunt. The cold steel caused her to flinch again, and he entered her pussy with the weapon.

"Yes, baby, I like it," she said, her face less than an inch from Emilio's deadly blade, while he roughly massaged the lips of her sex with the sight of the blue-black automatic.

"You want to get high, don't you?" he whispered, leaning over her. But she knew better than to respond positively.

"Whatever you want, baby," she replied.

"I want to coat my dick with drugs and have you suck it off," he said, teasing her. He pulled the pistol out of her cunt, and aimed it at one of the back skylights. He laughed and pulled the trigger, shattering the fixture, and Maria gasped, knowing the cocked weapon had been inside her. Emilio set the gun on the counter, dumped the contents of a small baggie on the mirror, and drew four huge lines, each 4 inches long. Maria was weak with fear, and her knees almost gave way as some shards of glass not dislodged when Emilio had fired the shot, fell to the hard concrete in the back of the warehouse. She was exactly where he wanted her.

He turned her head to the mirror and she inhaled through a silver straw. He did the same, then held her in his arms. "I love the way you respond to me," he said. He could feel her heart pounding against her chest, her lungs gasping for breath. "Here, have a shot of tequila." He poured a large shot for each of them, and they gulped. He felt the strong liquid, like high-octane fuel, enter his system. She prayed it would numb his senses, and that he wouldn't be too rough. She turned and picked up one of the bottles of Corona and took a swallow, but he grabbed the beer out of her hand. "Did I tell you to drink that just yet?"

"No, baby," she said abjectly. "I'm sorry."

The beer ran down her torso, foaming over her pert breasts. He grabbed her ponytail and untied it, allowing her long, shiny mane to fall over her shoulders. "Ladies shouldn't drink out of bottles," he said menacingly, spinning her away from him again. He grabbed the hem of her blouse and raised it over her head. He snapped her bra open and, pulling on one end, spun her to face him while ripping the bra from her body. Her breasts jumped and quivered and, since the coke had sensitized her brain, she responded to him readily.

He pushed her to the mirror and she snorted again, her buzz lifting her higher, her inhibitions melting. He poured tequila down her throat, cut the miniskirt off her body, and kicked her high heels across the floor.

"I'll teach you how to drink beer," he stated. She was quivering like a volcano ready to erupt as he lifted her onto the widest portion of the counter, and slid her crotch to his face. He leaned over as if to kiss her there, then grabbed the bottle and poured the beer between her young, supple tits. Her legs were spread wide, and the foamy liquid slid between them, down across her flat tummy, and over her crotch. He leaned and drank. She arched her back, and felt his tongue against her clit. Suddenly, she felt the neck of the bottle enter her pussy. At first, she was racked with fear as the cold glass slid inside her, then she felt his tongue again. One thumb and forefinger played harshly with her nipples, and she savored the sensation of the cold liquid entering her as her body exploded. She climaxed fiercely as he pulled the neck of the bottle from the depths of her vagina, then drank as the foamy brew cascaded from her crotch along her inner thighs. He drank and licked hungrily at the liquid mixed with her warm fluids running over his mouth and down his face, neck, and through the fine, dark hairs on his chest. She came again, almost passing out.

Emilio stood back from Maria, and assessed her form, perched on the countertop, legs spread wide, her pubic hairs carefully trimmed to a diamond around the lips of her sex. Her waist was so small that he could almost encircle it with his hands, and her chest heaved as she attempted to catch her breath, sprawled before him wet with beer, sex, and sweat. Her hair was matted against her classically beautiful, Mexican, high cheek-boned, features. With her make-up running slightly, Emilio watched her breathe as he disrobed, hanging his clothes neatly over the back of the couch. Naked, he sat on the edge of the bed with the mirror beside him, and two shots of tequila on the small stand beside the bed. The counter was 40 feet from the bed, in the middle of the 100 by 100-foot room. Maria remained draped across the countertop, still wet, her eyes closed, in a lewdly awkward, half-sitting, half-lying position. "Hey, baby," Emilio called to her, his words slightly slurred, "now it's my turn."

Maria, drunk, dazed, and high all at once, opened her eyes slowly, then hopped down from the counter, only to fall to the floor when her legs failed to support her. Emilio, observing her from the bed, smiled wickedly. "Crawl," he commanded, and she obeyed, her tits wobbling and her arms quivering as she tried to grovel across the floor to the bed, where Emilio sat massaging his hardening dick, and urging her to hurry up. Occasionally, Maria looked up to see him stroking his cock, as he watched her, and her alcohol-and-coke-saturated brain flooded with distorted images of the sex acts he would command her to perform. Emilio was 28, with a narrow frame, long, black hair, and skinny legs. As she drew closer, he pointed the head of his swollen cock at the mound of glistening white powder, and rubbed it in the fine granules. It came away covered with an uneven layer of fine crystals just as Maria reached the edge of the bed. She crawled between his legs and began to lick the head of his stiff penis, slowly taking more of it into her mouth. As the drugs slipped down her throat, she felt her high intensify, cascading her into a world of pure sexual pleasure. Everything tingled, and she could feel moistness build in her body again. "That's enough," Emilio shouted, pulling his dick from her mouth, and jerking her to her feet before tossing her soft frame on the smooth sheets, and handcuffing her wrists to the metal bedposts. He entered her roughly, driving against her, then uncuffing her in order to throw her to the hard concrete floor, where he fucked her doggy style. He seemed to pound into her forever, relentlessly slamming his dick into the deepest recesses of her pussy. Again, he forced her onto the bed, and handcuffed her to the steel frame. Just as he was about to enter her again, something happened. A loud knock on the door and screaming brought Maria back to reality. Emilio pulled out of her, got off the bed, crossed the room, and grabbed the boot .25 automatic, already chambered and cocked.

"Emilio, I know you're in there! Open the door!"

"Who the fuck is it?" Emilio demanded, angrily.

"Emilio, I must talk to you!" The screaming continued.

"Wait a fucking minute," Emilio shouted, his voice an infuriated snarl. He was nude, covered in perspiration, half erect, and with his hair matted to his head as he tore open the door. "What the hell is it?" he bellowed.

A girl in her mid-20s stood at the door, tears streaming down her face, and a newborn baby wailing in her arms.

Emilio became flaccid immediately. "This is your baby, Emilio," the girl sobbed. "Why don't I ever see you anymore?"

Emilio looked at her with contempt, and she backed away. She had tasted his rough love, and witnessed his violence, especially when she had told him she was pregnant. That was the last time she ever saw him until this moment. "Get the fuck away from me, bitch." Emilio spat. "I'm busy!" He opened the door wider, revealing Maria lying naked on the bed, squirming against the handcuffs. Emilio stood in the buff in front of her, and wiped the sweat from his face with one hand and held the small pistol with the other. "You were once beautiful, but now you're just another fat mama. If that's what you want, go for it. But don't come sniveling to me, or I'll blow your fucking head off!" Emilio grabbed Rosy by the jaw and squeezed. Striding out onto the sidewalk nude, the sun blazing down on both of them in the deserted industrial street, he stuck the barrel of the gun into one of her nostrils. "Maybe I should shoot you now, and the kid can make his own way alone." Rosy tried futilely to escape his grasp. "Or I'll tell you what—blow me right now, right here, and I'll give you 25 bucks, you fucking whore. You're all alike—bitches who use your bodies, then want some man to pay for your fucked-up lives." He shoved her into the street, where she stumbled and fell. "I'll kill you the next time you bother me, you fucking cunt!"

Emilio slammed the door and returned to Maria, handcuffed to the bed frame. Casually, he took a deep slug of the Cuervo, and another snort of coke, then wiped his face with Maria's miniskirt. He looked at her trapped form on the bed and began to get hard again. "I need to go," Maria said, praying to find the words to stop him.

"I'm not finished," he said, climbing onto the bed.

"No," she begged, a tear running down her face. She suspected the depth of his evil, but it was more than confirmed as he entered her, slapped her hard, called her a bitch, and finally, came on her face in an explosion of drug-laden semen. When he was finished, he got dressed while she sobbed on the bed, uncuffed her, and rode out of the building alone, leaving her to walk home in the tattered remnants of her clothing.

BAKERSFIELD BLUES

Danny rolled into the oil and agricultural town of Bakersfield in the cab of an uncomfortable truck owned by a one-time biker derrick man, Mick Karr.

"What the hell have you got yourself into?" Mick inquired, as he turned onto Wibble Road, heading north.

A moment ago, Danny had been smiling at the statement silk-screened on Mick's shirt, but the pleasure was fleeting. Breathing heavily, Danny placed his elbows on his knees and rested his sunburnt face in his hands. "I don't know," he said. "But goddammit, I'm going to find out. Where we headed?"

"I saw you coming up the off-ramp and knew you weren't going to make it, so I changed directions," Mick explained. "I'm headed back into Bakersfield to drop this trailer and go home. I been on the road for a couple of days."

Danny was glad to be off the highway, sad about the motorcycle, and he wondered what the hell was happening to him. "I've got to make a call," he said.

"No problem," Mick replied. "We'll be at the yard in 15 minutes. You can call from there."

Danny sat quietly as Mick's truck and cargo rumbled up Wibble Road to the Pumpkin Center at the Greenfield Junction, and rolled onto Highway 99 again. Danny got a chill as they entered the traffic, and it continued as they watched a constant stream of emergency vehicles fly by, heading south.

"That wouldn't have something to do with you, would it?" Mick asked. While his hair was gray and cropped short, his faced tan, tough, and wrinkled, he nonetheless had a youthfulness about his movements. Reading Mick's darting, light blue eyes, Danny had a hunch he'd be no slouch in a fight.

"Afraid so," Danny said. "You ever ride?"

"Yeah," Mick returned. "For about 20 years."

"Ever been in a club?" Danny asked.

"Yep," Mick said, shrugging his shoulders. "Can't talk

about it, but it sure weren't no brotherhood." Mick pulled off the freeway at Cutoff 58, and swung onto Rosedale Blvd., a street as wide as most highways. This was the center of the oil industry for the area. Each block contained oil well tool companies, machine shops, truck dealers, heavy equipment leasing agencies, and bars. Occasionally, there was a small truck-stop-style restaurant. Two miles down, Mick hung a left on Calloway, then onto a narrow side street, and into a four-acre dirt yard. A biker-looking guy came out of the office to meet Mick.

"How'd the run go partner?" Smiley asked. "Hot enough for ya?"

"It was fine," Mick responded. "Smiley, I'd like you to meet an old friend of mine, Danny." Mick's introduction was intended to keep questions from Smiley to a minimum.

Smiley reached in and shook Danny's hand, whereupon Danny immediately spotted Smiley's Harley tattoo and the black, H-D logo T-shirt he wore.

"Good to meet ya," Danny said.

"Mind if Danny uses the phone?" Mick inquired.

"No problem," Smiley replied, gesturing toward the yard's office. "Right through that door."

There was no one else in the office as Danny dialed Dixie. She answered immediately in her naturally sweet voice. "Hello," she said, expectantly, as if she had been waiting by the phone for the call.

"Hey," Danny said. "It's me."

"Are you all right?" Dixie asked, as if she expected bad news.

"I'm OK," Danny assured her. "I'm in Bakersfield. They shot my motorcycle right out from under me. I wish I could figure out what's going on. Have you heard anything?"

"All the brothers here are planning your membership party," she replied gleefully, ignoring his question. There was something in her voice and manner that didn't seem to ring true. "Where are you?"

"I don't know about any party," Danny snapped. "These people are trying to kill me—understand? They have no intention of letting me meet with the president of the Los Cuchillos."

"That can't be, baby," Dixie said, in an overly confident tone, followed by her baby-like giggles. "We know you'll make it. No one wants to have a problem with the Devils Own. That doesn't make sense. Just tell me where you are so I can call you back in a couple of minutes."

Danny picked a card off the desk and read the name of the company and the number to Dixie, "I'll probably be here a couple of hours," he told her.

"I love you, babe," Dixie said, pouring her sweetness into the receiver like honey over pancakes. "Don't worry, it'll be over quick."

Her voice trailed off as she hung up, as if she didn't believe what she was saying. Danny put the phone back in its cradle, and went outside in the blistering afternoon heat.

"Hey, give me a hand unloading this," Mick hollered, as Danny passed Smiley, the round, bearded biker heading for the office. "Undo the chain locks on that side of the tool," Mick ordered, moving up and down the half-ton directional drilling tool, while another worker in gray overalls maneuvered a fork lift into position. The yard was open to the elements, and the noonday sun was relentless. Everything in the yard, including winches, gooseneck trailers, cranes, and trucks was coated in faded paint.

The yard was nothing more than dirt surrounded by a six-foot chain link fence. A wide steel gate allowed entrance, and concertina wire uncoiled along the top of the fence discouraged thieves. One steel warehouse was rented to a woodworker, and a small tin office was planted in the dust, alongside the gate. The heat was all but unbearable, but the workers were forced to wear gloves to handle the scorching, heavy steel equipment. Tools, pipes, and raw steel are unforgiving when it comes to mortals. A smart man stands clear when two tons of pipe is being hoisted from one truck to another. A finger caught between a stand of pipe and a truck bed will be snapped off instantly. The tools were carefully removed from the back of the trailer, then the trailer was moved and disconnected. Danny stood aside while Mick handled the forklift, chain hoists, and the process of tying down properly.

Danny could feel the sweat running down his back as he wiped his brow with a club bandanna. He looked at the colors and what they represented, and he wondered what went wrong. For a moment, with Mick, the world seemed all right, almost normal, but the square of linen reminded him of his growing dilemma. Instinctively, he knew he had to keep moving. With his bedroll thrown over his shoulder, he prepared to leave. "Hey," Mick called out after him, "where do you think you're going?"

"I better get moving," Danny said. "Thanks for the help."

"Where you gotta go?" Mick inquired.

"Fresno, first," Danny said, looking at Mick across a truck bed. He wasn't sure whether or not to tell the man anything. His world was rapidly falling apart, and he didn't want anyone else involved until he knew more.

"If you can hang on for a day, I'll be heading north tomorrow," Mick said, "I can drop you off."

Danny did a quick mental inventory of his problems. He had a gun in his bedroll, his motorcycle was gone, he had no transportation, he didn't know his way around, he knew someone was out to kill him, his prospect patch was ripped with road rash abuse, and he wondered if it wasn't a target anyway. Mick watched Danny ponder his next move. "Would you like to talk about it, brother?" he asked.

"You got a family, Mick?" Danny asked.

"Yeah, I got an ol' lady, her kids, and one of mine," Mick replied.

"Then I don't think it would be a good idea just yet," Danny said. "Just like I don't think it's a wonderful fucking idea to continue to wear this."

Danny set his bedroll in the bed of the truck and was removing his vest when a loud crack filled the air, and the passenger-side window of Mick's truck exploded. Both men hit the dirt. They heard the crack again, and a bullet pierced the door in a downward arc. Mick crawled in the dirt to the front wheel, where he spotted a black sedan moving along the fence. A gun barrel protruded from the slightly lowered rear window. Mick scrambled to the back of the truck, and then across the back of the trailer.

Danny tried to move under the truck, but he couldn't tell where the bullets were coming from—only that they were getting closer. Just then, the diesel motor fired in the fork lift and the smell of exhaust filled the broiling air as the machine lurched toward Danny, lying in the dirt. The bullets kept getting closer, until the assailants realized that the fork lift was going to block their view of Danny. As the fork lift sped up, the bullets began spitting at the lift controls. Mick was running alongside, steering it from a secure position even as sparks flew around his hands. "Danny," Mick hollered, "get the hell out of the way. I'll cover you."

Danny rolled under the bed of the truck and out the other side, pulled out the .38 Miguel had given him, aimed at the sedan, and pumped the trigger. For a moment, he thought his shots were missing, but he quickly realized that something was dreadfully wrong. Even amidst the volleys of gunfire, he could tell that there had been no report from his pistol, nor any recoil. He popped out the cylinder and dumped out the shells. But even as they dropped to the dirt, Danny saw the problem—the firing pin had been filed away, so that the weapon was rendered inoperative. Danny had only the briefest moment to offer up one curse for himself for being so careless and naive as to have failed to test-fire the weapon before needing it. He offered a second curse for the treachery of Miguel and the Devils, who clearly anticipated that Danny's trip might involve some serious confrontation, and wanted to make sure that if such confrontation occurred, Danny would be, practically speaking, unarmed. His angry train of thought was interrupted by another bullet's piercing the truck three inches from his head. Danny tossed the .38 in the weeds just as the sedan began squealing toward the corner. He clawed desperately at his bedroll to retrieve the ivory-handled 9mm Browning, finding it just as a bullet hit the bedroll, knocking it out of his hands. Holding the Browning tightly, Danny half ran, half crawled to the opposite end of the rig as Mick rounded the corner of the truck, and the sedan squealed past the chain-link fence. The late '60s, slammed-to-the-ground, Chevy with tinted windows churned down the dirt alley, spewing rounds from an assault rifle thrust out the window.

The first bullet blew a hole in the tailgate, 6 inches from where Mick was heading. Danny came around the opposite side of the tailgate as another bullet shattered Mick's taillight. Danny went down on one knee and fired on the sedan, his first bullet blowing out the passenger-side window, and the next piercing the rear window 4 inches below the protruding barrel. Danny tried to center himself, to stay calm, and to aim accurately, but the car sped up and disappeared around the corner of the warehouse. Mick lay in the dust and Danny ran to his side.

"You OK, you hit?" Danny asked frantically.

"Takes more than a couple of lowlifes in a Chevy to kill me," Mick said, getting to his feet and dusting himself off. "You've only been here a half hour. Word gets out fast." Mick raised his eyebrows, and his piercing blue eyes ground into Danny's.

"I've got to get the fuck out of here, before they come back," Danny said, his face half covered in dirt, the redness of the constant sun shining on his forehead. He was tired, his shoulders drooped, his resolve dwindled, while his confusion increased.

"Listen, you're beat," Mick said. "Stay at my place tonight, get some rest, kick some ass tomorrow."

"I can't risk staying with you," Danny said. "They might come back—obviously, somebody knew I was here." He looked suspiciously at the scruffy biker coming out of the office to see what had happened. "I'm going somewhere safe for the night, but you'll hear from me. I won't forget what you did."

"It was nothin'," Mick spouted. "Hell, you saved my dusty ass during the next round. And if I ain't mistaken, you scored some hits."

They shook hands, Danny rolled his patch into the bedroll, threw it over his shoulder, stuffed the warm 9mm semi-auto in his waistband at the small of his back, and walked out the gate, around the perimeter of the fence, following the tracks of the sedan.

Mick watched him with a certain degree of envy. He knew what Danny was facing. He too had endured the rigors of warring clubs in his younger days. He watched Danny round the corner of the fence in this blistering Bakersfield heat, his shoulders burning under the sun, his tank top torn, his oil-stained Levis covered in dust, his thick, sandy-blond hair knotted and tangled from the wind. But his muscles rippled, and his forehead was furrowed with questions. Mick knew this man had heart, and he wasn't going to let up until he had answers.

Danny walked to the end of the block, past the faded tin warehouse, to the corner where the car had stopped momentarily. Fresh blood dripped in the dirt grooves of the alley, wetting the tips of his fingers when he touched it. The car had turned north, so Danny faced south, walking briskly for two blocks to Calloway, then left, east, toward the hills.

Looking over his shoulder, and walking backwards from time to time, Danny kept up the fast pace for Rosedale Avenue. At the main intersection, he found a pay phone strapped to a post on the corner. He walked to it and lifted the receiver, immediately dropping it when it proved to be hot enough to burn his hand. "Shit," he murmured. "Sonuvabitch."

Danny thought about the call, the only one he would make, the only number he knew. None of the members had given him a card or phone number. The only one he had was Dixie's, and he was beginning to form doubts about her. But it couldn't be, he thought, remembering how she sobbed when he left. Big flowing tears ran over her plump cheeks, her eyes deep pools of concern. She whimpered as if about to lose him forever, and her troubled eyebrows were furrowed with anxiety. He saw honesty in her soft eyes then ... or did he? He looked at the receiver hanging by the cord in the stifling heat. Taking out one of his leather gloves from his back pocket, he used it to insulate his hand from the sizzling black plastic. He returned it to its cradle, and passed on the call.

Danny crossed the street and went into a gas station to look at a map. Sweat dripped in his eyes as he tried to figure out where the hell he was, or what the fuck he planned to do. He drank a bottle of water and bought a candy bar, concerned about dipping into his limited budget. The water didn't stop the sweat running into his eyes, and he used his grimy bandanna to dab at his burning blue eyes.

The map was taped to the window separating the station's service area from the office. The sun had faded and dehydrated the paper until it had the look of cracked parchment. Danny studied it, as if it might reveal some answers to his perplexing questions. Nothing seemed to add up. He needed to get to Fresno, but he couldn't walk up 99.

"Hey, mister," the teenage attendant said. "Ya dropped

these. Can I help ya find something?" The freckle-faced kid in the Grateful Dead ball cap handed Danny the pack of matches from Dolly's restaurant in Gorman. Danny opened the bright red flap, already faded from the sun, and saw Elizabeth's phone number.

"Thanks, kid," Danny said, eyeing the youngster in the Texaco shirt. "You may have saved more than the day." The kid brightened, and Danny could smell the aroma of marijuana emanating from the kid's breath and clothes. "Where's your phone?" Danny asked.

"By the heads at the back of the building," the kid answered. "Wanna smoke a joint?"

"Let's see how this call goes first," Danny replied heading for the phone. Donning his gloves, he picked up the receiver, dialed, and fed in the change. The phone rattled and pinged, then he heard it ring.

"Dolly's restaurant." The voice sounded feminine, but seasoned and old.

"Is Elizabeth there?" Danny said trying not to allow expectation filter into his voice.

"She may have left already." The voice sounded irritated. "Her shift ended fifteen minutes ago."

"Could you check?" Danny asked, trying to console and cajole simultaneously. "It would mean a lot to me."

"This isn't her husband, is it?" The woman's voice brightened somewhat.

"No," Danny returned. "And I'm nothing like him."

"Hold on." Danny heard the woman put the phone down on the counter.

"Elizabeth!" Danny could hear the woman shouting out the door of the diner, and he waited for what seemed an eternity before sensing a door opening.

"Hell;o," Elizabeth said, in a voice riddled with trepidation.

"Elizabeth, this is Danny," he said. "I'm the biker in the restaurant this morn—"

"Danny," she interrupted him, "are you all right? I was worried."

"No, I'm not," Danny said. "And I need a place to hide. Can you help me?"

"Yes," she said without hesitation. "Where are you?"

"I'm at the corner of Rosedale and Calloway, but I can't stay in town," Danny replied.

"See if you can get to the junction of Highway 65 and Famoso Road," she said quietly into the phone. "There's an abandoned grocery store there. Out back are a couple of pepper trees where I used to have ice cream with my mom when I was a kid. Wait there for me. I live in Pine Flat. No one will bother you there. Most people don't even know how to get there. I'll be there about 5 p.m."

"Are you sure it's okay?" Danny asked. "It's been—"

"I suspected," she interrupted again. "I've been listening to the news. Someone died in a shoot-out an hour ago. You better move." She hung up without waiting for good-byes.

Danny hung up, hearing sirens blaring off in the distance. He picked up the bedroll and headed back to the map with the kid following him. "Hey, aren't you gonna smoke a joint with me?" the kid asked.

"Save me one. I'll be back in a couple of days," Danny said, still walking. "Which way to Highway 65?"

"Just go down to Fruitvale and hang a left," the kid happily offered. "It's not too far. Ain't ya got a car?"

"Nope," Danny said, turning his back on the kid and walking briskly to the busy intersection. "Had a motorcycle, but it's gone."

The kid looked stunned. He too had been following the police reports about the mayhem on the highway all day, and he wondered if this could be the guy whose motorcycle was left in flames on the off ramp. He twisted the thin, crumpled joint in his hands and watched the grubby, young biker walk on down the street. His imagination roared even before he took his first puff.

Danny walked hard—a difficult task with one boot heel gone and his feet hurting. The flesh wound in his neck burned, his motorcycle was gone, and he had only 180 bucks in his pocket. Indeed, he was a man without a club, a home, and perhaps, a girlfriend. He needed answers. One other aspect of his tenuous life troubled him—several people were desperately trying to kill him.

Danny's vulnerability haunted him as he walked along, lost in thought. A cop car appeared and slowed down, rolling alongside him. Danny froze. He was packing, he was a convicted felon out of his probation region, and he had been involved in two, maybe three, felonies so far that day. When the cruiser sped up again, Danny's knees almost buckled, and when a lowered pickup cruised by slowly, Danny knew he needed to get off Rosedale, a busy, major thoroughfare, with two lanes going in each direction, and a median 25 feet wide. Almost all the commercial and industrial buildings were set back from the curb to allow for parking lots, and the sun was still blazing hot. He felt like a lone shrimp, about to fry on a skillet. He crossed the thoroughfare, and walked down a side street to a small, dusty one-laner that paralleled Rosedale.

He walked more aware now, more keen to movements around him. He moved his Browning to an easily reachable spot inside the bedroll. The houses around him were built in the mid-'50s, boxes of stucco and wood, extremely small and faded. Multiple families lived in these tiny, scorched cracker boxes, most of which sported swamp coolers in windows and on roofs. The hard-working cooler dripped water, rust, and mildew on roofs and down the sides of the building. Danny wandered past one unruly lawn after another. Dented and abandoned cars and pickups were strewn across the lawns of houses that hadn't been repainted in 15 years.

Danny walked faster. He managed to remain centered throughout the day, but his resolve was fading, and his fear was rising. Looking at his reflection in the sideview mirror of a parked car, he saw the battered, road-worn image of himself. Caked blood clung to the back of his tank top, road rash coated one arm, and asphalt had ripped holes in his Levis and left red bloodstains along the tattered edges. He was soiled with dust and grime from his boots to his tangled mass of sandy hair. He pulled a the knotted strands with his free hand and continued walking.

Walking briskly past another car, he noticed a ragged bedroll and the length of hemp twine forming the shoulder strap. For a brief moment, Danny saw a homeless man, destitute, lost in a strange town reflected back at him from the car's side windows. Then he passed a biker's home. It was destroyed, from the split door and tattered screens, tot he motorcycles nd trucks parked in he small, sunburnt yard.

Danny scanned the dump until his gaze fell on the garage, and the four men sitting on bikes and benches drinking beer.

The four Mexican riders topped drinking as Danny walked past. One of the men said something to a smaller one, and he went in the house. The other two overheard the conversation and fearful expressions crossed their faces. Danny had learned to read people, and he knew instantly from the exchange that he had been recognized. At first, he thought about running for it, but his prison instructor, and even before that, when trained with Officer Black, he learned that one of the first rules of close-quarter combat is "Attack the attacker."

Danny stopped and turned toward the three men standing in the shade of the garage. As he did, the eight rules of close-quarter combat rolled through his mind: "Fight dirty, attack the attacker, attack vital areas, momentum of attack, simplicity of attack, expect to get hurt, mental preparation, and don't go down." Something clicked in Danny, and he was ashamed for his moments of self-doubt. It angered him to have lowered himself to the low levels of his environment. He was mad.

Danny had seen the biggest of the crew start down the driveway, but when he turned, the man hesitated and stopped. Danny let the bedroll drop to the ground in a cloud of dust. The yard was surrounded by a 4-foot chain link fence that was bent and rusting, The gates hung loosely on their hinges, but were chained shut. Danny took the top galvanized rail in both hands and vaulted the short fence to face the man "You got a problem with me walking down your street?" he asked challengingly.

"I got a problem with any gringo in my part of town," the big Mexican with the 19-inch arms said, in his best menacing voice.

Danny kept walking toward him until he was in striking distance. "That's too bad," Danny said, flying into a fighting stance and striking the big slob in the neck with a claw punch. The flabby Mexican grabbed his throat just as Danny kicked him in the balls with a snapped slap kick, then split his nose with a palm hand-thrust. The man passed out, and Danny leapt to the side as he collapsed to the dirt driveway, face first. Another south of the border biker charged into the fray, wielding a pool cue. As he drew back to swing, Danny ran at the man, trapped the cue, and hit him three times. The remaining rider bolted for the house.

Inside the ramshackle garage, a Los Cuchillos flag hung from the rafters. Danny found a can of gas in the corner, and splashed some of the contents on the pool table, then ran for the other exit. As he crossed the yard, bullets sang out from the interior.

"You're going to come out one way or another," Danny shouted. "Come out on your own, and let's do it like men. Ya got 30 seconds." Danny began to count as he rounded the corner to the front door, pouring the liquid on the front porch, then darting to the back door. In the 100-degree heat, with not so much as a drop of humidity in the still air, the gasoline began to evaporate into the atmosphere immediately, and as the thick waves left the surface and floated alongside the house, the smell filled the area. It was the smell of danger, like a leaky gas stove. Danny found the back door alongside an exposed water heater. He sought to stay clear of the pilot light as bullets crashed out of the small window in the kitchen. Whoever was shooting wasn't taking the time to aim. The semi-automatic rounds tore into the adjacent house, followed by screaming. Danny had hit a zone. He was poised, moving carefully with grace and tone, but he was mad.

When Danny reached the count of 30, he spun and rolled in the dry lawn on his return trip around the house, pulled the truck stop matches out of his pocket, and while lying on the ground face down, with bullets flying out of the living room windows, and glass shattering overhead, he folded the flap of the matches behind the sulfur heads, lit the whole squadron of fire makers, tossed it against the front door, and rolled away from the building. The front of the cracker box house exploded in a ball of fire, and a ripple of the flames followed a path along the lawn to the garage. Like the explosions before top dead center in an engine, the blast lifted the roof off the garage.

Danny rolled toward the gate, jumped to his sore feet, and leapt the fence. He grabbed his bedroll and ran, hearing squealing tires coming closer from the opposite direction. Danny rounded the corner into an alley as he heard the water heater blow, and screams from the interior as the house became engulfed in flames. The explosion in the garage drove a ball of fire into the house through a flimsy interior garage door. The biker with the automatic weapon was on his knees on the rusty, inoperative dryer, pointing the rifle out the window above him as the flames swept him off the porcelain top and onto the floor.

The Mexican on the phone heard the first explosion and hung up at once. Emilio had instructed him and his cohorts to hold the gringo at the house until they arrived. He dropped the receiver as the first blast took out the front door, and he headed to the kitchen as the front door swung open and flames licked their way into the interior of the house. The heat and the capacity of the flames to ignite anything flammable caused small explosions until the whole living room was ablaze. Miko, the snitch on the phone, moved quickly through the glass in the kitchen to the side door. He could feel the blast-furnace heat chase him, the smell of gasoline now mixed with burning filth and soiled fabric. His lungs burned and malfunctioned. He gagged, reaching for the door, but as he turned the knob in desperation to breathe the fresh air outside, he heard a crack, sounding like the shell of a large egg splitting. Instantly, the door burst open, slamming him to the floor against the old, rusting refrigerator. In a reflex movement, Danny extended his hands to break his fall. The jagged shards of sharp glass sliced his palms, pierced his Levi's, and cut his thighs as the water heater exploded next to the open door. The small service porch ignited immediately, and the metal frame of the screen door melted before Miko's very eyes. As the flames crept inside the kitchen, he attempted to stand. But as he pushed his hands against the deck, lancets of glass pierced the calluses and fatty tissue of his palms to break apart against his bones. He screamed and thrashed about uncontrollably, and yet more glass cut into his thighs and knees. Then the smoke from myriad chemicals and plastics burning in the living room came into contact with the new kitchen flames. Miko couldn't breathe in the toxic atmosphere filling the room, and as he attempted to crawl in the glass, unaware which way to turn, the room exploded in a spectacular meeting of fire from the kitchen and dense chemical fumes from the living room. The house had almost burnt to the ground as two carloads of Los Cuchillos pulled up in front.

Danny ran down the alley with his bedroll flapping behind him. His feet were killing him, making running excruciatingly difficult. Cutting over to another street, he spotted Fruitvale. As he walked down the alley, trying to stay out of sight, he spotted a barber shop, vacant except for the old coot who ran the joint. The 68-year-old, balding man in his white, professional barber's smock sat reading a newspaper in air-conditioned comfort. Danny ducked inside, startling the old man with his bruised and cut body, as well as his filthy clothes smelling of gasoline and burnt wood. Clearly, the barber was shocked. "Ain't got enough in the till to make donations today, son," the old man said, folding his paper.

"I got cash, pops," Danny responded, pulling a wad of twenties from his pocket. "Just clean me up quick. I gotta meet my girl."

"Sure, son," the old man said, eyeing the money. "You been working on a construction site?"

"Yes sir," Danny replied. "You might say that. A wall caved in on us, so I quit."

A small television across from Danny on a narrow coffee table strewn with magazines was dispensing the news. "Mind if I leave the set on?" the old man asked. "There's some kind of motorcycle gang war going on, and I've been following it."

Danny noticed the black and white television for the first time as he rummaged through his bedroll for a clean T-shirt. Just as he pulled one out, a good-looking Hispanic woman came on the screen. "We interrupt our regular programming for this special report. What began as just another blistering Bakersfield day has turned into a countywide manhunt and war between rival outlaw biker factions."

"Actually, if you don't mind," Danny said, leaning over and turning off the set, "I'd like a little quiet for a few minutes. They'll cover the same shit all day long anyway." Danny rummaged everywhere in his bedroll, but every T-shirt he pulled out bore some kind of motorcycle insignia or commemorated some biking event. The first he pulled out had "Snitches Are A Dying Breed" silk screened on the black surface. The next was a "Support Your Local Devils Own" shirt. Frustrated, Danny asked, "Is there a fitness store close by? I need another pair of running shoes." He tried to keep the veteran barber occupied with anything other than bikers, but the old guy could hardly miss the blood-soaked biker tank top he was wearing, and his black boots and belt.

"Yeah, just down the street on the right," the barber said.

Since his survival depended on concealing his biker background and club affiliation, Danny decided that his long hair implied those connections to the local yokels, especially in a town currently ass-deep in a biker crises. It was time to make a change. Cruisers and fire trucks poured in from all directions while the old man chopped at Danny's hair and shaved away his stubble, leaving his face clean, except for a shortened, well-manicured mustache. Finally, the old guy couldn't hold it in any longer. "Say, son, you a biker?"

"No way," Danny replied. "There were lots of bikers working the construction site. One of them gave me the T-shirt. Hell, no self-respecting biker would be caught dead on foot." The barber chuckled at Danny's joke, although he wasn't entirely convinced by his denial.

"So far today," the old guy remarked, continuing to shave the back of Danny's neck, "they've killed four members of the Los Cuchillos. That's a big motorsickle gang around here, case you don't know."

"Who did it?" Danny asked, uneasily.

"The authorities don't know whether it's another gang or not," the old haircutter replied. "Personally, I wish they'd take all those bastards out in a field, and shoot the whole lot."

Danny bristled as the old man finished. He paid his bill, and looked in the mirror quickly. The man had given him a short, but full, businessman's haircut, a shampoo, and had trimmed and shaved his face. "Thank you, son," he said, as Danny tipped him. "Uh ... it's none of my business, but you don't want to be mistaken for a biker. Just to be safe, you might want to go out my back door to the alley. The fitness store has a back entrance too, and there's also a gym upstairs." The old man gave Danny a conspiratorial wink as he showed him the back door to the small shop.

Danny felt better, but under pressure as he made his way down the alley to the fitness store. With each step, he felt dangerously conspicuous. Danny stashed his bedroll behind a trash container belonging to the fitness store, taking only his cash. The haircut cost 15 bucks, and was well worth it, but his budget was tight. He was down to $160 now. Inside the store, he headed first to the clothing and T-shirt racks, grabbing a small assortment of black workout gear, the cheapest they sold, and headed toward the change rooms. He tried on black workout shorts, a set of long sweat pants, also black, and a couple of inexpensive, black T-shirts. He ditched his street clothes in a store bag and left the dressing room wearing the new clothes, his biker identity hidden. He grabbed a package of black cotton socks, then, still wearing his boots, he made a beeline for the training shoes department. Danny looked odd wearing black sweat pants, a black T-shirt, and biker boots, but he quickly removed his battered boots, slipped on a pair of new cotton socks, and tried on running shoes, quickly and efficiently. He selected the third pair he tried on. With the additional purchase of a gym bag, the total came to just over $92. He flinched, paid the bill, and headed for the gym. The upstairs training facility was packed as he walked up to the desk, inhaling the smells of clean, new carpet, sex, and sweat, mingled in an almost hospital-like facility. He wanted to stay.

"Can I help you?" the young attendant asked, eyeing the tall, good-looking man as Danny took in her petite, perfectly shaped form.

"Yes, I'd like a towel and a one-day pass," Danny replied.

"We don't generally have one-day passes," she said, professionally.

"Well, I'm just visiting town for a couple of days," Danny said, disappointed. "Hey, does it count that I just spent 90 bucks downstairs?"

She looked deeply into his blue eyes and said, "Sure, why not?" She handed Danny a towel and a locker key. "Enjoy yourself, and if there's anything I can do, don't hesitate to ask."

Danny looked at her smooth-as-a-baby's-ass features, and knew he was right about staying. He threw his towel over his shoulder, and walked to the well-kept showers. Inside, he stripped and showered, examining his wounds in the process, which didn't appear to be serious. The Mexican's knife had cut a shallow flesh wound, and his road rash and bruises wouldn't kill him. Nonetheless, he knew from the multitude of scrapes and bruises that he would be plenty sore the next morning. Danny looked at the clock on the tiled wall, and then at the pristine facility he could train in. The equipment was freshly finished, and there were a surprising number of Nautilus machines, free weights, and punching bags to work on. He hadn't hit the gym or performed his strict katas since his last day in the joint, and he was already feeling the slack in his muscles. Danny knew that time was running out. The clock indicated that he had less than two hours to skirt through the streets of Oildale, on the outskirts of Bakersfield, without getting arrested or shot, in order to rendezvous with Elizabeth. He didn't even know how far he had to go, or if she would actually be there when he arrived. Not one to wait passively for something to happen, he dressed and went back to the small blonde at the reception desk. "Could you tell me how far it is to James Road and Highway 65?" Danny asked.

"About seven miles," she answered.

"Might as well ask directions, if you don't mind my asking," Danny said.

"Another couple of blocks on Fruitvale, you'll hit Olive which leads into the roughest section of Oildale," she said, cooing slightly. Danny felt the connection. "Go right on Olive until it hits James, and turn left. What's out there? I've never been to that area in my life, and I was born here."

"Oil," Danny shot back. "What else?"

"You're right," she returned.

"I don't have much time," Danny said, holding out his hand to her, "but I want to thank you for all your help." He bowed slightly, and turned, walking toward the thick wrestling mats in front of a wall of mirrors. He found his emotions taking a roller coaster ride, and he needed to center himself.

He sat Indian-style, with his heels tucked into his thighs, and closed his eyes. He allowed himself 15 minutes before he had to leave. For two minutes, he meditated, palms up in his lap, eyes shut, clearing his mind. His brain cells whirled with unanswered questions, but he was taught by Tong in prison not to dwell on problems, but to take your mind away from them for new and clear perspectives.

After two minutes, he stretched and rehearsed five katas

four times apiece, then stretched again, and quickly returned to the showers. He showered again, and pulled on a pair of black sweat pants, the training shoes, and black socks. He loaded the extra tank top and shorts into the gym bag, and thanked the young blonde once more. Behind the building, he retrieved the bedroll and unrolled it. Taking his extra skivvies, he rolled them in the gym clothes, then put the clothes in the bag. The heavy 9mm went into the bag's only outside pocket. He stretched briefly, then tied the pack on his back and began to jog.

Danny could feel his muscles resist the movement, and the bruises flared, but he knew his options were few. As he put one foot in front of another on the hot concrete, his body began to respond, loosen, and pick up the pace.

Meditation always worked for Danny. For him, it was like a drug to the anxiety-ridden, a plan for the frustrated, and answers for the curious. He felt a certain cunning come over him like confidence returning to a wounded mountain cat. He liked the feel of the sneakers on his feet, the looseness of the clothing, and soon a natural rhythm took over. The town seemed to be in a state of siege, as emergency vehicles and cop cars sped past him. He could sense the presence of plainclothes cops in unmarked sedans cruising along Fruitvale by the way they drove—like human street sweepers looking for discarded bodies lying in the gutters. He was thankful that he had no visible tattoos.

Jogging like this was a daily ritual, and he paid no attention to the cops or to the occasional lowered truck or van as he crossed Fruitvale to the right, and caught Olive Drive. The neighborhood seemed to deteriorate as he left Bakersfield and skirted Oildale. The homes were smaller, of poorer quality, and badly maintained. Many had been abandoned and vacant since the oil crisis. The industry seemed in disarray as the prices skyrocketed. Danny continued to pump his legs, and he began to sweat freely as he made his way toward James Road. Crossing the intersection of Olive and Pegasus Drive, he heard more sirens, all headed in his direction, but it took a moment to determine where they came from. Then he heard rubber tearing against pavement, followed by the sound of a car coming up from behind him on Olive from

Fruitvale. On his right, old dogs behind poorly maintained homes howled in canine harmony, kids abandoned their television sets and spilled out onto front porches and lawns to see what had happened in their small town of 25,000. Danny didn't dare turn around for fear of being recognized, but the sounds and excitement made his body tense, and sharpened his senses. He concentrated all his energy on the vibrations of the first car, an old '62 Ford Econoline van, painted primer gray, that passed him, closely followed by an unmarked Plymouth cop car painted a dull bronze, trailed by two black-and-whites. The van attempted to turn left on Pegasus, but the driver hesitated and hit the brakes.

Danny had just reached the intersection and he could see the horror in the eyes of the biker riding shotgun. Watching the vehicle squeal into the turn, Danny prayed that it would make it, and take the pursuing cops far down the road. But once the truck began its abrupt turn and the brake lights flashed, he knew that it was in trouble. He watched the left wheels lift and the van tumble over on its side, showering the pavement with sparks. Immediately, the hot night air filled with the smell of gasoline and the sirens were momentarily drowned out by the sounds of tearing metal, shattering glass, and the screech of steel against concrete.

The cops slid to a stop behind the overturned van, the three vehicles forming a barrier around the wrecked Econoline. "Get out with your hands up—now!" one cop shouted over a bullhorn, his adrenaline level peaking. The smell of fuel, rubber, and exhaust filled the air as the other cops took positions over their hoods and trunks, weapons drawn. An officer left the scene and walked directly toward Danny. "You!" he said, excitedly. "I'll have to ask you–" Danny looked directly into the cop's eyes and stopped running. He froze momentarily, trying to determine what the man wanted. A crowd of kids and onlookers gathered on the sidewalk around Danny. The cop spread out his arms and waved them. "Everybody needs to move back," he barked, authoritatively. "And you kids need to go back in your houses. This is a dangerous situation."

Danny saw his clue and turned to face the kids. "Come on," he said, the picture of a cooperative citizen. "Do like the officer said. Move back—way back. C'mon, let's move it." The kids were mesmerized by the smoldering vehicle lying on its side in the middle of the intersection. They had watched the reports on television, and wanted desperately to be part of the exploding saga in their otherwise dull town.

"You in the van," the cop called over the bullhorn. "you don't have much time. Your vehicle may explode at any moment. Show us your hands and get out of the van slowly. Don't make us do this the hard way. It's your choice—you have one minute."

Some squealing and arguing could be heard inside the van, then the rear door popped open, and an assault rifle clattered to the pavement, followed by a stout member of the Los Cuchillos. Danny stared at the young man for a frozen instant, then turned back to the kids who were slowly backing away. The outlaw was one from the rent-a-car on the highway. He was bruised and bleeding. Shortly, another member emerged. Soon, four Los Cuchillos faced the sideways roof of the van with their legs spread and a cache of automatic rifles, ammunition, and various pistols were laid out on the hot asphalt. A fire truck arrived, and the firefighters sprayed the engine compartment with foam.

Danny knew he had to move, but the officers had taped off the corner, making it awkward for him to fade into the night. He had to avoid acting suspicious around all these keyed-up cops. The police and the firefighters set up barricades, blocking Pegasus Street to through traffic. Cars were cruising slowly down adjacent streets, the people inside checking out the action and turning around to go past the scene again. A uniformed cop stood in the center of each merging road, directing traffic. Danny was running out of time. He studied the young uniformed cop motioning to traffic eastbound on Pegasus. The rookie officer was obviously involved in one of his first major cases and was very pumped, breathing so fast in the heat that he seemed in danger of passing out, especially wearing that navy blue uniform. Danny turned and spied an old Mexican woman returning to her home. "Excuse me, ma'am," Danny said, accosting her on the lawn. "*Agua, por favor?*" The squat woman with the mass of straight salt-and-pepper hair pulled into a long ponytail nodded, and motioned for Danny to follow her. He took a long drink of the icy liquid in her neat kitchen, and made gestures, asking for permission to take the glass out to the policeman,

"Aqua para policia?"

She nodded again, and he bolted for the door with the frosty glass. When he reached the curb, the street was open, and he waved for the officer to come to him. "Here, man," Danny said, holding out the glass of water, "you need to take a few slow breaths, or you'll pass out in this heat."

The neophyte cop had only recently graduated from the Sheriff's Academy in Los Angeles, and his insecurity and uncertainty were obvious as he looked Danny over carefully. In his jogging togs and with Danny's build, the officer figured he was some fitness expert, and he actually tried to slow his breathing. He gulped at the water.

"Not so fast, officer." Danny said, smiling broadly. "Looks as though you have everything under control here. By the way, I was jogging along here when all hell broke lose—could I impose on you to escort me across the street, so I can get moving again and out of your hair?"

"Sure, come on," the gullible young cop said, lifting the yellow police line ribbon allowing Danny to duck under it with no possibility that anyone could think he was trying to slip away without police permission.

"That glass belongs to the old woman in the house there," Danny informed the cop, pointing out the small bungalow on the corner.

As Danny turned to face the painted walkway across the intersection, he glanced over at the van just as the handcuffed outlaws were being placed into patrol cars. As each of the four was pulled away from the van, he faced Danny and the officer crossing the street. Danny glanced over, and inadvertently looked straight into the eyes of the stocky biker from the highway, the Cuchillo who he saw reach for a gun in the back seat as Danny fought to maintain control of his bike. For a second, they were frozen in eye contact. Danny wanted to avert his eyes, but any sign of cowardice would have inflamed the tough guy, and given him even more reason to hate Danny. So he stared at the man as if he was marked for

Danny's next victim. If the biker had uttered a word, Danny intended to cross the tape in front of the entire world, and tear his throat out. The man was stunned to recognize the clean-cut guy walking with the cop as Danny. But when one of the officers pushed him toward the patrol car, and eye contact was broken, the prisoner began to speak. "I'll get you, you goddam—" He attempted to shout and turn again toward Danny, but was unceremoniously shoved into the patrol car. Danny took advantage of the broken stare and hustled to the curb with his back intentionally toward the Los Cuchillos. The commotion caught the attention of the officer escorting Danny, and he turned toward the noise. The young Mexican's shouts were muffled behind the cop car window. He struggled against the handcuffs and seat belt. Muffled, but distinct enough to understand, came the words, "You killed my brothers!"

The cop looked at the biker, then tried to follow his gaze, as Danny ducked under the tape on the opposite end of the intersection and began to jog away.

Chapter 18

FRESNO FURY

As the sun began to set and the rich, fiery hues streaked the bright blue sky like the fire of war shattering the tranquillity of the blue Pacific, the clam-baked Central Valley was exploding in turmoil. Every off-duty cop for 200 miles had been called in to man surveillance teams on the Los Cuchillos. The FBI had sent a team from the Bay Area, and the DEA flew in a squad from Los Angeles. Terrified that they were witnessing the beginning of an all-out war, police agencies attempted to run down and watch every known member of the Los Cuchillos. Pito Flores, the acknowledged president of the group, had been taken in for questioning.

Emilio and a group of his followers were hiding out in the warehouse district of Fresno, since the focus of the investigation was Bakersfield. Those members, including Emilio, who weren't being watched, set up a police scanner in an abandoned freight station next to the Southern Pacific Railroad tracks, two blocks from Emilio's warehouse. Four members of the Los Cuchillos sat on milk crates in the vast, filthy building. They pulled their bikes and cars inside, and shut the massive cargo doors. It was still hot in the dark, empty, wooden-slate structure. Emilio sat and listened to the scanner flip from one law enforcement frequency to another. Emergency vehicles were still being called to the fire in Oildale. Other cars had been dispatched to the homes of known Los Cuchillos in Bakersfield, and the tentacles of the law were beginning to reach north. Shit was happening fast, and pressure was mounting from the Devils Own chapters to the north.

Emilio stood up, and dust clouds exploded around his polished boots on the hard-packed dirt-and-concrete floor upon which rested uncountable millions of hay bales over the years. Now and then, a rat ran across the long expanse of the building, scurrying to another hideaway. Bats lived in the wooden, webbed structure far above the men's heads. Any sudden movement caused them to screech and chirp. "Don, you watch the front door for cops," Emilio said, motioning him to the opposite end of the building. "Marko, keep an eye on the rear, while I discuss our next move with Romeo." Emilio turned up the volume on the scanner, and it hissed and squawked, jumping from one frequency to another. "I got two phone calls we need to talk about. One from the Devils Own, who want this bullshit over with, and one from Al. He was arrested in the crashed van in Bakersfield. He said he saw our boy in a jogging suit."

"Is he sure?" Romeo jumped in.

"He says he is, says he looked him right in the eyes," Emilio replied. "We've got to get this shit wrapped up, or we're gonna have more trouble than we'll know what to do with. This *gringo* asshole is being hunted all over the valley. I say we hit Pito when they release him. The cops will blame it on the *gringo*, and we can forget that white bastard. Let him live, he'll never get out of this valley without being arrested. And they'll blame him for everything that went down today."

Romeo sat on his milk crate and held a cold longneck Bud in two fingers, rolling it back and forth. He took a sip, brushed back his long, tangled hair, and pulled on his scruffy black beard. "We haven't had much luck getting rid of that shithead gringo," Romeo observed. "He must be one lucky motherfucker. Either that, or smart." He paused for a moment, then said, "I like your plan. We can let the cops take care of him. He's too much trouble, and we're losing too many members over him. Let's just end it. When will the cops cut Pito loose?"

"Not sure," Emilio said. "Maybe late tonight, or in the morning. I told him that we'd pick him up, but he wanted that punk Gil Luna to do it. He said we're too hot these days."

"Where's Gil?" Romeo asked.

"He's at home, with his fat ol' lady and his kids," Emilio said. "Isn't one of these guys friendly with him?"

"Yeah, Marko over there," Romeo said, setting the bottle of beer on the dust-covered floor, then pulling and snapping open his Buck knife. He tested the sharpness of the knife by shaving some of the hairs off the back of his hand before beginning to clean his dirty fingernails with the point. "Maybe we need to have a party." Romeo raised his dark eyes to Emilio's in a knowing look.

"Hey, Marko," Emilio shouted, his words echoing down the vast length of the huge building, "come over here." The young biker broke into a jog at the summons.

Marko was a young and inexperienced member. In the club for less than a year, he was unaware of the ropes—as in hangman's nooses—tied to the lifestyle. He had joined for the brotherhood he read about in biker magazines, and for the pride of wearing the Cuchillo patch. "Whaddaya need?" Marko asked, obligingly. Of average build, with long, straight hair over a clean-cut face, Marko stood 5 feet 8 inches tall, and had only recently turned 25. He could fight with his fists, and would die for any club brother. His creed was simple: The Los Cuchillos stuck together as a hard-core brotherhood, picked on by law enforcement, cowboys, rednecks, and *gringo* truck drivers. It was the Los Cuchillos against these *gavacho* motherfuckers, and that was the end of it. As far as he was concerned, the Los Cuchillos were the good guys. They rode hard, played hard, and fought hard for their brothers and families. He had a lot to learn.

"Is your pickup clean?" Emilio asked Marko. "That punk is causing more shit—"

"I wish I could get my hands on him," Marko interrupted, puffing out his small chest against his white Los Cuchillos T-shirt, and pulling on his denim cutoff vest.

"You may still get your chance," Emilio assured him. "We need to talk to Gil Luna. Could you go find him and bring him here? Tell him we can't use the phones, but there's more trouble in Bakersfield."

"Sure," Marko said, turning to the task immediately. He ran to his compact Ford pickup, jumped in, and fired up the engine in a single aim-to-please hustle. "Back in a half an hour." Another member opened the door, and Marko pulled into the street, showering his door-holding brother with dust and dirt.

Gil was one of the older members of the Los Cuchillos, an outlaw from the old school, a maverick rider before the media discovered its fascination with the anti-social, violent subculture of biker life. He ran a few scams when he was younger, got loaded as much as possible, pushed people around, and collected money for pot dealers. But that was a long time ago. Now, with his collection of kids, a wife, and a small, frame house on a tree-lined street in the suburbs, he had become legit. All the family crap had rubbed off on the big outlaw, and he wanted the club to follow suit. So he lobbied for less self-destructive activities, a more family-oriented organization, and fewer bullies in the club. His political agenda was routinely wadded up and tossed in the trash with the beer bottles—when he wasn't around.

Marko rolled to a stop in front of Gil's house, and one of Gil's kids dashed outside to greet him. "Marko, where's your bike?" the youngest of the clan hollered, excitedly. Little Franko was barely eight years old, but already he loved to see the bikes pull up in front of his dad's house. He loved the smell, the powerful sound, and the way the neighbors looked out their windows at the mean-looking men in their rough clothing.

"Where's your dad, kid?" Marko asked, roughing the kid's hair.

"He's inside," little Franko said. "I can't get him away from the television."

Marko pulled open the screen door and walked into the biker's home. It was a domestic mess with toys and children's clothing scattered everywhere, several more kids running in and out of rooms, the smell of menudo wafting from the kitchen, and a large Los Cuchillos MC flag nailed above the couch. Gil sat in a threadbare armchair and stared at the small black and white television. "I told these bastards, never to get involved with the Devils Own," he mumbled, in a gruff voice.

On the TV screen, a pretty Hispanic woman faced the camera with the van behind her. "And in another violent incident today, four members of the Los Cuchillos motorcycle gang overturned their van trying to escape the police. A search of the van produced numerous automatic assault weapons and over one thousand rounds of ammunition. Because of the violent reputation of the Los Cuchillos organization, the bomb squad was called in to partially dismantle the vehicle before it was taken to the police impound facility. Members of the club refused our request for a statement, but police say that additional arrests are expected as their investigation continues." The report cut to shots of the handcuffed bikers being loaded into patrol cars with the reporter providing the voice-over. "This is the fourth incident since the tragic accident on Highway 99 this morning. Lupe Delgado, reporting live from WCBS in Bakersfield. Back to you, Ron."

"Gil," Marko began, "something else happened in Bakersfield, and some of the brothers are meeting at the northside docks. They want your advice."

Gil, unable to resist the ego boost of his brothers needing his advice, turned to Marko and said, emphatically, "They need more than my advice. They need to get the fuck out of this state."

"Whaddaya mean, brother?" Marko asked.

"I mean just what the fuck I said," Gil snapped, getting to his feet. "These jerkoffs wind up with their ass in a crack that they can't get out of, and finally, they want my advice."

"Yeah, maybe. But still, I think you need to talk to them," Marko said, backing away from the big man, averting his eyes from Gil's.

"I'll go, goddammit," Gil said, pulling his cutoff from the back of one of the dining room chairs, and grabbing a beer from the refrigerator in the kitchen. As he put on his shades and pulled his long salt-and-pepper hair through a tie at the back of his head, he turned to Marko, "It's about time they wanted my advice. Maria," he shouted to his wife in the next room, "watch the kids. I'll be back in an hour."

Marko's truck rumbled up to the weathered wooden door at the front of the abandoned building on a vacant street in the industrial wasteland of Fresno. Ironically, this most desolate, uninhabited, section of town had more rubbish strewn along its curbs than any sleazy street downtown where throngs of pimps, whores, criminals, junkies, lunatics, and weirdoes congregated daily. Old couches, refrigerator crates, and wine bottles choked the gutters and piled up against fences like sand dunes. As they pulled up to the building, Romeo opened the creaking wooden door. Behind the thick, dark glasses in the solid black plastic frames, Romeo's eyes were hollow and cold. The man seemed to be pure menace, and he gave Gil the chills as they pulled in under the arch of the door, 25 feet above their heads. Like a colossal guillotine, the door dropped closed behind them. There were no lights in the building, the little light filtering in through the smudged skylights and cracks in the wooden slat exterior was fading fast.

Emilio lit a small Coleman lantern and placed it on the tailgate of his El Camino. The dazzling white light threw grotesque shadows along the walls and on the floor, while the steady hiss of the pressurized combustion seemed somehow ominous as night descended. Waiting in the silence of the building's vast darkness were just the two of them, Emilio and Romeo, Gil's understated enemies, the only two men who wanted to lead the club in a diametrically opposite direction from Gil's wholesome agenda. Gil didn't like the audience he came to speak to, and furthermore, the building began to stink. "Where are the other members?" Gil asked the kid who brought him to the meeting.

"Don was here when I left," Marko said. "Maybe he'll be back."

Gil thought for a moment about Marko, and was relieved to have at least one other member with him who could think for himself. Marko pulled his small pickup against one of the walls, and shut off the engine.

"I thought we were meeting with an actual group of members," Gil said, a touch of annoyance in this voice as he got out of the truck.

"Nope," Emilio said, standing up. "We need to come to an understanding with you."

"What kind of understanding?" Gil asked. "You motherfuckers have screwed up everything. Sooner or later, we'll all be arrested because of your bullshit. How the fuck will that help you and your fucking deals with the Devils Own?"

In a gesture of utter contempt, Emilio worked his jaws for a moment, then spit a bolus of saliva that landed two inches from Gil's left boot. "Fuck you, man," Emilio said. "I'm sick and tired of your chickenshit family crap. Either you're an outlaw, or a pussy motherfucker. You shouldn't be in a bike club, you should be in the Boy Scouts."

Fuming, Gil walked toward Emilio. "You miserable little

prick—you just want to take the entire club down the shithole you've dug for them."

Emilio advanced on Gil until they were face-to-face. "Kiss my *culo*, you lardass piece of refried shit," Emilio snarled. "Fuck with me, and I'll pull your fucking patch right now, and you can go back to changing diapers with that tub of guts you're married to."

Gil grabbed Emilio by the throat. "No one talks to me like that, you pencil-dick bastard. If you ever again..." Gil's voice faded away, replaced by a guttural gurgle from somewhere deep in his throat. His eyes widened in pain as Emilio's knife entered below his sternum, cut through the top of his stomach, slid underneath his ribs, and sliced through his heart. With his eyes rolled back, Gil heaved an agonized sigh, then collapsed, blood pouring from his wound onto the dirt floor beneath his lifeless body. The bats overhead sensed the violence and began to squeal and flutter about, their dark shadows dancing through the fleeting light.

"What the fuck," Marko said, coming into the light and kneeling beside his downed brother. He stood abruptly, his face flushed, tears streaming down his cheeks. He was just a kid, and Gil had been one of his wise mentors. This was alien to his heart. Brothers didn't fight brothers in his world.

"How could you do this?" he screamed "He was..."

Marko's impassioned words were cut short by a sound, an abrupt, sharp sound like the spit of an air hose disconnected from its coupling to a compressor. It came again, and the bats fluttered about wildly as young Marko pitched forward onto the floor. Two .22 magnum rounds pierced the base of his skull an inch apart, like a massive rattlesnake bite. The silencer at the end of the Ruger's barrel was about the size of a can of frozen orange juice, and it transformed the .22's report from a loud crack to a hollow pop, like the sound of a stifled sneeze. The bullets didn't explode into Marko's skull, but rather they hissed through his brain. Emilio was facing his younger brother as the first bullet exited through his sinuses, splattering Emilio with blood, bits of shredded tissue, and bone fragments. The second bullet exited through his eye socket, the eyeball exploding in a shower of bloody vitreous humor. The young rider was dead before he hit the floor.

While unscrewing the silencer from the long-barreled, .22 mag revolver, Romeo moved into the light to inspect his handiwork. "Let's get the fuck out of here," Emilio said.

"What can we leave to tie this to the *gringo*?" Romeo said.

"I got it covered," Emilio murmured, pulling from his vest five books of Dolly's Restaurant matches he picked up in Gorman. The matchbooks were held together by a rubber band, and he ignited the entire bunch, then dropped the flaming bundle to the floor of the warehouse. Emilio climbed in his El Camino as Romeo walked to the front of the building and opened the door. As they drove away, the leftover hay ignited like tinder, the flames at first hardly more than an inch or two tall, but moving inexorably across the floor toward the 50-year-old walls. Soon the interior of the building was engulfed by the fire, sending thousands of bats into a frenzied hysteria of chaotic flight, squealing and flapping their wings in terror. Rats poured out of their hiding places, scrambling across the burning floor to cracks in the walls, where they escaped into the streets.

On those same streets, two Mexican outlaws sat in silence as they drove toward the county lockup to meet with their president.

PINE FLATS

*D*anny felt a quiet stillness in the sultry air. It was still 90 degrees as he jogged toward his destination to meet Elizabeth, almost 45 minutes late. He hadn't jogged in years. In fact, he had never been an avid runner, and now his legs ached, his tank top was completely sweat-soaked, and his breathing labored like a dying water pump, chugging away after the well has run dry. A strong dose of fear kept him driving one foot out in front of the other, but he knew he couldn't keep this up much longer. He also knew that the Mexican outlaw had recognized him, and that could only mean reinforcements would be on their way. He wiped his sunburnt brow as he plodded ahead, along the desolate, deserted road.

The sun was setting, and the change of watch between the sun and the moon created an eerie stillness in the air, as if the earth was waiting for something to happen. The heat rose off the concrete in waves, and the acres and acres of hay fields gently swayed, like couples on a dance floor, waiting for the next song to begin. In spite of the pain and weariness, Danny kept moving onward with the determination of a marathon runner in training, even though he had no way of knowing if he was headed in the right direction, or if the girl would be waiting for him if and when he arrived at the agreed-upon location. The farther he got from town, the more bizarre the landscape became. Initially, Danny was impressed with the rolling fields of hay, sliced by only a single band of asphalt, a reminder of civilization's ceaseless efforts to improve and speed up transportation. Abruptly, the fields of hay ended, and acres of grapevines replaced the grain. Then, out of nowhere, oil pumping units and scattered derricks rose out of the vast, empty plains, and less than 50 feet from the road, running parallel to it, were strange-looking steel expansion pipes, with large, otherworldly loops to allow the natural gas to expand as it was pumped from the derricks to the refineries.

Danny began to feel like he was going to pass out as he struggled to run up a rise in the road. His breathing was seriously labored by the time he reached the crest, and he considered walking for a spell. A large co-generation plant tucked into the hillside like the Emerald City of Oz jumped out at Danny without warning, as though it was some strange, secret plant for making weapons or bizarre chemicals. The co-generation plant burns coal and turns turbines with steam to create power, which is transferred across the state through huge power lines. Danny was on the brink of exhaustion, although the unexpected sight of the power plant, with its myriad pipes, tubes, tall smoke stacks, and strange, lifeless-looking edifices momentarily distracted him from his otherwise acute awareness of his barely functioning body, his aching joints, and his burning lungs. He pushed ahead for another mile on this road that seemed to go nowhere. Few cars went by, and for that, Danny was glad. He no longer had the strength to watch out for cops or more outlaw bikers, and the road provided no cover to hide in case of an attack. He was open to his enemies, an easy target. Because of the heat and his exhausted condition, when the occasional truck or car passed, the pungent smell of its exhaust nauseated him, and he tried to take shallow breaths until the fumes dispersed.

Then he heard it—the unmistakable sound of a Harley, the only sound on the road. Nothing in the world resembled that throaty roar of thundering power, although Danny was surprised that it sounded alone, a single V-twin on the open road. He stumbled, looking for a place to hide as the sound came closer. The bike was behind the rise he had struggled past a half-mile back, and he could hear the noise reaching the crest of the hill. The bike would be upon him soon. The sound of its exhaust clapped effortlessly up the hill, and the scoot revved its delight as it descended the grade. Danny's emotions ran the gamut from concerned, to afraid, to terrified, to angry, and back again. He was in the open, with no place to hide, as the sound drummed closer, until it was on him. Danny pulled the gym bag around to his front, and reached inside for the 9mm. And as he suspected, he could hear the motorcycle downshifting, and the revs dropping as the bike grew nearer. He wanted to turn, to run, to hide, to fight, but in truth, the fight was gone from him, his energy depleted. As he stopped running, he realized how totally vulnerable he was on the desolate road, surrounded by these open fields, and he suddenly remembered all the stories about shallow graves between Los Angeles and Las Vegas. The rarely traversed road was shouldered by soft sand, centuries old. A short shovel could easily dig a small grave that might never be discovered. Danny stopped running and turned to meet his fate, when, to his surprise and relief, he was confronted by a Volkswagen with a faded, British racing green paint job—the only 4-wheeler that could be mistaken for a Harley-Davidson, usually because its muffler was defective, as was the case with Elizabeth's bug. The worn and rusted VW pulled alongside Danny.

"Get in," Elizabeth said. "We need to hide, the cops are coming." Danny didn't utter a word, but took off the backpack and tossed it into the back seat, then climbed in. She immediately shifted gears, and the 20-year-old bug jerked and shuddered, slowly climbing back to speed.

"Put your head down," Elizabeth said, glancing in the rearview mirror. Then, realizing that her passenger was immobile, she shoved the back of his sweat soaked head toward her lap as a cruiser topped the crest behind them, red light flashing, blasting over the hill. Elizabeth stared straight ahead and pulled slightly to the side of the road to let the speeding law enforcement vehicle pass. But instead of roaring quickly by, it slowed and pulled alongside.

The young, immaculate cop on the passenger side rolled the window down, grimaced in reaction to the severe evening heat, and peered into the frayed interior of the VW. "'Scuse me, ma'am, seen anybody jogging out here?" the cop shouted over the roar of the VW's exhaust.

"No, sir," Elizabeth said, "I haven't."

The officer stared at her with a look reeking of young testosterone. His blue eyes flickered, but Elizabeth faced forward again, and he escaped back into the air-conditioned interior of the patrol car, rolling up his window, then running his fingers through his wind-blown hair. His partner punched him in the arm as he took one more longing look at

Elizabeth's thick blond hair and warm, inviting features. She was tall for the Volkswagen, and far too statuesque—basically, the gnarly bug was beneath her beauty, unworthy of her bright, intelligent eyes. As Danny turned his sweaty head to face her, he first saw her delicate feet operating the controls of the VW flawlessly, like she was performing some sort of dance. Her calves were soft and gently sculptured, as her muscles instinctively tightened and released on command. Her skirt, hiked 10 inches above her knees, revealed tanned thighs. Danny felt a warm, sensual feeling rise in him as he sat up, and she, too, warmed to Danny's new clean-cut features. The Volkswagen labored up and over another rolling hill in the middle of what seemed a no man's land, and there before them was the junction of Famoso Road and Highway 65. On one corner stood a series of grain silos, rusting and abandoned. Across from the once bustling business, stood a small grocery store. The screen door hung by one rusting hinge, creaking in the evening heat. A once-white awning, designed to reflect some of the sun's rays away from the display windows on either side of the front door, drooped over the face of the building, and the rusting Pepsi sign still stood as a promotional reminder from the '50s, sporting the fading name of the store, "Evan's Grocery." Although it had been abandoned for years, a closed sign still hung in the front window. Behind the building stood a pair of testaments to the strength of nature—two massive pepper trees bearing healthy limbs and thick manes of rich, green foliage.

Elizabeth pulled around back to the cover of the trees. "We might need to wait here until those cops head back," she said, looking to Danny for approval.

"That's fine," Danny said, still breathing hard. "Thank you for coming to get me. I wasn't sure..." His voice trailed off as he realized he wasn't sure what he intended to say.

"No problem," Elizabeth said, getting out of the bug and plucking a small bag from behind her seat. "I brought you something to eat and a couple of sodas." She spread out a white paper napkin on the warped and chipped picnic table, then reached into the bag, before placing a tuna sandwich and a piece of apple pie on a paper plate. She pulled out two cokes in paper cups, opened the straws, and put them carefully into place.

"Aren't you eating?" Danny asked, looking at an old pickup truck in the weeds behind the store, gradually becoming part of the land again, as the tires rotted and peeled away from the rims, and the wheels sank into the hot, dry soil. Its paint was all but gone, and rust was taking the old, classic carcass home.

"No," Elizabeth said, sweeping the area with a napkin to make a clear place for Danny to eat. "I get plenty at the restaurant."

Without staring, Danny watched Elizabeth's movements. He enjoyed the care she brought to everything she did, tentative about her moves, but nonetheless efficient. "I used to come here as a kid," she said. "My folks brought me to Evan's Grocery on the way to our favorite campsite. It was always hot, it seemed, and we needed a break from the road, so we got sodas or ice cream, and came out here where it was cooler to relax. I'll never forget it. Listen, I know you've been through some kind of hell today, and I don't want you to tell me about it. But I should tell you that members of the Los Cuchillos were with members of the Devils Own in Gorman before you got there. Basically, that's all I know, except that I believe instinctively that you're a good person, so if I can do anything to help, I will."

Elizabeth spoke so forcefully that Danny was momentarily taken aback. He looked at her across the table, and as he reached for the frosty cup of soda, she took his hand in hers. Surprised, he felt a tightness in his chest and a lump in his throat as he looked deep into her brilliant blue eyes, and placed his other hand on hers. "I want to tell you everything," Danny said, gently squeezing her soft hands. "But right now I need answers, one in particular."

The sound of an approaching car filled the air, and two headlights burst over the hill from the direction of Porterville. The car slowed at the intersection, and Elizabeth jumped to her feet, dashing around the corner of the dilapidated building. It was the police cruiser on its way back to Bakersfield. She watched the taillights disappear over the hill, then returned to Danny. "Let's go get some answers," she said. Danny finished the last bite of apple pie, stood up, and followed her to the VW.

"Where do we need to go?" Elizabeth asked, pulling out of the dusty parking lot and onto the highway.

"I need a map," Danny said.

"There's one in here," Elizabeth said, reaching across the dash to open the door of the glove compartment, extracting a creased and worn rectangle of folded paper. Danny spread out the tattered map in front of him. As he squinted down at the crisscross maze of intersecting lines, she handed him a small penlight. Danny studied the roads and the small towns between Bakersfield and Fresno. "I need a town between here and Fresno that we can get out of quick. We also need a good vantage point to watch from."

"Watch what?" Elizabeth asked.

"I'm not sure," Danny replied. "It's sort of a test."

Elizabeth didn't understand, but knew that she'd find out before long. "How about Visalia?" she suggested. "I know the town like the back of my hand, and we can get out of there without a hassle."

"OK," Danny replied. "Let's get to the outskirts, and we can look things over." Elizabeth turned north on Highway 65, the little bug picking up speed toward another small town. "I'm not sure what I've got myself into, but..." Danny's voice trailed off as he realized he didn't know how to finish the sentence he'd begun.

Elizabeth slipped her hand over his, reassuringly, and Danny stopped trying to make conversation. His breathing changed, slowing to a more regular tempo than the erratic, edgy pace of the past few hours. "You've been through hell, today," Elizabeth said, soothingly. "Just relax for half an hour and think. You don't need to explain anything to me unless you want to."

Danny leaned back against the tattered seat and closed his eyes. His heart rate had accelerated with Elizabeth's initial touch, then slowed as she talked. "Thank you," he said, slipping deeper into his seat. The little German classic buzzed along the dark roads and through the vast fields, heading north toward Visalia. The road meandered up and over hills, and through row after row of table grapevines, which became eerie silhouettes in the dark, like battalions of dead soldiers coming to assault the hill once more. Danny rested fitfully, his mind packed with vivid memories, turmoil, questions, and the electricity of hate. He could see the expanding whites of the rider's eyes when he smacked the stern of the heavy CalTrans vehicle, he could feel the gunshots behind him, and it made him shudder. He thought over what Elizabeth had told him at the picnic table, savoring the memory of the touch of her hands. Why would members of the Devils Own and the Los Cuchillos meet in Gorman? He thought about what Tong had taught him about human nature while he did his time in the joint. He tossed and turned in the uncomfortable seat, trying to separate emotion from rational thought. He thought about this club president he was supposed to meet, and wondered what he had to do with what was going on. He knew for sure that any president who was losing members at the rate he was, couldn't be happy.

The VW rattled across a set of railroad tracks, and Danny jumped, scanning the darkness for danger. "It's OK," Elizabeth said. "Just some railroad tracks. We're entering Porterville." Danny scanned the small town in the darkness, the lone bar easily identifiable by the accumulation of trucks and old cars out front, and the garish neon glow from the shaded windows. "We'll be in Lindsay soon, then Visalia," she said quietly. "Should I be looking for anything in particular?"

Danny pushed his shortened hair back. "Here's the deal," he said. "I don't know who to believe, or who's behind trying to kill me, or who my real friends are, but we're gonna find out the answer to one question tonight. I need to find a small building somewhere where no one innocent can get hurt. I'll need a phone, and then a place we can go to watch the building."

"I'm not sure I understand," Elizabeth said, as Danny bent forward to open his backpack and pull out the 9mm. "But I'm sure I'm about to find out."

On the outskirts of Visalia, the couple arrived at an intersection. A small, tin warehouse teetered on one corner, a fading, gray hardware store sign hanging askew from the metal exterior. On the opposite corner was a pay phone with a single street lamp above it. "Pull in there," Danny said, checking that the pistol's 13-shot clip was full. Elizabeth watched, her eyes widening. "I need to make sure the phone is working, then check out the interior of the building."

"I'll check the phone," Elizabeth, said. "You check the building."

Carrying Elizabeth's penlight, Danny pushed open the back delivery door to the ramshackle tin shed and went inside. The building was empty, except for a large quantity of broken glass, two mattresses, and beer cans and old bottles scattered around the floor. He went back outside and scanned the area. In the darkness, he couldn't see far, but across the street, he was able to make out a Richfield Oil yard, fenced with 10-foot chain link, behind which were rows of trucks and equipment. Two dim lights weakly illuminated the front of the small mobile home on stilts that served as the office. In each corner of the yard, 150-watt floodlights threw a faint halo over the still machinery. He could smell the oil residue from the equipment, the old, rotting wood inside the building, and the wafting scents of the hayfields beyond the intersection. Danny could see that the road rose slightly past the oil field equipment yard. "Let's go up that road," he said, moving toward the bug parked alongside the phone booth. Danny looked the car over. It was obviously a remnant of a divorce. The "Proud To Be A Marine" sticker on the bumper was faded and scratched. Under the dim shroud of illumination around the phone booth, the car didn't appear to be in bad shape, the unnatural light giving the '65 bug a new hue. Like magic, the dents were gone, the imperfections softened, and the chrome glowed. Danny and Elizabeth got in the car and drove up the incline Danny had observed from the intersection. The hill really wasn't much more than a large bump in the road, but nestled on its top, behind a border of shrub trees and bushes, were the remains of a weathered, wood-framed house, long abandoned. Danny got out of the car and opened the crumbling gate in the battered fence. Elizabeth pulled the car inside, and shut it off. "Relax here for a couple of minutes," Danny said. "I've got to make a call." Feeling somewhat revived, he jogged down the hill to the phone booth, dropped a quarter in the slot, and dialed. It rang only once.

"Hello," Dixie said, in her child-like voice.

"Dixie, I'm tired and wounded," Danny gasped into the receiver. "But I think I'm OK for the night. I'm just tryin' to hide out till morning."

"Where are you?" Dixie asked. "I don't know what's going on."

"I'm at the intersection of Highway 65 and Strathmore,

south of Fresno. I've been through hell today. People are trying to kill me, and I gotta get some sleep." Danny grunted out the words, breathing heavily. "I'll be OK if I can rest for awhile. I found an old hardware store to hide in. I probably shouldn't talk on the phone, but I'll call you in the morning."

"I love you," Dixie said, halfheartedly.

"I love you too, baby," Danny said, then hung up.

Danny backed away from the phone as if he had done something terribly wrong. He couldn't hurt her—it just wasn't in him. He was young, and the idea of being betrayed by a woman was alien to him. But he had to rely on his pragmatic side. One more mistake could be his last, and besides, this "test" would answer some questions, though he couldn't be certain which ones.

As Danny backed away from the phone booth, the whole scene seemed like a dream. The single light, 50-feet above the dusty parking area, cast a warm glow over the vacant lot and the front of the building. He wished he could stand back and sketch a drawing of the lonely building, lifeless, alone, and neglected even as society passes it by daily. He walked to the front door, pushed, and it swung open. Danny left it ajar while he looked around for something to use to sweep away his shoe prints. He found a couple of sections from a faded newspaper, wadded a few sheets into a ball, and swept away his footprints and the tracks of the VW before making one clean set of prints from the road to the front door. Danny walked through the building, gathering debris and newspapers, and stuffed everything tightly into a chunk of red ceramic sewer pipe. He stood it upright, 6 feet from a window, and lit the material. Once the fire was going well, he turned to the mattresses and formed a crude mannequin of newspapers and rubble, then made it difficult to see by partially obscuring it with the other mattress. He exited the building from the rear, moved across the parking lot, and jogged back to the top of the hill, where Elizabeth was waiting.

"She was your girlfriend?" Elizabeth asked in a whisper from the rickety porch.

"Yeah," Danny replied, looking down at the building an eighth of a mile away. "In fact, I guess she still is, in some respects."

"That so?" Elizabeth responded. She hadn't intended to

question him about the other woman, but her curiosity got the best of her.

"I've had my doubts," Danny said, searching the distance for headlights. "And this is the acid test."

"I'm sorry," Elizabeth said, placing her arm around him. "For the sake of your faith in women, I hope she's all right. Selfishly, I hope she's a bitch." Danny and Elizabeth turned simultaneously and faced each other. Against his 6-foot, 4-inch height, she was only 7 inches shorter. He looked down only slightly into her sparkling blue eyes. For long moments, they stared into each other's souls, then Danny began to fade. The emotional strain of the day was wrestling with the thunder and questioning in his heart, leaving him drained and spent. Feeling his knees give slightly, he put his left hand against the wall of the wind-worn wooden slats, feeling and hearing the chipped paint collapsing under the pressure. Instinctively, she reached for his waist to stabilize his body. His right arm encircled her shoulders, and for the first time she could feel the tightness of his muscles and the broad expanse of his frame. She was impressed by the trained-to-tautness mass of his body and its absence of fat. "You've got to get some sleep," she said, grappling with his sagging form. They sat on the porch, and he rested his head in her lap. Danny knew there was something erotic about being this close to her, but his body had no energy left to respond. As he fell asleep, he felt her hand gently stroke his hair.

An hour passed with no activity, except for the incessant chirping of the multitudes of grasshoppers in the nearby fields. Elizabeth looked out at the night, wondering about the man whose head rested peacefully in her lap. She was young, but she had been discouraged by her first marriage. The customers who flowed in and out of the truck stop diner winked at her and flirted with her, then got back into their flashy pickups, into their semis hauling produce to hell and back, into their RVs, with dogs and wives, and onto their motorcycles, all headed off to one adventure after another. At least, that's how it looked when she remained, living and working in a world of transient men, mostly. Elizabeth often wondered what women were doing with their lives, and she shuddered at the thought that a growing number of them were divorced, disenfranchised from the commercial world, holding down subservient jobs, and going home to single apartments or guest houses. And the single mothers struggled even harder to make ends meet, their standard of living a fraction above abject poverty, with nothing except their children to entertain them. She wondered about those humble offspring, growing up without hope, without security, and only an occasional stranger briefly walking into, then out of, their lives. She knew the life, because she was living it, and many of the people around her were trapped in it. At least the girls who weren't mothers could go to school if they had the self-discipline, if they weren't alcoholics, drug addicts, or whores.

Suddenly Elizabeth's somber reverie was broken and she was instantly alert. Something had caught her eye—a flicker, a glow. Something changed. She shook Danny.

"Huh?" Danny said, groggily. "What is it?"

"I don't know," Elizabeth replied, her eyes darting back and forth along the road. As Danny sat up on the porch, she began to stand up, in order to look down on the dark intersection below. Danny grabbed her, wrapping his arms around her tender thighs. She fell to the side, and Danny caught her to keep her from getting hurt.

Elizabeth jerked around to face Danny. "Why did you-" she began, but her words were cut short by Danny's firm hand clamped across her mouth. She squirmed against his grip, suddenly fearful that she might have made the worst judgment call of her life. Then she heard a voice and immediately went limp in his arms, ceasing to struggle.

"Is that the building?" The voice was heavy and slow.

"Must be. Let's go back and get the car." The other voice was smaller and higher.

"No, let's get closer. This time, we need to make sure." The voice was a snake's hiss in the night. Danny lay motionless, except for removing his palm from Elizabeth's mouth. His forearm rested against her chest, and for a moment, he felt the softness of her breasts. Two bikers walked along the edge of the street below, headed toward the desolate intersection. Danny and Elizabeth were uncomfortably intertwined on the dilapidated wood porch, unable to move a muscle. One creak, one cracking board, could be heard a quarter-mile from where they huddled together.

"See, there's a light burning in the window," the younger voice said, the biker trying to convince his partner. "Let's get the car, and we'll blow that fucking pieceashit building into the next county." There was no response from the other biker.

Danny kept his head down, pressed against Elizabeth's thigh. Her legs were twisted underneath her, and the position was growing painful. Just as she realized she needed to straighten her legs, her muscles began to tighten and cramp.

"Bullshit!" the hard voice snapped at the shorter of the two men. "We've got to finish this shit. I want to cut his throat and watch him bleed. He's killed four of our brothers, goddammit!"

"But we've got to get back before Pito finds out," the smaller voice said pleadingly.

"Fuck him," the other biker snapped again. "He's next."

The house had been built in the '30s, probably the home of a migrant family with enough wealth to own several hundred acres of the hot, dry land. The decrepit old home was built of wood lath and plaster, strong enough to withstand bitterly cold winters and brutally hot summers. But over the years, the expansion and contraction of the wood had loosened the fasteners at the joints until the house almost swayed when a wind whipped up, and the noises it made were eerie and unsettling—a squirrel's death screech in the jaws of a cat. Lonely, mournful sounds that made you think of lost hopes and dead dreams, or the desperate, steady keening of a family drawn together at the hospital, knowing that the expression on the doctors' faces mean terminal news. By now, Elizabeth's leg was cramping, and the pain was growing unbearable. She tried to adjust with minimum movement, but the weather-beaten porch refused to remain quiet any longer, creaking and groaning as she attempted to relieve the knotted muscles in her thigh and leg.

Everyone froze, alert, waiting.

"What was that?" the smaller of the two bikers asked, rattled by the unexpected sound.

"Shut up!" his companion hissed, in a loud whisper, while quickly drawing a snub-nosed S & W .38 Detective's Special from his waistband at the small of his back, and turning toward the house, kneeling. "Circle around behind the house up that way," the big Mexican whispered, pointing to one side of the shrubbery obscuring a clear view of the house from below. "We may have gotten lucky." A sliver of light faintly illuminated the narrow, expressionless face of Gonzalo Sainz and his equally nervous partner, Perdo Padilla. Earlier, Emilio had received the call from Fast Eddie, who was busy packing Dixie's nose and consoling her with assurances that her betrayal of Danny was justified. Emilio grabbed Gonzalo and gave him the order, "Kill the bastard, or don't come back."

Gonzalo wasn't worried about the threat accompanying the order; he was just pleased to have been given the assignment. He needed an opportunity to look strong to Emilio and Romeo, to stand out among the ranks of members. The way he figured it, killing the *gringo* would make him one of the stars of the club. Gonzalo was tall and skinny, with narrow features. Once he started school, this combination of physical traits caused him to be dubbed "Gonzalo Gusano." *Gusano* is the Spanish word for worm, and it fit Gonzalo both literally and figuratively. He was a slimy, repulsive, featureless creature, with all the personality of an earthworm. Even as an adult, he was unable to shake the name. From his first day as a hangaround with the Devils, he was known as El Gusano. Pedro, Gonzalo's partner on the mission, began to round the building, as Gonzalo had instructed. He was scared. But then, he was always frightened when he wasn't high, so he jumped at the chance to get away from Gonzalo, duck around the corner of the building, and dig into the vial in the pocket of his tattered denim vest. At the edge of the property in the back yard was a bare, wooden slat fence 3 feet high. At random intervals, slats were missing, or lying in the weeds growing all around the rotting fence. The yard contained a dying assortment of skinny, neglected, fruit trees. Facing the street at each corner of the front of the house, were two massive, overgrown olive trees. There were no bushes or other cover for the two on the porch. Danny attempted to tug the heavy 9mm automatic free from his shorts, and as he did so, he turned his hip in order to reach his pocket, causing the gun to slip out and fall to the wood floor of the porch with a loud clunk. Danny twisted and desperately tried to grab the weapon before it slipped through a large crack between two rotted and chipped boards. But he was too late. He jammed his hand into the jagged gap between the two slats, but he couldn't reach the pistol no matter how much he strained.

Crouching near the fence, Gonzalo saw vague forms moving on the porch, and he opened fire. Bullets exploded into the wall around Danny and Elizabeth, shattering the old panels in an eruption of splintered oak. Danny, in a low crouch, with his back to the Cuchillo firing at him, lifted the horrified woman. With Danny half-holding, half-dragging Elizabeth, they ran toward the corner of the unprotected porch. Bullets shattered the pane in the window above Danny's head, showering the pair with fragments of glass, as he dived for the corner, with Elizabeth in his arms, screaming in terror.

"After I kill you, *gringo*," Gonzalo shouted while he reloaded his gun, "I give your girl an *adios* fuck before I blow her fuckin' brains out!"

Danny and Elizabeth crashed to the ground, and squirmed around the corner, crawling in the dirt toward the back of the house. "Stay here," Danny whispered in her ear. "One second." In shock, her eyes wide with fear, she lay near the side of the house, on the stretch of ground between the building and her Volkswagen. Danny was in a cross. He wanted combat with the two Los Cuchillos, but his first priority was to protect the girl. He knew that if the Cuchillo reached the corner, he'd have a clear shot at them, and even then he could hear the stout Mexican working his way along the fence.

Houses built in the '30s rarely had concrete foundations, but were raised off of the ground by supporting posts or a similar substructure, leaving crawl spaces beneath. Latticework covered the empty gaps between the house and the ground. Danny crawled over to a section of the crisscrossed strips and kicked his way through the flimsy wood. Backing into the dark, narrow space, he pulled Elizabeth in after him. She resisted at first, recoiling from the spider webs, the filth, and the impenetrable darkness. But she relented, and let herself be hauled through the demolished latticework, primarily because she had little choice, and yet also because she felt an attraction and a caring for the man tugging on her wrists that she had never experienced before. Suddenly, she was acutely, brutally, aware of the level of danger she was in. Beneath the floor of the house, thick clouds of dust and dirt rose to choke their air passages and block their vision. "Keep your eyes closed and don't move," Danny whispered into Elizabeth's ear and kissed her cheek. "I got more answers in the last five minutes than I got all day. I'll be right back."

Elizabeth squeezed his arm as he moved away, crawling toward the porch. From outside the fence, Gonzalo peered intently at the dark house. Pale moonlight allowed him to make out the outline of the structure, and the bodies moving along its face, but once Danny and Elizabeth rounded the corner, they disappeared into the deep shadows between the house and the VW. Beyond an ink-black stretch of ground, Gonzalo could see the vast yard behind the house, a reminder that at one time this dwelling sat alone in the center of 200 acres, with one small, unpaved road running from the front door, to the highway, a quarter-mile distant. Much had changed since then.

Danny crawled on his belly beneath floor braces and around studs, ducking under retaining beams to reach the porch, built half as high as the 18-inch crawl space under the main portion of the house. He squeezed himself under the dividing structure, and under the slouching porch. Because it wouldn't need to bear the kind of weight the rest of the house had to withstand, the porch wasn't built to the same heavy-duty specs as the rest of the one-story structure. Not surprisingly, it sagged from 40 years of age and abuse. Danny strained his eyes against the dark until he caught the glint off the cold blue surface and ivory grips of his weapon lying in the dirt.

Since Pedro was circling the house, Gonzalo expected to come face-to-face with him at any moment. But as he squinted into the eerie darkness, there was no sign of his less-than-violent brother. Nothing moved, nothing creaked, and even the warm breeze ceased. It all seemed too still, Gonzalo thought, his index finger twitching nervously on the trigger of the snub-nosed .38 he held.

Danny shoved the automatic into the waist of his pants at the small of his back, and inched his way back toward Elizabeth, who lay perfectly still, awaiting his return. "I'm going out the back door," he whispered in her ear, while touching her arm tenderly. "Lie still, and don't move." Danny groped toward a dim opening in the back of the house, probably an entrance hole dug by the family dog. Moving steadily under the house, he peered into the night, watching for Pedro. He saw him crouching behind a narrow tree trunk in the back yard, packing his nose. Danny waited as Pedro scooped a large mound of coke out of the vial and held it to his nostril. The blast from the drug rocked the young Mexican so that he almost lost his balance. "Don't move," Danny said, quietly, leaning in close to Pedro's ear as the outlaw felt the first rushing wave of the high. Danny pressed the automatic against the ear he'd just whispered into. "Drop the shit and your gun." Abruptly, Pedro stood up, dropping his gun and the vial, paranoia exploding inside him, obliterating the anticipated euphoria.

A rustle in the brush at the corner of the building was followed by a harsh crack, accompanied by a flash of light. Danny was still low to the ground when the young outlaw jerked and fell backward. Danny moved behind the tree. As Pedro toppled backward, he cried out in pain to the man on the other side of the yard. "Brother," he gasped, "why?" He was dead before he hit the dirt.

Danny moved around the trunk of the apricot tree and squeezed off two quick shots in the direction of his assailant. As Gonzalo emerged from the protection of the corner of the building, toward the trees planted 30 years earlier by kids hoping to grow up in the golden glow of the California dream, El Gusano was an indistinct silhouette in the darkness. "Come on, you white cocksucker!" Gonzalo snarled, his voice a raspy whisper. "Let's face off like men, you chickenshit *cabron!*"

Danny watched Gonzalo take a step, observing that it was heavy, and off balance. "Hey, you shit-for-brains badass," Danny shouted mockingly, "your people killed two of your own brothers today, trying to get to me! So what's the big fuckin' deal, man? Why me? I'm just a damned prospect."

"You ain't shit," the Mexican barked, swaying noticeably. "I spit on your miserable ass!" Danny stepped around the tree trunk into full view. He had taken Pedro's revolver, and now raised both weapons. "Chance of a lifetime, asshole," he said, and both men fired simultaneously. Danny dropped to one knee and fired again. The big man stumbled, then collapsed, pitching forward into the dirt.

Elizabeth crawled out from under the house as Danny rounded the corner. "They don't hold you in high regard, do they?" she said, embracing him, and then jumping into the driver's seat of the battered Volkswagen. Danny ran for the gate. "Maybe it has something to do with my hygiene," he joked over his shoulder, almost giddy with exhilaration and relief. Opening the gate as she turned on the headlights and put the bug in gear, Danny was illuminated, covered with dirt, dust, and soaked in sweat. As she pulled up beside him and he jumped into the car, she said, "You could use a shower."

"Hold it," Danny said, forcing himself to haul his tired, beat-up ass out of the car in order to destroy the car tracks with the dead tree limb. Once they were on the highway, he slumped back into the worn-out seat and laid the two pistols on the floor between his feet. "This time, I pick the location for our next event," Elizabeth said, pressing the rattling accelerator pedal to the floor.

"OK, your call," Danny mumbled, slumping deeper into the tired seat cover. Then he sat up straight. "Wait." he said, and Elizabeth brought the car to a lurching stop. "What is it?" she asked.

Danny reached his hand toward her, and gently turned Elizabeth's face toward his. Leaning close, he kissed her, then collapsed back into the seat.

He was asleep in two minutes, while she steered the little vehicle south to Ducor, then turned left, winding east and deeper into the hills. From the flats, the road began to swing over rolling hills, and soon began to cut between boulders and manzanita shrubs. Scrub oak became more prevalent as the curves grew tighter and the elevation increased. While Danny slept, she maneuvered them past Fountain Springs, a one-store intersection, and through California Springs to the spot where the winding road reached the base of the mountains and the California Pines flourished. Danny and Elizabeth entered the Green Horn Mountains where that range collided with the southern Sierra Nevada Mountains, and it was midnight before the sputtering VW pulled into a community lost in the mountains of Pine Flat. She wound through the town of 300, with less than a half dozen businesses, past the Rabbit's Foot Trail Inn, the tiny Pine Flat Resort Bar, and a couple of real estate offices. Turning right beyond the mobile home park, she entered a community of aging hippies and escapees from the cities below. The streets narrowed, and she navigated the dusty vehicle from one small road to another even smaller dirt path, until she pulled up in front of a small A-frame home tucked back alongside a creek. She parked the bug behind the house, hauled her stuff, Danny's bag, and his guns inside, then returned for the fatigued man, folded awkwardly into her front seat.

Chapter 20

TIGHT SQUEEZE

Darkness shrouded the wide streets of Fresno as Emilio drove the El Camino past the county lockup, slowing a block from the entrance, then stopping. It was an enormous, armored-looking structure, built in the late '40s. With two huge, traditional iron sconces leaning away from the block edifice, wide stairs began at the sidewalk and tapered smaller, finally funneling into two bulletproof glass doors. Inside, a huge oak desk sat on a large dais, raising it above the reception area, and protecting the desk sergeant, who was perched behind its thick polished exterior, showering all who entered with an immediate sense of his power.

Outside in the shadows, the two outlaws waited in the car. Emilio and Romeo sat silently in the late evening heat. They didn't really need to talk, or to plan, or to speculate. Instinctively, they knew that once they had Pito in the car sitting between them, it was just a matter of picking the right moment. They would strike fast, with deadly force, and it would be over. Then they could restructure the club, kick out all the punks and family types, and run the valley with a sharpened blade while reaping a harvest of cocaine profits.

The two men watched the front door of the building with cat-like intensity, as straggling prisoners were released, and cops emerged, talking intensely with each another. A constant line of suits went in and out of the building—undercover cops, FBI, and DEA agents. From time to time, black-and-whites pulled into the side entrance of the building. New prisoners sat handcuffed in the back of the cars. Some wept, but many sat silently, wondering what the hell they were thinking when they made the wrong move. Some watched expectantly for friends coming to bail them out. The air was thick with negative vibes. There were no celebrations or affirmations associated with the immense block edifice, just the gray, somber feeling of uncertainty. An hour had passed when a slender biker strolled down the steps rubbing his wrists. He was short, but his engineer boots, filthy cutoff, and tattered denims showed his affiliation. He walked to the curb and looked both ways.

"It's Don," Romeo said, cracking a smile.

Emilio flashed his parking lights and Don saw the El Camino. He turned and walked in their direction, but he didn't cross the street. Instead, he just kept walking toward the corner.

"What's he doing?" Romeo asked.

"Must be something's up," Emilio muttered, starting the car and driving in the opposite direction. They drove a couple of blocks past spray-painted industrial buildings. When Emilio was confident that no one was following, he spun the wheel to the left for another city block. Two blocks down, Don stepped from behind a primered van with the windows shot out, abandoned on the street. He got into the cab, and pushed Romeo to the center. "You shouldn't be here," Don said. "But since you are ... well, I can use a ride."

"What's the deal?" Emilio asked.

"It's hot, way hot," Don replied. "They've got more agencies hanging around than I have spokes on my bike."

"When is Pito getting out?" Emilio asked, looking at Don directly. "I've got a plan to end this bullshit, and put all this heat on the *gringo*."

"I'd love to kill that pissant *puta*," Don said, rubbing his hands together eagerly. "Anyone heard where that little white boy is? I saw him kill my brother, and I want him. He's mine."

"Hey, asshole," Emilio said, leaning sideways to poke Don in the chest. "I asked you a question." "I don't know, boss," Don said respectfully. Don was a new member, and lacked street smarts. He had joined the club under Pito's rule, and his attitude was not cutthroat enough for Emilio. And besides, he didn't do drugs—always a bad sign. Emilio wasn't sure he could trust the man, which is why he had sent him home earlier.

Emilio thought for a moment. "We haven't heard from the *gringo*, but it's time we checked in with Los Angeles." He changed directions again. "Is your place hot?"

"Yes sir," Don said, setting his emotions aside, and

respecting Emilio's toughness. "I'm sure it is. They picked me up right after I left the warehouse. The *gringo* is in Visalia."

"How'd you find out?" Emilio inquired, paranoia running high.

"In the jail," Don said, uneasy because of the suspicious vibes darting his way from Emilio. Romeo began sharpening a blade slowly and quietly, while watching Don with a stern, unsmiling expression. "The cops said they found Gonzalo and Pedro in Visalia, dead."

"No!" Emilio blurted, involuntarily. He looked at Romeo, and both men experienced a fearful chill. Emilio knew the cops had also discovered the charred bodies in the burnt-out warehouse. And he had fully expected Gonzalo to waste the gringo. That was the sixth brother down. "How?"

"They were both shot," Don said. "That's all I know."

Suddenly, Romeo felt alone and hunted. The need for more support caused him to abandon his violent facade. "You need a weapon," Romeo said, more as a statement of fact than as advice.

"Yeah, I do," Don replied. "What do you want me to do?" Don was young and confused. Emilio sent him home when Marko went for Gil. He was behind the young immigrant, but wasn't sure of the depth of his commitment.

"Take this," Emilio said, leaning forward to pull a plastic bag from under the seat, before handing it to Romeo, who glanced at him knowingly. Handing Don a .22 caliber Ruger fitted with a silencer, Emilio said, "Here, and take this .38. If you kill the gringo, leave the .22 with him."

"What's this?" Don asked, unwrapping the revolver.

"It's insurance," Emilio replied, reassuringly.

Don nodded, and re-wrapped the weapon as they pulled into a corner mall with a movie theater. "I'm makin' a call," Emilio said, getting out of the lowered vehicle. He had parked in the mall lot, in the midst of a sea of other cars and a constant flow of people from the nearby movie theater. No one paid attention to the outlaw as he entered the lobby and used the pay phone. Inserting the coins, he dialed and waited. This was the part of his life that Emilio enjoyed least. In his own territory, he was king—tough and mean. No one could tell him what to do or when, but the Devils Own were a different breed. They had a creed of vengeance and violence.

They were more overtly violent than he ever imagined. They were the green berets of outlaw bikers. They took no prisoners and their motto was, "When in doubt, knock 'em out." There was no slack when it came to these people. A shudder of fear crept up his spine as he listened to the phone ring, over and over, without being answered.

Abruptly, someone on the other end picked up the receiver. But Emilio heard only silence, a terrifying, intimidating silence. He waited. "Well?" a voice hissed into his ear.

"Well, what?" Emilio snapped, trying to keep his confidence high.

"Did your brother finish it?" the voice asked. "I bet you don't even know what your brothers are doing."

"I know more than you do, pal," Emilio shot back, feeling strong for the first time in the presence of these cutthroats. "The gringo is still alive, as far as I know, and you got two more of my people killed." Emilio was still bothered that Don was tipped off before he knew about it. Cold silence again emanated from the other end of the line.

"Well, smartass," Miguel sneered, menacingly, "whaddaya gonna do now?"

"I've got a plan, and..." Emilio began, trying to regain his self-assurance.

"You better, motherfucker," Miguel interrupted, slapping Emilio with the words as a challenge.

"I should have handled this my way from the beginning," Emilio shouted into the receiver. He began to sweat. People were emerging from a completed show, and the lobby was filling with citizens. Only one or two glanced in his direction, though it hardly mattered, since his nerves were on overload.

"Handle it, shit!" Miguel screamed into the phone. "You and the rest of your pussyass bunch got 24 hours—24 hours, asswipe, you understand? Just 24 hours, and then I'm coming with the rest of the whole goddamn club, and when we're finished with your sorry asses, there won't be enough left of you slimeballs to fill a taco shell. You got that?" Miguel slammed the phone into its cradle.

Emilio hung up the receiver slowly, looking around as if everyone in the brightly illuminated lobby saw him get his ass kicked over the phone. Emilio's hand twisted the receiver, slowly resting it in the chromed cradle. His eyebrow lifted slightly as a young Mexican girl leaving the lobby caught his eye. He knew he was knee-deep in danger from all quarters, and although he was now in even greater jeopardy than before, he was enjoying the experience. His muscles tightened and twitched. The young, dark outlaw was attracted to the saucy Hispanic *muchacha* with a full mane of jet-black hair, narrow waist, jutting tits, and a wicked smile. And the glint in her eye indicated that the attraction was mutual. For a moment, he licked his lips in lascivious fantasy. But then her boyfriend emerged from the men's room and swept her away, although she looked back and winked. Emilio knew he still had it as he looked into the glass of a coming attractions display case, and checked his reflection. He was together, clean, and slick with his long, black hair, his lithe body, and his narrow mustache and immaculate imperial. All in all, he was the living image of the devil on a motorcycle.

Outside, Emilio got into the car feeling frustrated. He had no confidence that Don could do anything to help, but as long as the silenced weapon was out of his own possession, that was enough for the time being.

"Drop me off in the alley up ahead," Don said. "Call me at home if you need anything, or if you find out exactly where the *gringo* is."

Emilio braked the El Camino to a stop at the mouth of a dirt alley, behind a line of barrio bungalows. Don got out without a word and, along with his package of weapons, disappeared into the smoldering night.

On the way out of the area, Emilio and Romeo thought for sure that they saw at least half a dozen unmarked cop cars. New tan, and deep blue four-door, full-sized Fords and Dodge sedans seemed perched about in great numbers, at various corners and along streets that usually contained nothing but old, rusting pickups and lowrider vehicles. The plain Fords and Dodges carried too many antennas, rolled along on blackwall tires, had small, cheap hubcaps, incongruous for such new vehicles, little or no trim, and contained two white men in suits. No one on the planet drives cars looking like that, except undercover cops. Emilio had Romeo duck down in his seat, so it appeared as if he was alone. Nonetheless, he received a number of suspicious looks.

"Where we goin'?" Romeo asked, sitting low enough in the seat so that he wasn't visible to anyone unless they were right outside the car door.

"To Gil's place," Emilio said. "Pito will call there, and I need to know when the old man is gettin' out."

"Hey, man," Romeo stammered at the announcement. "I don't want to go there. You know—his kids, the ol' lady, that damned dog of his, and if..."

"Fuck you, punk!" Emilio shouted, interrupting Romeo's Top Ten List of Why He Didn't Want To Go To Gil's House. Emilio stomped on the brakes and the truck skidded to a halt. Emilio slid over the vinyl bench seat, and jammed Romeo against the passenger door, his knife out, and at Romeo's throat. "So what's the problem?" he hissed into Romeo's face. "You can shoot your younger brother in the back, but you can't face that fat fuck's little squirts, and his lardass ol' lady?"

"Sorry, brother," Romeo stammered. "I'm with you, man. It's just that, for a moment, I..."

"We're close to finishing this," Emilio said, interrupting again. He re-sheathed his stiletto and slid behind the wheel once more. "One more piece of business," Emilio continued, "and we own this fucking hellhole." He shifted the car into drive and moved closer to the old middle-class bungalow area that contained Gil's home. It was almost midnight when they pulled up in front of the stucco, Spanish-style home. The house lights were out as Emilio turned off the truck's headlights and killed the engine.

"I'll talk to the ol' lady," Emilio said. "You stay in the living room, and see to it that the kids don't wake up."

Although Emilio opened the rusting screen door extremely carefully, it creaked and whined like hell. He knocked lightly. After three tries, a light came on inside the house, and a small, barred window in the upper center of the door opened. "Who is it?" Gil's wife, Maria, whispered. "The kids are asleep."

"Maria, this is Emilio. Can I come in?"

"What's up?" Maria asked, unlatching the myriad chains and deadbolts on the door. "Where's Gil?"

"He's all right, but he may have been arrested," Emilio

said, in a soft and consoling voice. Padded words rolled like small, comfortable pillows off his tongue, and soothed the most acerbic of women. Maria backed away from the door, and let the two men come inside. Romeo nodded, but said nothing, making his way to the couch in the dark room, and sat down. Emilio followed Maria into the kitchen. She was 35 and plump. Under her flimsy nightgown, her tits hung heavy and large, with large, dark nipples. She could feel his eyes evaluating her form as she prepared to make coffee.

"What was he arrested for, Emilio?" she asked.

"There's some shit going down in Bakersfield," Emilio replied. "And they're questioning everyone. We just picked up Don at the jail and took him home."

"Why haven't you been picked up?" she asked. Emilio was growing annoyed with her questions.

"Just lucky, I guess," Emilio said, moving to her side. Her form was silhouetted against the night sky outside the kitchen window, her body clearly visible through the diaphanous material of the nightgown.

"You're not lucky," Maria said, turning toward him after sliding a large butcher knife out of the block holding the kitchen cutlery, and pointing it at Emilio's throat. "You're up to no good, Emilio. What do you want?"

Emilio shifted to the side, and his eyes widened as he thrust the blade aside, twisting her small wrist until she squirmed and dropped the knife. It clattered against the linoleum floor. Emilio crushed her body against the counter, and slipped his own stainless stiletto under her chin, then licked the side of her face—a long, slurping, wet lick. "You so much as breathe loud, and I'll cut your fucking throat," Emilio warned. "And I'll cut the throats of any of your bastard kids who wake up, too—you understand what I'm saying?" Emilio's body was crushing her vertebrae against the tile counter and the blade of his knife rested against the soft flesh of her throat. Her breathing came in spurts and gasps as Emilio reached down and lifted one of her large, unharnessed breasts out of her gown and squeezed it in his hand.

"I want only one thing," Emilio said, softly, "and then I'll leave your family alone forever. Has Pito called?"

She looked at him with fear in her eyes as he slid a rough

hand under the hem of her nightgown. "Yes," she stammered.

"What did he say?" Emilio asked, running his hand up her round thigh, over her supple ass, then down between her legs.

"He said they would let him out in the morning," she replied, feeling the razor-sharp blade against her throat each time she spoke. "Please let me go." She squirmed against Emilio's body.

He jabbed a finger inside her, and a tear ran down her cheek. Then he left.

FRESNO RUN

*T*heir two bodies lay together like silver spoons shining on each other. Danny awoke with a start, then calmed as he realized who was between his arms. Elizabeth sensed his arousal and rolled over to meet him. Naked, they melted into one another, and their lips tasted the other's for the first time. "We need to move on, don't we?" Elizabeth asked in a sad whisper.

"Yeah, I'm afraid so," Danny said. "I'm concerned that the president is in as much in trouble as I am." They kissed again, and Elizabeth could sense the immediate effect she had on him. She ran her hand down his side to his crotch and grasped him gently. Climbing on top of him, she slipped his cock inside her, and slowly lowered herself until they were one. As she leaned forward, her large, hard, rosy nipples grazed his torso, and his strong, taut chest swelled to meet her breasts as he surged deeper inside her. She felt him peak against her. They kissed again, their tongues searching for some unknown substance.

"I thought we were leaving," Elizabeth said, breathing heavily.

"Same here, but ... I can't," Danny gasped. "We've got to get to..."

"OK," Elizabeth said, understanding his meaning in the fragmented words of his passion. She began to roll off him, and as he followed, they both rolled slowly off the mattress and onto the floor, landing with Danny on top. The slight bump on the carpet pumped him even deeper into her. His eyes widened, and he looked down at the beautiful image beneath him. Elizabeth arched her back, and her creamy tits pointed up at him. Her face, soft as feathers, was surrounded in a sea of naturally blond hair, cascading around her bright features in golden waves. She was a dream, from the nape of her neck, to the firm roundness of her breasts, to the way her hands stroked his waist, and up over the sculpted pecs of his chest, to his parted lips. Elizabeth looked down her body to where he disappeared deep inside her. She pulled her legs up high, and he seemed to slip in even deeper. Then she slid her beautifully manicured nails down the inside of her thighs to her pussy, touching it slightly, then moving daintily around her belly button and up to the base of her breasts. Slowly, she licked her lips and let her fingers move over the cool flesh of her breasts to her nipples. Danny hadn't moved inside her, except to billow even more, but as her soft hands grazed her taut nipples, he began to move slowly in and out. She arched to meet each thrust, her body reaching and reacting quickly toward orgasm. His cock peaked and gushed, and her body responded simultaneously. "Oh, my god!" Danny screamed.

"Come on, baby," Elizabeth urged. "Fill me up."

Arching to meet him, Elizabeth drove herself to a deep, rumbling, jerking climax that seemed to last longer than any either of them had ever experienced. Danny felt every fiber in his body react to the woman under him, wanting to stay connected forever. They collapsed together, still in each other's arms. "I know we must go," she whispered into his ear.

"That's easy for you to say," Danny murmured, licking her earlobe. He was still throbbing inside her as they started giggling. He straightened his arms and lifted himself, torso first. Slowly, he began to easy out of her body. With each movement, he throbbed and she gasped, then they laughed again. As the head emerged from her swollen lips, they gasped in unison. "Let's do this again, soon," Elizabeth said, softly, pulling herself up and kissing him again. Their lips met quickly, lingered, but as he pulled back, he bent down to her wetness and kissed her on the top of her mound, letting his tongue slip quickly between her lips. She jumped.

"I suppose so," Danny said, pretending indifference, and she laughed and kicked at him as he leaped to his feet. For the first time, he saw the trappings of Elizabeth's life. The bedroom was small and rustic, but clean and neat, with a large king-sized mattress, surrounded by numerous large, fluffy pillows. At 23, she was handling the task of taking care of herself. The A-frame building contained odd, angular rooms, but she had brought them to life with plants and tasteful antiques, although she did have her share of crystals and incense burners. Danny located the bathroom, showered, shaved, and only then realized he had little to wear. Stumbling out of the bathroom wrapped in a towel, he inhaled the rich aroma of toast and freshly brewed coffee.

"Have a cup and some toast while I shower," Elizabeth said. "I called the sheriff's station for you. He's still there. It's almost 7 a.m., so that gives us just an hour before they begin to release prisoners."

"You shouldn't go," Danny said. "It's dangerous." He moved to intercept her on her way to the shower. "I'm buried in doubts and worries about this whole affair, but the one solid thing among all the shattered chunks of my life right this second, is you. I couldn't stand to lose you."

"You need to get to town," Elizabeth said.

"Then I want you to drive me there, then come back here and wait for my call." Danny insisted. "All right," Elizabeth said, looking at the soft carpet at her feet, feeling the emotions growing inside her. "There's some of my husband's old clothes in that box beside the door. I was about to trash them."

"Let's move," Danny muttered, reaching for the wheat toast on the multicolored Spanish pottery plate. "I have a plan." He rummaged through the box and found a gray, Marine sweatshirt and a pair of Levis. He pulled on the garments, then slipped his running shoes back on.

Elizabeth was out of the shower in less than 10 minutes, and within 15, they were on the road. Coming out of the mountains, Danny had a chance to absorb the beauty of the region, the massive Sierra Mountain ranges, peppered with majestic pines, twisting manzanitas, and massive granite boulders. As the road dropped into the valley, the temperature rose. They stopped in Fountain Springs near a saloon that had withstood railroad treachery, as well as wars between the farmers and field workers since 1858. Refueling the VW, Danny leaned against the run-down bug and thought about where they were headed and what might occur at their destination. Anger crept into his thoughts, replacing the flood of emotion toward Elizabeth he had felt only an hour ago. Yanking the nozzle out of the tank, he slammed it back onto the pump. Every muscle in his body jerked and spasmed. "Let's get the hell out of here," he barked, and she shoved the loose gearshift into first. The faded Volkswagen lurched onto the main road heading out from the mountains and into the blistering heat of the valley. It was as if they were two soldiers lumbering from the protection of the hills into the open fire of the front line.

Danny sat in Zen-like silence for the rest of the trip. By the time they reached the outskirts of Fresno, the temperature was peaking over 110 degrees. Elizabeth drove directly to the jail and parked. Looking into a small compact mirror, she straightened her hair and freshened her make-up, then got out of the car and strode up the stairs to the ominous front entrance. Inside, the air-conditioning hissed away, and her nerves were momentarily relieved by the cool air. She was dressed in a professional-looking tan suit and low pumps, with her hair pulled back into a ponytail. Her makeup was minimal, but enough to enhance her natural beauty without calling undue attention to her looks. A folder tucked under her arm, she strode to the massive desk behind which the duty sergeant directed the endless daily traffic of lawyers, prisoners, visitors, reporters, and cops. Elizabeth could have been any attorney's assistant in the county, except that she was a knockout, whether nude, disheveled, dressed in Levis and T-shirt, or in the professional outfit she wore today as she stood in front of the leering sergeant. Her sand-colored skirt hugged her narrow waist, draped becomingly over her supple hips, and ended at mid-thigh. A matching jacket concealed her large, firm breasts pressing against the white blouse she wore buttoned to the neck. Nonetheless, her form was discernible beneath the conservative exterior. "Excuse me, sergeant," Elizabeth said, sounding altogether professional. "When are you releasing Mr. Pito Flores?"

The cop glanced down at a list resting on the desk in front of him. "In ten minutes, lady," he replied. "If you like, you can have a seat in the waiting room across the hall."

"Thank you, but I should move my car," she returned. "Will he come out here?"

"That's correct," the officer said, staring at her chest, then at her glistening blue eyes. "He'll come right through those doors." He gestured toward a set of metal-reinforced, featureless doors to the right of the desk. A sign above them read, "Holding Area."

To the left were courtrooms with hardwood floors and impressive high ceilings bearing the California Bear Crest above massive oak podiums where the judges sat. The sight of one of these courtrooms was immediately intimidating. To the opposite direction was the jail, its sterile, concrete walls painted in high-gloss enamel, free of any sign of life at all. With their lifeless, cold exteriors the rooms and holding tanks seem to trap time and freeze all movement.

From the moment Pito entered the building, with its plain, polished floors and Formica counters, it was as if he were a rat trapped in a laboratory environment for testing, no longer a human with loves, and desires, and hopes. All traces of humanity were erased inside these walls with no pictures, no windows, and no sign of life, except other inmates who were immersed in the same experience—and they exuded nothing but hate, fear, doubt, and confusion.

Pito supposed that one reason the facility had been designed drained of all human touches was to influence the prisoner's reaction when he was questioned. But Pito had been downtown many times in the past, and so remained relatively unaffected by his surroundings. Handcuffed, he sat in a cold chair made of steel and stared back stoically at investigators half his age, while they drummed him for information. They had threatened his freedom, told of brothers supposedly snitching on him, and accused him of everything from rape, to murder, to destruction of public property on a freeway, which they claimed over and over was a federal offense, and that, under the RICO act, he would be forced to spend the rest of his life in a federal penitentiary, far from his family and brothers. Until midnight, Pito had pretended to speak almost no English, but then an officer who had known Pito for years came on duty. For the next four hours the cops rephrased their questions. Pito grew weary, but his will was strong, and he held his mud. As long as they couldn't charge him with anything, he knew they would be forced to cut him lose eventually.

Elizabeth exited through the mammoth front doors of the courthouse into the heat, and got in the car. "Ten minutes," she said. Danny lay curled in the back seat, waiting, a loaded 9mm auto in one hand, and a Taurus .357 magnum with a 4-

inch barrel, in the other. The .357 had belonged to Elizabeth's husband, and she ended up with it in the fallout of the divorce. A riot shotgun and several boxes of ammunition were stashed on the floor, behind the front seats.

"Drive around the block," Danny instructed, looking for Mexican bikers in cars who might be waiting for Pito to hit the street. As Elizabeth pulled away from the jailhouse, she noticed an El Camino parked across the street facing her. Two rough-looking characters sat in the front seat, both studying the stairs to the building's entrance intently. "They're here," she whispered, not moving her lips and staring straight ahead as she drove past the car.

"Did they notice you?" Danny asked.

"I don't think so," Elizabeth replied, attempting to reach behind the seat to touch Danny comfortingly.

He was as tense as a bow string, the muscles in his leg tight and unforgiving. "Good," Danny remarked. "We need to circle the building and park where we can watch them. If they stay in their car, get out and stop Pito. You'll somehow have to talk him into coming with us, then get in the car and drive—but keep your head down, 'cause the shit's probably gonna fly. If they get out of the car and go toward the building, don't go—stay in the car."

"What if he won't come with us?" Elizabeth asked, hesitantly.

"Then get as far from him as fast as possible," Danny replied. "I doubt that they're stupid enough to try to off him in front of a building full of police, but ya never know. You'll need to get back in the car, and we'll follow as soon as things shake out."

Elizabeth drove around the building and stopped near a parking lot for a few minutes. The fierce heat hammered down on the tiny car with no air conditioning, and little left of its dried and cracked insulation. They were both nervous, unsure, and tentative. Danny wiped his brow repeatedly, trying his best to center himself, and then attempted to do abdominal crunches in the back of the car to get his mind off the next hour. "Let's go," he said, finally, looking at his watch. "Pull up just down from the front doors, and park. But leave the keys in the ignition."

"You're not going to leave me, are you?" Elizabeth asked, turning around to look at him anxiously.

Without responding, Danny sat bolt upright as they reached the corner. "Stop the car," he said, forcefully.

When the car was motionless, Danny leaned over the front seat to face Elizabeth as best he could. He dropped the weapons on the seat, then took her firmly by the shoulders. "Listen, you are absolutely the best thing that has ever happened to me," he told her, looking directly into her eyes. "I should be walking away from all this, but I can't. I don't want you here, or anywhere near these people, or—"

"I know," Elizabeth interrupted. "But I *am* here and I'm going to stay." This was the first indication of her desire to be with him permanently, and the first time she spoke of her uncertainty that they would remain attached.

Danny leaned forward to kiss her, then spotted a group of people leaving the jail. "They're getting out!" he exclaimed.

"What does he look like?" Elizabeth asked.

"I don't know," Danny replied, with sudden realization, stunned at his oversight. "All I know is that he's the president of this club, and has been for a while. He's probably big, maybe in his forties."

Elizabeth pulled the VW to the curb and killed the engine. "Keep your eye on the guys in the El Camino," Danny warned from the back seat. Across the street from the jail, the dark El Camino sat motionless at the curb. In the driver's seat, Emilio waited patiently, tugging at his jet-black imperial, while Romeo fumbled with his weapon and sipped on a beer. "It's hot—too fuckin' hot to be here," he said to Emilio, whose steely-eyed gaze remained fixed on the building across the two-lane street.

Emilio could sense the power within his grasp. "It won't be long now, my brother," he said, his tongue slippery with confidence. Romeo shuddered at the words. He had been with Emilio since the beginning. In fact, Emilio had sponsored young Romeo for membership in the club, recognizing the murderous glint in the youthful biker's eyes, but confident from the start that he could control the shorter man. And Emilio was right—a soldier through and through, Romeo wanted nothing more than to enforce someone else's rule. He had no interest in club politics, and lacked the mental capacity for leadership. All Romeo wanted to know was who needed a beating or a bullet, and when.

Although Emilio's demeanor had remained cool, as if someone had iced down the lowered, black El Camino, he flinched slightly and his black eyes widened when a stream of released jailbirds began to emerge from lock-up. Some looked scared, their eyes darting up and down the street, hoping someone was coming to rescue them from further embarrassment in one of the most demeaning experiences of their lives. Some were met by girlfriends and relatives. One man, from all appearances an oil well hand in grimy, denim bib overalls, was met by an entire family, although it was obvious that the woman had been battered—doubtless the reason behind his incarceration. A pair of young punks, making loud, defiant boasts, light-footed down the stairs, as if they had just gotten away with the crime of the century. Then came the veteran lawbreakers, taking their time, letting the cocky kids and the unlucky straights proceed them. They had been hardened by the system, and were fully aware of the consequences and the risks their lifestyle entailed. Pito was among this group walking slowly down the steps into the blistering sun. Pito put on a pair of dark glasses, then donned his leather vest, appearing small on the big man.

Elizabeth spotted him and saw the vest identifying his club. It was made from traditional black leather, with white backgrounds behind the rockers above and below the club's emblem. "That must be him," she said, starting the VW. The car's loud rumble caught Pito's attention, and for a moment, he glanced in the direction of the battered bug creeping up his side of the street. The big man turned away, spotting the El Camino and recognizing the brothers inside. But he had been expecting Gil. Unsure how to read the circumstance, he slowed, then stopped when he reached the sidewalk.

"Stop here," Danny said, and Elizabeth pulled the bug to the curb 10 feet from where Pito stood lighting a cigarette. She stepped from the car and immediately captured the big biker's attention. "Excuse me," she said, slightly disconcerted, but struggling to look poised. "It's not safe for you to go with those men."

Pito's first impression was that this woman probably worked for the local newspaper, although she wasn't carrying a pad or tape recorder. Meanwhile, across the steaming asphalt, Emilio opened the door of the El Camino and began to get out. Then, spotting the trashed VW and the woman talking to Pito, he hesitated, uncertain how to handle this unexpected development.

"We'll take you anywhere you want to go," Elizabeth assured Pito, earnestly.

"What?" Pito said, puzzled, looking at the car. "Who's with you?"

"It doesn't matter," Elizabeth replied, beginning to feel twinges of panic. "We just want to help."

Inside the Volkswagen, Danny was sweating bullets, trying to watch all the players simultaneously. Observing Pito's skeptical reluctance to agree to Elizabeth's pleadings, he tried to keep his eye on the El Camino, all but lost in the crowd of pedestrians, criminals, and family members milling about on the sidewalk and on the street. The blazing sun reflected off a dozen shiny surfaces to blind him, but he kept trying.

"Who's the bitch?" Emilio shouted back to Romeo. "What the fuck is she doing here?"

"She's trying to get the old bastard to go with her," Romeo replied, guessing. Emilio turned and got back in the car.

"I'll kill that cunt right here, dammit" Emilio hissed, taking another silencer-equipped .22 from Romeo and aiming it out the window.

Danny spotted the small cylinder creeping out the driver's side window, and instantly sprang upright.

"Please," Elizabeth said, tugging on the big leader's shirt sleeve. "You've got to get out of here."

Abruptly, Danny burst from the VW. Pito was the first to spot him, and turned to run, his heart suddenly in his throat. Danny held the riot pump at the ready, safety off, and was chambering a round as he leapt from the car. Pito, certain that Danny intended to kill him, jerked free of Elizabeth's grasp, and ran down the sidewalk, knocking people aside like bowling pins in his desperate attempt to avoid death. Danny tackled Elizabeth, sending both of them sprawling to the pavement as the first round spit from the .22 automatic crashed into the concrete building behind him. With

Elizabeth still underneath him, Danny unsteadily pointed the shotgun toward the El Camino and fired, blowing out the truck's windshield and reducing the outside mirror on the passenger side to a twisted tangle of metal.

"Get back to the car!" Danny shouted to Elizabeth, rolling off her while jacking another round into the weapon's smoking chamber. Prisoners and bystanders dropped to the ground or ran in terror as the El Camino pulled away from the curb in a scream of burning tire tread, flying up the street, laying down rubber all the way. Danny and Elizabeth jumped into the VW and followed Pito, who was rounding the corner, heading for the alley. "We've got to get to him before they do!" Danny hollered over the noise of the fleeing truck and the confused screams of the crowd. Elizabeth spun the wheel, and the bug slid into the alley.

The big biker knew the town well, and had already darted between two buildings by the time the VW turned into the alley. Convinced that the anglo following him was the prospect from the Devils Own who was sent to sell drugs in his territory and to carry out their treacherous orders, he efficiently eluded his pursuers along the narrow brick walls and through the maze of old and new downtown structures.

Emilio knew the area, and could make a knowledgeable guess about the escape route Pito might follow. Once away from the gunfire and the courthouse, he turned left, drove two blocks, then turned left again, stopping the El Camino in front of the Midnight Saloon. The bar was one of the last remnants of old town Fresno, a single-story brick building, worn and dingy from years of abuse. The neon sign was dark, cracked, and broken, and the door had been nailed shut after the last in a lengthy series of stabbings. On the street, the place had been known as the "Junkie's Joint," because its trembling, desperate patrons came for only one reason—to score and get loaded.

Pito squeezed between the new bank building on the left of the Midnight Saloon and the corroded bricks and crumbling concrete grout of the abandoned bar's exterior wall. He wasn't as young, thin, or agile as he once was, and the newer buildings were constructed even closer to each other than in the past. He could smell the urine and stale beer absorbed in the soft dirt around him for years, and he sensed the fear and pain of the countless addicts and winos cornered here in the dark, beaten, stabbed, then left to die in a puddle of piss. His mind spun with hate and uncertainty. A number of his brothers were dead, and he was no longer sure whom to trust. And this enigmatic gringo, with his ferocity and unrelenting drive, puzzled him greatly. What made the man survive, what made him keep coming back?

Pito burst free of the reeking confines of the space between the two walls, stumbling into the rubble and trash in front of the neglected brick building, surprised to discover the waiting El Camino. For an instant, he was relieved to see Emilio emerging from the vehicle, but then he spotted the shattered windshield. Perplexed, he stopped, waiting for some sign of welcome—or even recognition. There were only two seats in the passenger portion of the car-turned-truck, and Romeo wasn't getting out. Emilio had the same cold glint in his eyes as he did when the smell of drugs or power was in the air. His left hand rested on the vehicle's open door, while his right hand remained at his side, out of sight. Emilio, unsmiling and silent, made no move to come forward, or to demonstrate any degree of friendship whatsoever. The color drained from Pito's face as he stood, exposed and unarmed, less than 12 feet from this inscrutable, ruthless biker, and with nowhere to run. With mounting panic, he looked around, but he was trapped, unless he wanted to retreat to the coffin of so many drug users and winos over the years. Just as he heard sirens howling from the courthouse two blocks away, he spotted the glint of blue steel in Emilio's hand. He knew then that there would be no negotiation, no discussion, no mercy.

Elizabeth downshifted and floorboarded the accelerator as they rounded the corner into the alley, only to discover Pito nowhere in sight. "What do we do now?" she said, shaking.

"Slow down," Danny said from the seat beside her. As they crept past two older buildings, Danny spotted the path between them. "Stop," he said. "I'm gonna get out. Leave town now and go home. I'll call you."

Danny jumped out and quickly stuffed both the 9mm and the stainless .357 into his waistband. Elizabeth drove away without hesitation, too frightened to argue. Danny thrust himself between the two buildings, hoping he hadn't offended her, and that she would understand that he had acted out of concern for her safety. He pushed and struggled between one set of buildings and into the next street. Looking both ways, he saw nothing but parked cars and small buildings housing law offices, bail bond agencies, and pawn shops. Nothing moved except the shimmering waves of heat from the pavement. He ran across the street, assessing each building as he passed, until he recognized the oldest among them, a hair salon built into a teetering wooden structure. He found an opening between it and the offices of Cohen, England, and Whittfield next door, a contrast in vocations, eras, and lifestyles.

Danny carefully made his way between the buildings and into yet another alley. It held only trash containers and rubble, but he could smell the tell-tale odor of a nearby bar. He examined each building until he found the back door of the saloon and the narrow open space between its crumbling brick wall and the tight construction of the bank next door. As he shoved himself into the constricted opening, he observed the dark tailgate of a vehicle parked in the street ahead, where Emilio faced Pito coldly.

Just beyond Danny's field of vision, Pito tried to shrug off his fears. "Let's get the hell out of here," he said, nervously, to the stone-faced biker in front of him. "Thanks for coming to get me."

"Por nada, jefe," Emilio said, bringing the silenced automatic into view from behind his black Levi's. Holding his breath against the pungent, stifling stench, Danny fought to scramble through the soft muddy soil beneath his feet, aware that he was running out of time. In desperation, he pulled the .357 from his waistband and rapidly fired shots into the tailgate of the truck, the only part of it visible to him from the tight confines of his position.

Emilio held his weapon aimed directly at the center of Pito's forehead, just when three startlingly loud gunshots filled the air in rapid succession, followed by the sound of tearing metal as the blasts struck the tailgate of his truck. Pito, backpedaling rapidly while trying to keep Emilio in sight, fell backwards into a stack of broken barstools, shattered Formica tabletops, and construction rubble stacked in front of the stripped saloon. Pito clawed at the debris frantically, scrambling for cover. Emilio, his ears still ringing from the report of Danny's .357, fired wildly at the pile of rubbish that had once been part of the old saloon. The scream of sirens grew louder, and two more heavy slugs ripped into his truck, fired by an unseen enemy. Emilio pulled the trigger again and again, the .22 bullets from the silenced pistol kicking up small clouds of dust and trash around Pito as he desperately scrambled deeper into the pile of saloon rubbish.

"Old man," Emilio shouted, jumping into the El Camino with his empty weapon, and tossing it across the seat at Romeo, "you better be dying, 'cause your fuckin' time is up!" Danny, his sweatshirt ripped and smeared with brick dust, emerged from the narrow strip between the buildings just as the El Camino sped away, fishtailing down the alley. He dug into the rubble in front of the bar, where Pito lay face-down in the dirt, wide-eyed and breathing heavily. "Get up," Danny said. "He's gone and we've gotta get the hell out of here."

Pito was mad as hell and scared shitless at the same time. "If you're going to kill me, gringo, get it over with," he growled wearily. "I'm sick of this shit."

"I'm not here to kill you" Danny said, reassuringly. "Now get up, before the cops are all over us." Suddenly hearing a rumble behind them, Danny spun around, amazed to see Elizabeth in the thumping VW, screeching to a halt in the deserted alley. "Come on," she called. "The cops are everywhere!"

Danny helped the big man to his feet. "Are you hit?" he asked.

"Hell, I don't know," Pito said, following Danny to the VW. Danny pitched himself into the back seat of the Volkswagen, and Pito clambered into the seat next to the driver, both men crouching down as low as the tight space allowed. Elizabeth put the little car with the big load into first gear, and gunned down the street, headed for the outskirts of town.

THE DEVILS OWN

*T*he burdened VW rumbled east out of the city. No one said a word as both Danny and Pito slumped deeply into their seats, watching intently for police. Elizabeth turned north on Blackstone, near the Smuggler's Inn, a historic watering hole known for the unsavory clientele who patronized the joint in the late 1800s.

Elizabeth stopped for a red light at the corner of Blackstone and Shaw, turning on the car's right-turn directional signal, blinking intermittently under the charge of the weak 6-volt German electrical system. Pito had just begun to sit up when Elizabeth simultaneously noted his movement and a Fresno Police car pulling up on her left. She leaned forward slightly and winked at the officer. Across the intersection, two county cop cars idled, and another entered the left-hand turn lane just beyond the patrol car next to her. The sound of a siren filled her ears, confusing her. She could feel perspiration beading up along her hairline.

Another siren joined the first, and the ear-splitting din grew closer. All at once, the sirens seemed to merge, and a loud, unsettling squawking blared from the car less than a yard from Elizabeth's door. "I'm not sure I can make it," she murmured under her breath, as another patrol car roared up behind her, siren shrieking. Danny sensed her mounting panic. She was frozen in her seat, immobile, unable to think or move.

Elizabeth had never been in trouble with the law. Her ex had served as a member of the Military Police at one time, and had told her countless stories of chasing bad guys, apprehending remorseless criminals, and assisting local cops with arrests. The man being chased was always some idiot without the sense to live a normal life, and according to her ex-husband, each one was a wife beater or drug smuggler, not worth the powder to blow him to hell.

The cop in the car behind her honked his horn, then the brittle crack of a loudspeaker filled the air. The officer in the car next to her rolled his window down and shouted, "Hey, lady, pull that piece of shit over."

"Elizabeth," Danny said, just loudly enough to be heard over the ambient noise from where he lay flat on his back in the back seat, "let out the clutch and pull around the corner." He touched her arm gently. "I'll be with you all the way." She reached out and grabbed his hand, squeezing it tightly, then eased out the clutch as Danny had instructed. The crackling from the radio intensified, and the driver of the police car alongside Elizabeth suddenly fired up both his siren and his lights. Just at the very moment she began her turn, another cop car blazed toward the intersection at 70 mph. Seeing the VW bug pulling into his lane, the cop behind the wheel sent the car into a slide. By then, all four cop cars at the intersection had their sirens going full blast. Rocketing and fishtailing into the intersection one after the other, the police cruisers slid right in behind the slow-moving bug. The first black-and-white downshifted, spun into the center lane, and passed her. Elizabeth cringed, pulling the steering wheel so hard that the VW rammed into the curb in front of the Texaco station. "They got us," she cried, burying her face against the steering wheel.

Pito and Danny lay motionless, as each patrol car shot past and continued down Shaw toward the town of Clovis. "OK, baby," Pito said, comfortingly. "You can roll."

Elizabeth's blood pounded in her ears in rhythm with her hammering heart. She began to sob, but pulled herself together enough to back the bug off the curb and proceed along Shaw to 1st Street. "Turn here," Pito instructed, pointing to the left, and she turned left. When he first got into the car, Pito wasn't sure whether or not he had just signed his own death warrant. Danny had plenty of opportunities over the last few minutes to shoot him, drive to the edge of town, and dump his body, but he hadn't. In fact, he'd left the pump shotgun in back, and he hadn't said a word, except to help Elizabeth through her panic. Then again, they weren't out of the woods yet.

"Turn right on Herndon," Pito said. "I know a place where we'll be safe for a while."

Two miles out on Herndon, signs of the community came less and less frequently, dwindling to little more than an occasional grape orchard and scattered industrial buildings. Pito pointed out one of the latter, a new building combining several units, with roll-up metal doors in front of each. Elizabeth pulled up to the entrance, and Pito got out and unlocked a side door. He entered the building and yanked the chain that controlled the 15-foot segmented door. He then stepped into the opening and indicated for Elizabeth to pull the bug inside the building. As she pulled in, Danny sat up and saw several motorcycles lined up against the back wall. A fully-equipped, commercial paint booth occupied one corner, along with a large tool chest, a drill press, and several benches. Toward the back of the huge, open room was a rust-red picnic bench on which rested a few empty Bud cans, a black pepper shaker, a small glass jar of red pepper flakes, and a larger one containing jalapeño peppers. A full-size refrigerator stood against the side wall separating this unit from the next. Pito opened the refrigerator and pulled out three beers and three burritos rolled in tin foil. He opened the door of a small toaster oven, inserted the burritos, set the timer, then returned to the table with the beers.

Elizabeth and Danny got out of the car and fell into each other's arms. Tears of fear still streamed down her face as they embraced. "Are you all right?" Danny inquired.

"Yes, yes," Elizabeth said, her resolve returning. "It's just that I've never been in that position before. All of a sudden, everything inside me seemed wrong."

"If this isn't for you," Danny said, consolingly, "you can split now. I'll call you when it's over."

"What do you mean?" Pito asked, leaning over his beer. "What more could there be? You've killed most of my members."

"Always in self-defense," Danny replied. "And I didn't kill the first one in that bar fight in L.A., even though I did the time for it."

"Then why did you come up here?" Pito asked, skeptically.

"I was told to meet with you to settle our differences," Danny explained. "Then I'd get my patch and become a member of the Devils Own. I went for it, but if I'm not totally out to lunch, we were both set up. If you killed me, the Devils

Own could kill you in retaliation. And if I killed you, then your people could kill me for the same reason. There's a scheme behind all this, and I'm positive it's got something to do with drugs. They wanted me to bring a bag of coke to you, but I wouldn't do it."

"They wanted you to carry the coke 'cause they knew that I'd kill anyone who brought drugs into my territory," Pito said, beginning to understand. He got up from the picnic table and took a pack of Camels and a turquoise-inlaid Zippo lighter from a pocket of his vest. He tapped a cigarette loose from the pack and lit it. He placed the Zippo on the table alongside the pack of cigarettes, took a drag, and stared off into the vastness of the room. Danny watched the big man think.

Reaching inside his vest, Pito pulled out a narrow stiletto and, with a few deft slices, removed his colors. His face was drawn and sad as he turned and tossed his patch into an empty 55-gallon steel drum. It had once been his strength, his allegiance, his family. He was born to be a patch-holding outlaw, but he had come to recognize the changes the club had undergone, and he knew what they meant. He dragged the cumbersome drum to the center of the room, and Danny followed him, tossing his prospect patch on top of Pito's weathered vest as the big man squirted lighter fluid into the drum and ignited the contents.

The two men stood watching the flames consume their once-treasured patches. Becoming a member of the Devils Own had been Danny's lifelong dream. Leading his family of bikers was Pito's only life. As the two men quietly sipped their beers, and Elizabeth sat at the table wondering what was going to happen next, the room filled with the odor of burning leather and denim. Elizabeth understood the passion these men felt for what they loved, and she knew that burning their patches was a symbolic act, and wasn't going to destroy their drive, sap their strength, or turn them into straight-as-a-string insurance agents. She watched and waited patiently.

Pito finished his beer first, retrieved the burritos from the toaster oven, and dropped them on paper plates, placing one in front of Elizabeth, and another in front of Danny. He then returned to the fridge, pulled out another round of beers, and turned on the exhaust vent to clear out the cloud of smoke hovering near the ceiling. "So," Pito began, looking at Danny while popping the tabs on the three beer cans he held, "what did you mean by 'when it's over?'"

"I meant I'm gonna find out who's behind this," Danny said. "And I'm not gonna let up until I do. That's when it'll be over."

"You know they'll kill your family if you pursue a war with them," Pito said, grimly.

"I don't have a family," Danny replied. "My brothers turned against me, the girl I loved set me up, strangers destroyed my motorcycle. I have nothing."

"That's not exactly true," Pito objected, glancing at Elizabeth.

"You're right," Danny said, pulling Elizabeth close to him. "I do have a someone." He reached across the table, his open hand extended. "And I do have a brother."

"Good," Pito said, shaking Danny's hand. "So are we the lions that will take on the warlords?"

"In so many words," Danny said, excitedly, "yes, goddammit!" "I've worn that patch all my adult life," Pito said, looking at the smoldering trash can. "And I have my suspicions about who and what made it worthless." To emphasize his anger, he drove his fist against the table as he finished speaking.

"Let's start this brotherhood with something permanent," Danny suggested. "And this time, I'm letting a woman join us, stand together with us, side by side." Danny pulled his heavy wallet, connected by a chain to one of his belt loops, from his back pocket. Opening it, he extracted a folded sketch of a lion's head with a gleaming diamond inset for his eye, and his mane flowing into a motorcycle wheel.

"What do you think?" Danny asked, showing it to Pito and Elizabeth. "I drew this in prison."

"Tattoos, no patches," Elizabeth said. Although she had never been tattooed, and feared the sting of a tattoo gun, she had never felt so close to anything in her life as she did to the union of the three of them. "You're right," Pito said. "Patches label us. We don't need them." He got up from the table, made a call, and returned to the table. "It's someone I can trust," he said.

"We need some rest," Danny stated. "Then we'll take this lion to the Bay Area and see what we can find out."

"Are we riding?" Pito asked with a sense of longing in his voice.

"If you have the bikes," Danny said, "we ride."

"I'll find a way through the mountains to keep you off Highway 99 and I-5," Elizabeth said, rising from the table to look for maps in her VW.

Throughout the night, the trio took turns under the tattoo gun, sleeping on cots and working on two choppers in the back of the shop for the ride ahead. Elizabeth's tat graced the inner thigh of her left leg, and the two men wore the intricate skin art on the right arm, the lion facing right, a ruby gleaming from each eye. A chain partially encircled the biceps, its ends to be linked only when the final battle had been fought and all matters had been resolved.

As morning broke, Elizabeth lay sleeping on a tattered army cot, and the two bikers were tightening the final bolts after a night of intense work and fitful catnaps. Danny examined his motorcycle appreciatively. The Glide front end was wide, extended slightly, and stripped. The shotgun pipes ran parallel to each other down the side of the engine, and Pito had done a magnificent job of hiding most of the electrical components with the battery under the seat. Earlier, while Danny had assembled components, Pito shot the final coats of clear over the long lightning bolts on either side of the tank and front fender. The bike went together like a dream, components fitting handily, fasteners readily available. An 80-inch stroker, the Shovel was equipped with UL wheels from the Flathead era, and ran an S.U. carb copped from an English sports car in a junkyard. By mutual agreement, Danny didn't wake Elizabeth. They knew that it would be easier on both of them to avoid an emotional parting, so they had said their farewells when Elizabeth finally turned in. Both bikers pushed their machines into the street and started them. Danny had over 250 miles to ride, while Pito had only a dozen. Danny looked down at the Shovelhead engine beneath him in the stock swingarm frame, the fender mounted to the swingarm, hugging the rowdy 18-inch wheel and tire. The silver machine was all performance, and Danny would need all the horses the bike could pump out to get to L.A., take care of business, and return by the following morning to meet with Pito. Pito and Danny shook hands at the curb and hugged, then admired the lions on their arms. Danny dropped the Shovel into gear and pulled into the street. Elizabeth had carefully prepared a map for him, his route skirting the fringes of Fresno to highway 65, rolling south to 155, east to 178 at Lake Isabella, then south on the 14 at Freeman, heading toward Lancaster, Palmdale, and on into San Fernando.

They would be waiting for him.

Pito had two members to deal with, and throughout the night, as he finished the final touches to his angry black Panhead, he planned for the time they would meet. The intimidating bike boasted a stretched frame, and Pito savored the symbolism of the fierce flames licking the spot on the tank where his club emblem was once proudly displayed. During a night marked by erratic sleep, the buzz of the ink-slinger, and talk of club politics, rumors, and threats, Pito became keenly aware of how far his club had fallen into the hands of drug factions to the north and south. He realized that his Hispanic brothers were only pawns in a game that had no winner. With a kind of grim satisfaction, he sharpened his stiletto, loaded his Smith and Wesson, 4-inch barrel revolver, and donned an old dungaree jacket with inside pockets for each weapon. As they struck out on their respective missions that day, neither Danny nor Pito wore vests. Vests were for club members, and they no longer fit into that category. Each man was well aware that every law enforcement officer along their route would be looking for any rider in a vest, and wearing a patch would likely mean arrest and incarceration.

Pito gently nudged Elizabeth as she slept, kissed her hand, and whispered to her that both her lover and her brother would return. She had her own responsibilities in the effort to make their plan succeed. She was their fail-safe, their single-handed emergency rescue operation, and their cook. The two bikers would need quick nourishment and rest upon their return—if they returned. This would prove to be the longest, hottest, most frustrating day of Elizabeth's life.

Chapter 23

SANTA MONICA

As Danny rolled into the outskirts of Los Angeles, moving from the 14, to the mammoth 5 interstate, to the 405 freeway, rolling south and west to the coast, he watched the traffic grow denser, the homeless multiply, and the air stagnate. It was then that he realized that he had no home and no family in this Southern California metropolis of four million. And now, he was about to find out if he had any friends left. He wanted all the deceit and violence to stop, but he knew that it wouldn't without the answers he needed, or without confronting his brothers.

Brothers. The word had lost its comforting ring. The club had become a business, composed of ambitious fools scraping and clawing their way to the top. They had risked everything in the pursuit of their goals of wealth and power—including the very brotherhood that was the essence of being a biker—and now they would face the consequences of their actions. Involuntarily, Danny tightened his grip on the handlebars.

When he reached Van Nuys about noon, Danny was hungry, so he pulled up to Cafe '50s. As he shut off the bike and dismounted, he was aware of the attention he drew with his short, but wild-looking hair, the U.S. Marines sweatshirt, the jeans once belonging to Elizabeth's ex, and his road-battered Levi's jacket that provided little armor against the elements, but as the summer continued to broil, the jacket became the perfect garment, as constant sweltering temperatures dictated light clothing.

Danny took a window booth from which he could observe his motorcycle. He relaxed on the booth's bright red, tuck-and-roll vinyl seat while he ate. Mounted to the front of the building, housing the restaurant and the artifacts on display to create its rock and roll theme, was a huge black and white clock. Above it, in long, sweeping tubes of neon, were the words, "Time To Eat." Inside, the walls were covered with Elvis movie posters, promotional photos from old biker movies, and 45- and 78-rpm records. The chrome and vinyl-cushioned counter held small, individually-mounted jukeboxes at each stool, while the tables were graced with marble vinyl, and the floors with checkered linoleum. But Danny was oblivious to the trendy decor and the be-bop trappings.

When Danny's gaze happened to sweep across the small jukebox on the table, his attention was caught by the title of a song by the Temptations, "I Wish It Would Rain," and in spite of himself, the tune diverted his concentration on the plans ahead. As a motorcyclist, wishing it would rain was against his religion. But as a heartbroken man, it was the perfect solution. He dropped a quarter into the 20-year-old machine, and pondered the words of the song, realizing that since the moment he was released from prison his entire existence had revolved around staying alive and avoiding the treachery and deceit all around him. He looked around the café and studied the posters, enjoying the celebrity black and whites, and the garish colors of the ones featuring hot rods. The theme of the restaurant seemed somehow to underscore Danny's unproductive life, and a new determination coursed through his body. For the last four days, he hadn't been living; he had simply been endeavoring to survive. He couldn't see or enjoy the neon artwork affixed to the window pane in front of him; he saw only police cars. He wasn't tasting the food, because he was watching his back for the Mexican outlaw bikers hunting him. And he couldn't relax or check out the paint job on a passing hot rod without looking for outlaws in vans. He had been swallowed up in a fight for survival, losing all touch with the normal world, and it pissed him off. Other than the moments alone with Elizabeth, he hadn't tasted, seen, or smelled anything besides blood, beer, and violence. He needed to center himself—badly.

Knowing the day would be long and dangerous, Danny concluded that he needed some sort of quick distraction, something to take him away from the life-numbing influences that had consumed him from the instant he stepped through the prison gate to freedom. He decided to find a dojo and train for a while. He walked outside the restaurant and stretched, feeling his muscles move again after the ride from Fresno. The tightness in his traps and back was deep, and would require more stretching and work to unlock. Rolling south on Van Nuys Boulevard for two blocks, he came upon busy Ventura Boulevard, where he turned left and soon thereafter spotted a storefront with a sign reading, "Billy Chen's Martial Arts Studio." Inside, the walls were black except for expansive mirrors and long stretching bars. Above the mirrors were plaques and trophies attesting to Mr. Chen's expertise and accomplishments. Danny approached the counter respectfully. "Excuse me, sir," Danny began, hesitantly. "I was hoping I might train for a while today. But, unfortunately, I can train here only once. I'm just passing through."

Billy Chen was a small, lithe Chinese man who had trained with Bruce Lee and worked in several of his movies. Caught up in the Hollywood scene, Billy moved to California at the age of 20 and set up shop, dreaming of becoming as popular and successful as Bruce. Martial arts was his love, and he supplemented his dedication to them by studying the spiritual world of Zen, in order to maintain his balance and perspective. At a glance, he sensed the turmoil of disturbance swirling within the tall, muscular anglo standing before him. "Here," Billy said, reaching under the counter, and offering a used Karate Gi to the big motorcyclist. "And may I suggest," he added, humbly, "that you begin with some meditation." Danny followed Billy to a small corner of the training facility, where the wiry Asian offered the stranger a spot on a large, woven-straw mat. Danny assumed the lotus position and closed his eyes. From behind Danny, Master Chen, touched and firmly squeezed the seated man's traps. "Think of the future beyond what bothers you," Chen said, softly, yet forcefully. "Think of the flowers, and think of your form."

Ten minutes passed before Danny was able to sort through

all the bullshit and focus first on the future, then on the beauty of the earth, and finally, on his martial arts form. Billy returned, and again touched Danny's traps. "You are confident, calm, and fearless," he whispered in the biker's ear. "Repeat it, feel it, then open your eyes and look at yourself in the mirror. Continue to repeat it until you have convinced your image."

Without hesitating, Danny began the ritual. When he finished, he moved to the stretching exercises, beginning by extending his legs as widely apart as possible. At once, he became aware of yet another indication of the tension in his life—his lack of flexibility. His muscles screamed, his joints howled, and his unforgiving tendons raged. Observing Danny's difficulties, Billy came to his aid. "Breathe," he told the young biker. "Take deep breaths and close your eyes." As he spoke, he lifted one of Danny's legs while he lay prone on a soft workout mat. "Now release your breath and release the muscle." Danny did as instructed, and his thigh muscles relaxed. He moved through each arduous task with considerable strain, but gradually, his body began to loosen, and he felt it responding for the first time in weeks.

Standing up after the final stretch, Danny inadvertently stepped onto the sparring mat, and Mr. Chen bowed instinctively, as did Danny. Billy was lean and quick, bounding across the mat with the apparent weightlessness of a butterfly, flicking at the air with grace and purpose. Danny adopted a fighting stance, but he was too late to block the master's first kick, which slapped Danny hard in the face, twisting his neck. Two lessons returned to Danny in a flash: "Attack the attacker, and don't go down." He spun, almost stumbling and falling to the mat before regaining his balance. He shifted his bare feet along the mat in an aggressive move toward his assailant. Again, the master was much faster than the awkward Anglo with his large muscles and slow movements. Chen set his feet on the mat in perfect form, regained full balance, and shifted forward as his feet slid effortlessly along the mat to within striking range, where both fists snapped in a quick blur of motion. One fist landed in the center of Danny's surprised face, and the other jabbed deeply into his solar plexus. Perfectly placed, the first punch bloodied Danny's nose, while the second relieved him of his wind. Nearly doubled over, Danny gasped, and then remembered another rule of close-quarter combat: "Expect to get hurt."

Danny moved quickly to straighten, and the master spun away from arm's length and into a position to kick him from the side. Blocking the out-thrust leg, Danny trapped the man's ankle and hammered his trainer's knee joint, then thrust his left elbow to the man's jaw. Billy dropped to the mat, and Danny stepped back and bowed in respect. They continued to spar for an hour. With each set, Danny felt his focus, his confidence, and his center returning. Walking out of the gym freshly showered and relaxed, he enjoyed the feel of the sun against his shoulders, savored the shape of a woman in exercise tights, and relished the smell of fresh chocolate chip cookie batter emanating from a corner bakery. He took a long, deep breath and started the Shovelhead, slapped it into gear, and pulled a wheelie leaving the parking lot—and he would also soon be leaving the last valley before reaching the coast.

A mist of fog lay over the seashore as Danny leaned off the 405, the San Diego Freeway, and then onto the 10, the Santa Monica Freeway. He sped to the end of the freeway at the beach, weaving through coastal traffic along the Pacific Coast Highway, passing myriad multicolored hippie havens, sorority houses, well-kept California bungalows, and surfer pads on his way to the Army-Navy store in Venice. After parking the motorcycle, he searched the store for both a left- and right-handed shoulder holster. With the help of a camouflaged attendant, he found what he was looking for. As the sun began to settle over the street vendors, tattoo artists, and reggae singers performing their final gigs for the tourists on the boardwalk, Danny made his way inland to the house where Dixie lived.

The house was a tiny crackerbox affair. Dixie was just waking up, and she struggled a bit, getting to her feet at 4 p.m., when Danny walked in the door.

A small mirror with a pile of white powder, a rusty, single-edged razor blade, and portion of a Jack In The Box straw on it rested on the dining room table. "Hello," a feeble voice called from the back of the guest home. Danny stood quietly in the living room, waiting for the tiny woman to emerge from the bathroom.

The size of the house seemed appropriate for Dixie. It too was diminutive, the living room barely able to hold a small couch, an armchair, and a television. No objects in the room aligned, no patterns matched, and the television was a black-and-white set, covered with dust. It was the home of a constant drug user. Dixie obviously didn't care much about anything but the drugs, and staying high. Wrapped in a towel as she entered the small, tiled kitchen, she was stooped and gaunt from her incessant consumption of cocaine.

For Dixie, looking at Danny was like seeing Santa Claus and a ghost at the same time. She had expected to hear of his death at any time, yet she silently prayed to hold him again. Her big eyes captured his form, and she let the towel drop, running to embrace him. His body remembered the better times and the touch of her skin against his. As he gazed down at her nakedness, over her plump breasts and pert tummy, to her shaved pussy and stout little legs, he remembered, mellowing. But as she attempted to embrace longer, he pushed her away, spinning her damp body and shoving her plump little form against the wall.

"What are you doing?" she squawked, as he handcuffed her with a pair of the military's finest from the war surplus store. He bent her over the linoleum table in the kitchen and slammed her face into the mound of coke on the mirror. The powder lifted in small clouds, spreading out over the table. Her eyes widened.

"I should kill you," Danny said, spanking her chubby bottom, as she squealed.

"But I love you," Dixie whimpered, as he spanked her again, then turned her round body, and shoved her into a chair.

"You love this shit more," Danny said, lifting the mirror

and pouring the powder on her buxom chest, over her nipples, and down her pudgy tummy. She watched in horror.

"Where are they hanging out, now?" Danny asked, coolly.

"I don't associate with them anymore," Dixie replied, looking longingly at the white powder on her chest, and at the rivulets of water dribbling down her soaking-wet red mane, then falling onto her chest, washing the dissolving drug down past her stomach and abdomen, then disappearing into the soft pubic region of her crotch.

"Just tell me where they are," Danny said, "and I'll leave. Then you can snort all this shit you want." He waited for an answer standing over her.

"You won't hurt me?" Dixie asked, beginning to cry.

"Not if you tell me what I need to know," Danny answered.

"You would never hurt me," she said, whimpering. "But they do."

"Bad decision," Danny commented, flatly. "But it's not one you can change this time."

"I can try, can't I?" Dixie sobbed.

"Just tell me where they hang out," Danny insisted.

"They're still going to the warehouse by the Hughes buildings," Dixie sighed. "They'll be there tonight for church. Honey, I need to get high. If they find out I told you, they'll hurt me bad."

"Your decision," Danny said. He uncuffed her, then cuffed one of her hands to the small kitchen table, the only place to eat in the house, although Danny doubted that any meals had been served on that table since the current tenant moved in.

Danny watched Dixie as she lifted one breast at a time and snorted loudly, then licked the white residue off her nipples. Her small, pink nipples hardened and she instinctively parted her legs and leaned back in her chair. Danny could see the glistening wetness form between her thighs. After she licked her fingers clean, she traced the coke to her pussy and massaged her clit, arching to meet her fingers. Danny watched her, momentarily recalling the wild nights they spent in sexual suspended animation, feeling the constant tingling in their loins. Those glorious nights, followed by terrible, come-down days, were like going to heaven, enjoying the show, then being transferred to hell.

Danny backed away from Dixie, found the phone in the bedroom, and cut the cord. The sun was setting as he walked down the alley behind Dixie's pad to his motorcycle, parked at the end of the block. He rode across town to a residential area overlooking the sprawling 15-acre Hughes production complex. Pulling to a stop, he could see one bike parked outside the facility entrance, and the long, narrow warehouse that had once been used to shoot movies starring Lana Turner. He scanned the area for a vantage point and an escape route if his plan happened to go awry.

He found a maze of buildings facing several directions. The complex was constructed in the '40s, and resembled a military installation built in the post-war era. The industrial units resembled airplane hangers, and the smaller buildings looked like office buildings in the Philippines—four feet off the ground, with large porches and asphalt tile roofs. Danny rode to the bottom of the hill and coasted into the complex with his engine off. Hiding the bike behind one of the utility buildings near the gate, he turned the machine toward the entrance, and left the gas petcock on.

The buildings were mostly abandoned now, and Danny moved to his best vantage point, 50 yards from the large sliding steel doors at the front of the 20-year-old structure. Danny attempted to nap on a picnic table bench, knowing that the sound of arriving motorcycles would be all the wake-up call he would need. But he managed only to doze fitfully. Shortly after 8:30, the staccato roar of V-twins filled the night air. Danny sat bolt upright, and turned to watch the proceedings. The large steel doors were opened every time a bike arrived, then shut behind the rider. Danny counted five bikes and two hangarounds, who were assigned to operate the doors. Inside, the members milled around until 9, when the meeting was called to order, and the two hangarounds were required to go outside and guard the facility.

Chapter 24

FINAL RUN

*T*wo o'clock in the morning. Danny finally pulled up outside Pito's faceless hideaway, followed by Jesse and the rumbling of a Mac semi cab, piloted by Mick Karr, from Bakersfield. Both Jesse and Mick were sporting the new Gilded Lion tattoo. Danny spotted blood on the tarmac, dismounted quickly, and hammered his fist against the steel door adjacent to the truck-sized roll-up entrance. Elizabeth opened the door cautiously, and they embraced. Danny grimaced from his bandaged wounds, but it felt like heaven to have her in his arms. Throughout this ordeal, she had been his salvation.

"Are you all right?" Danny asked, fearfully, with an apprehensive thumping in his heart.

"I'm fine," Elizabeth answered, hugging him. "Pito was wounded, but he's OK, I was worried about you."

"We're all right," Danny said, relieved. "But let's get this door open and these vehicles out of the street." He kissed her on the lips, deeply. "We're almost there, baby." Danny stepped inside and pulled the chain hand-over-hand, lifting and rolling up the large sheet metal door. With the bikes and the truck securely inside the vast hall, Danny let the steel-linked door unravel and close like a guillotine on a condemned man's neck. It slammed against the unforgiving concrete and echoed in the steel, uninsulated cavern. Danny introduced the respective players, and everyone downed a cold beer around the rust-colored picnic table.

The light banter reminded Danny of more relaxed times, times he could barely remember anymore. Now he sat sipping the icy brew and feeling Elizabeth's thigh against his, while he nervously stared at one man after the other. He was faced with one more insidious adversary, and he couldn't rest until the final battle was done. He wished no harm to this assembly of talent and heart. In fact, for the first time since he was in prison, he felt that he had met and mustered people who had no criminal motivation, people who cared because it was part of their nature, who lived for the sheer joy of living. He felt a pang of guilt from a sense that they had no business being involved in this dark world he found himself fighting.

As the conversation lagged, Danny said a silent prayer and got down to business. "Tomorrow we ride to Menlo Park," he explained. "We'll meet our toughest adversaries there and the source of all the problems we've encountered. We will need all our resources and faculties, so let's get some sleep."

"Hold on," Mick protested. "Don't you think we should move, before the heat and the information get to all the wrong sources?"

"Yeah," Elizabeth agreed, snuggling closer to Danny. "I want this over as soon as possible. And Mick's right, the word will spread quickly."

"I'm sure someone has already dropped a dime," Jesse piped up. He had been working out since Danny had last seen him, and was more thick and stocky than ever. "If we don't move, they'll move on us. I'd just as soon get them before they send someone."

Danny looked at the cot where Pito lay, his neck and shoulder bandaged. "What about Pito-" Danny began

"What about me?" Pito broke in. "*Vamanos muchachos y muchacha. No hay tiempo perder.*"

Danny spread out a map on the table, and the four members of the New Order of the Lions studied the San Francisco Bay region as Jesse described the area that housed the Devils Own club building, its structure, and the defenses. "We can only hope that the word spreads and they'll have a meeting tomorrow," Jesse said, wincing. "This is like taking on the LAPD. When we go, there'll be no turning back."

"They've caused all the murders and all the trouble I've encountered," Danny snapped. "It won't stop unless someone takes a goddamned stand."

"I'm with you, brother," Jesse replied. "But it ain't gonna be easy. My pappy was a cop for 25 years, and he taught me street tactics. This will take all ya got."

"They won't expect aggression," Pito said from the couch. "They're the big boys, after all. They'll expect to put together a hit crew and send 'em into our barrio looking for us. They won't be expecting no siege on their own clubhouse."

Elizabeth thought about the angry nature of her ex, a man who had lived the life of a warrior. His skills were honed, and he had trained and studied constantly, but she had never seen him calmly discuss stepping into a deadly situation. He was insecure of his abilities in the field, so he beat her to prove himself. She was sure of that now—and even more sure of her belief in, and love for, Danny.

Danny listened intently to everything each member of the group had to say. He had known and ridden with Jesse for years. He knew about Jesse's father's past, the beatings Jesse endured as a child, and the abandonment when his father died. Jesse's long, dirt-brown hair was pulled tightly into a ponytail, which somehow seemed symbolic of his defiance of his father and the man's hatred of his biker ways. Jesse learned toughness from the Southern cops. They may have lacked technology, cunning, and expertise, but they were unrelenting, strong as the alligators that lived in the swamps, and tough as rattlesnakes. Although Jesse was a rebel, he knew the ways and attitudes of cops.

Elizabeth looked at Pito lying still on the cot, recharging his batteries for the final battle. He had been a biker and an outlaw leader for 20 years. In all that time, he had never been a slouch, never backed away from a fight, was invariably defiant in the face of authority, and was as cold as a mountain lion when it came to defending his family. His role would be to provide leadership in the field. He would know instinctively what to do in the heat of battle, and he would not hesitate.

Mick was sharp, but emotional, and would need to be controlled. He came from a long line of drunks and street brawlers, growing up under the tutelage of an oil well pusher, the boss on the rig. He was thick-boned, thick-headed, and tough as nails. But he was a charger, and when the best tactic was to hold back, he could be tough to reign in. When he was younger, Mick once rode 400 miles in the rain to fix a friend's points, an act which was indicative of the level of his commitment to his friends.

Elizabeth looked at Danny adoringly. He was obviously the glue, as well as the most handsome of the bunch, with his neatly cropped, sandy-blond hair, carefully trimmed mustache, and new forced tan. His emotions were high, but his thoughts were with every person on the team. His concern for Pito was evident. Although he had come to confront the longtime leader, and possibly fight him, he had found the truth and he had acted on it.

Danny was obviously protective of Elizabeth, and wanted to spend more time with her, but his sense of right and wrong as an outlaw had been pushed to the limit, and that fact consumed him—there was no stopping him now. He had gone to jail for his so-called brothers, only to have been deceived, shot at, beaten, threatened, and lied to, all because of greed and drugs. At this point, nothing would stop the mission he was about to undertake—including his blossoming relationship with Elizabeth. She understood, and was prepared to support him all the way, secure in the belief that her time would come.

Jesse sketched a rough layout of the target. He had been there only once, but he recalled well the vile clubhouse, the massive front doors, and the chain link around back, topped with coils of concertina wire. It was a fortress, and Jesse figured they'd be outnumbered four-to-one.

Danny tallied the odds with the group, discussed the scarcity of weapons on their side, and touched on their overall lack of experience in such assaults. The group sat quietly and stared at the sketch of the huge stronghold.

"It's essential to understand the enemy's strengths," Danny said, squeezing Elizabeth close, and punching Jesse in the biceps to break the icy stillness. "It's also necessary to grasp our own weaknesses. Now that we've got all the cards on the table, let's form a plan."

"Not much to go on," Jesse said, and Danny slapped him. Although it was intended as a playful gesture, the tension suddenly became as thick as the dense smoke in a nightclub. Without speaking, Danny extended his hand to

Jesse, and with their handshake, the tension seemed to dissipate. Nonetheless, the realization of their opponents' strengths in contrast to their own striking weaknesses had sunk in, and the group sat listlessly, each wishing that this was some kind of bad dream from which they would awake, and return to their normal lives.

"We're here to win," Danny said loudly. "I'm not leaving this building until we all feel the same as I do. Now, we have work to do. Tong taught me the art of dealing with combat when you're outnumbered. Four principles apply: speed, surprise, shock action, and diversion."

Danny paused, looking intently at each member of the group. "So here's how we're going to expand our arsenal," he continued. "First, clear all the shit off this table and lay all the guns and ammo on it." Danny drew his 9mm automatic from his waistband and laid it on the table. The others followed suit. "Now, I need all the glass bottles we can get our hands on." Pito gestured to Elizabeth to look in the trash cans. As she started piling quart beer bottles and empty tequila bottles on the table, Danny instructed her to find caps whenever possible.

"Where can we find sandbags and gasoline?" Danny asked Pito.

"Big gas can in the corner," Pito replied. "And at the intersection, two blocks down, is a building supply yard."

"OK, listen everyone," Danny said. "It's 2:30 now. We need to be on the road at 3:30 to get there as the sun's coming up. Elizabeth and I will fill bottles with gas. Mick, you and Jesse see if you can't use your truck to get into that yard and get as many sandbags as you can load in a few minutes. Those places usually have some ready-to-go, full bags available for landscapers who don't want to hassle with filling empty ones. Pito, you got some old motor oil around here?"

Pito pointed to a steel cabinet, and Danny instructed Elizabeth on how much oil to mix into each bottle of gasoline. Danny took some of the bottles filled with gas and oil, capped them, then wrapped them with rags. Others, he filled with gas and stuffed rags down the neck, while others, he just filled with gas and capped. He filled the luggage compartment of the VW with capped bottles, then he filled a carton with bottles and loaded it into the back seat of the bug.

Jesse climbed on top of the cab, and Mick pulled the truck out of the industrial unit, heading up the street. Soon, Mick pulled the diesel into the alley adjacent to the building supply yard, and Jesse went over the fence from the roof of the cab. Three minutes passed, then Jesse signaled Mick, who climbed out of the dusty cab and onto the back of the truck. Jesse threw him the bags, and he stacked them around the massive trailer hitch.

The smell of gasoline filled the huge building. Pito could no longer stand lying idle, so he began to dig through his war chest for more ammunition and weapons. Mick hauled along a 12-gauge High Standard pump shotgun and one box of double-ought buck. Pito loaded the weapon and slipped the safety on. He then loaded a long canvas bandoleer with spare rounds until the box was empty. He loaded spare clips for the Browning 9mm, stacking them alongside the weapon. He loaded the one speed-loader for his own .357 mag, then poured the rest of the shells into a baggie he could slip into his pocket.

Danny took the .22 long rifle, semi-auto Ruger from the floor beside Hank when he died. He had no ammunition for it when he arrived, but Pito's war chest was littered with .22 LRs. Danny scooped them off the bottom of the old military chest and fed them into the belt of a western holster designed for an 8-inch-barrel six-shooter target pistol. This would be Jesse's piece. That left Elizabeth and one extra gun, Pito's favorite weapon, which he hadn't used since a street gang tried to invade his area with angel dust. The 9mm submachine gun still was strapped to the bulkhead above his war chest. Pito groaned as he reached for it, but took it down with respect, and dusted it off with a clean terrycloth rag. The military weapon, with its cooling cowling and 30-round straight clip protruding from the bottom, needed little to make it battle-ready. Inside the war chest were five loaded clips and a convenient olive drab shoulder bag to carry them. He grimaced as he slid the woven strap over his head and felt the weight around his neck. Then he looked at the table, did a few mental calculations, and glanced at Elizabeth, who studied him carefully.

Pito reached into his chest and rummaged around, looked at Elizabeth expectantly, and searched some more, finally coming up with a Smith & Wesson .38 revolver with a 6-inch barrel. The piece was already loaded, and he handed it to her, along with a small leather pouch filled with spare cartridges. As she spun the cylinder and checked the pull on the trigger, they heard the revving diesel outside. Danny went to open the roll-up door.

"Got all the bags we could carry," Mick hollered from the cab. "What're they for?"

"Never mind," Danny shouted over the noisy rattling of the injector tappets, hammering into oblivion. "Lock and load—we gotta move. I'll explain on the way."

Midnight at the Devils Own clubhouse, and the air was quiet. Four members sat around a man tied to a chair and toyed with his life. Ronnie Rickman, known as "Rickshaw" for the hint of Chinese in his heritage and looks, dealt drugs on a big scale. But he also played with fire. Not a big man, Ronnie stood 5 feet, 8 inches of thin, out-of-shape wannabe. He curried the approval and company of the Devils Own, looked for love with whores, and sought prestige with drug lords. He was unsuccessful in all three endeavors. He didn't have the balls or power to cope with the club, nor the assurance to exercise command over women, and in spite of the volume of drugs he moved, would always be lightweight in that world.

Rickshaw's delicate, almost translucent skin seemed in odd contrast to its pockmarked surface, the result of a severe bout with acne during puberty. Years of drug abuse had left his limbs flaccid and weak, and his vastly fluctuating income made him gaunt, both in the wallet and in the cheeks. His final downfall came about because of his weakness for sampling his own wares, a fatal flaw that left him bereft of resources and deeply in debt.

"You owe us, dickhead," Miguel said, sneering at the helpless man strapped haphazardly to the chair in front of him. "You've owed us in the past, but by God, you'll never owe us again." Miguel stepped forward and stared into the sweating man's eyes that reflected sheer terror. Then, without warning, he twisted Rickshaw's left wrist over, palm up, snapped open a 3-inch Spyderco folding knife with a slight flick of his wrist, and sliced off the top layer of the man's skinny wrist like peeling a potato. Rickshaw screamed in agony, while Miguel poured drugs directly into the bleeding wound, except this time it wasn't the relatively mild effects of cocaine that would swim in his veins toward his heart, but the hi-test racing impact of speed, pure methamphetamine, $C_{10}H_{15}N$, to chemists, crank to users, death to the careless. As Rickshaw's pain mounted, another member, who had been preparing something behind the club bar, came around the massive oak structure carrying a hypodermic needle. Clamping his hand around Rickshaw's upper arm until a fat vein protruded, he thrust the needle home, waiting for blood to back up in the syringe before slowly injecting the contents of the syringe, a mixture of pure speed and a few thousand micrograms of LSD. Almost instantly, Rickshaw sat up straight, eyes bulging, as if he had freshly mixed cement running through his veins. The first rush of speed hit his weary brain like a runaway freight train.

"You're too crude," Sprocket said to Miguel, in a superior tone. "I'll make him fly while he's lying in the gutter." The two men sat down on a couch across from their prisoner and watched with anticipation. Rickshaw had gone beyond his normal range of fuck-ups. He hadn't snitched anyone off. On the contrary, he consistently kept his mouth shut—even after a Devils Own member broke all the fingers on one of his hands, simply because he saw Rickshaw talking to a traffic cop. At the time, Rickshaw was receiving a citation for double parking while selling drugs to a street whore. He had tried to explain, but received the harsh club lesson anyway. But this time, Rickshaw had bought a pound of coke, and paid for only half of it. Now he wanted to be fronted more, assuring the club that he was good for the money. But he caught Miguel on an off day, and he decided that Rickshaw had run out of credit—and luck.

The bikers watched Rickshaw writhe in wave after wave of drug rush. His temples pounded like kettle drums, and sweat drenched his body. In his intermittent moments of lucidity, he could feel his heart working overtime. After a few minutes, the acid began to work, and his mind gathered momentum. Shortly, he experienced a spectacular blast-off. Miguel and Sprocket watched as Rickshaw's eyes rolled back in his head and he began to mumble, then cry, then laugh. He opened his eyes, but saw only pulsating blobs of color, unrecognizable, constantly changing amorphous forms. He tried to focus, to resolve what he saw into some coherent pattern, but his brain could grasp an object for only a millisecond. Then it erupted into swirling tumbles of color and sound, a Technicolor roller coaster ride into madness. All the while, the meth fed his paranoia and amplified his fear, causing his limbs to thrash and struggle against his restraints—to no avail. He was blinded by his own sweat pouring into his eyes.

The clubhouse was dark, stark and quiet, except for Rickshaw's squirming, incoherent pleading, and deranged giggling. Sprocket and Miguel fired up a joint and passed it back and forth. The ember at the end of the joint captured Rickshaw's intensely acute attention. The glow in the dark became freeways of light to the thin man who was losing all color, and whose heart was beginning to race and flutter. Rickshaw didn't know that he was dying as the clubhouse phone began to ring. Rotten Ron and Rico were witnesses on the other side of the room, sharing a small mirror and a pile of coke on the bar, while watching Ricky's last minutes. Ron, the oldest of the bunch, and carrying the most seniority told Rico, "Get up and answer it."

"Aye, captain," Rico said, pushing his massive, steroid-enhanced body to its feet. Rico always wore the same thing—skin-tight Levi's to accentuate his narrow waist, and a leather cutoff without a shirt. His muscles rippled beneath the leather vest, and his mammoth forearms were larger than Ricky's thighs. "Yeah?" he bellowed into the receiver. "Who the fuck is it?"

"It's Fireball, from L.A." came the reply.

"Hold on," Rico said, cupping the receiver with his massive palm, as he called across the open room. "Miguel, this is your problem. One of the guys from L.A."

Miguel nodded as he accepted the joint from Ron. Rico turned back to the receiver. "Wait a minute," he snapped, dropping the phone and leaving it swinging on its cord.

Miguel got up from his chair while taking a long hit on the joint. While he did so, he looked down at Ricky, who was still alive but fading fast. His color was almost gone, his lips were turning blue, although his eyes still darted back and forth, looking at nothing in particular. Miguel leaned down close to the man's face, stared into his eyes, and exhaled the pungent smoke into the dying man's face. Miguel's features were as cold as his demeanor—angular and tan, his jet-black hair making him look almost American Indian as he picked up the dangling receiver. "Better get the body bag ready. This clown's a goner. What's up?" he said into the phone, dryly.

"Danny came to the clubhouse a few hours ago and shot Hank and Eddie," Fireball blurted into the phone.

"So, why didn't you kill him?" Miguel barked back.

"I didn't have a gun," Fireball returned, stuttering.

"So why didn't he kill you? Miguel demanded.

"I don't know..." Fireball began, not knowing how to respond. "He took my patch."

"He should have," Miguel responded, fuming. "In fact, I should have ripped it offa your ass a long time ago." He smashed the receiver into the cradle.

As Fireball set the phone down, he marveled at his own stupidity, wondering why he had made the call in the first place.

Danny rode in the VW beside Elizabeth, fanning the gasoline fumes away from the driver. Behind them, Jesse held a wet towel over his mouth and nose. Ahead, the semi led the way with Mick and Pito. They pushed only slightly past the posted speed limit. Taking Highway 58 across to I-5, they headed north, past the vast, open cattle ranches and farmlands scattered between Los Angeles and San Francisco. The 5 freeway was a straight shot, with breaks at 30-mile intervals. Past Colingua, they began to look for Highway 152, which would take them to the near-coastal route of 101 and on into the Bay Area. The small caravan pulled out of the industrial park on time, 3:30 a.m. With luck, they would arrive at Menlo Park around 7:30 to 7:45. At 60 mph, it would take them over four hours to make the 250-mile trek.

Elizabeth followed the semi closely, drafting the big truck, increasing her gas mileage. From time to time, members of the VW squadron leaned out the windows to gasp for fresh air. There was little talk. The strategy had been reviewed several times, although no one could be certain that it would work. Every member had memorized his or her assignment and the timing necessary to bring the plan off.

About 10 miles north of Coalinga, and just past a sign reading, "Next Services 42 Miles," the VW's engine suddenly coughed, and each passenger gasped involuntarily. The bug seemed OK for 45 seconds or so, then it stumbled again, and then again. Then it died. Frantically, Elizabeth hit the highbeams to attract the attention of the men in the semi. Mick noticed the flickering behind him and pulled over.

"This bug has never given me a lick of trouble in ten years," Elizabeth said, pounding the steering wheel in frustration and pumping the gas. She twisted the key in the ignition, and occasionally, the car would sputter and spring back to life—but only to die again. She coasted to the side of the road and turned the ignition off. Danny was silent as the big semi shifted gears into reverse, then carefully backed down to where the VW and its passengers were stranded.

"You out of gas?" Mick inquired.

"I couldn't be," Elizabeth replied, on the verge of tears. "I fill it up all the time." She began to sob. "Where are we going to get gas this late?"

Jesse burst out laughing, then handed Elizabeth a one-gallon glass bottle with a rag stuck in the end of it. In a matter of minutes, the VW had been refueled from the quantity of various-sized bottles stuffed around Jesse in the seat and on the floor. They pulled onto the highway again. At the next exit, they topped off the tank, refilled some of the bottles, and got back on the road. They were less than 125 miles from their destination.

The group felt a mounting anxiety as they pulled onto Highway 101, and all talk ceased as they swung onto Highway 82, less than 30 miles from Menlo Park. Pulling off the freeway, the group watched the sun appear over the buildings in the small industrial/aging hippie town. They pulled to a stop behind the first gas station they saw. "This is it. Get out of the car, Elizabeth," Danny ordered. He exited the idling bug, walked to her side of the car, and embraced her. They both reeked of gasoline. "This is the final fight," he said, holding her close and staring into her deep pools of blue. "I love you." His eyes drifted, and he paused, as though he wanted to say more, but couldn't. Elizabeth and Jesse jogged to the truck and began arranging sandbags on the tail. The remaining heavy bags were formed into the shape of a bunker around the trailer hitch and the framework behind the cab. Mick drove the semi, while Elizabeth and Pito climbed into the makeshift bunker. Jesse climbed on top of the rig, and Danny dressed for the final ride in the VW.

At 6 a.m., Miguel returned to the clubhouse after dumping Ricky's body outside a rundown suburban hotel. As he arrived back, Sprocket met him at the door.

"Could be serious, asshole," Sprocket said, wiping his massive, callused-from-weight-lifting hands after cleaning up the mess caused by their deadly game with Ricky. "The bastard burned down the L.A. clubhouse."

"Who the fuck are you talking about?" Miguel asked, sneeringly, though knowing full well who Sprocket meant.

"That Danny guy," Sprocket said. "He also hit the Cuchillos in Fresno. I called a security meeting."

"You did *what*?" Miguel said, his chubby features reddening. The rest of the club had criticized his handling of the Los Angeles scene from the beginning, and the whole L.A. Central Valley project was unraveling. "I don't need no fucking security meeting! I'll go kill that sonuvabitch and Pito myself, goddammit!"

Just then, other bikes and cars began to pull up to the building. A large, fat man peeled himself out of a black, lowered pickup and threw on his club vest. "Miguel," he barked, "you fucked this thing up. Stash all these bikes and get ready for a meeting."

Miguel's power faded as he moved motorcycles into the shed behind the house while other members showed up. Even the new, inexperienced brothers ignored him as they arrived, dismounted, and went inside. Inside, Miguel set out the meeting tables with the help of Sprocket, while some of the other members met in private rooms behind the bar. Others leaned against the ornate bar and talked, whispering quietly.

The yard behind the clubhouse was protected by a chain link fence topped with concertina wire. Within its confines was a two-car, stucco garage and enough room to park a dozen cars. Miguel had neatly housed the bikes in the garage, then shut the door. He parked the cars and three trucks, including the president's, then locked the gates to the fence. Ordinarily, the rule was to park cars against the gates but, certain more members would be coming, he left room for the gates to be opened. There were no windows in the clubhouse—only gun slits in the doors, front and rear. The single-story building had a rounded tar roof, with an interior ladder leading through the ceiling.

Inside the clubhouse, Big Al took his acknowledged position at the front of the U-shaped arrangement of folding tables. He shouted at the 15 men in front of him while ignoring Miguel. "What's the problem in the Central Valley and L.A.?" he barked. "We've been doing increased business with that area for a couple of years now, and all of a sudden, with the release of one fucking prisoner, we're cut off. I got five calls this morning. Four people are dead since last night, six more since Friday."

Miguel knew that if he didn't respond, someone else would begin to throw shit in his direction. "It's all under control," he said, striving to sound confident. "I'm gonna roll south and..." Miguel's reassuring speech was cut short by a terrible screeching noise outside, and a muffled explosion that rocked the rear of the building.

Danny, wrapped in wet blankets behind the steering wheel of the bug, prayed that the little machine wouldn't explode when he started the motor. Two boxes of Molotov cocktails had been loaded onto the back of the semi, and Danny had stuffed rag wicks into the 20 bottles in the forward trunk of the VW. The interior of the bug was like an internal combustion chamber with a speeding piston headed toward the compression stroke—after grabbing all the air and fuel it can, the piston heads perilously close to that crucial point, 30 degrees before top dead center, while the points spin to fire the plug. Danny knew he was running out of time as he pulled into the street and revved the engine only a city block from the clubhouse.

The engine was unaccustomed to this sort of abuse, but Danny pressed the pedal to the floor, and wound through the gears. Adjacent to the clubhouse was a mammoth, 80,000-square-foot printing plant with a vast parking lot spread out before it, joining with the one next to the clubhouse building. On weekends, when the plant was closed and the Devils Own were hosting a large gathering, they had access to another 100,000 square feet of parking space.

Danny used the vast parking area as a runway, bouncing up the driveway into Pacific Printing's parking lot at almost 50 mph, slamming his head into the bug's roof while heading directly toward the clubhouse. The jolt of clearing the curb caused the glass bottles in the trunk to jostle and smash against each other. Danny's eyes widened apprehensively, but he kept his foot firmly on the gas as he gained momentum toward the chain link fence, followed by the semi. Targeting the center of the chained and locked gates, Danny hit them dead-on, springing the lock and wrapping the gates over the top of the bug. He had less than 20 feet to go before colliding with the rear door to the clubhouse. The chain link squealed and strained like a fisherman's net capturing an unexpected killer whale. When it was 15 feet from the target, the VW slowed under the strain of snapping poles and fasteners. Realizing the bug might be halted before he could reach the doors, Danny feared he might find himself trapped inside the explosive machine by a barrier of chain link net. At 10 feet, something let go. The front bumper of the bug tore loose of its mountings and whipped back over the hood, shattering the windshield before disappearing over the thin roof of the abused Volkswagen. In a final surge, the car sprung forward and bashed into the clubhouse doors. The heavy, locked entrance cracked and splintered, ripping the hinges away from the jambs. Danny's head smacked against the steering wheel, as he groped for the door handle while simultaneously reaching for the Zippo lighter on the passenger seat. Flipping open the stainless steel lid, he spun the knurled wheel, striking the flint. The lighter sparked, but failed to light the wick. Just as he set his gloved thumb firmly against the abrasive wheel to try again to ignite the gasoline-soaked passenger seat, a powerful explosion tore through the vehicle. Whatever it was, something in the back seat, or volatile fumes reaching the power plant, the blast launched Danny through the driver's side door and onto the pavement. At that moment, the trunk exploded, spewing jets of flames through the shattered doors and into the clubhouse. The oily mixture clung to the building's stucco walls, allowing the fire to take hold and spread. Danny rolled away from the blazing bug, then sprung to his feet, running to back up his crew, barreling through the parking lot.

"What the hell was that?" Big Al shouted, leaping to his feet and slamming a meaty fist against the table. "Get the weapons!" He turned to Miguel. "We'll deal with you later."

The club had fashioned an artillery wall behind the oak bar. With the opening of a simple latch at each end of the mirror behind the oak pillars, the entire facade opened to reveal a cache of automatic pistols, conventional handguns, and assault rifles. As the men scrambled to grab a weapon, the rear door blew off its hinges and small explosions sounded from the rooftop above. Three men headed for the ladder leading to the roof, but dripping flames ran down around the hatch and down into the building's interior. In an instant, the clubhouse was filled with billowing smoke. Panicking, the disoriented bikers scrambled for the last exit, the ornate steel-sided doors of the main entrance.

Mick backed the semi up against the front entry, shearing away the hinges, crushing the doors with the truck's frame rails, and throwing the confused members of the Devils Own back into the smoky abyss. Pito lit the wicks on several bottles, then kicked an entire box of Molotov cocktails off the back of the truck into the clubhouse. The crate of glass bottles shattered onto the concrete floor, sending a wave of flaming gasoline surging throughout the interior of the hall. Meanwhile, from atop the truck's cab, Jesse launched one rag-stuffed bottle after another onto the roof of the building, each exploding and bursting into flames. As the sound of sporadic gunfire filtered through the chaos, club members, like fear-crazed rats, ran in circles, vainly trying to escape. Mick pulled the semi away from the fiery door enough to have an overview of the street-front and parking lot side of the building and its roof.

Inside, men were dying of smoke inhalation. Realizing that there was no escape to the rear, since that portion of the building was already engulfed in flames and the Volkswagen plugged the exit like a cork in a bottle, the bikers had no choice but to run through the flames in an effort to flee through the two main doors. The first two members who tried, burst through the doors only to encounter Mick in the semi's cab, holding the 12-gauge, and Pito, behind a heap of sandbags on the back, with his zeroed assault rifle. The two on the truck took careful aim and fired as the two members of the Devils Own tried to escape, their clothes ablaze. Other patchholders emerged from the passageway, coughing and gagging, only to be shot. Danny's plan to take advantage of the element of surprise was working, as the first six members were taken down handily.

Jesse jumped down from the cab and quickly escorted Elizabeth away from the action, crouching down behind a lone compact parked in the center of the parking lot. Danny met them there.

The club members had no idea what they would encounter on the outside, so they fired their weapons erratically as they ran from the flames. Inside the building was total pandemonium, every man for himself. One club member tried to climb the ladder to freedom on the roof, but was engulfed in fire. Screaming and writhing in pain, he fell to the hardwood floor and died. Another member launched himself through the flames to the sunlight outside. As his eyes tried to focus, he kneeled on the pavement and shot at any form in front of him. Pito reloaded and returned the fire, hitting the man in the left shoulder and hand. The outlaw dropped his weapon and fell backward, screaming. Unable to see, he nonetheless knew the next bullet would soon be coming. His mind racing, he struggled to his feet, turned, and ran back into the death-shelter of the blazing building.

Inside, Big Al had dragged Miguel and Rotten Ron into an inner chamber where officers decided the fate of lesser men. "This is your problem, motherfuckers," Al spat. "And you're gonna get me out of this, or I'll kill you both with my bare hands."

"Fuck you, fat man!" Miguel shot back. "If you'd given me more support with this operation from the beginning, we wouldn't be up shit creek right now!" He pulled a stainless PPK from his vest and shot his president squarely in the chest. In wide-eyed astonishment, the man looked at his killer with surprise and hatred as he took his last breath.

"What the fuck did you do that for?" Ron asked, dumbfounded.

"Never mind, fuckface," Miguel replied. "If we survive this, we'll take over this pieceashit organization and have it to ourselves."

"How the fuck are we going to get out of here?" Ron screamed in desperation. "The goddamned building is burning down!"

"But we're not," Miguel said, confidently. "This room is fortified and separately ventilated. Just hold on. Let's see if they have the balls to come get us."

Kneeling behind the parked compact, Danny studied the fleeing men for the ones Jesse had described. He had no way of knowing how many members were in the building, but he knew he had to make decisions fast, and then get the hell out. Soon cops, and possibly more Devils Own members, might arrive. The smell of burning flesh and oil smoke, coupled with the intense heat, was turning his stomach. As the roof began to collapse beneath the blaze, a black figure appeared at the door. Virtually unrecognizable, the smoldering man emerged like an inky specter, the Grim Reaper holding an automatic weapon instead of a scythe. In the enveloping smoke, the man's eyes stood out like two white crystals in a sea of black volcanic ash. It was Sprocket, his patch having burnt completely off his back. As he raised his rifle, he opened his mouth and a wisp of gray smoke floated into the air. "Die, you cocksuckers!" he shouted, firing his weapon in all directions. Hearing Sprocket's imprecations, Pito grasped his smoking assault rifle tighter and peeked over his barrier of sandbags. He was hit immediately by an armor-piercing bullet that blew him off the framework of the truck and onto the asphalt below.

The unearthly screaming, the unbearable heat, and the hellish smells permeated the truck, bringing each member of Danny's team to the verge of nausea. No sleep, coupled with nights of abject terror, had reduced the freshly tattooed crew to edgy exhaustion, with one exception. All this was just enough to set Mick off. He had seen the powerful bullet lift Pito from his protected perch like a doll, hurling him to the pavement in the open, less than 25 feet from the smoldering body of one of the Devils Own. Blood spewed from Pito's destroyed shoulder. Mick snapped. "Motherfuckers!" he screamed. "I'll fucking show you what dying is all about!" He stomped his foot down on the stiff clutch pedal, jammed the shift lever into reverse, and popped the clutch. As bullets pierced the cab, shattering the truck's rear window, Sprocket stood completely still, like a statue commemorating dead outlaws, firing his gun until he was out of ammunition. The sharp rails of the screeching semi caught Sprocket in the chest, driving him back into the flaming building. But Mick didn't stop there. He kept going, even though the engulfed structure was collapsing around him.

"Mick, don't!" Danny screamed, then turning to Jesse, who was frozen, his back against the side of the small foreign car.

"I can't do it anymore," Jesse sputtered, his hands shaking like leaves in a gale.

Danny yanked Jesse to his feet by his collar and slapped him hard. "You've got to stay with us," he barked into the exhausted man's face. "We need a vehicle to get the hell out of here! Go get that pickup truck! I'll take care of the fighting here."

Jesse regained a measure of composure and ran for the shattered gates. "Are you all right?" Danny asked Elizabeth, touching her shoulder and grasping her hand. She nodded confidently. "I'm going to get Pito. Cover me." He released her hand and ran toward the veteran outlaw who lay bleeding on the tarmac.

Kneeling beside him, Danny could see that Pito was still conscious. "Hold on, *cholo*," Danny said. "We'll get you out of this, brother." Danny pulled off his belt and tied Pito's shredded arm to his side, stuffing the wound in his shoulder with his T-shirt. Grabbing his injured partner's feet, Danny began to pull him toward safety, as the sound of more gunshots filled the air. Panting heavily, he dragged Pito 20 feet to the protection of the compact. "Watch him," he said to Elizabeth. "See if you can slow the bleeding. I'm going after Mick."

As Danny approached the building, he heard a roar. He couldn't tell if it was the sound of the semi, an explosion inside the building, or the structure crumbling beneath the flames. He ran toward the collapsing building, barely able to withstand the heat from the inferno ahead. Then, as if the specter had returned in the form of a smoldering truck, the semi crashed out the side wall of the blazing building. Danny dived to the pavement, as smoke and flames consumed the building's blistering exterior. Two men were in the cab. Neither of them was Mick.

Danny scrambled to his feet as Miguel leaned out of the side of the burning vehicle, firing an M1 carbine. Danny rolled aside as the truck sped past him, through the blinding smoke. He couldn't believe what he was seeing—where was Mick?

The semi shot past in a blur of smoke and flames, but something fell from beneath the careening truck. It was another smoldering man, a man without a vest. It was Mick, letting go of the screaming truck. Danny ran to his side. He was shot, hurt bad, and gasping for air, but not dying. Just then Jesse pulled up in a black, lowered pickup belonging to the former president of the Devils Own. "Load him up," Jesse hollered. "The hospital isn't far from here."

Danny lifted Mick's writhing form and set him gently in the truck's bed. "Man," he said, trying to divert Mick's attention from his injuries, "you're heavy for being cooked."

A smirking smile crossed Mick's strained features.

"Danny," Jesse said under his breath, "the guys in the semi are the ones." He pointed over his shoulder. "There are bikes in the back." Elizabeth helped Danny load Pito onto the bed of the pickup, then she climbed in on the passenger side.

"I'll meet you at the hospital," Danny said, as he set off, jogging to the rear of the building. Sirens blared in the distance. Danny fired one of the bikes to life and looked down at the Devils Own decal on the tank. He jammed the motorcycle into gear and pulled into the street in hot pursuit.

The truck turned right at the end of the street, then took the on-ramp onto the freeway. Danny, his eyes bleary from the smoke and his brain weary from the fight, couldn't see the pickup, but he whiffed the air for the smell of the burning truck and followed his instincts onto the freeway. The performance bike sped through the gears until it was splitting lanes at over 100 mph.

As he rounded a sweeping freeway curve, Danny detected the familiar scent of oily smoke in the air, and spotted the smoking semi ahead. At the same moment, the two outlaws in the cab caught sight of the screaming rider. Miguel turned to the blown-out rear window with the M1 carbine, and began firing.

Danny was gaining fast, making him an easy target. As he crushed himself against the tank, he saw flashing lights in the rearview mirror. Two Highway Patrol cruisers were flying up the freeway. Danny, certain that he was their target, shut down, easing off the throttle. His last check of the speedo revealed a velocity of well over 120 mph. But now he slowed to 80 mph. The inevitable was approaching at over 100. Danny was at a loss to know what to do—he was armed, in violation of his parole on several counts, and guilty of crimes too numerous to mention. Worst of all, he was caught.

The cruisers were on top of him, one on either side. Then, to Danny's astonishment, just as quickly they passed him. He made no move, kept his speed steady, awestruck to see the patrol cars blast by him. Frozen to the tank, his white-knuckled fists in a death grip locked on the bars, he watched the cruisers cut off the semi ahead. Danny drifted to the right as he spied more cruisers in his mirrors, gratefully pulling off at the next off-ramp. He doubled back toward the hospital and Elizabeth, remembering one of the eight rules of close-quarters combat as he weaved down the side streets heading toward his wounded crew: "Don't go down." For the first time, Danny truly understood what it meant.

WATCH FOR UPCOMING BIKER FICTION FROM K. RANDALL BALL AND VISIT HIS WEB SITE, BANDIT'S BIKERNET. HTTP:// WWW. BIKER NET. COM

CHOPPER ORWELL

Regular readers of *Easyriders* magazine are already familiar with *Chopper Orwell* and K. Randall Ball's apocalyptic vision of a world in which bikes have been outlawed and only outlaws have bikes. Read the whole story in this one-of-a-kind novel of a future that may be closer than we realize. In a completely unique format, Bandit is publishing chapters of this novel on Bandit's Bikernet, affording you a sneak preview of the book as it's written. In this interactive world, Randall Ball gives readers the opportunity to comment on the structure and character of the book as he creates each chapter. In this light, readers can see if he responds to their suggestions by changes in the manuscript.

CROSS COUNTRY

Readers of *Easyriders* have also been forewarned about Randall Ball's next book *Cross Country* which takes a group of young rowdies on their first trip across the country. What are they running from, where are they going and who do they love? All that and more will be answered in this fast-paced book that has already been turned into a screenplay by Conrad Goody *(ConAir)* and may reach the screen before the book is published. Look for updates on the movie project in *Easyriders*.

OTHER MOTORCYCLE WORKS BY K. RANDALL BALL

THE ART OF DAVID MANN
Paisano Publications

THE ART OF DAVID MANN II
Artist's selection,
Paisano Publications

EASYRIDERS ULTIMATE CUSTOM BIKES
Carlton Books U.K.
Thunders Mouth Press U.S.

PRIZE POSSESSION
5-Ball, Inc.